SENTINALS AWAKEN

SENTINALS AWAKEN

BOOK ONE OF THE SENTINAL SERIES

HELEN GARRAWAY

ALSO BY HELEN GARRAWAY

Sentinal Series

Sentinals Awaken

Sentinals Rising

Sentinals Justice

Sentinals Recovery (novella)

Sentinals Across Time

Sentinals Banished

Sentinals Destiny

SoulMist series

SoulBreather

DragonBound

Published by Jerven Publishing

Cover by Jeff Brown Graphics

Map by Fictive Designs

This is a work of fiction. Names, characters, organisations, places, events, and incidents are either products of the author's imagination or are used fictitiously. Any resemblance to actual events or persons, living or dead, is entirely coincidental.

Registered with the British Library.

eBook ISBN: 978-1-8381559-3-3

Print ISBN: 978-1-8381559-1-9

Print hardcover: 978-1-8381559-2-6

Sign up to my mailing list to join my magical world and for further information about forthcoming books and latest news at: www.helengarraway.com

First Edition

For my Mum,

Margaret

I miss you every day

CONTENTS

GLOSSARY

Deities

    Leyandrii (Lay-ann-dree): Guardian of Vespiri

    Marguerite (Mar-guh-reet): Leyandrii's sister, Guardian of the Land

    Guerlaire (Guh-LAIR): Original Lady's Captain

Old Vespers

    Jerrol Haven: Captain of the King's Rangers

        Zin'talia (Zin-tar-lee-ah): Darian mare

        Ari: Arifel

        Lin: Arifel

    King Benedict: Ruling monarch of Vespiri

    Crown Prince Kharel (Car-ell): King Benedict's son

    Birlerion (Bur-lair-rion):   Sentinal - Old Vespers

    Leander Jennery: Lieutenant in King's Guard

    Princess Selvia: Kharel's wife

    Prince Anders: King Benedict's youngest son

    Lady Miranda: Princess Selvia's lady in waiting

    Darris: King Benedict's steward

    Commander Nikols: Commnader of the King's Rangers

Commander Fenton: Commander of King's Justice

Chapterhouse
Liliian: Scholar Deane of the Chapterhouse
Taelia (Tay-lee-ah):   Scholar
Torsion (Tor-zh-on):   Scholar, Jerrol's mentor and friend
        She'vanne (Shuh-van): Torsion's Darian mare

Greenswatch
Lord Hugh: Lord of Greenswatch
Lord   Simeon   Descelles   (Sim-e-on   Duh-shells): Hugh's son
Lady Alyssa Descelles (A-liss-ah): Hugh's daughter
Garrick: Simeon's steward
Oscar Landis: Captain of Greenswatch Guards
Versillion (Ver-sill-i-on): Sentinal Birlerion's brother
Serillion (Sair-ill-i-on): Sentinal – The Grove
Frenerion (Fren-er-i-on): Sentinal – The Grove
Parsillion (Par-sill-i-on): Sentinal – The Grove
Darllion (Dar-li-on):   Sentinal - The Grove
Fonorion (Fuh-nor-i-on): Sentinal – The Grove

Deepwater Watch
Lord Aaron: Lord of Deepwater
Lady Olivia: Aaron's mother
Denirion (Duh-near-ion): Sentinal

Stoneford
Lord Jason   Lord of Stoneford
Bryce: Captain of Stoneford Guards
Tagerillion (Tagerill) (Taj-er-rill-i-on): Sentinal - Birlerion
and Versillion's brother
Chryllion (K-rill-i-on):   Sentinal

Saerille (Say-er-rill) :   Sentinal

Marchwood
Lord William: Lord of Marchwood
Anterion (Ant-air-i-on):   Sentinal
Tianerille (Tee-ann-er-rill) :   Sentinal
Venterion (Vent-air-i-on):   Sentinal
Laerille (Lay-er-rill):   Sentinal

Ascendants
    Ain'uncer (A-nunce-er):   Warden at Watch Towers
    Var'geris (Var-gair-is):
    Fortes/For'teras   (For-tez/For-tair-as):   Velmouth
Councillor
    Meritas/Mer'itas (M-air-i-tas):   Deepwater Councillor
    Pevrill/Pev'eril (Pev-er-il): Lord Aaron's steward

    Other Sentinals mentioned
    Marianille (M-a-ri-an-ill)   Sentinal – Versillion, Tagerill
and Birlerion's sister
    Niallerion (N-i-al-air-i-on) :   Sentinal
    Lorillion (Lore-ill-i-on):   Sentinal

1

LADY'S TEMPLE GARDENS, OLD VESPERS

The sword missed his nose by an inch, if that. A momentary relief as solid steel thunked into the ground and Jerrol jerked back like a snake about to strike and then slithered away, inhaling the scent of soggy grass, dirt and roses. Roses? His brow wrinkled in confusion as he scuttled away and regained his feet. Backing towards the tall sentinal tree arching over the Lady's temple, he strained to see his assailants.

He leaned against the trunk as he scanned the gardens. He would have to apologise later; staying alive was more important than the sanctity of the temple gardens. There were three guards, large and brutal: chancellor's men eager to deliver him up more dead than alive.

The complaint of him snooping around the chancellor's business would be enough to get him placed on report, if not demoted. He wasn't supposed to be near Chancellor Isseran, let alone follow him.

Gritting his teeth, Jerrol considered his options. He couldn't kill them, not on the Lady's soil, yet he couldn't let them report back, either. The satin-smooth bark of the tree beneath his fingers warmed for a moment as he hesitated. The image of a tall, black-haired man stood before him. This apparition wore a silvery green high-necked uniform that glimmered in the swirling mist. He was striking to look at, unnaturally pale with distinctive features and straight, black eyebrows over silver eyes that gleamed in the dim light.

Jerrol gaped at him, unable to stop staring. It wasn't possible. Lady help him, it wasn't possible, was it? He recoiled as the man spoke.

"Captain? Is it time?" the man asked, his silver eyes burning bright.

He was young—younger than he was, Jerrol thought. Yet his expression was grave. There was a sense of a burden understood and accepted, of experience over youth. He had a sword strapped to his hip and a bow across his back, and he looked like he knew how to use them.

Jerrol frowned. *"Time?"* he asked, and the image faded. He took a deep, steadying breath and turned into one of the guards rushing him. Blocking the blow, he spun towards his attacker instead of away. Deep grunts and the thwack of punches broke the silence of the garden. Jerrol twisted out of the man's grip and drew his knife.

He hesitated, remembering he was on the Lady's ground, and instead landed a punch that dropped the man as he retreated. More men arrived, crowding the gate. Jerrol flinched as something buzzed by him, and one of the men grunted in pain and fell back. Audible thuds followed, and the men jinked back from the gate.

Jerrol took the opportunity to fade into the night, circling the temple and up towards the Justice buildings. The tower bells chimed, deep and resonant on the still night air. The sky was beginning to lighten to a steel grey. If he didn't return to the barracks soon, it would be evident to everyone that he had been out that night.

Keeping to the shadows, he made for the rear wall of the garrison. The small pack still nestled at the foot of the oak tree where he had hidden it. Assessing the height, he pulled the grappling hook out and slung it over the wall. The soft clank was loud in the quiet night air. He pulled it tight and was over before anyone noticed him; gathering up his rope, he dropped to the ground behind the stables.

Jerrol reached his room undetected; as a captain of the King's Rangers, he rated his own space. Sometimes he missed the camaraderie of the shared sleeping quarters but not on nights like this, when he was returning from an unsanctioned venture, battered and bruised.

He dropped his bag in the corner and lit the lantern with the candle he had picked up from the hallway. Fishing the notebook he had found in his hurried search of the warehouse, out of his pocket, he shed his clothes, lay down on the bed with an exhausted sigh and began flipping through the pages. His fingers slowed as he realised it was the chancellor's handwriting. He recognised the looping tails Isseran used. A list of names and words. Nothing else, nothing to explain what they meant. Most of the names in the book were known to him, a scattering of administrators, lords and courtiers, as well as high-ranking officers from both the rangers and the King's Justice.

He snapped the notebook shut and lay frowning in thought as the sky lightened. Had he seen a man in the sentinal tree? Legend said that Lady Leyandrii's Sentinals, her personal guards, had all vanished with her when she sundered the Bloodstone and brought down the Veil nearly three thousand years ago. The trees appeared at the same time—it was said in memory of them—and that's where the name came from. Some said the guards slept inside them, unable to cross the Veil with the Lady.

No, it couldn't be true. It was all myth and legends.

Shrugging off the possibility, his thoughts returned to his unsanctioned foray into the warehouse district of Old Vespers which raised more questions than answers. If Isseran was involved in smuggling goods across Vespiri, then they were in more trouble than he'd realised. According to the notebook he'd found, the chancellor was colluding with a network of influential individuals.

Rising before sixth chime, he showered and dressed in the grey and black of a King's Ranger. The only visible sign of his overnight excursion were his reddened knuckles, and a slight bruise discolouring his right cheek. At least they could be explained easily enough. Everyone gained bruises in the sparring ring.

Commander Nikols was in his office when Jerrol arrived. Nikols was a career soldier; he had risen through the ranks uninterrupted and had been tenured as the Commander of the King's Rangers, and Jerrol's commanding officer since Jerrol had first joined, seven years previously. He was a large man, towering over Jerrol's slight stature, and twice as wide.

He was also intelligent. Jerrol respected the sharp mind that sat behind the piercing brown eyes that saw through every ragtag, desperate excuse. He could cut through bull faster than any commander Jerrol knew. Nikols was a staunch supporter of the Lady and Jerrol trusted him.

Nikols' brow darkened as Jerrol reported. He glared at Jerrol as he took the notebook he offered him. Jerrol knew the names, having memorised them during his sleepless hours. He stiffened under Nikols' inspection and knew his nondescript appearance belied his competency. After all, he had been on Isseran's detail because he was tenacious and discreet. It was his tenacity that got him in trouble, and that usually meant trouble for Nikols.

Nikols flipped through the notebook. "This doesn't tell us much. It certainly wasn't worth drawing Isseran's attention to you any more than it already is. You're not supposed to be anywhere near him."

"I didn't expect him to be there, sir. I left him in the arms of his latest floozy. He should have been there for the night."

Nikols glanced up from the notebook and Jerrol winced.

"If the chancellor is at the root of our recent troubles, then we have no choice but to go to the king," Jerrol said, watching his commander. "If these people are his supporters, then most of the administration is corrupted."

"If you can get through the Crown Prince first. He guards his father's peace with a tenacity equal to yours."

"Depends if the king wants it guarded so," Jerrol said, considering the astute monarch that ruled their kingdom. He didn't think the king would accept his son's scheming for long.

"Unless he says otherwise, that is what we have to accept." Nikols glared at Jerrol in warning. "Do not offend the prince, Haven. Your life will become much more difficult if you do. You think Isseran is a pain? Kharel would be ten times worse."

"But it's not like the king to allow others to speak for him," Jerrol argued.

Nikols shrugged. "It's time the prince was more involved, and I expect Benedict is preparing him for the throne."

"Still, it doesn't seem right to me."

"Good job it's not down to you, isn't it? Leave this with me. I'll see if I can get an audience with the prince. Keep your head down. You're supposed to be off Isseran's rotation, so stay away from him. Let's not rile him any more than necessary. Keep to the barracks." Nikols stood and leant on his desk. "Understood?"

"Yes, sir." Jerrol saluted and left the office. He didn't think arguing would get him anywhere. He knew Isseran was up to no good—look at his attempts to lose Jerrol. If he didn't have anything to hide, he wouldn't try so hard. His turning up at the warehouse, which was totally unexpected, sealed it for Jerrol. He wondered why Nikols wasn't so sure.

The days passed, and Jerrol kept to the barracks, leaving once to visit the Lady's temple to apologise for fighting in her gardens. When he arrived, a young man was kneeling before the altar and Jerrol halted in surprise. The white marble was shimmering; it solidified as he watched, and soft voices drifted on the air.

"Dearest Birlerion, please, be a diversion, protect him."

"But my Lady..." The man broke off as he looked around, aware of someone behind him. He rose in one fluid motion, bowed towards the altar and turned away, keeping his eyes downcast as he left the temple, but Jerrol recognised him even without his bow strapped to his back. The glimpse of silver eyes and the archaic uniform—those were distinctive.

"Hey, wait." Jerrol ran after him, but he had disappeared; the gardens were empty. Returning to the temple, Jerrol knelt before the Lady's altar. He stared at the lifelike statue of a young woman, standing barefoot by a stream surrounded by flowers. The Lady Leyandrii, the deity who helped create the world of Remargaren.

The white marble gleamed in the soft light of the temple, the statue shimmered, and the flowers rustled, giving off a heady scent.

"You are late, my Captain."

Jerrol stiffened, glancing around the empty temple, and his stomach fluttered as he stared at the statue. *"Late?"*

"Events quicken, and we are unprepared."

He swayed, grappling with her words. *"Unprepared for what?"*

"The forgotten stir. It is time."

Jerrol braced a hand on the stone step. What was going on? Was he hallucinating? He flicked another glance around him and back to the statue. *"The forgotten?"*

"They wait patiently, my Captain."

"Who does?"

A tinkling laugh filled the air. *"Who do you think?"* The shimmering statue solidified, and the laugh faded. The statue gleamed in the subdued light, watching him.

Jerrol rose, staring about him wildly, his heart thrumming in his chest. He backed away from the altar and hurried out of the temple. He stopped before the tall sentinal. It couldn't be, the myths could not be real. The silvery trunk glistened in the sunlight, and he placed a tentative hand against it. Nothing happened.

He shook his head. He was an idiot. What had he expected to happen? Did he really think a man would step out of the tree?

The sentinal stood as it had for the last century and more. Records stated that the temple had been buried beneath the land for nearly three thousand years, and all that time the sentinal had been sheltering it. As the soil was excavated and the temple revealed, the sentinal had slowly straightened, its pointed leaves reaching for the sky. One of many sentinals scattered across Remargaren, though the only one in Old Vespers.

Deep in thought, Jerrol paused at the entrance of the Chapterhouse. After a fleeting glance back at the temple, he entered and approached the duty scholar.

"History of the Sentinals? First floor, section twelve, you won't find much though. No one's been able to explain them," the duty scholar said, pointing the way.

· · ·

Jerrol leaned back in his chair and scrunched his face up. His eyes were sore from trying to decipher the faded text in the oldest document he could find. According to the dusty journal, the Lady Leyandrii had called forth her Sentinals in 1122, and nearly one hundred men and women had responded, committing their lives to her. Then she had dispersed them throughout Remargaren. She had kept an arm at the palace. An arm? He frowned at the unfamiliar term and returned to the parchment, searching for references to an arm.

He stilled as he read the list of twelve strange names that comprised the 'arm': the Sentinals posted to the Lady's Palace. His breath hissed out as he found what he was searching for. The name he had heard for the first time only a few hours earlier. "Birlerion," he whispered.

As Jerrol returned to the barracks, his mind was spinning. Questions bounced off one another, and there were no ready answers. He wasn't sure if the Lady had spoken to him, or if he had imagined her and the man. Could a man exist within a tree for three thousand years? And if he could, why had he awoken now? And a more disturbing thought, were there others?

2

RANGERS GARRISON, OLD VESPERS

I t was much later by the time he slept, and early when a
tapping woke him from a dream about the Sentinals,
the Lady's Guard. Tall, silver-eyed men and women
lost when the Lady banished all magic from the world,
immortalised by the silver-trunked trees which had appeared
overnight in their place. The Sentinals awaited his
command.

A young page in palace livery stood outside his door, a
missive in his hand. "Captain Haven? Message for you."

Jerrol pushed his hair out of his face and flipped open the
note. The page waited, trying to suppress a yawn. The king
expected his presence in the throne room, immediately. As he
dressed, he speculated on why King Benedict of Vespiri was
granting an audience at this time of the night. The page led
him to the dimly lit courtyard, where horses waited patiently
in the darkness.

On arrival at the palace, a sleepy groom took his horse,
and the page led Jerrol through the silent corridors to the
throne room. King Benedict was already seated on his throne

when Jerrol arrived, which was unusual. He was also unattended.

Behind the king, engraved in the wall, were the words of the King's Oath. The oath that bound the king to the Lady and the Land, and the protection of his people. A gleaming black and white mosaic of a sentinal tree and a crescent moon covered the floor.

Jerrol entered and knelt before the king. He bowed his head, waiting for permission to rise. It didn't come, and he remained kneeling, getting stiffer as the minutes passed. He swallowed; was the king that angry with him? He reported what he found. It was not his fault if it wasn't what the king wanted to hear.

As he continued to wait, he realised the king was muttering to himself, but he couldn't make out the words. The mosaic floor began to burn his knee, and he squirmed into a more comfortable position, but it didn't help.

He hadn't seen the king for a few weeks; his last report had not been received well, and the king had not been pleased. Discreetly peering up at the king, Jerrol could see those few weeks had not been kind to him. He looked as if he had lost weight, and Jerrol's frown deepened in concern.

"Do your Duty. Never Falter. Never Fail."

Jerrol jerked his head up as the first line of the King's Oath rang around the throne room. He inhaled sharply as the words vibrated in the air. Was the king trying to invoke the Oath?

He stared at the king, noting now how dishevelled he appeared. King Benedict was usually immaculate no matter the time, but now his shirt was wrinkled; his brown hair looked as if he had dragged his hands through it a few times, and his face was lined and pale. He mumbled under his breath; he seemed agitated and not quite himself.

Jerrol held his breath as King Benedict's unwavering eyes

stared into his. The king rambled about oaths, the King's Oath in particular. He kept changing topics: he talked about the Watches and his responsibility, and then back round to his Oath before he veered off talking about his concern for the guardians, the tall sentinel trees that were located across Vespiri. The king struggled with himself, and then he spoke again. "Lady, Land and Liege obey."

Jerrol gasped out loud, recognising the second line of the Oath. The king's eyes bore into his as he gripped the arms of his throne. He looked, dare Jerrol say it, a bit desperate. The king was rambling about time when he cut himself off and started to speak the third line. "All are one, entwined ascend..." The throne room doors crashed open and interrupted him, and a stocky young man in an ornate uniform of navy blue and gold trimmings entered.

"Father." The king's eldest son, Crown Prince Kharel, strode up to the throne. The king faltered, the words dying on his lips.

Jerrol flinched as a loud crack ricocheted around the throne room and the floor trembled. Jerrol caught the king's eye. "Sire, if it is your wish, I accept your oath. I will guard the Watches for you."

The king dipped his head in what Jerrol hoped was acknowledgement rather than despair. Jerrol was positive the words of the Oath flashed as he spoke.

Prince Kharel grabbed Jerrol roughly by the shoulder and spun him around. His numb legs failed to take his weight as he tried to rise. Staring at the wall, the prince growled, "Haven, you are under arrest for treason."

Jerrol struggled to his feet and glared at the prince. "For what?" A shiver of fear flashed down his spine.

"For plotting against the Crown and the Administration," the prince replied, his face stern. "Guards, arrest this man."

Jerrol turned to the king, who leaned back on his throne

and closed his eyes as if exhausted. "Your Majesty, I swear, I have done no such thing."

"All lies," the prince said. "Take him away." He waved the guards forward, and they gripped Jerrol's arms firmly between them. Jerrol had no choice but to let them steer him out of the throne room; their grip was unyielding. The prince was telling his father he had it all under control as Jerrol was escorted away.

Jerrol sat on the floor of the cell and stared at the bare rock wall opposite him. It was good for interrogations, he assumed, as he'd collected a few cuts and bruises as the guards bounced him off it when he first arrived. They weren't taking any risks. He must have quite a reputation for being difficult.

Not only had they shackled his hands behind his back, but his cell was also on the lowest level. A solid oak door barred his escape. His lips twitched. He had to admit he had been a thorn in Chancellor Isseran's side; this must be payback.

He frowned in thought. Was the prince's action connected to Isseran? It must be. Nikols must have gone to the prince with the notebook. There had been more than enough time for the prince to speak to Isseran, and the prince must have believed his lies. There was no other reason to arrest him.

The situation was far worse than he had reported if the Crown Prince supported Isseran. After the king, they were the two most powerful men in the Kingdom of Vespiri. The prince had moved fast. Nikols could only have shown him the notebook in the last few days.

He sighed as he tried to get more comfortable. His shoulders ached along with his head as his mind spun, trying to figure a way out. Why had the king not spoken up for him? Why would the king try to invoke an oath that as far as Jerrol knew had never, ever been invoked, and yet allow the person he was entrusting it with to be arrested? It didn't make sense.

The cell door rattled as it was unlocked. It opened, revealing Commander Nikols. Jerrol struggled to his feet as his commanding officer raked him with a no-nonsense glare and folded his arms as the guard locked the door behind him. It was clear he wouldn't be amused by Jerrol's blood-stained jacket and bruised face.

"You are a disgrace to the uniform," Nikols began, his voice deep and hard, just as Jerrol had expected. "That a King's Ranger is arrested for treason, manacled as a common criminal—words fail me."

Jerrol grimaced; he wished they would.

"Look at me when I am speaking to you."

Jerrol raised his eyes to his commander's furious brown ones.

"The prince has ordered you executed at dawn. I wonder at his eagerness, but from his reports, you have been stringing us along for months. Your actions have finally caught up with you." The commander's eyes flicked down to his hands, and Jerrol's eyes followed. He was holding a set of metal lock picks in front of him.

"I don't know whether to beat you myself or offer you to the dogs, but I suppose the prince has made that decision for me." He leaned forward and slapped the wall, before pushing Jerrol back against it. "You are no longer a King's Ranger. Maybe that will remind you not to embarrass me before the king." He slapped the wall again as he lent over Jerrol and stuffed the bundle of metal down the back of his trousers. He stood away as Jerrol slid down the wall. "You're not worth the effort," he spat, turning back to the door. "Open up; this reprobate won't even make the first dawn."

The door rattled, and the commander left. Jerrol lay stunned for a moment, the picks digging into his back. The guard leered at him before locking the door again. Jerrol considered what his now ex-commander had said; he had to get out before dawn. Trying to ignore the creeping sense of failure, he worked the picks out of his waistband and felt the thin metal rods to find which would be best to unlock his manacles.

After much cursing and awkward fumbling, Jerrol managed to shuck the manacles off on the floor, he rubbed his wrists and rolled his shoulders, easing the tension in his muscles. He froze as a sharp voice penetrated the wooden door.

"A cat? You've had your nose in too many jars, mate."

"I swear, a black and white one, with ... um ... with wings! It just flew down the steps."

"Yer having a laugh. Try and pull the other one."

"I swear, I saw it. It appeared out of thin air. A cat with wings."

The other guard burst out laughing. "You think you can gull me? You'd have to come up with something better than that."

There was a clatter of boots as one of the guards clumped down the stairs to the lower level–presumably to chase the cat. Jerrol grinned at the thought. The guard slid the peephole back and peered in; he saw Jerrol laid out on the floor and turned back to the hunt. Boots clattered back up the steps. "Did yer see it? The bloody thing's greased, slid right out of my hands it did."

"There's no such thing as a flying cat."

"I swear, look, it's over there."

There was the echoing sound of a chair falling over. "Bleeding 'ell. Well, catch it then you idiot; it can't stay down 'ere." Muffled curses floated down the stairs.

The older guard groaned. "Only you could make such a ball ache out of it. It's just a bleedin' cat."

"Well, you catch it then." The younger guard sounded annoyed.

"If this costs me my rotation, you'll regret it. I've got just one more watch, and I'm out of 'ere. One more soddin' night of making sure locked doors stay locked and you have to find a bleedin' cat ..." His grumbling voice faded as he climbed the stairs.

Jerrol peered through the peephole; the younger guard had his back to him, and at an exclamation from above, he climbed the first few steps. "Did you get it?"

Jerrol knelt by the door and selecting his picks, set to work. Sliding out of the cell, he shut the door behind him, and as he crept along the wall, he listened. The older guard cursed. "The bastard's slippier than the first frost. Get up 'ere. I'll chase it to you, and you grab it."

The guard on the stairs hurried up, and Jerrol silently followed. Chairs scraped across the floor as they shoved furniture out the way. "There it is, go on, chase it up the stairs, quick. It's just a cat. It ain't got no wings; you need to get yer eyes checked."

Jerrol peered through the doorway. Both guards were herding a small black and white cat up the curved stairway to the upper level. He squinted at it. He was seeing things. It did have wings, and a scaly tail which was flicking in agitation. Jerrol hid behind the desk, rubbing his eyes.

"Which idiot let it in? That door shouldn't be open," the older man said, stomping back down the stairs. "Whatever next. You go down and check the lower cells. I'll do this floor." The guards dispersed and Jerrol fled up the stairs. His eyes widened as he reached the top; the door was open again.

He eased out of the opening and after a quick scan of

the dark expanse of the parade ground, he closed the door behind him and knelt to lock it. Once the lock clicked shut, he didn't hesitate; he straightened his jacket and strolled towards the outer wall of the palace, the darkened parade ground behind him.

A low hooting, like that of an owl, made him stop and peer up at the wall. A knotted rope dropped down, almost braining him. He tugged it and climbed up and onto the gantry and then, flipping the rope over the wall, down the other side. He peered around for his helper, but he couldn't see anyone.

The torches lining the palace walls flickered as patrolling guards moved in front of them. Jerrol waited, counting as the guards reached the end of their patrol, and as they exchanged words, he slid down the steep slope into the scrub.

He waited, expecting a hue and cry as they realised he had escaped. But the night was silent, and after a moment to calm his racing heart, he worked his way deeper into the bushes and retreated into the murky darkness. He made slow progress across the shadowed landscape, listening for whoever had helped him, but there was only his heavy breathing, loud in the silence. He worked his way towards the edge of the city as the faint grey dawn began to steal across the sky.

3

OLD VESPERS

J errol paused in his flight across the rooftops; his grey and black uniform blending into the velvety shadows lurking in the corners of the brick chimney stacks. Not that he needed them, as no one was looking up; in fact, they were very focused on charging down the Port Road. As if he would be that obvious! You would think they had higher expectations of his capabilities. He watched as two more units of guards came charging out of the garrison and raised his eyebrows.

He eased further back into the shadows as his ex-commander exited the gate and scowled after his men. Nikols' glance swept the surrounding buildings, and even reached as far as the upper windows; then he abruptly about-faced and passed back into the garrison courtyard.

Jerrol rubbed his stubbled chin as he considered. Nikols never did anything without an excellent reason. He wouldn't have emptied the whole garrison without cause; and Jerrol thought, with a wry grin, he was a cause that could use all the help he could get.

His heart rate spiked a moment as he thought about the

last few chimes. One night was all it took to rip his comfortable life apart and force him out. Shutting the thoughts out, he refocused on his immediate problem. He needed to get out of Old Vespers alive, then he could worry about the rest.

Spying the drainpipe at the end of the terraced roofs nearest the garrison he shinned down, dropping the last few feet to the ground. A quick sweep of the entrance showed the courtyard was clear. He brushed down his uniform and strolled through the garrison's main gates as if he belonged there, which of course he had.

Jerrol entered the adjutant's office and picked an order pad up from the desk. Listening intently, he dashed off a few words before addressing the front and slipping it into the worn, leather courier bag stacked on a chair by the wall. He padded up the stairs and down unnaturally quiet corridors to his room in the officers' barracks.

Collecting his travel pack and daggers that were unaccountably still where he had left them, and regretting the loss of his dress sword, which the prince had taken a liking to, he grabbed his spare. He froze as he heard pounding feet in the distance. Time to go, but maybe not via the stable as he had first intended. He picked up his overcoat and slipped out of the garrison without a soul seeing him.

Jerrol observed the entrance to the Chapterhouse of the Lady's Order of Remargaren. It looked perfectly normal, with scholars entering and leaving the stone archway unhindered. It didn't appear to be under surveillance, but he couldn't be sure. Few people knew of his relationship with the scholars, but that didn't mean the connection hadn't been made; after all, it hadn't been a secret. He slipped out of the shadows, following the dirt track around the golden-coloured stone walls to the rear gate. His timing was perfect—the supply cart was entering the Chapter-house, and he managed to slip in with the cart before the gate closed.

The Remargaren Chapterhouse was the centre of learning in Vespiri. It was a sprawling set of two-storey build-ings above ground which split into colleges focused on a variety of disciplines. The Chapterhouse contained scholars from all over Remargaren learning the skills of research and interpretation. Below ground was a catacomb of archives and tunnels still being excavated and catalogued by the schol-ars, and—Jerrol was sure—not yet fully discovered.

Scholar Deane Liliian was a formidable, angular woman. Grey-haired and sharp-eyed, she had been a close confidant of the king for many years. As head of the Chapterhouse, Liliian was the one that Jerrol sought. He sauntered through the cloisters which led out of the courtyard and through the walled garden. He reached the stone stairs at the base of the tower which led up to Liliian's office. Hoping she would be in residence, he acknowledged the portly scholar-secretary seated at the desk in the outer office.

"Is the Deane in?"

"Captain Haven! We weren't expecting you!" His eyes widened as he took in Jerrol's dishevelled appearance. "Is everything alright?"

"Yes, fine," Jerrol lied.

"She has people with her, and there is no free time until much later today." He spread his hands. "Her calendar is solid, and she has to go up to the palace this afternoon."

"I can't wait. If you could keep my visit between us three, I'd appreciate it. I need to leave the Deane a message; I have to leave town, and I'm not sure when I'll be back."

The scholar smiled, used to keeping the captain's visits under wraps. "What is it this time?"

"Can't say. Is Scholar Torsion here, do you know?" Jerrol

scribbled a note explaining his situation, before folding the paper and handing it back.

The scholar shook his head. "No, I'm afraid not. Scholar Torsion left for Velmouth about four or five months ago. Haven't seen him since."

"Keep it close. I wasn't here!" Jerrol left the office hoping to escape the Chapterhouse without being seen, but he should have known better. She always seemed to know where he was.

She was waiting for him outside the tower. A slender silver-robed figure, a broad smile across her face. A mass of curly brown hair tumbled around her shoulders, framing a precious heart-shaped face, dominated by enormous sparkling turquoise eyes.

"Taelia," he said as he scanned the courtyard, and wrapping her in a hug, steered her out of view behind a stone column. He indulged in breathing in the fragrance of her hair and his tension eased.

"Jerrol, you weren't going to sneak out without seeing me, were you?" Her smile slipped as her hands fluttered over his face. "What's happened?" Her fingers paused at the heat of his bruises.

"How many times do I have to tell you not to look out for me? It's safer if you stay away from me; I'm nothing but trouble. Torsion's told you enough times."

"Rubbish. I can choose my friends."

"You don't need friends like me." Jerrol forced the words out. "I've been dishonourably discharged. The prince and no doubt the chancellor are after my head. I have to leave before they track me down. It would have been safer for you if you hadn't known I was here. I don't want to get the scholars in trouble."

Taelia gasped, her eyes widening in shock. "But what about the king? He can't want you to leave. He relies on you." She tilted her head. "In fact, there's something else, isn't there? I can feel it. The king's charged you with something, hasn't he?"

"Hush, ask Liliian to make sure she speaks to the king every day. Prince Kharel is trying to isolate the king and banishing me helps his cause." Jerrol memorised her face. His troubles melted away when he was with her. He set her apart from him, resisting the urge to bury his face in her hair. "I have to go. Don't tell anyone except Liliian you found me here." He placed her hand on the wall and left her there, staring sightlessly after him.

Jerrol made it out of the Chapterhouse without anyone else seeing him. He hunkered down in the shelter of a small copse of beech trees on the outskirts of Old Vespers, the thick screen of green leaves providing cover. The king had been concerned about the Watches; therefore, the Watches would be his destination. It would be a few weeks before the orders he had sent would reach his friend Jennery in the King's Guard; he was on the Elothian borders to the north.

He would do the short circuit. That would give him enough time to return to the port in time to meet Jennery. By then, he would have an idea of what they were facing. He would swing through Greenswatch and Deepwater, maybe even as far as Marchwood if he didn't dawdle, before cutting back along the East Road to Lowalstall. That would take him a month on foot. The recent settled weather meant the roads would be in reasonable condition. Unless he could find a horse. A Terolian Darian would be nice. He twisted his lips. Darians were telepathic horses and very rare outside of the neighbouring country of Terolia. A Lady's gift, some said, because the horses chose their riders and bonded for life.

Pulling his purse out, he looked at the paltry handful of coins he'd emptied into his hand. He sighed. That would not get him very far. He could offer to do some stable work for a meal or two; after all, he'd spent enough hours in the stables at Stoneford as a lad. For a moment he thought of returning home, but discarded that idea immediately. He didn't want to drag Lord Jason nor the Watch into his troubles.

He stowed his purse away and started down the trail towards the Guardian mountain range which curved around the city of Old Vespers. He would avoid the port, especially with the number of guards Nikols had sent in that direction. Hopefully, he would reach Greenswatch by sun-up, and then he could lose himself in the forests.

Decision made, Jerrol focused on the path ahead of him. He needed to get through the range before the guards reversed their direction. Amongst this sparse vegetation, there was nowhere to hide, and he would be exposed as he climbed the trail. At least he had a head start—in theory at least.

The narrow trail wound up into the foothills, past drystone walls edging empty fields. Some were ploughed, ready for late planting, the rich, red loamy soil drying in the breeze. Others were full of knee-high waving golden stalks of some crop or other.

Catching his breath, he looked down and out towards the city of Old Vespers. It was his home. For the past seven years, he had lived amongst the hodgepodge of buildings and spires, part of the royal court, comfortable in its rhythms. The solid golden towers of the Chapterhouse rose above the buildings, sturdy and practical, a counterpoint to the silvery spires of the palace. A movement caught his eye and he stiffened, but he couldn't see what it was, and he hurried onwards.

Old Vespers passed from view as Jerrol entered the first of the dim, narrow passes that cut through the base of the hills and wound its way through to the Greenswatch. As he walked, all sound was deadened in the confining space, and the air was unnaturally still. His pack caught on the crowding rock as the trail narrowed and widened again. He hurried on, eager to leave the oppressive atmosphere behind. It echoed his thoughts.

The narrow walls of the trail finally opened onto a plateau, surrounded by tall pine trees providing a natural windbreak and an oasis of calm air which felt pleasantly warm in the evening sun. It had taken all day to get through the pass.

After some searching, he found a small cave tucked up in the ridge. A wiry green-leafed bush disguised the entrance. He squeezed his way in, pushing his pack in front of him, glad for once that he was not a large man. There was a slight alkaline scent lingering after some creature had moved on.

He hunkered down in the dim light, and chewing on a strip of dried meat out of his travel rations, contemplated his immediate future. He was poorly provisioned for any trip, let alone one travelling around the Watches for a month. His rations would last a few days; he would need to find food, especially if he was going on foot.

His mind spun with unease. He didn't like leaving the king. Not that the king was unprotected; he had his guards and other rangers after all. But he was the only ranger that seemed concerned about the chancellor's sudden elevation or believed that he was up to no good. For him to be accused of treason and removed from the board so easily was worrying.

And then the king had tried to invoke the Oath. He wasn't sure what the Oath *did*. No one had ever used it before. The fact that the king thought he needed it meant the king was concerned about something.

The king hadn't completed the Oath; did that mean it wasn't in force? Or was it? He was sure the words had flashed in the throne room. Could an oath be half sworn?

He rehashed the scene in the throne room, not making it any clearer.

And who had helped him escape? And why? He couldn't think of anyone he knew who would have taken such a risk, except maybe Jennery and he was still miles away. As he pondered, exhaustion from stress as well as his flight finally caught up with him, and Jerrol dozed off.

4

GREENSWATCH

J errol awoke at the rattle of stones outside his cave. Someone was searching nearby. Stiffening, he felt for his daggers which were within easy reach. He waited, tense and alert, but no one tried to enter the cave, and after a while, all sounds faded away. He relaxed his grip on his daggers and sat listening for the rest of the night. Before the sun came up, his meagre belongings were packed, and he left the cave, daggers at the ready.

After two days of trudging south towards the big river, Jerrol's feet were blistered, his body ached, and his mood was tense and murderous. If Isseran stood before him now, Jerrol wouldn't hesitate to take him down. He clenched his fists at the thought.

Someone was following him. He knew it. They kept their distance, but he couldn't relax. His senses were on high alert, keeping him tense and jittery. What were they waiting for? Maybe more reinforcements. If so, he couldn't afford to wait for them to arrive.

On the third night, Jerrol set up camp. The gleam of the

large river flickered through the trees that led down to the water's edge. Following the routine of the previous two nights, he found a small copse of trees and bent them into a shelter with his bedroll. As darkness descended, he melted into the trees.

Circling back around his route, he paused, listening for his trackers. He heard a slight scuff off to his left and froze. The forest floor was carpeted by a soft layer of mulch and decaying leaves, muffling the sound of footsteps. He peered into the impenetrable gloom, but he couldn't see anything.

He wasn't sure what gave him away, maybe he was over-tired, but he was on the defensive as a knife-wielding shadow attacked him. Allowing the momentum to take him back, he accepted the initial slash as his due and twisted into the man. Displacing his opponent, he attacked. They jostled for position, back and forth, daggers clashing and chinging off each other. Blades flickered between them until Jerrol saw the slightest opening and took it, committing himself to the move and the kill.

Gasping for breath and feeling a little light-headed, he levered himself off the still body. Tensing, he listened for the others; he knew they were out there. Why had they dropped back and not charged him? He circled as he searched the deepening gloom and stumbled over a body. Frowning, he felt for a pulse, but the man was dead, though he couldn't find a wound. Recent as well—one of his trackers? Had they had a falling out?

He spun as shadowy forms rushed him all together, getting in each other's way. They were larger and persistent, and although he disabled two of them, he began to tire. When an unexpected fifth man jumped him from behind, delivering a stunning blow to his head, he sagged, dazed.

The remaining men stood, sides heaving. "I never saw

such a scrapper," one of them said, a tinge of respect in his voice.

"Scrapper or no, he's done for the 'atchet, we ain't gonna get our money now," a low voice complained.

"Yeah, stick 'im one and toss him in the river, no point dragging him back," another rough voice agreed.

The men grunted in agreement and Jerrol was dragged across the ground, the matting of pine needles pricking his skin. From what felt like the bottom of a deep well, he heard a low-voiced argument going on around him as to who would get to stick 'im one. The voices echoed painfully in his temples.

A high thrum, a low curse, and one of his captors let go of him. An unexplained stumble and another man lost his balance, and they slipped and skidded down the steep slope. The men flailed, trying to grab the thin saplings that bent under their weight, and they lost their grip on Jerrol. His body rolled the last few feet and splashed into the water, sucked under as the men watched.

The water roiled and then calmed, returning to its smooth deep green flow, and continued on its way as if nothing untoward had happened, all traces of infamy gone. The men stared around them with caution before beginning the climb back up the steep bank.

Jerrol had a vague memory of rough handling and then the shock of being consumed by cold water. He was sucked down by the current, out of sight and out of breath.

As he struggled to reach the surface, the realisation sank in that he wasn't in the water, he was kneeling on solid land. He coughed out water and dragged in a breath. He sensed a presence and opened his eyes. Thin saplings grew in a curve up to the riverbank, blocking the sky and the moonlight, providing a dim glade lit by a soft green glow filtering through the leaves.

In the centre, a slender young woman stood in front of him, patiently waiting. "Where am I?" he asked, clearing his throat as his voice cracked. He wiped his face with his dripping sleeve.

The woman mused for a moment. "There is a place betwixt life and death where the essence of time shimmers like a mist and allows me to reach your soul and bespeak it."

"Am I dead?" Jerrol asked, confused by her words.

"Not quite, you are my Captain, and you have yet to fulfil your duty."

Jerrol stiffened and lifted his eyes to her face, taking in her flawless complexion and sparkling emerald-green eyes. He swallowed as he realised who stood before him, speaking of his death so casually. She was the Lady Leyandrii, the deity worshipped by at least three of the four kingdoms of Remargaren.

"The Ascendants grow bold," she said.

"The Ascendants?"

"They return to finish the deed."

"Deed? My Lady, why am I here?" Jerrol staggered to his feet and stood, swaying.

"Bend your head." Stepping towards him, she reached out and placed her hands either side of his face. Jerrol tensed as her power surged through him, almost dropping him to his knees, but he was held in place by her will alone. "You are *my* Captain," she repeated. "You have the sight. You have the depths. Only you can find the truth. Restore the forgotten, heal the wounded."

Leyandrii raised Jerrol's head and stared deep into his eyes as if she could see straight to his heart and his innermost self. He felt exposed to the core. "Soothe the Land and make her your ally. She misses us as we miss her. You have the knowledge, the courage, the heart and sight. What was sundered cannot be reformed, but a true heart may restore."

She looked off into the distance, a small smile curving her lips. "Help is at hand. You are relieved of your immediate assailants, my Captain. You do seem to be able to put yourself in danger's way. You should be more adept at avoiding trouble."

Jerrol stared at her, stunned and confused. He had always followed the Lady, been hers to command, but this felt a bit more definite. She spoke in riddles; he was unsure what it all meant. Warmth suffused him as she stepped back. "Wake my guards. They will help you. There is one I cannot see, the deceiver. Watch for him, my Captain. He stirs. There is one who waits for you up ahead. She will be good company, I think. Be well," she said as everything started to shimmer, and he felt himself spinning and tumbling against the current.

His shoulder glanced off a submerged rock, the shock making him inhale a mouthful of water. He choked. He was still in the river, attempting to drown. He struck out, pushing himself back to the surface. Gasping for air, he treaded water as he frantically tried to see if anyone still haunted the riverbanks. It appeared that he was alone. The water calmed as his breathing slowed, his frantic panic subsiding.

The river deposited him on a small gritty beach, where he lay retching up water, his chest heaving. His stomach fluttered on the edge of panic, surprised that he was still alive, as the current tugged at his legs as if to coax him back in. His throat burned as he struggled to inhale air between retching up water, until at last he lay limp and exhausted.

Jerrol stirred as the cold seeped into his bones. His

clothes clung to his blue-tinged skin. Sharp grit dug into the palms of his hands as he pushed himself up. The Lady's assistance was double-edged, it seemed. He didn't know where he was, and he had lost his pack and another sword—and, curse it, his daggers as well.

He sat up, groggily, and brushed the grit from his hands. He surveyed his surroundings. In front of him, the slow-moving mass of brooding darkness lapped at his feet and the exposed roots of leafy trees clung to the bank. Rank upon rank of trees rose from the water's edge up the steep slopes on either side of the river, which was much broader here. He must have been swept some distance downstream, maybe even as far as Deepwater.

The only piece of good news that he could see was the fact that he was now on the other side of the river, though that must have been the most uncomfortable river crossing he had ever made, hopefully never to be repeated. He peered into the impenetrable darkness rising around him. The night air was thick and heavy. No lights shone to ease the depths. No sounds broke the stillness, not a leaf stirred. He shivered.

Jerrol began the climb up the riverbank, grabbing the thin trunks to help pull him up. As his feet slid on the decaying detritus, the noise of his passage reverberated in his ears. He slowed as he worked his way up through the trees; his breath was coming in gasps as his abused lungs struggled to cope.

He tried to figure out where he was, to find a landmark that would give him some indication of which direction he needed to go in, but the trees were thickening ahead of him. His wet clothes made his skin clammy and chill, and he shivered in the cold night air. He wrung his shirt out, but it didn't improve the situation much.

He kept moving. The Lady's words filled his mind, but they made no more sense now than when she had said them.

He couldn't put this down to imagination, even if he had been hit over the head and half-drowned.

The ground levelled out, and the trees grew sturdier, their thick trunks blocking his view. He paused and leaned against a huge tree, whose roots tangled in the undergrowth. He stared up through the leafy branches, thinking of Sentinals as he tried to catch his breath. His chest ached. If hadn't imagined the Lady, then the silver-eyed man in the tree must be real too. He wondered where he was.

If he could recognise the stars, he might get a sense of direction. He cursed under his breath as he peered about him. The thick matrix of branches above him defeated his eyes, so he stared into the darkness ahead instead. Maybe he should stop until the sun came up.

He hesitated as he saw a pale shape in the lightening gloom. As he approached, he realised it was a horse. What was a horse doing here? It was a pure white mare, her hide gleaming in the dim light, with elegant lines and a long swishing tail, tacked up with a saddle and bridle. Where was its rider?

Searching the surroundings, he tried to quiet his laboured breathing, but there was no movement except for the slight chink of the bridle as the mare chomped on the bit. He placed his hand on her neck and reached for the bridle. "Where did you come from?" he asked, his voice a soft murmur in the night. "Are you lost?"

She shook her head, her dark eyes gleaming as she watched him. She sighed and rolled her lips, and he couldn't help the smile that crept over his face. Breathing in the musky scent of her skin, he felt a tension deep inside him ease at the familiar smell. He stroked her neck with long, firm strokes, enjoying the contact with another living creature that wasn't trying to kill him.

Thanking the Lady, he rummaged through the saddlebags. A bedroll was tied on the back of her saddle, with a sword strapped in place. "Shall we see what treasures we have?" he murmured as the gloom began to lift. Pale streaks of grey light pierced the canopies and eased the darkness. "Hopefully, some money. Otherwise, you are going to have to make do with roadside grass." He laughed at her expression and then sobered at the sound. It had been a long time since he'd had reason to laugh out loud.

The pack yielded not only a welcome, plump purse but also a cloth-wrapped sandwich. He inhaled the mouthwatering aroma and wondered who had provisioned her.

"Should we stay or go? Do you think it is safe here?" His voice echoed in the gloom as the mare shook her head. "I agree. We ought to go." He rifled through the rest of the pack: dry clothes, a useful flick knife, a flint, and a canteen of water. He found a set of daggers, and he breathed a heartfelt sigh of relief. He hefted one in his hand; the balance was perfect.

Thankful for the dry clothes, he stripped off his wet ones. He hesitated at the fine texture of the shirt, before quickly dressing. The tension across his shoulders eased as the warmth from the clothes penetrated his chill skin. He strapped the sword around his waist, reassured by its familiar weight. Slipping the daggers into his belt, he wrapped the warm cloak around himself and reluctantly stamped back into his soggy boots; the wet clothes he wrung out and shoved into the saddlebag.

He led the mare out of the trees, towards a faint trail which he hoped led down to some sort of road. A road should help him get his bearings. As they reached the trail, he turned back to the mare. With a deep breath, he pulled himself up into the saddle, hissing at the deep ache in his shoulder and chest. He rubbed his side where the assassin had slashed at him not so long ago. Fortunately, the knife had not penetrated through to his skin; he had been lucky.

The chattering screech of rising birds in the trees behind him had Jerrol moving off with alacrity. He glanced back as the mare wended her way through the undergrowth, but the trees closed behind him, obscuring whatever had disturbed the birds.

5

MARCHWOOD WATCH

Jerrol slogged through the mud wishing he hadn't bothered to visit the hamlet. That had been a waste of time and effort, but after a month on the road, keeping out of sight and dodging the local Watch guards, he had wanted to find somewhere warm and dry. Somewhere safe.

The feeling of being watched had grown stronger, as had the fleeting glimpses of a dark figure intervening whenever he had found trouble. The only reason he wasn't hunting the person down was because he had an inkling of who it was, no matter how impossible the idea was, and so far the person following him had been intent on keeping Jerrol alive.

Jerrol glanced down at himself. He could have been anyone. A slight man, drably dressed in a muddy cloak and trousers, both of which had seen better days. The edges of his rough shirt were frayed and trapped the water dripping down the threads in the soft rain. His boots were thick with mud and well-worn. A nondescript hat was pulled down over his face, offering some protection from the elements.

Over his shoulder was a burlap sack which might once

have been waterproof but was now sadly waterlogged. His cloak, though, was dark and warm. It was the item of most value to those who stalked him.

Jerrol didn't acknowledge the three commoners who paused as they watched him struggle through the thick mud. He was an easy mark, a lonely figure who posed little threat and would not be missed, focused on keeping his feet in the treacherous conditions. He sighed under his breath. If only they knew. In unison, they closed on him, daggers in hand, the squelching of mud betraying their position.

Forewarned, Jerrol spun in one fluid move. The glint of steel carved an arc that sliced through the air. It came to a halt just in front of the lead man, a broad-chested, blond-haired man, who flailed desperately to avoid skewering himself on the vicious-looking blade. The man's feet slid out from under him at his sudden change in momentum. He landed in the mud on his backside as the sword skimmed his lank hair and came to rest at his throat. The man gulped, the silver scar on his chin prominent, his blue eyes wide with fear.

Jerrol's gaze raked across the other two bandits as they slithered to an uncertain stop. "I could pierce you like a suckling pig." Jerrol cleared his throat. His voice was low and gravelly not having used it in a while. "If you were worth the effort."

There was a muted whirr, and the man on the left cried out and dropped his knife. He hugged his hand to his chest as he stumbled away, squelching through the mud, and the other man scurried after him.

Jerrol scanned the undergrowth. His silent protector was still following him, then. Appearing at opportune moments and as mysteriously disappearing before he had a chance to accost him. The stranger had been following him since he left Old Vespers; who was it? "Show yourself. I know you're there, so you may as well come out."

He looked back at the man sinking into the gloopy mud. His sword followed the man's slow descent as the glutinous muck restrained him better than any ropes could. A quick flick of the eyes confirmed that the others had turned tail and fled back into the dripping trees.

Glancing back at the bushes, Jerrol waited, and the lean, silver-eyed man from the temple gardens stepped out. His grey-green uniform was showing signs of wear and tear, but he looked nowhere near as disreputable as Jerrol.

"You've been following me for nearly a month. What do you want?"

The man's alert eyes flitted around them before returning to the man in the mud. "I do the Lady's bidding."

"The Lady does not bid you kill innocent people."

"No, only those trying to kill her Captain."

"Do you think we can continue this conversation some-where dry, and warmer?" the man stuck in the mud asked through chattering teeth.

Jerrol looked down and grinned. "Well, if you will consort with bandits, what do you expect?" He wiped his sword on his cloak and sheathed it, and then he began to chuckle. "Not the rendezvous I was expecting, Jennery," he said as he reached out a hand to help pull his friend to his feet. The mud released Jennery with an enormous squelch; Jerrol's grip inexorably pulled him up and out of the mucky suction. Jennery staggered as his legs took back his weight and trembled back to life. Looking down at his clothes, he scowled.

"Rendezvous," he barked with laughter, "in this godfor-saken place? You could drown in this, and no one would ever know!"

"There are worse fates, you know," Jerrol replied as he moved to the firmer ground at the side of the road.

"Who is your friend? He won't stick me with one of those arrows, will he?"

Jerrol flicked a glance at the man watching them. His bow was still strapped to his back. "Not unless you try to attack me again."

"Jerrol!" Jennery followed him. "What happened? Why all the secrecy? And why are we flailing about in all this mud?"

Jerrol turned away. "Not here," he said. "Let's get out of the rain first. There's a barn back aways down the track. It's empty for now, and you can clean up." He gestured to the silent bowman. "Will you join us?"

It wasn't much of a barn, more a temporary shield from the rain. The screens were crude: a simple weave that wasn't tight enough to prevent the water from dribbling through the many gaps and collecting on the mud floor. The damp smell of saturated soil and drenched foliage permeated the air.

Adjacent to the shelter was a lean-to providing just as primitive protection to a rug-covered horse tethered to the wall. Jennery drifted over to the unfamiliar mare, admiring her sleek lines visible even under the grubby rug. He gently rubbed her nose in greeting. "Where did he find you?" he murmured as she tossed her head. Jennery sighed as he glanced around. "A bit of luxury for a change. I'd forgotten what it was like."

Jennery observed the bowman hovering by the door, half in and half out. He looked lean and dangerous, his face sharp and observant, his eyes never still, watching. He made Jennery feel on edge as if something terrible were about to happen.

A soft snort from behind him showed him how much sympathy he was going to get. "Stop complaining," Jerrol said as he threw over a bundle of cloth. "Get changed. I want to know why you were with those bandits and attacking innocent strangers as well." He shook his head. "I thought you would come in by the Port Road."

"I did come in by the Port Road, for what it's worth," Jennery grunted as he peeled off his sodden clothes. He used them to rub the mud off his muscular body, but they didn't help much. He gave up, dropping them on the floor. "But the port was closed. The dockers were protesting about something or other, so I tagged on to a mule train." He struggled to get a clean shirt on over damp skin, the cloth muffling his voice. "From the tone of your very short and uninformative message, I guessed you didn't want to advertise our presence here?" He ended with an upturn of his voice. He looked across the shelter at Jerrol, who was kneeling over a small fire pit, trying to coax a spark out of his flint.

The man in the doorway gave a soft exclamation. He was watching Jerrol with a strange expression on his face, but Jennery didn't think it was a conversation gambit, so he looked back at Jerrol, pausing as he watched the spark catch and the flames grow. He continued with his report. "The chancellor posted guards at all the entry points; he controls the wharves and the headland. The king won't get support from the dock hands when their livelihood is at risk."

Jerrol sighed as he rested the tin pot over the fire. "I know," he replied, glancing up. The flickering flames slanted a soft yellow light across his face which was drawn and strained. The dark shadows under his eyes made him look a lot older than his twenty-two years, but his grey eyes were clear and sharp.

Jennery's mouth tightened with concern. Jerrol was thinner, having lost weight in the few months they had been apart. The arms master had raised his slight build as a concern when he had first been inducted into the rangers, but his wiry, stubborn constitution had always proved true.

He rubbed his chin, remembering the one time Jerrol had managed to beat him in the sparring ring. The scar was an annoying reminder. Their foster mother Hannah had had conniptions sewing him up, berating both of them for their carelessness. "What happened?" he asked as he squatted next to the tiny fire and inhaled the intoxicating smell of coffee. "Coffee," he exclaimed, "you've got real coffee?"

The bowman shifted as the aroma reached him, his eyes brightening. "Kafinee?" he murmured.

Jerrol grinned, the corners of his eyes crinkling as the tightness in his face eased. "The last bag. I couldn't get any more so make the most of it. I hope you brought some money with you as I'm just about out." He handed a mug to the bowman and then one to Jennery.

"Bliss." Jennery communed with his mug and sipped the steaming black coffee. It was pungent but smooth, and more importantly hot. He relaxed as the warmth crept down his limbs.

The unusual bowman still hovering in the doorway drew his attention. Even with the coffee in hand, he held himself alertly. He looked as if he could deal with whatever came through the door. His silver eyes never stopped moving, continually scanning the surroundings. He wore an archaic silvery-green uniform, with a high-necked collar, which made him look mysterious, foreign. The material shimmered even though there was little light.

"Who's this in the fancy get-up?" Jennery jerked his head at the man at the door.

"I don't know." Jerrol stared at the dark-haired young man. "I first saw you in the temple in Old Vespers. Who are you?"

The man ducked his head. "The Lady bid me protect you; you have too many enemies, Captain."

"You're a Sentinal, aren't you?" Jerrol said slowly. The man stilled, and Jennery gasped.

"He can't be. They all died," Jennery blurted, and the man flinched, his face paling.

"No, they didn't. The Lady encased her guards in the sentinal trees to protect them. You've been sleeping, haven't you? You're Birlerion. One of the forgotten."

The man deliberated, staring at Jerrol, his face unnaturally stiff. "Yes, the Lady named me Birlerion. I am one of her Guards."

"But that would mean he's over three thousand years old," Jennery gasped, his mouth dropping. He didn't believe it; it wasn't possible. Birlerion stepped back, his eyes flitting around him.

"Why didn't you come forward before?" Jerrol said, his voice calm.

Birlerion flicked a glance out the doorway. "If they didn't know I was there, easier to take them out."

Jennery scoffed, watching the man who looked ready to flee. "And how many have you taken out?" he asked with morbid interest.

Birlerion clamped his lips shut and turned away.

"Enough, Jennery, drink your coffee."

Jennery dragged his gaze away from the strange Sentinal and looked at Jerrol. His friend was on edge and greatly worn down. His brown hair was much longer than usual, his uniform was grubby, mud-splashed and unrecognisable except for the badge on his tunic. For the third time, Jennery asked, "What happened?"

Jerrol hesitated, delaying his response by sipping his coffee. Eventually, he raised his head and looked at Jennery. "There was a misunderstanding. I haven't figured it all out yet, but the upshot is ..." He hesitated again and gave a slight shrug. "The Crown Prince arrested me for treason."

Jennery gasped. "What?"

"He sentenced me to death." Jerrol stared into his mug.

"But, but why?" Jennery couldn't grasp what he was saying.

"It seems that Prince Kharel has the ear of the king and has convinced him that I am working against the crown and not to be trusted. Oh, and Isseran has levied some such accusation or other that I've been trying to discredit him." Jerrol rubbed his face, and Jennery saw his hand tremble. "The king is ill; he has some palsy that is eroding his strength. Prince Kharel is feeling vulnerable. Instead of relying on his greatest weapon, the King's Rangers, he is sowing dissension. At least Prince Anders is out of Vespers with the army. By casting me out, he thinks he can strengthen his grip, reduce the rangers' influence on the king."

"But you are one of the king's most trusted advisors! He wouldn't send anyone but you to Birtoli; he refused to consider anyone else. The resolution was acclaimed by all; even the princess acceded to the agreement. If anyone were going to get upset, it would have been her. And collusion against the chancellor?" Jennery paused, trying to find a foul enough word to use. He gave up. "I don't believe it," he said. "Nor will anyone else."

"I had been on Isseran's detail for the last two months, remember. He is rumoured to be negotiating with a high-level party for support, and I have been seen in his vicinity. It doesn't take much for most people to assume the worst."

"If you are no longer part of the court, there is no benefit to Isseran."

"Of course there is. The king has lost a trusted advisor. He wins either way."

"It doesn't make sense. Isseran knows you would never

betray the king. I don't believe he would even waste his time trying. The king knows it too, and nothing you say will make me believe differently." Jennery glared at Jerrol.

Jerrol laughed, though there was little humour in it. "I don't think the tale of my arrest was bandied about that much." A pained expression passed over his face. "I think the prince was hoping to kill me off quietly, without anyone noticing."

Jennery's breath hissed out in dismay; there was something not quite right, but he just couldn't put his finger on it. "What did Nikols say?"

"Well, seeing as he was the one who helped me escape, I assume he thought that the accusations would hold. I thought it would be best if I kept my head down, maybe check out the Watches whilst the furore dies down. Incognito, you know." Jerrol paused, waiting.

"Incognito! I'll have his head on a pike, the bastard. You wait till I get my hands on him. How dare he treat you so. To let the prince arrest you ..." Jennery broke off, appalled. No wonder his friend looked so wrung out.

Jerrol held up his hands, fending Jennery off. "I know, I know," he said. "Calm down, think of it as a break, time to relax," he added with a slight smile.

The comment gave Jennery pause. "What? In all this mud? Not the sort of place I'd choose," he huffed. "How come I'm here? If you are not on king's business, how did you manage to wangle my orders? I am an important member of the king's army, you know. Those orders were official, though now I think on it, they were a bit vague."

Jerrol laughed and gripped his friend's arm. "I've missed you."

Jennery squinted at him. "Hmm. Are you going to tell me what's really going on here? Or do I have to beat it out of you? And where did you find that mare? There is no way she is a garrison horse, and quite frankly, there is no way you could afford to buy her."

"I told you; I've been discharged. I managed to get out of Old Vespers before the prince could do anything more permanent, though it was a near thing. He was very enthusiastic in his pursuit!" Jerrol paused. "I believe I have Birlerion to thank for making it this far. The mare found me on the road and decided to stay." He shrugged. "I wasn't going to argue, I'd walked far enough. The only good thing all this mud is good for is disguising what she is, though even then she is still quite eye-catching, no matter what I say to her. The Darian breed is rare in Vespiri. I'm hoping most people won't recognise her for what she is."

"And how successful has that been?" Jennery asked, his voice bland. "The Darians make lifelong bonds, don't they? Has she accepted you as her rider?" He snapped his fingers. "She must have. I bet she's given you her name, hasn't she!"

Birlerion stiffened. "Never share her name," he said, his voice edged with an emotion Jennery couldn't identify. "She is the Lady's gift."

"She did," Jerrol admitted. "The first time she spoke to me, I almost fell off her in shock. That was a surprise; it's almost as if she were looking for me. I must admit I don't think I would have survived without her; she's been good company." He stared bleakly into the fire, his face taut.

Jennery shifted as the silence drew out, and discreetly observed Birlerion. Considering how fraught his friend looked, he wondered how the Sentinal had managed to cope with being abruptly woken and shoved into a situation not of his making, nor of his time. He didn't say much. They knew nothing about him, and the thought of him silently following Jerrol these last few weeks made his gut tighten.

At least he was here now; he could protect Jerrol. "So

now I'm here, what's the plan? I need to pick up my horse and saddlebags from the village."

"I thought I'd disguise myself as a King's Ranger seeing as I am so experienced," Jerrol said. "No one will recognise me. It worked quite well earlier." He grew serious. "We need to check out the King's Watches; it appears the administration is under threat. Too many have forgotten the promises, the guardians are failing, and we need to discover why. A gentle jaunt exploring the countryside, what more could you ask for?"

"Less mud," came the grumpy response.

6

GREENSWATCH

Jerrol waited his turn at the water hole, digesting the news that Lord Hugh of Greenswatch had travelled to Deepwater for the confirmation of Lord Aaron. Zin'talia had tugged her reins free and wandered over to the pond whilst they had been talking to the teamsters and was now cropping the short, wiry grass around the edges. He could sense her impatience; she wanted to get off the road and find a warm stable.

Frowning, he squatted down at the water's edge to scoop up a handful and splash his face. What to do next? He rubbed his face over and rinsed again. He unstopped his water skin and dunked it in the pool. Jennery leaned against his horse, waiting for him to finish drinking from the water. Birlerion hovered on the edge of the road, watching the wagon train disappear around the bend.

"I think we'll swing around south by the Grove before heading across to Stoneford. No point going to Greenswatch if Lord Hugh isn't going to be home. We can stop off there and report to Lord Hugh on the way back. "

"I can't wait. I need a bath, all this dipping in rivers can't be good for you." Jennery bared his teeth. "I need a few comforts on this merry jaunt of ours. Can't you find a hostelry for once? There's one about ten miles further on, Mucky Duck or something; it's on the outskirts of the Lady's Grove. Let's make for that and have a good meal; you're wasting away, lad."

Jerrol tilted his head, a slight smile on his face. "You mean the Black Hen? I assume it has a taproom?"

"It would be rude not to, now wouldn't it?" Jennery grinned.

"Alright," Jerrol agreed. "Let's do that. The horses could do with a rest; we've covered some miles this last week. Now we are in the Greenswatch we need to keep a closer eye out, ask a few questions. Though that does not mean we are going to crawl from one taproom to the next," he said with a mock scowl as Jennery's grin deepened.

Jerrol shook his head, stoppered the water skin and hooked it back under his saddlebag. "You all finished here? Birlerion, do you need to top up your water?" He gestured to the pool as he prepared to remount Zin'talia.

Birlerion took his place at the water's edge as Jerrol swung himself up into the saddle, and Jennery gathered up his reins and pulled his horse away from the pond. Jerrol turned onto the muddy track that would lead them north towards the tall sentinal trees that stood in the Grove.

Jennery glanced at the mysterious Sentinal as they rode. He rarely spoke. On occasion, he graced them with his presence, like now, but usually, he was a shadow on their trail, silent and deadly. "So, Birlerion. Where were you from? Where did you call home?"

Birlerion hesitated before answering. "I was born in Vespers, but I called Greens home."

"Vespers. Yeah? Which one? Old or New?"

"There was only one Vespers."

Jennery nodded sagely. "Old, then. What was it like three thousand years ago?"

Birlerion's face was stiff, but he answered. "A lot smaller."

"We could've guessed that. Tell us something we don't know."

Birlerion glared at Jennery, and Jennery gave him a bright smile. He made a silent bet the Sentinal wouldn't tell them anything. He rarely spoke as it was.

Birlerion gritted his teeth and stared ahead over his horse's ears. After a moment, his shoulders relaxed, and he began speaking, his voice low, and both Jennery and Jerrol listened.

"Vespers was more compact than it is today. Narrow twisty streets that led down to the harbour, which wasn't much more than a beach and a jetty, with a few barns behind it, nothing like your warehouses. Leyandrii's palace was closer to the city than the king's is, closer to her people. Her temple was newly built. She was always present, part of daily life.

"Guerlaire was her Captain. He was an intense and practical man." Birlerion grimaced. "Stubborn too; once he made a decision, he wouldn't budge. Very clever. He built Leyandrii the most beautiful bridge, connecting her palace to the Chapterhouse, a sparkling edifice that amazed everyone, even his harshest critics. You had to see it to believe it; it was breathtaking." He paused a moment, remembering, a slight smile on his face.

His voice softened as he continued. "She watched over everyone, and you could feel her presence. Her roses grew everywhere; the scent was relaxing at times, and at others uplifting, but always comforting." His lips quirked. "Depended on what she thought you needed, I suppose."

"So you were based at the palace with Leyandrii?" Jerrol asked.

"Yes, with a few others."

"How did you become a Sentinal?" Jennery asked, trying to keep the conversation moving. "Did she have a recruiting effort going?"

Birlerion's lips tightened, but he answered. "She asked very nicely."

Jennery snorted. "That was it? She just asked?"

"That was all that was needed," Birlerion replied.

"And you dropped everything? What were you before you were a Sentinal?"

"A ranger."

"And they just let you go?" Jennery asked, the disbelief evident in his voice.

Birlerion cast him a withering glance. "It was different then. The rangers were hers, too. The Lady was part of our daily lives. It was an honour to serve her, as it still is."

"No one would just walk away from the rangers. Not after the effort it takes to get in in the first place."

Birlerion shrugged. "If the Lady asked you, and you heard her voice, I doubt you would be able to refuse her."

"Alright then, where were you at the end? What happened?"

There was a short silence before Birlerion replied. "A lot of things happened. Considering Vespers was destroyed, I'm surprised you have to ask."

"That's no answer. Where were you? What did you do? How did you end up in the tree?"

Birlerion's horse came to a halt as he clenched the reins, and Jennery turned, eyebrows raised. He swallowed at the sight of the Sentinal's face. "I'm sorry, I didn't mean to ..." His voice trailed off.

The Sentinal was so rigid he could have been carved

from stone, except for his eyes; they were full of pain and loss before he looked away and hid his emotions behind his considerable wall of reserve. But not before Jennery saw a flash of fear—was it? Or remorse?

"Enough, Jennery," Jerrol said. "No more."

Birlerion slowly relaxed his grip, and his horse began to move again.

They rode on in silence.

The sun was setting as they finally reached the Black Hen. The evening sky was burnished bronze and gold with fiery red tints flashing across the horizon. The Black Hen was a sprawling inn that showed recent signs of expansion. Lighter-coloured brick walls extended further back than Jerrol remembered, and the frames of another building stood blackly silhouetted in the burning sunset.

In the distance, dwellings were set back on either side of the track as it curved around the bend. The Grove boasted a simple temple dedicated to the Lady, as well as a meeting hall, a thriving market place, and a smithy connected to a hostelry near the group of sentinal trees.

Jerrol swung his leg over and dismounted with a tired grunt. He handed the reins up to Jennery as he unstrapped his saddlebags. "Jennery, take the horses down to the hostelry, and Birlerion and I will sort out the rooms. It may make sense to get them checked over while we are here; it's been some time since we've been near a smithy."

"I'll take care of it," Jennery said as he led Zin'talia and Birlerion's hack down the road and round the bend out of sight. Jerrol peered at the swinging sign of a somewhat faded, grubby-looking bird. It did look more duck-like, he thought with a grin. He strolled into the cool dimness of the taproom, breathing a sigh of relief to be out of the glare of the blazing sunset.

"Evening." He inclined his head towards the tall man standing behind the bar, polishing a glass. The taproom was empty, and the tables and chairs all tidily arranged in rows awaiting the evening crowd.

"After rooms?" the barkeep asked with a quirk of his bushy grey eyebrows. "And maybe a bath?" he added, observing Jerrol's grimy appearance and Birlerion's mud-splashed travelling cloak.

"Both would be welcome," Jerrol said. "It's been a long week."

"Just you?" asked the man as he reached for a numbered tag hanging on the wall behind him.

"There's three of us. We can share a room if you have one handy."

The 'keep tossed a tag on the bar and selected another off its hook. "One's got two beds, the other is a single," he said as he pulled a long draught of ale which he plonked on the bar in front of Jerrol and then Birlerion in turn. "Gets rid of the dust," he said. "We're quiet tonight so you can have as many rooms as you like," he continued. "Be busy later, though, as one of the old'uns passed; they're all up at the landing saying their goodbyes."

Jerrol gulped his ale. It was dark and intense, pungent enough to clear the road grime from his throat. Birlerion sniffed it suspiciously before taking a sip.

"Where you from then, travelling a week? Been up north?" the 'keep asked. He had knowing blue eyes that assessed them quickly.

"Just passing through. A bit of comfort makes a change; the ground gets harder this time of year."

The 'keep snorted in agreement. "Dinner's served in an hour. You can have the bathhouse to yourselves tonight, so I recommend you make the most of it. The girls can sort your clothes if you want. They'll have them ready for you in the morning if you leave them out."

Jerrol stared at him. "Bathhouse?" he repeated.

The 'keep grinned and pointed out the window towards the strange silhouette. "Bathhouse, hot water and all for an extra copper. Wife's idea," he added with a satisfied smile.

Birlerion straightened up in interest.

Jerrol finished his drink and made to place a copper on the bar, but the 'keep shooed him off. "First ones are on the house. I'll let the girls know to start the fire. Yer rooms on the second floor, at the top of the stairs."

Jerrol led Birlerion up the stairs to drop his bags. The first key opened the door to the twin. The room was small and narrow with most of the space taken up by two single beds, but it was clean and bright with whitewashed walls. He handed the other key to Birlerion and entered the room.

The linen smelt fresh, and a small reed rug separated the beds. He grinned; they'd better not both be trying to get out of bed at the same time. A small window let the evening air in to blow away any mustiness. The inviting bed was tempting, but the bath won. He dropped his cloak on the bed and dug out clean britches, a shirt and his last piece of soap. *Note to self*, he thought, get soap. Heading down the stairs, he met Jennery stumping up.

Jennery squeezed past, sliding his saddlebag off his shoulder. "Well, and where are you off to?"

"The same place as you, I expect," Jerrol grinned. Eyes alight, he waved the piece of soap under Jennery's nose. "Bathhouse," he gloated and sped off down the stairs.

"What?" Jennery spun to watch a rather energetic Jerrol disappear. "Bathhouse?" He dropped his bags on the floor next to the unoccupied bed and was soon following Jerrol out towards the wondrous structure which provided hot water on tap. "Lady be blessed," he murmured as he watched Jerrol ease himself into the steaming water with an immense sigh of relief. The clean clothes he had piled on the bench; the travel-stained were dropped in a heap on the floor.

Jennery shucked his clothes off as quick as he could. He sluiced off the worst of the dirt under the shower, shuddering as the cold water rinsed him down, and soon he was groaning in pleasure as he slid under the warm water. "Bliss," he said as he submerged up to his neck. "Whoever came up with this idea has to be raking it in," he said as he relaxed bonelessly in the warm embrace.

Jerrol opened an eye when a young lad bobbed into the room. "Sir, I'm here for the washing."

Jerrol waved a lazy arm over towards the bench. "Take it," he said and closed his eyes again.

Time passed peacefully. The water steamed, making the air hazy until Jerrol stirred. "Time for food," he said as his tummy grumbled. He ducked his head under the water one last time. Lady, when was the last time he had felt this clean? He reached for his towel and levered himself out of the tub. He rubbed himself down, grinning at Jennery who had relaxed even further into the water, supine, drifting. It wasn't often Jennery let his guard down. They both needed a recharge.

Jerrol dressed, and on leaving the shelter, he quartered the yard alert once more as he rubbed his hair dry. He needed to get it cut. "Thank you, my Lady, for this moment," he murmured as he caught sight of the nearly full moon beginning its ascent. His hand automatically spread over his heart and touched the smooth green stone hanging around his neck. He felt the weight of her presence; she was almost at full strength. Time was passing, and things were not going well.

He glanced back at Jennery still supine in the tub and

wondered where Birlerion had got to. "Bet I finish the first ale before you," he teased.

Jennery opened one eye. "Yeah?" he drawled. "Then you better have one on the bar for me when you do."

Jerrol waved an airy hand and left.

The sentinal trees had been standing tall and proud since the cracking of the Bloodstone nearly three thousand years ago. He now knew that the myth that they were the Lady's personal guard, unable to follow her across the Veil which had descended around Remargaren, was true. There were men and women inside the sentinals who stood guard over the Lady's sacred groves, preserving her people's place of worship. He knew where he would find Birlerion, and the question he would ask.

7

THE GROVE, GREENSWATCH

Jerrol walked along the avenue of beech trees that led up to the Lady's temple. The towering sentinals dwarfed them, and Jerrol's blood stirred as he approached. He reached out to touch one, and his stomach fluttered.

The sentinals guarded her altar—a stone table on which burnt-out candles sat in each of the four corners. Here families lived under the watchful gaze of the Lady, celebrating life and the passing of the seasons, marking the passage of time in rituals handed down from mother to daughter.

Jerrol leant against the tallest sentinal and breathed in the fresh greenness of the bark. As he inhaled deeply, the clean scent zinged through his body, vibrating through his bones and settling as a gentle hum at the back of his mind. If he flung his arms around the tree, he would not embrace even a quarter of the girth. These trees were immense.

How could people not believe when all they had to do was reach out and touch. Yet that was what was happening: people turning away from the Lady, challenging age-old beliefs. The stories and rumours were gathering strength and beginning to spread, taking root and growing like weeds. Jerrol wondered sourly who was sponsoring such an effective spread of blasphemy and how he was supposed to stop it.

He mused for a moment. The Ascendants had been banished when the Lady had cracked the Bloodstone. The destruction of the stone had been her last defence against the wild magic of the Ascendants. She had pulled down a veil through which magic couldn't penetrate and so protected her people from the world destruction the Ascendants threatened. Since then, there had been no sign of magic in the Four Kingdoms. The Lady, her guards and the Ascendants had all disappeared, leaving the world in peace and without magic.

And yet, the sentinals were magical. How could people doubt, when the trees stood as proof before them? The tall silvery trunks were smooth and silky to the touch, unviolated. No child could scamper up these trunks.

Jerrol peered up into the canopy high overhead where the branches sprouted, festooned with large pointy leaves that blocked the setting sun. A deep, deep green filtered the sunlight into a cool silvery-green glow. A broad canopy that protected from storms and brutal sun alike, the colour of the Lady's eyes, so the storytellers said, and to which Jerrol could now attest.

As he embraced the sentinal, breathing in the green life, breathing out doubt, he felt comforted, invigorated, revitalised. The presence of the Lady resonated within him, binding his belief, rooted in his core and unshakeable. He heard the echo of a voice; a question lingered on the air.

Reluctantly, he broke the link with the tree and took a deep breath as the thrum hummed through his veins. Turning, he walked through the grove. The evening sun pierced the canopy with shafts of brilliant light illuminating the trail that led to the circle. The path was straight, edged by sparse clumps of grass and shade-loving fronds of feathering ferns, mimicking the pointy leaves above.

The blaze of the evening sun made him blink, orange skies bleeding to a deeper red nearer the horizon. His eyes teared against the brilliant glare, and he ducked behind the monolith that marked the beginning of the circle and rubbed his eyes. The granite stone was rough to his touch, covered by moss and lichens softening the sharp edges to a resplendent orange in the evening glow.

Birlerion knelt before the altar and prayed. He begged the Lady to forgive him as he prayed every day. But she hadn't answered, and he was adrift in a strange world that he was supposed to know but didn't recognise.

His gut twisted, and his heart fluttered somewhere about the base of his throat as memories flooded him. He had failed her. He was supposed to be her protector, and she was gone, lost with Guerlaire. The memory of Leyandrii's final moments cut through him, and only his need for forgiveness kept him rooted to the spot. He didn't deserve to wear her uniform.

The only comfort was the fact she hadn't forsaken him: she had asked him to protect her Captain. He clung to the command; once he had known how to do that, maybe he could redeem himself in her eyes if he was successful.

A soft voice intruded on his thoughts, and he opened his eyes and saw a young woman kneeling over one of the stone fragments. Her fingers were busy exploring the stonework. She had masses of brown hair clouding around her face.

"Which one are you?" she asked, raising her face.

Birlerion lurched to his feet, disorientated. "What?"

The woman smiled as she rose, her fingers questing for the stone altar. "There were four recorded here: four children of Greens, four of the Lady's guards. Which one are you?"

"Birlerion."

"Ah, the youngest. Much missed, but never forgotten. Greens waits for you."

"Who are you?"

"I'm a scholar. By name, Taelia."

"Where did you come from? Did you find the waystone?"

"Waystone? I know nothing of waystones. I am here at the Lady's bidding." She considered him for a moment, and Birlerion felt flensed by turquoise eyes that looked straight through him; she might not see the surface, but in that moment, she saw more than any outer shell. "I don't believe the Lady is wroth with you; you did all she asked of you and more."

Birlerion inhaled. "I failed her. I couldn't protect her. She is lost to this world."

Taelia's skirts swirled as she took a step towards him. "You're wrong. The Lady is not lost to those who believe."

"Where is she, then?"

Taelia tutted as she approached him, her hand questing in the air; Birlerion grasped it. "Inside, of course. I can see her; she is rooted deep in you, isn't she? She said you needed reassurance, but I don't think you do. You won't falter. You won't be alone for long, Birlerion. Jerrol will wake the others from their protective sleep."

"How do you know?"

"Because the Lady told me. Her sentinals truly are amazing, aren't they?" She tilted her head back, staring up at the canopies as if she could see them. "She protected you well. What are they like inside?"

Birlerion's tension eased at her eager interest. "It would be an honour, my lady, to introduce you to my sentinal on my return to Vespers."

"I'll hold you to that. We scholars never pass up a chance to learn." Her face grew pensive. "You must warn Jerrol that Prince Kharel has placed a bounty on his head. He must be careful."

"He makes his way here. You could tell him yourself," Birlerion said, glancing towards the path.

Taelia grimaced. "I'm not sure he's ready for this. You can tell him for me, and anyway, the Lady brought me to you, not him." She rested her hand against his chest, as if in benediction. "We'll meet again, Birlerion. Look after him for me." She gave him a brilliant smile, and she was gone.

Jerrol gazed around the unbroken circle. Another four monoliths completed the circuit, surrounding the stone table in the centre. Broken fragments of stone poked through the grass, the exposed faces covered in lichen nearly hidden from view.

The faintest of markings were visible on the surface. Taelia ought to visit and see what she could make of it all. She was the expert on engravings, her sensitive fingers teasing out the most worn remnants. Birlerion knelt before the altar, his dark head bent. His clothes glowed in the evening light.

"They still sleep," Birlerion said, not turning around.

"When will they wake?"

"When you tell them to."

"But I don't know how."

"You woke me."

Jerrol wrinkled his nose. "That was the Lady, not me."

"You said it was time, and I stepped out of my tree. I didn't expect to come out next to the temple."

"Where did you expect to be?"

"With Leyandrii at the palace – that's where we were when the Ascendants attacked."

Jerrol swallowed. "You were with the Lady?"

"And Guerlaire." Birlerion paused, his voice low. "I don't remember how I got into the tree. We were defending the palace, Guerlaire broke cover ..." He faltered to a stop.

"I'm sorry, Birlerion, this must be difficult for you."

"Nothing looks like it should, even the names of things and places are different. Warren was Lord of Greens, but there is nothing here in memory of him or his family. I searched."

"It was a long time ago."

"Not for me, they would be expecting me to visit if I was passing; they were my family. I would be in serious trouble if I didn't stop by."

Jerrol froze; he hadn't considered that Birlerion must have had family somewhere, now all lost. "I thought you said you were born in Vespers?" he asked, not sure what to say.

"Yes, but a friend of mine, Tagerill, was Warren's son; he dragged me into his family, and they wouldn't let me go. They adopted me. So, Greens is home." His face softened in memory, and then he stood, his eyes shining with unshed tears. "I'll go find the baths. The Lady waits for you. She left you a message: Apparently, the prince has placed a bounty on your head. She bids you be careful."

Jerrol watched Birlerion leave. He touched each sentinal as he passed. The air flickered above him, and he raised his hand as the dusk embraced him, and he faded out of sight.

Jerrol peered after him, before dropping to his knees in front of the altar. He rested his hand on the granite tabletop.

His fingers strayed to the green stone at his throat; it was polished smooth from constant wear. He had found it in a time of need when he was a child. Once he had created a shrine to the Lady, with sticks for the monoliths and a flat stone for the table.

His aunt found him and hounded him out of the woods as a malingerer; after that she had washed her hands of him, and he had been fostered to the keep at Stoneford. The Lady had set his feet on another path.

Head bent, he reaffirmed his commitment to her cause and offered up his prayers and his support.

Her acknowledgement caressed his face and resonated through his body—along with a touch of possessiveness? No, that couldn't be right. He gave a shuddering sigh as he grew conscious of the growing chill as the sunset faded. The moon's glow strengthened above him. He had been communing with the stones for longer than he realised.

As he straightened, he saw an older woman pause as she entered the stone circle. She was slightly built, shorter than him even, with silver curls framing a youthful face. She held her hand up in apology. "Sorry, lad, I didn't mean to intrude." Her voice was low and velvety. "Folks don't normally stay this late."

Jerrol rested a hand on the tabletop in farewell. "I was about to leave. I've been longer than I intended."

The woman approached the table, her arms full of late-blooming flowers. "I was just bringing the crumbs for the critters," she said as she scattered some pulses and grains on the table and laid the flowers in the centre. "They'll be gone by morning."

"The Lady watches," he murmured, spreading his hand across his heart.

The woman glanced at him and finished the catechism: "...as the Line protects." She mirrored his action. "Not too many invoke the Lady these days," she said, watching him closely.

His head jerked back. "What, even here in the heart?"

"Especially here, it seems. Sometimes familiarity breeds contempt, I think. Folk say it, but there is no conviction behind the words, no depth, not like you did. I could feel it, deep inside, that you meant it. If I can tell, then I'm sure the Lady knows," she said. "It's even worse when the council encourages it."

"The council?" He considered her words. "Of course!" He smacked his palm against his forehead. "That explains how fast it is spreading. The easiest way to instigate change is to say it is the rule of law, through the council. They are actively withdrawing support for the Lady?"

"Oh, not so obvious yet, not plain-spoken like, but more folks are sniggering at those who invoke the Lady, making them out to be soft in the head like, to believe such a story. As if the Lady was just a story," she huffed, beginning to get distressed. She took a deep breath and grimaced. "Sorry, lad, didn't mean to dump my cares on you. I'm just worriting about the lads." She gestured at the sentinals.

Jerrol smiled at her affectionate term. "I don't think you need to worry about these trees. They are sentinals, and they can protect themselves. You need to take care of you and yours." He glanced around the circle; they were still alone. "How many know you are a Guardian?" he asked.

She jerked back, raising her hand to her mouth, and she glanced around the circle. Jerrol reached out a reassuring hand. "We are alone," he murmured. "You will need to dissemble better when the next person comes by. I agree there is a risk, not just yet, but the pressure is building. The

Guardians are the Lady's power here; she cannot afford to lose them and nor can the rest of us."

"Who are you?" the woman asked, her eyes large in the dim light. "How do you know so much?"

"Jerrol Haven is my name, lately a King's Ranger, though for my sins not anymore," he said as she gasped. "I think the same powers that are trying to discredit the Lady are working from the top down as well. I'm a follower, no more, aware that she is under siege and trying to help where I can. I have permission to travel and assist where possible. I was working my way towards Scholar Torsion at Velmouth. I thought he would have a clearer idea of what is going on, but if you are saying the councils are wavering …" He paused, frowning in thought.

"You know Torsion? He won't waver, no matter what he has to say publicly," the woman remarked. "He should have an idea of what is being said and by whom, and maybe even why."

"Good point, I think I need to visit him next." Jerrol tucked her hand in his arm and turned her back toward the gap in the stones. "I think you will be missed soon," he said, steering her out of the circle.

"They know where I am if they need me," she said, but the air was starting to cool now the sun had set. She gripped his arm more tightly. "The smith is my son. I live with him now, close to the trees." She smiled in greeting as they passed under the broad leaves, which rustled as they walked. "My name is Sylvie, though just mention the smith and you'll find me. Come to dinner tomorrow, Mr Haven, and we can talk more. It's a relief to talk with someone without having to curb your tongue."

Jerrol ducked his head. "Thank you kindly, a meal would be welcome and the good company," he said. "I'm travelling with friends." He paused as she waved her hand.

"Bring them too." She looked at him sharply. "I can't see you travelling with a veil-shredder."

"A veil-shredder?" he said with concern.

"Hush, I'll tell you more tomorrow," she whispered as they turned into the high street, and she pushed him away as their paths separated.

8

BLACK HEN, GREENSWATCH

Jennery was sitting on a stool at the bar nursing a mug of ale when Jerrol entered the taproom. The barkeep inspected him. "Well, you're looking better," he said as he placed a mug on the bar in front of him.

"Lady's blessings on your wife," Jerrol said, hand splayed over his heart. "She is a miracle worker."

The 'keep grinned. "Oh, aye? Don't tell her that she'll be crowing for the rest of the year."

"And so she should." Jerrol prepared to move off to a table.

"You're a follower of the Lady?" the 'keep asked.

"You are not?"

"Oh, aye, I am. There's not many around here who admit to it, though; many are questioning, and newcomers scoff at the legends."

Jerrol raised his brows. "Here? Where Her presence is felt the most strongly?"

The 'keep bobbed his head. "Be careful what you say. The doubters are creeping in and causing strife. If the Lady is struggling in Her stronghold, what is it like elsewhere?"

"Thanks for the warning," Jerrol said as he joined Jennery in an alcove near the roaring fire. He relaxed back in the seat out of the glare opposite Jennery and considered the barkeep's warning.

"Where's Birlerion?" Jennery asked, leaning forward to rest his arms on the table. The shadows flickered over his rugged face as the flames danced, and his bright blue eyes gleamed as he watched Jerrol.

"He went for a bath. I expect he'll be along soon."

"Have you had a chance to speak to him? Properly, I mean. He doesn't say much, does he? Even when he does speak, he tells you nothing."

"Would you, in his situation? He is disorientated; the only thing he is clinging to is the fact that the Lady told him to protect me for some reason."

"You think he really is a Sentinal?"

Jerrol choked on his ale. "You don't?"

Before Jennery had a chance to answer, the food arrived. A steaming roast and freshly baked bread, closely followed by Birlerion looking even younger, newly shaved and with his damp hair slicked back and dressed in clean shirt and trousers.

"Well, the Dirty Duck is exceeding all expectations," Jennery said as they tucked in.

Jerrol eyed Birlerion as he ate. He was neat and economical, focused on his food, and for such a distinctive-looking man, he seemed to blend into the shadows. He turned his attention to the room as it began to fill with locals, returning from the service at the Landing.

Birlerion glanced across at Jerrol, as if aware of his inspection. "What are you expecting to achieve here? What exactly are you searching for?"

"The circuit is a periodic check on the Guardians and the Watches. They are tied to the Lady, the Land and our Liege.

The health of the country and the king is enshrined in the Guardians that protect us." Jerrol paused, struck by a thought, before continuing. "Makes you wonder if this is tied to the king's illness. It's said that the first responsibility of the crown is to protect the Guardians for the Lady. Rumour has it that some Guardians have disappeared and not been replaced. Our job is to check and solve where possible. To help the king keep his oath to the Lady."

"Solve what?" Birlerion asked, glancing at the fire as a log shifted on the hearth, causing sparks to fly up the chimney.

"That is what I hope you can help us find out, discreetly." Jerrol clapped Birlerion on the shoulder. "I would expect you to know who the Guardians are."

"The Watches had only just been created, the Lord Guardians confirmed. I'm not sure I will recognise them any better than you would," Birlerion replied as he gazed at the Captain. His expression grew withdrawn. "Once I knew this land well, not so much now."

"You'll learn it again. I have maps. You can study them later."

"It's not just the land. It's the people. It's the way of life. Everything is so much faster. People are always in a hurry. Moving things from one place to another. I saw a wood mill on the river near Deepwater. They were using the water to power the mill. I've never seen anything like it. They wouldn't let me inside to look."

Jerrol scowled. "There is progress, and then there is progress. I'm not sure Deepwater is a good example. The water mills have helped to speed up production, especially as the population grows because growth drives more demand for timber. But Deepwater seems to be taking it to extremes." He fell silent, considering the sudden ramp in timber production in the Watches.

A little later as Jennery stood at the bar waiting to get refills, the door gusted open, and a crowd of men blew in on the damp air. "Ugh, trust Mac to end the day with a bit o' rain. I bet he's laughing his socks off, watching us get wet sending him off."

"Ah, it's not his fault," a small elderly man replied. "I expect the Lady's grieving too; he was an ardent supporter, you know. The fires burned extra bright for him."

"Yeah, yeah, Father, was a nice service," a stocky, red-faced man replied, leaning on the bar. "Hey 'keep, three flagons of ale and ..." he paused, counting, "seven mugs," he finished. The men gathered around, holding out mugs ready to be filled; once served, they moved off to the tables around the fire. They hesitated when they saw strangers ensconced in the alcove, but the lure of the bright yellow flames drew them in, and they all settled down comfortably.

Jerrol dipped his head in greeting. "Turned into a damp night," he said.

"Yeah," sighed the stocky man who had ordered the beers. "And you are?" he asked, casting a suspicious glance at them.

"Just passing through. Had a wondrous experience this afternoon in that bath-tub," Jerrol replied, smiling with remembered pleasure.

The stocky man snorted. "Yeah, can you believe that fella listened to his wife and is building a room to put it in?"

"Lady's blessing on her head," intoned Jerrol. "That room will be a goldmine."

"Truly?" One of the lads, his damp clothes steaming gently, perked up at his words.

"Truly," Jerrol grinned. "I never felt so good."

"Good for business then?" another put in intently.

"Oh yes, once word gets around, you'll have people flocking here," Jerrol replied.

The men all grinned at each other and relaxed. Talk moved on to a general review of the service. The Father preened as the men complimented him on his sermon. An aroma of unwashed bodies and drying clothes mingled with the wood smoke. The ale kept flowing in memory of Mac and talk veered off to broodmares and the local bloodstock scene, till a slight altercation off to the side began to draw an audience.

"Yes, it is," reiterated a dark-headed, solid man, with very thick arms which were resting on the table in front of him.

"No, it isn't, that's just story telling," a smaller man said, his blond hair sticking up in all directions as it dried.

"Father," appealed the stocky man, "isn't it true the Lady climbed them sentinal trees to reach the moon?"

The Father sat up and straightened his robes.

"Now you've done it," someone muttered into his beer. "Here we go again!"

"The Sentinals," the Father said grandly. "Today, you find them tall and proud, leading the way to the Lady's heart. They have guarded the people since the end of the Bloodstone and the descent of the Veil, but they were guarding long before that." He glanced around the taproom and inclined his head importantly. "The Sentinals were the Lady's guard. She chose them herself, and they all pledged personal allegiance to her. All the Guardians had their protectors, but the Lady's were the most famous." He paused as he shuffled his thoughts into order.

"Why were they the most famous?" the pot boy asked.

"Why?" repeated the Father. "Because they were the most dedicated. No one, but no one, got past her Sentinals."

"Then why did she have to leave? They couldn't have been that good," scoffed one of the men from the shadows.

Jerrol gripped Birlerion's arm as he jerked.

The Father glared at the man. "I am telling this story."

He gathered himself and began again in a rhythmic tone of voice.

"In the time before the Veil descended, there were three Guardians of the realm. The Guardians lived in a beautiful palace. The walls were made of the whitest marble, threaded by veins of crystal which glistened in the golden sunshine. It towered over the city which sprawled down the hillsides below it, and the golden spires reached for the sky."

His audience sat listening wide-eyed; they were ensnared in his word pictures, enspelled by the magical world and the splendour he was describing. The fire flared unnoticed, casting shadows against the walls.

"When the Lady newly ascended to her Guardianship, she was advised to recruit a personal bodyguard for her safety. And with that, she stood and commanded, and fully two hundred and forty men and women stood forward and pledged their allegiance to her. And as each one pledged she accepted and blessed them, and as they straightened up before her their tabards shimmered a silver-green and their eyes took on a silvery hue."

Birlerion ducked his head, keeping his eyes shielded, and Jennery stared at him wide-eyed.

"They were hers for life. They protected her against all threats, but in the end, they were unable to protect themselves from her." The listening men stirred in expectation. Jerrol's brow creased, and he glanced at the barkeep. The 'keep raised his eyebrows and shrugged.

"As time passed, a group of educated men calling themselves the Ascendants began to share their idea for an alternative way of life. To challenge the grip the Guardians held over the world."

Jerrol shifted sharply at the blatant twisting of the story, staring in amazement as the men in the bar drank in his every word. His grip on Birlerion tightened; the Sentinal was rigid.

"But the Guardians would not release their hold," the Father proclaimed, his voice ringing across the bar, "and the Ascendants challenged the rule of the Guardians. In desperation, the Lady destroyed her family's power by shattering the Bloodstone. For when she cracked the Bloodstone, she caused the Veil to descend, forcing her family and the Ascendants out of this world and into exile. But her Sentinals could not follow where she led. She had placed a curse on them, tying them to the land, forcing them to stand in front of her altar and set down roots and never move again. They became the sentinal trees you see today scattered across Vespiri."

There was a short silence after the Father finished, just the sound of the wood crackling in the hearth. A few hands surreptitiously made the obeisance rather sheepishly to the Lady. Not many though, Jerrol noted as he watched the Father.

"Well told, Father." Jerrol lifted his mug in salute. "May I ask where that version originates from?"

"Version?" the Father spluttered. "That is the true story as validated by the council itself."

"It must be recent." Jerrol reached out to put another log on the fire, shielding Birlerion whose eyes were glittering with anger. "I haven't had the pleasure of hearing it before."

"Then you have been told lies, my son," the Father said, thrusting his chest out, "for this was the true story of the Sentinals."

Jennery grasped his sleeve as he was about to probe further and shook his head. Jerrol leaned back and took refuge in his mug; he was right. He was drawing attention to himself. Men peered towards him.

Fortunately, their attention was diverted. "You don't see

nobody from them towers up past Velmouth anymore," reminisced the man with the muscular arms, pausing to sip his ale. "Used to have a thriving trade back in my granddaddy's day, all sorts of knick-knacks and trinkets the ladies delighted in, he used to say. Them Watchers used to travel off to distant lands and return with saddlebags full of stuff you never saw before. And stories, what stories he used to tell, many a night my grandda used to roll in with a story to tell us kids." He paused again to take a sip of his ale and glance around the room. Men leaned closer, anticipating the start of another tale.

"Go on, Ben," one of the men prodded. "Don't stop there, there 'ent no knick-knacks around here no more, you're trying to gull us you are."

Ben smacked his lips and grinned. "I remember the day he gave m'grandma a moon catcher."

Jerrol stilled as the man burbled on; Jennery flicked him a glance before leaning forward like the other men to listen. Birlerion stared at the table, his knuckles white with the strength of his grip on his mug.

The pot boy went back to work and began to collect the empty mugs. As he reached for the mug in front of Jennery, Jerrol caught his eye by holding a copper coin between his fingers. "Boy, who's the moon catcher man and where does he live?"

"Him? That's the smith. He lives next to the hostelry." The boy reached for the coin before scampering off.

Jennery leaned forward. "What's the matter?"

"Can you follow that spiky-haired fellow showing an interest, and see if you can find out who he is and where he goes? Birlerion and I need to talk to the smith. He talks a little too freely about things that should not be mentioned. Meet us back here," Jerrol said, draining his mug.

9

BLACK HEN, GREENSWATCH

A t last, the barkeep called time, and his customers started to straggle out into the damp night. Many glanced at the glimpse of the moon peeping through the clouds surrounded by a glowing haze, maybe thinking about catching moonbeams for themselves.

Jerrol grasped the smith's sleeve. "Friend," he said. "Let me walk with you. I want to check on my horse which is in your stable." The smith squinted at him and lurched as the fresh air took its toll. He was grateful for the strong arm keeping him straight. Birlerion followed behind, watching the street.

"A word of warning," Jerrol said. "Old magic should be guarded, not bandied about in public alehouses. Do not underestimate its power to influence people."

"Old magic?" scoffed the smith. "None around here, there's nothing but stories, no matter what the Father says."

"Guardians protect and in turn are protected," Jerrol intoned. *"Keep the line. Watch for the Lady."*

The smith froze mid-step and rubbed the back of his neck. "I don't know what you are talking about."

Jerrol stopped beside the smith in the middle of the street, aware of Birlerion slinking through the shadows, his presence reassuring. "The Guardian will need protecting, as will the moon catcher. They are few. Too few," he said. "You shouldn't have spoken of it tonight. Men will covet it and expect you to lead them to it. Don't lead them to the Guardian." He placed his hand on the smith's chest. "The time is coming, you must hold your promise and guard the line."

The smith swallowed. "What line? There is no line."

"Jerrol? Come quickly. I smell smoke, lots of smoke!"

Jerrol stiffened, as Zin'talia's fearful voice reached him. An icy shiver flashed down his spine. "You fool," he whispered, "we are too late," and he took off, sprinting down the high street towards the hostelry situated at the junction at the bottom, Birlerion on his heels.

The smith staggered along behind him, straightening up as he smelled the wood smoke drifting in the cool night air. "No," he wailed as he rounded the corner and saw the flames licking up the side of the wooden boards that clad the hostelry. The squeals of agitated horses in the barn blended with the clanging of the emergency bell. People tumbled out of the nearest buildings, dressed in whatever clothes they could grab, as fire threatened all nearby buildings, being built from wood.

The people began forming a bucket line, from the well to the burning building, rushing to splash water on the hissing flames. Jerrol loomed up in front of the smith. "Sylvie, your mother, which room?"

"W-what?" The smith stared at him. "How do you know my mother?"

"Your family, man," Jerrol shook him, "whereabouts would your family be?" He flung his hand towards the burning building.

The colour drained even further from the man's face. He started towards the steps as two small girls came tumbling down into his outstretched arms. "Gilly," he shouted, over the roar of the flames, "where's your mother?" He hustled them away from the building.

"She went to help Grandma," the young girl cried, holding onto her father's arms as her body shuddered in terror.

His arms full of children, the smith looked at Jerrol. "Help them," he pleaded, "they'll be upstairs at the back. Her room looks over the courtyard towards the trees." He turned the children, leading them away from the heat of the scorching flames.

Jerrol paused long enough to divert a bucket of water to dump over his head, shuddering at the shock of the cold water, before running up the steps. He flinched as a roaring tendril of flame reached towards him. He gritted his teeth, tossed his dampened cloak over his head, and darted around the fire and into the house.

The smith handed his children off to one of the women hovering in horror. As he turned, he grabbed Birlerion's arm and pointed him towards the barn. "Quick," he yelled, "the horses!" Then he ran into the burning building after Jerrol.

The front door led into a communal living space. The hangings had all gone up in flames, and fiery tendrils ran greedily across the beams. Jerrol's cloak blocked most of the heat as he dashed through the parlour and headed for the stairs. The heat was intense, but the smoke was worse. It was thicker downstairs. It thinned as he reached the top of the stairs and stumbled across a woman collapsed on the floor.

He turned her over and searched for a pulse; she was still breathing. He levered her over his shoulder and, hand balanced against the wall, descended the stairs as fast as he could; he snatched his hand back as the heat scorched his palm. As he reached the bottom of the stairs, he ran into the smith. He passed the unconscious woman to him. "Take her," he gasped and turned and dashed back up the stairs.

The smith ran for the front door, bursting through a swirl of smoke and flames. Frantic hands reached for the smith and helped him lay his wife on the ground. They poured buckets of water over his head as he gasped for breath. He shook the water out of his eyes and turned back to the house. "No, you fool, it's too late." A man restrained him as they all looked towards the flames blocking the front door.

Without pausing, Jerrol bounded back up the stairs. Keeping his face muffled and his hands off the wall, he halted on the landing and kicked in the first door he came to. The room was smoke-filled but empty. He moved on to the next room, similarly filling with thick black smoke. Coughing, he tried to filter the air though the damp material of his cloak. A low groan caught his attention and he wafted the smoke away from his face. "Sylvie," he croaked, and clearing his raw throat, tried again. "Sylvie!"

He found her huddled in the corner under a sheet. She had managed to tip her water jug over her. The dampened material steamed, but she had been overwhelmed by the ever-thickening smoke. Jerrol ducked under the sheet and felt her neck. She lived. But not for long, he thought, desperately trying to see a way out.

The Guardian jerked under his hands. "Don't let them fail," she pleaded. Her grip on his arm was unexpectedly strong. "Gilly knows what to do, she just needs time." Her eyes streamed from the smoke, and she slumped in his arms. Jerrol scooped her up and staggered towards the door; she was much heavier than she looked.

Hot embers drifted in the hallway. Red tendrils of burning flame licked up the walls, scorching him. His shirt sleeves shrivelled; the flames blistered his skin, and he stumbled back into the bedroom towards the bed, hissing in pain. He laid Sylvie down and leaned out the window. Behind him, the flames extended up the wooden door frame. He turned back and slammed the door shut. Yanking down the curtains, he beat uselessly at the fire before stuffing the material along the bottom to block the smoke.

Returning to the window, he peered out. A pulley jutted out from above the hayloft in the adjacent barn. He leaned out, teetering over the windowsill; it was out of his reach.

The Guardian coughed behind him. "Stick."

Jerrol turned. She was pointing at a hooked stick propped up in the corner. He grabbed it and leant out the window, reaching for the rope. The hook caught and he pulled it towards him. Down below, Birlerion was leading the hysterical horses out of the barn.

"Birlerion," he bawled, "hayloft." He frantically pointed as he tossed the stick aside. Bless the man, he understood immediately and disappeared into the barn. Jerrol looped the rope around the Guardian's chest and dragged her over to the windowsill. He flinched back as flaming red embers caressed his cheek. He levered Sylvie out the window as fast as he could, and the rope took the strain as Birlerion gathered the slack.

Jerrol paused as Sylvie's hand cupped his face; her hand was silky soft and cool against his scorched skin. He leaned into it. "The Lady bless you, lad," she said in a husky whisper. She was staring right through him, her eyes glassy. "Aye, m'Lady, I'll give him what I can," she said as she focused on his face. She kissed him on the lips as the light faded from her eyes, and she was jerked out of his grasp as Birlerion worked the pulley.

Jerrol flinched back as her will zinged through his blood. His heart raced as a fresh green wash flowed through his body, meeting scorched skin on the outside, making his body a living battlefield. His heart stuttered as he tried to assimilate the opposing forces, and he dropped to his knees. Steam rose from his tattered clothes. His skin gleamed with sweat: the only sign of his body's internal struggle.

Leaning against the window frame, he gasped for breath as black smoke billowed around him. The rope swung in front of him, and he cast about for the stick and then realised the fire had consumed it. The room was alight. The fire roared like a furnace behind him, the heat intensifying on his back as the room was engulfed in flames. He looked up at the pulsing moon watching overhead, as distant rumbles heralded the start of the building's collapse.

Jerrol climbed out of the window and balanced as Birlerion took the slack, staring up at him in horror. He launched himself at the rope, swaying precariously away and then back towards the burning building; the flames leapt and caught the rope as he spun away. His palms stung as they slipped, but he tightened his grip and hung on grimly.

Above him, the flames ate their way through the rope as Birlerion frantically lowered him to the ground. His legs collapsed as he touched the ground and he lay trembling face down on the cold cobblestones, gasping for breath and choking out smoke, wheezing like an old man. He rolled over and let Birlerion unravel the rope. He stared up at the moon until his smoke-ridden eyes watered and his sight blurred.

Suddenly, Birlerion wrenched him upright, and frantic hands stripped off his steaming cloak and started on his clothes. A bucket was upended over his head as he gasped for breath. Birlerion wrapped him in a damp sheet, cool against his naked skin; hands patted him down as if putting out flames.

"Ascendants balls," Birlerion cursed, making Jerrol smile, "you're smouldering, you fool. You'll go up next."

"As the Lady wills." Jerrol coughed, trying to clear his

throat. His voice sounded like a whetstone rasping across rusty steel.

"That's as maybe," Birlerion snapped, "but you don't have to help her."

Jerrol sat back down on the cobblestones; his legs were trembling again. Reaction, he supposed. His body cooled as the internal greenness dampened all heat and soothed his scorched skin.

"You risked your life for nothing," Birlerion continued, his voice strained. "She was dead when we untied her."

"Ah no." Jerrol bowed his head in grief. "Never for nothing." He gripped Birlerion's arm. He knew he had given him a fright. "Not now," he said clearly and lay down on the cobbles, closing his sore eyes, shuddering intermittently. He steamed in the short silence.

Birlerion stood. "He can't stay there," he said, exasperation in his voice. "Bring his fool horse back here, and I'll take him back to the inn and get his burns treated."

The smith hovered next to Jerrol, hesitantly reaching for his shoulder. "Thank'ee for trying."

Jerrol opened his eyes. The grimy face of the smith wavered in front of him. "Later," he rasped. "We'll speak later."

The smith stared at him before nodding. He returned to his wife's embrace. They held each other as they walked back towards the street.

The sound of horse's hooves clopped into the yard as Zin'talia arrived, nostrils flaring and eyes rolling at the still-burning ruin. Jerrol opened his eyes, gritty with smoke and ash, as her fear reached him. Birlerion helped him stand, and he leant against her shoulder for support. Waves of concern rolled off her. He shuddered as his body tried to assimilate the Guardian's parting gift, and Birlerion's grip tightened as the tremors shook him.

"Ready?" Birlerion murmured in his ear, as he prepared to shove him into the saddle. Jerrol sagged forward against Zin'talia's neck, clutching her mane; he was thankful for Birlerion's firm grip on his leg, keeping him balanced, else he was sure he would have slithered straight off the other side.

10

THE GROVE, GREENSWATCH

Birlerion eyed him as he began to lead him back to the inn. "You're still smoking, you know," he said, as he led the horse up the street.

"Yeah." Jerrol's voice came from the vicinity of Zin'talia's neck. He was flopped over as if he hadn't the energy to sit upright. "Wait," he croaked, "turn back. We need to go to the trees. The s-sentinals."

"Later, we've got to get you cooled down."

"N-now," insisted Jerrol, preparing to swing his leg over.

A grumbling rumble interrupted them, echoing up the street, as the rest of the hostelry collapsed to the ground. Ashy motes sparkled in the moonlight until they settled, sifting to the ground, the gleams fading away by sun-up.

"Jerrol, you can't even stand, stay on the horse, man!" Birlerion gripped him to keep him still.

"Now," Jerrol repeated.

Releasing a long-suffering sigh, Birlerion reversed his direction, leading them towards the towering sentinals. All Captains were the same, stubborn through and through.

The sentinals greeted them like an array of flag poles

waving their deep green leafy flags. Their leaves rustled, even though there was little wind—a blessing for the other houses in the village which could have been engulfed by the fire.

Birlerion paused under the first overarching sentinal. Lifting his face, he listened to the murmurs in the leaves. The echoes of the collapsing hostelry were somewhat muffled in the still air. "What now?" he asked, watching Jerrol as he continued to shudder in his damp wrapper of grimy sheets, which still steamed.

Birlerion's face pinched as he took in Jerrol's glazed eyes, huge in his flushed face. This was not merely the effect of getting scorched in a fire. The Lady was at work here, he could feel it. His mouth grew taut as Jerrol tried to dismount. He caught him before he fell: a tattered figured covered in ash and sweat.

Jerrol staggered towards the nearest tree, trembling hands blindly questing before him. He embraced the tree, his arms spreading wide as he stilled and closed his eyes. In the soft green light, Jerrol seemed to relax into the tree, fading from sight until a stray shaft of silvery moonlight pierced the shadows and caressed his body, silhouetting him in the gloom.

"Ahhh." Jerrol breathed a sigh of relief. Birlerion watched as he inhaled an uninterrupted breath of air that shimmered down his limbs and straightened his cringing spine. Birlerion knew the sentinal soothed the crazy castanet of shudders, and Jerrol's shoulders dropped as the tension caused by the battle raging in his body died away. He sagged against the tree and breathed.

All was still, not a sound in the grove.

The Lady approached silently out of the gloom; her exquisite face illuminated by a subtle glow. She reached out and cupped Jerrol's face. "The journey is just beginning," she said. "It has been long arriving, but the first step has been taken. The forgotten are waiting, and the Guardianship must be protected." Her face was serene. "My Captain. With protectors like you, we will succeed. Do not be afraid to ask. We are all in this together." She dipped her head and kissed him lightly on the lips.

He inhaled sharply as she breathed into his mouth. "You are mine," she said with a small smile, and she turned to Birlerion and caressed his face. "Birlerion, you serve your Captain well. I thank you."

Birlerion swayed as her regard sifted through him. "My Lady," he choked, his throat tight as he watched her with some desperation; she looked just the same. Some of his distress eased as Leyandrii's touch spread through his body, wrapping him in her love.

She tutted, her fingers tracing his jaw. "Always blaming yourself, after all these years! You'd think you'd learn."

A slight movement caught Birlerion's eye. Someone was approaching along the path. When he looked back, the Lady had gone, and Jerrol appeared transfixed by his communion with the tree and surprisingly was still standing. The figure drew closer, and Birlerion recognised her as one of the smith's daughters: the elder, he thought.

Glancing back at Jerrol, he stifled a gasp. Jerrol stood clear of the tree, but he was linked by a soft glow which emanated from the bark and coalesced around him. His eyes were wide and gleamed silver in the dim light. His hand rose of its own accord as if to greet the young girl approaching him.

"Guardian." His voice resonated deep in Birlerion's bones.

"The line protects," she said in return, lifting her face towards him.

Jerrol bent his head, and their lips touched; the young girl jolted back with a gasp and fell to her knees.

The Lady's euphoria resonated in his bones. Birlerion couldn't help smiling in wonder as the girl braced herself as the Guardianship coursed through her body, relaxing as it settled as sloshing water stills in a cup. Joy transformed the girl's face to an unworldly beauty as she lifted her face to the sentinals and bathed in the moon's triumphant light. The Lady's joy rang in Birlerion's inner ear as his blood sang through his veins in counterpoint. A low murmur of voices stirred in surprise as if awoken out of deep sleep.

Birlerion watched Jerrol. "Are we done now, Captain?" he asked as he drew Zin'talia out into the moonlight.

"I sure hope so. This night has been plenty long enough for me."

Birlerion glanced up as the air shimmered and a rare smile lit up his face. He held his hand out. "Did you hear the Lady?" he asked.

Jerrol gasped as a small black and white, cat-like creature appeared. It flipped its scaly wings back and wrapped its thin tail around Birlerion's wrist. Birlerion ran a finger down its white chest.

"It's real," Jerrol gasped.

Birlerion smiled. "This is Lin. She's an Arifel. One of the Lady's messengers. They used to carry messages for the Guardians."

Jerrol gaped at him. "It was you. At the palace. It's been you all along, has't it?"

Birlerion eased his shoulders. "As the Lady wills," he murmured, dropping his face into the Arifel's soft fur, luxuriating in the creature's silky touch. The Arifel meeped and rubbed her face against Birlerion's and then disappeared.

Jerrol helped Gilly to her feet. As he straightened, he realised a variation of his rangers uniform had replaced his grimy sheet. His jacket and trousers were a greyish green, which gave off a subtle sheen in the moonlight. The cloak was soft and fleecy warm, yet supple and not bulky. He knew if he saw himself in a mirror, he would be wearing the same archaic uniform as Birlerion. He swallowed as a laughing voice breathed in his ear, "It's a long time since I had the dressing of a ranger," and faded away again.

"Come on, let's get Gilly home. We can talk later."

They escorted Gilly to the safety of her surprised father's arms, stabled Zin'talia back in her stall in the still-standing barn, and then strolled up the high street towards the Black Hen.

"I wonder if Jennery had as exciting a night as we have," Birlerion said with a happy grin. "He's going to be annoyed he missed all the fun."

"You never know, he might have found his own fun," Jerrol said, surprised as Birlerion laughed. He blinked, the Sentinal laughed.

"Ha! I'll bet it was nowhere near as exciting as ours: blazing fires, collapsing buildings, nearly getting burnt alive, the Lady's grace. Nothing beats that."

"Well, we'll find out shortly. Here he comes now," Jerrol said as Jennery came hurrying towards them.

Jennery looked like he was bursting with news, but none of it good by his expression. "Jerrol! You're not going to believe this."

"Let's get out of the street," Jerrol said. "I doubt any of this is for general consumption." He led the way back to their rooms at the inn. Once the door was shut behind them, Jennery fumbled to light the lantern with a spill from the banked fire.

"Don't you use firesticks?" Birlerion asked, watching Jennery struggle.

"A what?" he asked as the wick finally caught.

"A firestick, you just strike it, no messing with spills or flints."

Jerrol cleared his throat. "You'll have to tell us about them another time. Safe to say, I am quite sure we don't have them anymore."

Birlerion stared at him. "I thought the flint was bad enough, but no firesticks? I thought it was because we weren't in the city."

"What's wrong with a flint?" Jennery asked. "They may be expensive, but they are much faster. We're lucky Jerrol has one."

Jerrol laughed at Birlerion's expression. "Jennery, report."

Once Jennery was sure no one could overhear them, he dropped his voice and gave his report. "The blond-haired man accompanied the good Father, and they went straight to his home by the temple in the square. They didn't take any side turns, didn't stop at the temple, straight home. Five minutes after they arrived, they had a visitor. Tall, cloaked, appeared from nowhere, didn't see him enter, no horse.

"The Father was very nervous around him, very obsequious. They spoke for maybe half an hour. Unfortunately, I couldn't hear anything, and then the man left. Stepped into the dark and were gone. I couldn't see a trace of him. It was like magic.

"The interesting thing is that the Father immediately began writing out notes as if passing on instructions. There were five, which he addressed and sealed. He left them on his desk and after he went up to bed, I, ah, let myself in and checked who they were addressed to. They were for the town councillors, all five. Here." He handed over a sealed note.

"Won't the Father miss one?" Birlerion asked.

Jennery shrugged. "He used a plain seal, it's easy to reseal, he'll never know."

Jerrol tilted the note towards the light and inspected the

writing on the front. It was addressed to Councillor Forbes. He broke the seal, trying to keep the damage to the minimum, and read the contents. He whistled before handing the letter back to Jennery. "That is treason."

Jennery, scanning the words, nodded in agreement before handing it to Birlerion. "I don't see how it benefits them, though." His brow wrinkled. "Seceding from the king's rule, won't that expose them? I can't see what they gain."

"Not if it's a coordinated event and multiple councils secede at the same time. It is either a distraction or part of a larger purpose. I imagine this is not a localised action," Jerrol said. "The bigger concern is that the whole council has been turned, along with the town's spiritual leader. They control the voice of the town. Someone has been very busy, and no one has noticed."

"This has the feel of the Ascendants. They were very persuasive. They were able to make people do things that they would not normally do. And the person would have no memory of doing it," Birlerion said, his voice pensive. "But the Lady took all the Ascendants with her, or so I understand, so it can't be."

"We don't have enough information. Who was the visitor? Who are the new council advisors, and who sent them? There seems to be a network of new players involved, and we don't know anything about them. I think that is our first step. Find out who the advisors are and where they came from and most importantly of all, what they are saying.

"Someone is coordinating them. We need to find out who. Can you make a copy of this and return it, Jennery? Good work. And then, we need to get some sleep and start again in the morning. I've had enough excitement for one day!"

11

CHAPTERHOUSE, OLD VESPERS

The Chapterhouse was quiet. The scholars were slumbering, all except one. A slender wraith slipped through the corridors until she reached the open garden in the centre. Listening to the sounds of the fountain, she fumbled for the stone bench before seating herself. Turning her face up to the night sky, she waited.

The moonlight bathed her face, leaching the colour from her skin, from her robes. She sat as if carved from living stone, breathing in the night scents of rosemary and broom planted in the beds behind her, tasting the metallic tang of water.

Combined with the sound of the gentle patter of the water tumbling in the fountain, she knew where she was. She breathed in the quiet night as she listened; something had woken her up and sent her scurrying through the halls like a mouse. The singing tension that had been present since she had awoken faded. Taelia sat quietly, waiting for what she knew not.

She dreamed of tall men and women dressed in high-necked silvery-green uniforms. Their silver eyes glinted with purpose as they prepared for battle. They waited. They had been waiting for centuries. She dreamt of a Captain. Newly claimed with silver eyes in a precious face she had never seen yet knew. She reached out a gentle hand to caress his cheek, and his lips curved into a soft smile just for her.

She jumped as a hand gripped her shoulder. Taelia found herself curled up on the bench, her cheek lying on the gritty stone. She slowly sat up, swinging her legs over and steadied herself, gripping the seat with her hands on either side. Whatever had woken her up had gone.

"Taelia, what are you doing out here? Asleep, where all can see you?" Torsion's voice was sharp.

Taelia turned her head towards her friend's voice. Torsion was a fellow scholar of antiquities. "Something was wrong," she said, her voice blurred with confusion. "But I don't know what."

"Well, sleeping on the bench in public view won't help you figure it out."

Taelia blushed. "Am I? I don't remember, where am I?"

"You're in the central courtyard, and our fellow scholars are staring. Come, let me take you back to your room." Torsion lifted her to her feet, his fingers gripping her shoulders painfully.

"Where have you been? When did you return?" Taelia was confused. She remembered retiring to her room last night and awakening suddenly, but after that, she didn't remember leaving her room, nor had she expected Torsion to wake her.

Torsion hesitated before replying, the moment lost. "It's a little after six in the morning," he replied, guiding her tentative steps out of the courtyard. There were, in fact, a few curious scholars gathering at the refectory windows.

"Something woke me up," Taelia muttered.

"Do you remember what?"

Taelia's brow creased as she thought. "I heard Jerrol, or was it Jennery? Are they together? I thought Jerrol fled on his own."

"Jerrol? What need has he to flee? I thought the king kept him on a tight leash?" Taelia felt him tense as he steered her down the corridors back to her room.

"The prince accused him of treason, threatened to execute him."

"Then he's lucky he's not dead," Torsion said with exasperation. "How did he escape?"

"I don't know." Taelia turned her fearful face towards Torsion. "You can't believe it's true."

Torsion squeezed her arm and brought them to a halt outside her door. "I believe he is capable of anything. He always follows his own rules. You should know that, you've been there, you've paid the price for his mistakes." He pushed open the door and guided Taelia in.

"That's not true, and you know it." Taelia pulled her arm out of his grasp and turned to block the doorway.

Torsion huffed and pushed her in, his veiled strength easily overpowering her attempted stand. "You know what I mean. He is too eager to fight when he should talk. He defaults to the blade when reason should prevail."

Taelia drew herself up, her face pale. Her voice was hard when she spoke. "I thought better of you, Torsion. I thought you were his friend."

"I am his friend. Friends recognise faults. They don't ignore them. He is my friend despite his propensity for violence." He took a deep breath and softened his voice at the sight of her rigid face. "Taelia, I can help him. What did you see?"

Taelia shook her head; anger coursed through her, making her jaw ache.

"I'm sorry, Taelia. He is my friend; he's like a brother to

me. I'm just not as blind to his faults as you are. I can help him, but only if you tell me what you saw."

"I'm not sure. Something important was happening. I was scared for Jerrol, something wasn't right, but I don't know what." She took a step back and bumped into her bed; she sat down. "He's alright now though," she said as she closed her eyes.

"Where was he?"

"With his Sentinals."

"His *what?*" Taelia heard the shock in his voice.

She lifted her face and opened her eyes. "The Lady claims what is hers," she whispered, staring at him. Torsion took a step back as her brilliant turquoise eyes bored into his as if she could truly see him. They started to glow as Taelia began to speak; he strained to hear the words as Scholar Deane Liliian spoke from behind him.

"Scholar Torsion, you are not supposed to be in the female quarters," she snapped.

"Hush," he hissed over his shoulder as Taelia's voice overrode theirs. Her voice was full and rich, resonating through their bones as they stood frozen in her doorway.

> "The Captain of the Guards awakens,
> His Sentinals await his commands."

Liliian pulled Torsion out of Taelia's room. She was a strong woman, and her face was like thunder as Torsion opened his mouth to protest. He swallowed his words as his heated gaze clashed with her stormy glare, and he stepped back, bowing low. "My apologies, Deane. I was but offering assistance."

"I will speak to you in my office. Leave us." Liliian didn't wait to see if he obeyed; she stepped into Taelia's room and shut the door. Taelia's voice continued, her eyes fixed, the altercation unseen:

> "The forgotten are stirring,
> The time is at hand.
> Beware those who rise,
> Thy will to enslave.
> Stand firm and true
> My people to save."

"Taelia?" she whispered, gently touching the girl's shoulder. Taelia shuddered and blinked. Her eyes resumed their natural colour, and she lurched to her feet.

"Taelia, all is well, you are in your room."

"Where's Jerrol?" she gasped, her hands reaching.

Liliian gathered the questing hands. "He is not here. I don't know where he is. You were dreaming."

"I was?"

"Yes, all is well. It's time for you to go back to sleep." Liliian pulled back the covers and helped her back into bed. She rubbed Taelia's feet briskly; they were freezing. When she was sure Taelia was asleep and muttering no further portents, she left the room and shut the door.

12

DEEPWATER WATCH

Deepwater Watch was preparing for the confirmation of their new Lord Guardian, and Alyssa bubbled with excitement as Millie finished plaiting her auburn hair. The day had dawned bright and clear; the skies were a vivid blue outside her window. The Lady blessed the day. Her first Holder confirmation! She was going to witness her first Guardianship, and she could hardly sit still.

"Be still," snapped Millie yet again. "The more you fidget, the longer this will take." She was trying to weave green ribbons into Alyssa's plaited hair, the only way to control her stubborn curls.

"Oh Millie, isn't he handsome though?" Alyssa's eyes shone. Aaron had swept her off her feet the previous evening. "So attentive and he dances so well," she sighed, remembering such a pleasant evening. Aaron had been waiting to welcome the Lord Warden of Greenswatch and his daughter in the courtyard. A tall, fair-haired young man with broad shoulders, dressed in forest green from head to foot. He had flashed her a broad smile, and Alyssa had been captivated by his deep brown eyes, fringed by long black lashes.

"Lord Hugh, Lady Alyssa," Aaron greeted them. "Welcome to Deepwater." His voice was deep, and the rich tones made her shiver. He stepped forward to help her dismount onto the wooden block a page pushed into place. His strong arm assisted her to the ground, and she looked up into his smiling eyes. An answering smile hovered about his lips as he lifted her hand, and her skin tingled with the kiss he planted there.

He led the way into the shadowy halls. "My people will show you the way to your rooms to change and freshen up," he said with a quick nod at the waiting staff. "I look forward to starting the evening with a dance, Lady Alyssa," he said as she was escorted away.

And dance they had. The evening was a long whirl of partners and Aaron and meeting new people and dancing and Aaron. Aaron had been attentive all night, hovering protectively over her as he introduced her to his friends. He introduced his mother, Lady Olivia, at one point, a careworn lady who hardly spoke. She was dressed all in black, which made her look paler and more faded.

It was such a sad story. Alyssa heard snippets through the night and managed to piece it together. Her husband, Lord Stefan, had been killed in a hunting accident, shot by his men as he crossed their path. They had been very happily married, so the gossip went. She had been devastated by his loss and wouldn't believe the reports, appealing to the Lady for justice, pressing Aaron to question his men further.

There was even a subtle suggestion that her mind had been overly affected by it all and maybe Aaron would be better served, they said with knowing looks, sending her somewhere quiet to recover. And hands over mouths, they would giggle and move on.

"There, a certain young man is sure to be bowled over now." Millie grinned knowingly at Alyssa. Alyssa blushed but held her tongue and, shaking out her robes, led the way out of the room and down the stairs.

~

Lord Hugh paced. He had taken precautions, but now he was wondering if they would be enough. Could he trust his people still? Or had these invidious lies percolated everywhere? They were fast approaching the time for Aaron's confirmation, and he instinctively knew it was going to be a travesty. He hadn't quite decided what to do.

The previous evening had been a revelation and not a good one. Everyone he had spoken to had either been afraid to say anything or mouthed platitudes about the new councillors. He was beginning to regret bringing Alyssa with him.

Worst of all had been his brief conversation with Lord Stefan's wife, Olivia. She had been adamant her husband's death wasn't an accident, and although she hadn't gone as far as to implicate Aaron, it was apparent she had been considering it.

He had tried to reassure her that Aaron would never send her away from the Watch. But as the night progressed, and some of the circulating gossip reached his ears, he thought that maybe her concerns were not so far-fetched.

His gloomy thoughts were interrupted by Alyssa's arrival. She glowed with excitement and made a pretty picture with her hair elaborately plaited with ribbons that matched her gown of bronze and green. Hugh led her into the hall where a light breakfast was being served as the guests assembled. The feast would start after the ceremony.

Outside brilliant sunshine and vivid blue skies heralded a momentous day. Every corner of the keep was festooned in banners and flags. It seemed as if the Lady was trying to put on a bold face. Hugh thought she was optimistic.

Alyssa's excitement rose to a fever pitch. Attending a confirmation was a great privilege, and she understood how important it was for a new holder to secure the Lady's blessing. The link between the holder and the land was immutable.

The king protected the land, the land provided for the people, the people worshipped the Lady, the Lady blessed the Guardians, and the Guardians protected all. The Lady, Land and Liege.

She fairly hummed with expectation. Hugh glanced down at her. "Alyssa," he murmured, "contain yourself; you're not a child anymore."

"I know, but I'm so excited! To receive the Lady's blessing, I would be so proud!"

Hugh grimaced. "Somehow I don't think the Lady has been invited today. Watch and listen. You know what should happen; watch what does. Remember we are guests here and this is Aaron's day."

Alyssa stopped fidgeting and flashed him a sharp glance. "Something is awry, isn't it?" she asked, keeping her voice low.

"I am very much afraid so." He was pleased with her perceptive question. "But it is too late to do anything about it. Just be your usual scatterbrained self," he said with a grin.

"Papa!" she exclaimed as Peverill paused in front of her.

"Ah, Lady Alyssa, you look splendid, all ready for the ceremony?" He gave her a smarmy smile.

"Oh yes, Councillor Peverill," she gushed, giving him a blinding smile which made him blink rather rapidly before moving on.

"Don't overdo it," her father cautioned, though he couldn't help but smile at her.

At last, the procession from the manor began. Aaron and Lady Olivia led the way out of the house and down the slope towards the towering sentinal that guarded the deep lakes that gave the holding its name. There wasn't room for everyone, so the villagers were held back whilst holders and local dignitaries thronged around the sentinal.

The first thing Hugh noticed was the complete lack of reference to the Lady, even though they gathered under her sacred Guardian. No one invoked her name; few hands fluttered in homage, no flowers stood on her stone altar; in fact, it was bare. He watched as Councillor Peverill stepped up to the altar and barely stifled a gasp as he climbed up onto it and raised his hands. A horrified ripple spread out under the sentinal as word passed of the sacrilege.

"Welcome," he said. "Welcome all to this new age!" He flung his hands wide to embrace them all. "Welcome to the council's first confirmation: the confirmation of Lord Aaron of Deepwater." He paused dramatically to give time for his words to take effect. "We are here today to announce the end of the holding by Lord Stefan and to proclaim his successor, Lord Aaron." His voice droned on as he outlined the holding, its history and its dependencies until he finally invited Aaron to join him. Aaron hesitated before committing the ultimate insult to the Lady and stepping up onto the altar beside Peverill.

"In the name of the council do you swear to honour and protect the lands known as Deepwater?" Peverill intoned.

"I so swear," Aaron responded, his voice firm and committed.

"In the name of the council do you so swear allegiance and fealty to the council of all within Deepwater?'"

"I so swear," Aaron replied.

Hugh stiffened. These were not the incantations that he was expecting to hear. The council had made them meaningless, with no depth or commitment, just words that skittered off the surface and paid lip service to the true benedictions that should have been performed.

The correct words would have chimed through every believer's soul, resonated in pure harmony with the Lady and bound the Guardian to his people and the land. A binding as base and immutable as time itself which should have entwined with the Lady's blessing. They either didn't understand the intent, or they had deliberately destroyed that link and the power that went with it.

"In the name of the council do you swear to abide by the rules of law so laid down?"

"I so swear." Aaron's reply rang out with conviction.

And so it continued; Aaron handed over his holding, his people, his lands and the Lady without lifting a hand to protect any of it. A voice raised in protest was swiftly cut off under the sentinal, and the low murmur of dissent stilled. The house guards stepped up and subdued the dismay that rippled through the villagers. The grove was utterly silent, no birds sang, not even the sentinal rustled a single leaf. Lady Olivia stood stern-faced and pale; a single tear glistened on her cheek.

"So be it. In the name of the council," proclaimed Peverill resoundingly into the silence. "I give you Lord Aaron!" He blinked as he realised his words fell like stones into the deafening silence. He glared at the guards who rushed to motivate the dumbstruck people.

Aaron stood awkwardly on the stone altar, uncomfortable at the lacklustre cheering. His mother turned away and left the circle before he reached the ground, which left him hurrying to catch up with her.

"Mother." He gripped her elbow, forcing her to stop and face him. He flinched at what he saw in her face, but he steeled himself. "Now we will proceed," he said. He led the procession back to the manor, head held high, ignoring the guards forcibly encouraging his people to cheer.

The small quartet of musicians positioned at the top of the room was playing as they entered the ballroom. The guests were greeted with glasses of wine to smooth over any awkwardness. The atmosphere lightened as more people entered the hall and began to circulate. Alyssa held her father's arm, her face strained and pale, her excitement replaced by horror and acute disappointment. Lord Hugh looked grim, and the other guests avoided them after a glance at their faces.

"Papa, if I have to have a happy face, so do you," she said with a woeful smile.

He sighed. "I am so sorry, Alyssa. I should never have brought you here. If I had known..." His voice died away. He tried again. "Stefan was such a good friend. I thought Aaron had been following in his footsteps, such a solid lad, where did it all go wrong?" He shook his head. "Simeon is the same, challenging tradition, they aren't listening ... they don't understand the damage they are doing."

Alyssa stared at her father, horrified; he sounded so defeated.

"So serious? This cannot be, the most beautiful lady in Deepwater and not a smile in sight. Come dance with me," Aaron commanded. "By your leave," he said with a smile that didn't reach his eyes as he led Alyssa to the dance floor.

Hugh seethed, but he made a concerted effort to smooth his face. He looked around the room, pausing when he saw Aaron's warden and Councillor Peverill in deep conversation with a shadowed figure who seemed to be interjecting comments. Hugh drifted across the room and stopped next to the Lord William who managed Marchwood Watch, a large tract of forest south of Deepwater and Greenswatch which gave way to fertile arable lands and marshes towards the southern coastline of Vespiri. Lord William had been confirmed the previous year and had proved to be an excellent forester, embraced by the Lady, in tune with his land and his people.

"William, Imelda, well met." Hugh greeted the elegant woman standing beside William. "What did you make of the ceremony?"

"I don't think I want to comment," William replied, observing the room. "I think I need to mind my borders more closely," he said, lowering his voice.

Hugh nodded in agreement. "Be careful who you invoke the call with, the response may not be what you expect. If necessary, my steward Garrick knows the protocols." He flicked a glance back to where Peverill still stood in deep conversation. "Do you know who that is? The man in the black robes, speaking to Peverill. I haven't seen him before."

"He appeared about two months ago. They say he was assigned by the king to bring the latest rulings to the council, though he doesn't speak to anyone except Peverill or Aaron. An acolyte descended on us last week spouting a load of rubbish, trying to say it was the new rule of council, twisting the wording until it no longer makes sense." William was getting quite heated. He took a deep breath and stared across the room. "Peverill is on his way."

Hugh calmly changed the topic. "How are your saplings coping with the excessive rain over the last few weeks?"

William grimaced. "The ground is getting too soggy, we've had more rain in the last month than in the last half-year, much more and the roots will be escaping. There is already too much movement. We get a strong wind and ..."

"Now, now, no talking shop at this great event, you'll bore the ladies," Peverill interrupted with a small smile at Lady Imelda.

Lady Imelda heroically took her life in her hands and

said, "Why, Councillor Peverill, thank you, I would be delighted to dance." She passed her glass to her husband and dragged the bewildered councillor to the dance floor.

William choked as Hugh murmured, "Your wife is a diamond, William, a true diamond."

The evening crawled by. Alyssa twirled by with different partners, a fixed smile on her face and an unnatural glitter in her eyes. Aaron led her into dinner and Hugh could see that Aaron thought the glitter was for him, as he preened unbecomingly.

Just before the evening drew to a close Lady Olivia paused beside Hugh. She had managed to escape Peverill's attentions. "Save me!" she whispered before hurrying away, peering over her shoulder.

"Working on it," Hugh muttered in return.

Early the next morning, before the revellers from the evening before were stirring, Hugh crossed the damp courtyard and entered the stables. It was raining again: a light mist that looked to remain all day. He yearned to get on the road home. To get back to his lands and ensure that his borders were secure. There was so much to do. He needed to set up the new security protocols he had agreed with William the previous evening. He snared his young page, Norris, as he scampered towards the stalls with a bucket of apples. Hugh dropped a screw of paper into the bucket. The stable was quiet and still, the silence interrupted by the sound of gentle drips in the damp air and the horses shifting sleepily in their stalls.

"Boy. Listen to me," he said. Norris looked up and dropped his bucket. "Saddle up your horse and take that message to Garrick. You will do it discreetly; you won't tell anyone where you are going, and you will leave straight away, you understand?"

Norris bobbed his head, eyes wide.

"Make sure no one sees you, and under no circumstances should that message be placed in any hand except Garrick's."

"Yessir." The boy scuttled off into the stables. Hugh glanced around and, still unobserved, strolled back into the mansion. He stopped as a door off the foyer opened, and Lady Olivia peeped out. She beckoned to him, and after a quick sweep of the hallway, he joined her in a small sitting room.

"Oh! Thank goodness," she said. "I thought I would never have a chance to speak with you. I feel like a prisoner in my own home. I would have been so happy to see young Alyssa and Aaron get on so well, but well, after yesterday ..." Her eyes glistened. "Well, in different circumstances maybe."

Hugh watched her. "Olivia, I am sorry about Stefan, it was such a tragic accident. He will be sorely missed."

"Thank you," She gripped her hands together, a sheen of tears in her eyes. "I still can't believe it. Even now, after all these months, for the Lady to lose him and in such a manner." She stopped, unable to go on. She looked frail and sad, and Hugh's mouth tightened in concern.

"Deepwater still needs you. Aaron still needs you."

"I know, I know." She faltered, her hand going to her forehead, wisps of blonde hair escaped her cap. "But I can't believe it's true. I don't believe it's true," she said, her voice firm.

"What don't you believe?" Hugh watched her in concern as she tensed.

"Hugh, you cannot believe that Stefan would break cover and walk in front of a line of fire. I can't believe anyone else believes it either. Even Aaron."

"Accidents do happen. The Lady cannot be everywhere all the time."

"This was no accident. Stefan was killed by his own men! How could five of them be an accident?" She couldn't go on.

"I thought it was an unlucky shot, wrong place wrong time, just a hunting accident."

Olivia stilled. "That's the story the council spread around; they said they didn't want to cause bad feeling between the people and the guards. I'm telling you it's all lies."

"The report that went to the king said it was a hunting accident. I saw it."

"What is happening, Hugh? Why is my boy caught up in this? He needs his father's guidance, he needs the Lady, but yesterday, he lost it all." Olivia hugged her arms around her thin body.

"I don't know, but the councils speak with the king's voice, so the king must have a plan he hasn't widely shared yet. I crossed paths with a King's Ranger on the way here. He was checking the circuit; he was going to report back to me on our return to the Greenswatch, so I may find out more then." Hugh pursed his lips at her distress. "How long has Peverill been leading the council here?"

Olivia scowled in distaste. "He turned up about three months ago, and a month later his acolyte joined him, and now they think they rule Deepwater. Aaron is too weak to stand up to them. Peverill thinks he can step right into Stefan's place and act as Lord. As if!" She snorted. "I don't trust them at all. Stefan had this huge argument with them just before his death; he had banned them from Deepwater, said they spoke blasphemy. That has all been twisted now, and my words have no weight. Not even with Aaron." She rocked in her chair. "I've failed both of them."

"Olivia, you haven't failed anyone. As I said, I'll follow up with the ranger. You need to remain strong; your people still need whatever you can do to help them."

"Hugh, promise me, don't forget about me. They will lock me away. I know it, they are all trying to say I am mad. Promise me you'll come and get me."

"Olivia," Hugh said soothingly, "Aaron would never treat you so."

The door opened before she could reply. "Mother, this is where you are. The household has been looking for you all over." He gestured to the warden who hovered behind him.

Lady Olivia rose and held her hand out. "Safe journey home, Hugh," she said before leaving with the warden. The door closed behind her.

"I hope Mother hasn't been worrying you with her fancies. She's still upset about my father. She won't let it go," Aaron said.

Hugh's eyebrows rose. "Understandable, I'm sure," he murmured. "She needs time; over time, the Lady will ease her sorrows."

"She is stubborn, but she'll come around. She will welcome Peverill's advances once she gets to know him if she knows what's good for her."

Hugh kept silent, biting his lip to keep his words behind his teeth. He tilted his head invitingly.

Aaron pounced on the opportunity to talk. "You know I have great plans for the holding. Yes, the people will be thankful I've taken over. They will be prosperous again. Once we harvest the timber and repurpose the land, and with direct links to the council, my voice will have weight. They will support my plans. I won't alienate them the way my father did; they will listen to me," he said, thrusting his chest out.

"Where are you going to harvest?" Hugh asked with feigned interest.

"The Great Western Bank is prime timber, exactly what the King's shipwrights need. I received notice of their requirements today." He rubbed his hands in glee. "My holding will be one of the greatest in the Watch, even the king is watching, and a certain young lady would be happy to join with me as we grow."

"The Great Western Bank?" Hugh was aghast. "Lad, that is your core stock; you lose that, and your holding will be worthless. Once it's gone, it's gone. That timber took centuries to grow; it's part of the ecosystem around here. Your lands will lose the protection they provide from wind and rain. The water run-off alone will ruin your soil."

"Rubbish!" Aaron laughed, greed gleaming in his eyes. "It'll take months to clear that land, and then the peasants can help till it and rent it off me, double the return! I know what I'm doing. I look forward to introducing you and Lady Alyssa to my holding." He turned away, hurrying to open the door. "The horses will be ready out front," he tossed over his shoulder as he led the way out into the hall where servants bustled in preparation of the continued entertainment. Hugh could not wait for the day to be over, so they could get on the road and back to the safety of his holding.

13

GREENSWATCH

J errol awoke early feeling quite refreshed. The grey pre-dawn light was leaking into the room through the small window. The soft patter of rain explained the dampness in the air. It was raining again. The roads would be impassable.

He stretched, muscles protesting as a result of the exertions from the night before. Miraculously there were no burns on his skin. He felt luxuriously cool. As he sat up, he noticed the soft green glow emanating from his skin. A temporary after-effect of the Lady's presence? He hoped it was temporary.

As he pondered on the Lady's words from the previous night, the glow began to dim, and Jerrol breathed a little easier. He glanced across at Jennery, still snoring into his pillow. It had been late by the time they had stopped talking.

Jennery's news was more disconcerting. The Grove council had a shadowy overseer calling the shots. How many other councils were infected by the same disease? He wondered what Torsion thought of it all and whether his council in Velmouth was affected.

Sighing, he decided to return to Greenswatch and hope the Lord Captain had arrived. Lord Hugh would be a good source, to begin with, and then they would search out Torsion. Decision made, Jerrol levered himself out of bed and changed into his new clothes; he didn't dwell on where they came from. The material was soft and silky against his skin. He had never owned such fine linen before. They shimmered with a silvery grey-green hue that pulsed gently, a more tangible gift from the Lady.

It would be interesting to see if Jennery saw it the same way. His skin pulsed in rhythm but as he stamped into his boots, the two clicked in place, and the glow sank into his skin, much as he had absorbed that exaltation last night. He wondered what it all meant.

He had dreamt of the Lady last night. It was if she was determined to give him his orders all at once. He had a head full of information, and yet it was all just out of reach as his brain busily catalogued and filed it all away; maybe once he made sense of it all he might be able to access it.

He turned back to rouse Jennery and saw a small Arifel nestled on his pillow. Hesitating, he looked closer; it was a bizarre sight. A black and brown mackerel-striped kitten ending in a forked tail, and yes, those were scaly wings tucked in behind its forelegs. How long had it been there? Where had it come from? It looked young, newly hatched, another Arifel. Why were they suddenly appearing?

He tried to reconcile the cute, cuddly kitten with the fact that it had reptilian features. The creature opened large emerald green eyes and chittered in disapproval. It snuggled further into Jerrol's pillow and glared at him; its eyes were trying to convey a message.

Information kicked in. Arifels dated back to pre-cracking of the stone times. They hadn't been seen since the stone had cracked, and they were highly intelligent creatures used by the Guardians to pass messages, especially vital between remote regions. They were telepathic creatures, though not with ordinary men, and they were rare, highly prized companions of the Lady's court, or so his new memories provided him. The Arifel chittered in agreement and began to preen, flicking his forked tail in a gentle thump on the pillow.

Jerrol smiled in amusement at the creature's antics and yet, why was he here? He perched on the side of the bed and watched the little creature. The Arifel had a pointed face and a white nose. He meeped mournfully, and Jerrol's stomach growled. He stared into the Arifel's mesmerising green eyes which grew larger and more pleading as he watched. He didn't know what Arifels ate, but he could tell he needed to scrounge some food to keep him quiet.

With a resigned sigh, he rose from the bed and glanced across at Jennery. "I'll get food, but you have to stay there," he said as he glared at the creature. The Arifel kneaded the bed as he circled, and curled up on the pillow, tucking his scaly tail around his body.

Jerrol left Jennery sleeping and made his way down the stairs to the taproom. One of the young maids was trying to wash the floor with a grubby mop. He wasn't sure that she was making much difference. She paused as he entered the room and with a twitch of her lips which might have been a smile, she made a funny bob and spoke: "You're early for the morning meal, sir, but I could get you some bread. Fresh-baked this morning."

"Bread would be fine," he replied, and she bobbed again. Propping her mop against the wall, she disappeared out the back of the bar. She was back before he had a chance to move, holding a tray of bread twists and a mug of milk which she placed the tray on the nearest table; then she grabbed her mop and disappeared again.

Jerrol sat and inhaled the aroma of fresh-baked bread, remembering similar early mornings at Stoneford Keep, coaxing rolls from the overworked cook, his shoulders relaxed as he pulled the twist apart.

He mused over Jennery's report of the man with the spiky hair he had followed the previous evening. Who were these people who had so insidiously infiltrated the Watches? The news of the shadowy figures controlling the council and rewriting history didn't bode well for the people nor the Watches of Vespiri.

Jerrol drank some milk and then broke the rest of the bread into the liquid. He carried the mug back up to his room before the Arifel came in search of him. As he climbed the stairs, Birlerion appeared, his eyes sparkling. "Captain, there is another Arifel in your room."

Jerrol grimaced. "I know, where are they coming from?"

Birlerion led the way. "The Lady is calling them."

Jerrol quickened his step and entered his room; he had returned none too soon. Jennery was groggily trying to swat what he thought was a persistent bug, though Jerrol grinned at the thought of an insect the size of this hungry Arifel.

Jerrol offered the Arifel a soggy piece of bread to draw him away from Jennery. The Arifel guzzled up the sops. Perching on the side of the mug, he leant down inside to reach the rest. Slurping, he leaned further and further forward until inevitably with a started squawk he fell in. Fortunately, it sounded as if the mug was empty; well, there wasn't much splashing.

A rather sheepish face peered back over the rim of the mug at Jerrol. The creature's whiskers had milk drops glistening on the ends, and he hauled himself out and perched on the edge; then, much like a cat, he started to clean his whiskers.

Jerrol watched amused as the creature carefully groomed

himself. Jennery had woken up and was also watching wide-eyed. "By the Lady," he started before Jerrol could shush him.

"It's an Arifel."

"A what?"

"An Arifel, a creature of myth and legend. I didn't think they were real, though this one certainly is."

"They are the Lady's messengers, if you can get them to concentrate for long enough," Birlerion said with a grin.

Jerrol glanced at him; he seemed more relaxed in their company after all the excitement of the previous evening. Jennery sat up, watching closely as he swung his legs over the side of the bed. "Is this to do with last night?"

"I would think so," Jerrol whispered, not wanting to startle the small creature. "Both our Lady and our king are under siege, gentlemen, and she has chosen us as her protectors." Jerrol grimaced, "Let's hope she has chosen wisely."

"Umm, Jerrol? Do you realise that your eyes are silver, like Birlerion's? Did that happen last night as well?"

Jerrol rubbed his eyes; he hadn't thought to check. He rose and looked at himself in the mirror. Liquid silver eyes gleamed back at him. "Along with my uniform. The Lady is determined."

The creature finished grooming and settled back down in a crouch with a soft meep. His large emerald eyes stared at Jerrol.

"Better?" Jerrol reached out a careful finger to stroke his white chest.

The creature chittered in agreement and stretched his pink mouth in a jaw-cracking yawn, then walked up Jerrol's forearm and snuggled into the crook of his arm. He gave a soft contented burp before closing his eyes.

Their eyes met across the room, and Jennery snickered. "Looks like you are on babysitting duty."

"Looks like it, but he can't sleep there."

"Well, at least he's cute, it could be worse."

"How?" Jerrol growled.

"Well, he could be covered in spines and ten times bigger."

With a sigh, Jerrol scooped the little creature up and, stuffing a wash-cloth in his pocket, he placed the Arifel safely inside his new bed. He didn't seem to mind; he burrowed deeper into his nest. "Let's hope he stays there for now." He looked over at Jennery. "Get dressed, we need to speak to the smith."

They left the inn and started to walk down the muddy high street. The sky was overcast, the clouds low and heavy, and a steady drizzle persisted. Someone had laid down a few boards in an attempt to create a sidewalk, but the boards squelched in the mud, creating a more slippery hazard. They sensibly avoided them, skirting the muddy puddles and flooded cart ruts.

"Ah, Jerrol?" Jennery rubbed his forehead. "You think you can catch me up with what's going on? It's all very well saying we are part of it, but what does that mean? I mean, last night was pretty spectacular, and you've had a grin on your face ever since, and now this furry creature turns up?"

Jerrol took a deep breath. "I guess it has been piling up. I'm not sure I can explain last night, but I'll try and explain what I can." Where to start, he wondered. At the beginning, he supposed. He began to speak. "You know I returned from Birtoli about five months ago, and Nikols assigned me to the chancellor's detail. I think Nikols has been suspicious of Isseran for quite a while. He's been meeting with all sorts of people, in odd places, yet none of it is reported back to the King through the usual diplomatic channels.

"While I was with him, he tried to shake me off constantly, even though I was his security detail. I made quite a show of going off duty, but I know I was being followed." Jerrol's face tightened as he continued. "Well, let's just say I didn't go off duty and the chancellor knew, then Prince Kharel accused me of treason and had me arrested.

"I tried to protest my innocence, but Kharel had his men hustle me out. I'm not sure who was behind it either. The chancellor? Prince Kharel? It wasn't the king that I do know."

Jennery watched Jerrol in concern. "But you managed to escape. How did you do that? And how did you know you needed to go to the Watches?"

"Yes, well, let's just say the prince didn't watch closely enough. Having cleared all my immediate responsibilities to king and country out of the way, it seemed logical to head as far from Vespers as I could. There have been concerns about the Guardians, and well, the Lady guides my feet now.

"I believe there is a link between the king's palsy and the state of the land. The king is supposed to protect the people, and the people protect the land for him. You know the story about the Guardians and how they are linked to the Sentinals. They maintain the balance in the lands."

"Yes, everyone knows the importance. Lord Hugh is one, Guardian of the Greenswatch," Jennery said.

"Hmm," replied Jerrol, glancing around as they neared the ruins of the smithy; this probably wasn't the best place to discuss this. He veered off towards the tall sentinals guarding the Grove. "Let's talk here for a moment." He glanced around him. The Grove was still; not a bird chirped or a leaf stirred. In the dim green light, Jerrol stared at Jennery and Birlerion, a sense of expectancy in the air.

"That balance is out of kilter. The Guardians are dying, and I need to discover why and stop it. That's where we come in. The Lady has more Guardians than just the Lord Holders. The Guardians also protect the groves, the sentinals, and certain relics and lore records. They are scattered across all the four kingdoms – not just here in Vespiri. Some are in Terolia, Elothia and probably Birtoli as well, but they always follow the same family. The Guardianship passed from generation to generation."

He ran his hand through his hair, leaving it sticking up in tufts. "That's what happened last night. The Guardianship passed to Gilly. The smith's mother, Sylvie, passed it to me before she died, but I wasn't the right vessel. My body couldn't assimilate it; it was trying to reject me. I think ..."

He paused, thinking it through. "I think that's why the Lady intervened last night. She couldn't lose another Guardian, so she made me a temporary vessel until I could pass it on to Gilly. And as a result, you see ..." He gestured at his clothing. "Only I don't think the Lady sees it as temporary. The Lady claimed me before; I think she is stamping her mark. She said to me ..." He tried to remember her words exactly. "She said the journey was just starting, that the forgotten are waiting and that we must protect the Guardians. She called me her Captain."

Birlerion nodded. "There has to be a Lady's Captain. If Guerlaire cannot return, then she would have to appoint another. All Sentinals report to you."

Jennery began to laugh. "I think the Lady is definitely more appreciative than your last boss." He waved at Jerrol's clothes as if to validate the point. "The King's got no chance of getting you back." He collapsed into gales of helpless laughter at the sight of Jerrol's pained expression. Jennery tried to control his laughter, but whenever he glimpsed Jerrol's face, he burst out laughing again. Even Birlerion was grinning.

"Alright, alright, joke's on me, but in all seriousness." Jerrol glanced sternly at Jennery who was leaning against the smooth trunk of a sentinal to hold himself up, flapping his hand in a go on motion. "We need to find and protect the Guardians against whatever is hunting them. And to see how the councils are all connected in this."

Jennery sobered up at that. "The fire last night managed to flush one of them out," he said. "It caught immediately, you know, and spread fast, even though the timbers should've been wet through after all this rain."

"Yes, we need to find out where and how the fire started. It wasn't accidental, that's for sure. It couldn't have been that fellow you followed last night; he never went near the smithy. Unless it was some type of delayed reaction." Jerrol considered the possibility and shifted uneasily. "Let's go look at the ruins and see if we can tell anything from that." He looked at Birlerion. "I'd like you to have a closer look, you might spot something we've missed. We still need to speak to the smith as well."

"How in the Lady's name did you manage to send my orders to join you if you've been discharged from the service?" Jennery asked, starting to put things together.

"Ah." Jerrol grinned at him mischievously: time to get his own back. "I told you I sent them before I left. I didn't think word of my downfall would have reached them yet."

"What? You mean they are not official?"

"Well," drawled Jerrol, "that probably depends on your point of view. Your commander thought they were official, otherwise, he wouldn't have dispatched you, though what he's thinking now who knows!"

"They'll be calling me a deserter," Jennery complained though he didn't seem particularly bothered at the thought.

"I'm sure the Lady, now she's got the hang of recruiting, wouldn't mind adding you to her company. I could use the help." Before he finished speaking, Jennery's eyes widened in shock, and a soppy grin spread over his face. Jennery had been leaning against the nearest sentinal for support and as Jerrol watched a green glow spread up his arm and gradually transformed his clothes into the same grey-green uniform Jerrol was wearing. Birlerion began to chuckle.

"Well, at least we match now." Jerrol couldn't help but grin.

"What?" Jennery leapt away from the Sentinal. "You, you!" Jennery waggled his finger at Jerrol, but he couldn't get the expletive past his lips.

"Never mind." Jerrol patted his arm in sympathy. "I doubt the Lady will be prepared to give you up either, even once she gets to know you."

"A new brother. The Lady is pleased. I said you wouldn't be able to refuse her. Welcome, Leanderion," Birlerion said, gripping Jennery's arms and giving him a shake.

"No, no, call me Jennery," Jennery gasped, horrified. Birlerion started laughing.

A muted meep from his pocket reminded Jerrol of his passenger, and he carefully lifted the little Arifel out.

"Did you hear the Lady?" From the enthusiastic response, he assumed the answer was yes. The Arifel launched himself at Jennery, fluttering around his head and mussing his blond hair.

Jerrol watched the Arifel and wondered what would happen next. How was an Arifel going to help him, and an immature one at that? His gut told him he was here to help and in response to the Lady's promise. Was he one of the forgotten? A soft chuckle vibrated in his ear, and he knew precisely how the Arifel could help.

Information scrolled behind his eyes and he sighed in relief; he parsed the information, suddenly glad of the hours spent with Torsion learning his research methods in the depths of the Chapterhouse's archives. Arifels could recognise Guardians. They could make themselves invisible as well, so only those with the sight or Guardians could see them.

At least that would help them travel more discreetly and be the signal for Guardians to come forward, assuming that they recognised the Arifel for what it was. He hoped the Arifel knew how to become invisible. He was certain that was something beyond his skills to teach! The little Arifel popped out of sight, and Jerrol assumed he'd be able to find them if he wanted to.

Jerrol led the way back towards the blackened ruins of the hostelry, with Jennery still muttering under his breath and a surprisingly happy Birlerion; maybe this was all familiar to him. He glanced at them both with a wry smile. Jennery was fingering his new clothes with hesitant fingers, a smile of wonder on his face. He'd probably never worn such fine linen before either.

As they approached the ruins, Jerrol saw the smith moving about, dejectedly lifting beams that were still smouldering before letting them fall back to the ground with sodden puffs of ash. The site looked more depressing in the drizzly rain. The smell of charred wood and the tang of ash and water permeated the air along with fine fragments of dust stirred up by the smith's actions. Towards the front of the house, the ash was a pure white, darkening to a dirty grey towards the rear. Jennery continued round to the stables to check on the horses.

"Not much left," Jerrol said as he surveyed the ruins. It was a distressing sight. The smith grunted in response as he lifted another beam. "It caught straight away," Jerrol continued. "You were lucky your neighbours managed to save the barn and the smithy."

The smith stood up. "I suppose so. In all this rain you would have thought it would stop smoking. You can still feel the heat in the beams."

"I'm sorry about your mother," Jerrol said.

The smith screwed up his face before nodding at Jerrol. "Appreciate your help last night, you took a risk running back in there. My mother said she invited you to dinner today; I think we'll have to rearrange it for another time," he said, his face drawn.

Birlerion glanced sharply at Jerrol before starting his investigation of the ruins.

"Yes, I think you have other things to worry about today. When will you be able to hold the Leaving?"

"Just waiting on the Father, he's not been round yet. Hopefully tomorrow at the latest. If we could get him to agree to today that would be best, but that would be two Leavings in two days."

"Will the Father perform the full rite? He seems to be advocating a change in the usual way of things," Jerrol asked, worried for them.

"He will if he knows what's good for him," the smith said, his face grim. "They can talk about progress all they like, but even the Father would hesitate to change the Leaving." He scowled. "Can you believe those town idiots tried to introduce a new tithe? They graciously granted each grower another ten foot of land, which the family would have to clear, and then they upped the tithe to pay for the additional crops they would be able to grow.

"Even though nothing edible will grow for a year or more at least, if ever, considering the timber draws all the nutrients out of the soil. It would have to be left fallow and mulched first. Nearly caused a riot! They tried to tell us we should be grateful. Grateful for them giving us forest land which is not theirs to give! To cut down the new saplings! Wait till Lord Hugh hears about it." The smith shook his head, his shoulders drooping as he surveyed the mess. "I'm afraid they'll pass a law or something. What do we do then?"

"Who holds the council? Surely they have the good of the land at heart? Felling the future can't be in their interest?" Jerrol watched the smith as he stepped over a blackened beam and kicked a pile of ashy debris.

"The council leader is no longer the real power, he's getting old. He was going to retire, but he changed his mind when that smarmy envoy turned up." The smith spat to one side in disgust.

Birlerion paused in his inspection of the ruins at the bitterness in the smith's voice, but he smoothly bent back down at a flick of Jerrol's fingers.

"Envoy?" Jerrol prompted.

"Supposedly sent by the king, he had the council hanging off his every word before the end of the first session. He says he's the king's voice. He seems pretty flimsy to me, spouting a load of Ascendant rubbish, trying to convince folks that they can self-rule. I doubt the king is sponsoring that message. He's not going to do himself out of power, now is he?"

"When did he arrive?"

"About a month ago. He doesn't mix much with us peasants, just sends out his lackeys with his messages, spreading them like a sickness. I never thought to see folks so gullible." The smith sighed, glancing around the dreary ruins. "The king better start paying attention, or his people won't have a choice."

"Have you heard the term 'veil-shredder' before?" Jerrol asked.

The smith froze. "Don't," he exclaimed, glancing around. "Don't mention them. They can hear you, you know. Hear what you say – it's not safe." He gestured towards the smoking beams. "A warning, don't you think?"

"Why would you need a warning?" Birlerion asked, brushing the ash off his hands.

The smith curled his lip, but before he could answer his

wife called his name. "The Father's waiting for you," she called.

The smith turned to Jerrol and stuck out his hand. "Thank'ee again for your help last night. My mother would have been glad of your company. As it is, it's safer not to keep company with strangers. Lady bless you both. You'd best be watching your backs, though, because the lackeys will have reported on you."

Jerrol clasped his hand warmly. "Protect your family. Protect the line and if possible, keep the Lady close. Don't ever give up on her. She'll never give up on you, I promise." The smith nodded slowly and turned away, following his wife up the muddy street.

Birlerion let his breath out with a whoosh. "Well," he exclaimed, wiping his hands with a handkerchief in a futile attempt to clean off the ash.

Jerrol held up a hand. "Not here. Let's get our things and get ready to leave. I think we need to bring Jennery up to date and go visit Lord Hugh as soon as possible."

14

CHAPTERHOUSE, OLD VESPERS

Scholar Deane Liliian sat behind her desk and inspected the man seated before her. He had reverted to his studiously courteous manner. His brief outburst was a mere memory. But she remembered the viciousness in his expression clearly: his thin face transformed by his anger into a honed weapon, his black eyes spitting fury. In all the years she had known him, she had never seen him behave so.

"Explain yourself," she said.

"Scholar Deane, I offer my sincerest apologies. I was just helping Taelia back to her room."

"Oh? You have been absent these three or four months, with no word, no report of your whereabouts, and the first thing you do on your return is to invade the women's quarter?"

"Not at all, Deane. I found her asleep in the courtyard when I arrived; I was on my way to my room."

"Taelia was asleep in the courtyard," Liliian repeated.

"Yes, Deane, on the bench by the fountain. I woke her and escorted her back to her room, and then you interrupted us."

"Interrupted what, exactly?"

"I was asking her why she was in the courtyard. She didn't remember."

"I must advise you, scholar, that I will be speaking to Taelia later."

Torsion pursed his lips. "She said she was worried for Jerrol, but didn't remember getting up. I suppose she must have walked in her sleep. There were enough scholars in the refectory to confirm my words."

"Jerrol?"

"She was afraid for him. She said the prince had accused him of treason." Torsion grimaced, his eyes cold. "I'm not surprised. He was ever wont to be in trouble."

Liliian's eyes narrowed. "Where have you been?"

"I told you. I was going to Velmouth and then up to the Watch Towers."

"For three months? I expect a detailed report of your findings on my desk by tomorrow morning."

"Of course, Deane."

"And a report of exactly what you and Taelia were talking about."

"Yes, Deane."

Liliian watched him closely. He was submissive, his anger sheathed, but she knew it was bubbling under the surface by the tension in his muscles. "What is wrong, Torsion?"

Torsion stared at her and then exhaled heavily. He twisted his lips. "If I'd known..." He paused. "Even when he's not here, he is."

"He?"

"Jerrol. Taelia can't see passed her romanticised view of him. He is not for her. He is unreliable, absent most of the time. His hands are covered in blood, and yet she doesn't see any of it."

"And you do?"

"I've known him since he was an unformed child. I helped mould him into the man he is today. He is family even with all his faults, and I know them all. I wouldn't want Taelia hurt. She could do so much better."

"With you, I suppose?"

Torsion shrugged. "Why not? I would protect her."

"Maybe she doesn't need protecting. You can't force her, Torsion," Liliian said, her voice gentle.

"I don't intend to. She will see sense in the end."

Greenswatch

After settling their bill at the inn, Jerrol, Jennery and Birlerion mounted their horses. Zin'talia emanated relief at seeing Jerrol, and he soothed her as they started back up the road towards Greenswatch. Trees crowded along the side of the road and made the day seem even darker and gloomier than it was. The trees were dense and the undergrowth so thick you couldn't see into the gloom for more than a few feet. The muddy road wound down a slight inclination before veering off to the right into what seemed like a bank of trees at the end. An illusion, or so he hoped.

Their horses walking in step, Jennery peered around them and then up at the sky as a fine drizzle began misting down again, pooling in beads before running harmlessly off their cloaks. Jennery observed the effect thoughtfully and cast a weather eye at the sky. "The Lady must have known more rain was forecast."

"With the amount of rain lately, it's not a big leap to make," Jerrol agreed.

"I wonder if she could do anything about the mud."

"You'll have to ask her, though I'm not convinced it will be a priority. Birlerion, what did you see in the remains of the smithy? Was there anything obvious?"

Birlerion shifted in his saddle and wiped the rain off his face. "It's all a bit inconclusive. There was some lighter ash at the front of the building where it burnt hotter which would match someone adding an accelerant to start the fire, but no indications as to what it might have been. The rest looked pretty standard."

"And no proof that the fire spread any quicker than normal, except that it appears more intense at the front?" Jerrol asked.

"Fires generally have a spark point, where they first ignite," Birlerion said, "and if they used oil to start it, then it would burn fiercest there."

"The smith thought it was a warning, though a warning against what isn't clear," Jerrol reminded him.

"Yes, he shut up quick once his wife turned up. I wonder what he would have said if we had more time. The councils are certainly the mouthpiece, though whether they believe what they are spouting or are just misguided, I'm not sure. Someone is influencing them. I doubt any king would support such a message; it must be coming from someone else."

"The chancellor?" Jennery suggested. "Do you think he is trying to take the crown whilst the king is ill?"

"If Kharel thought the chancellor could help him, he would use him. Though whether Kharel could prevent the chancellor from overthrowing him in turn would be the sticking point," Jerrol mused. "From what I heard at the Grove, it is more discrediting the Lady than the king. I can't see Kharel giving up his chance at the crown that easily. Even if King Benedict is distracted, I can't see him neglecting his duties; his belief in the Lady is absolute. He would never give her up. No," Jerrol muttered to himself, "something else is happening."

The miles passed. The roads were deteriorating further

as the unseasonal rain continued to fall. They resorted to cutting through the edge of the forest tracts, searching for woodland trails that weren't so waterlogged, but getting caught instead in intractable bracken that snared whatever passed.

As the clouds thickened, the rain grew harder, and the forest grew impassable as the light faded in the constant downpour. Jerrol finally called a stop. "We're not going to make Greenswatch in these conditions, let's stop and at least try to find some shelter. If I remember rightly there is a ridge just up ahead, before we reach the turnoff. Let's see if we can find any shelter there."

Jennery grunted and, hunching his shoulder against the inclement weather, he kept his head down under his hood and pulled his horse behind Zin'talia's sodden tail. The trees crowded them, blocking what little light there was and making them stumble over the first of the rocky outcrops. "This way," called Jerrol, veering off into the darkness ahead, "there's an overhang, it's quite deep, not quite a cave, but enough to give us some shelter."

They rigged an awning to keep the worst of the rain off the horses and stacked the saddles and saddlebags in the deepest corner to keep them as dry as possible. Birlerion bent over the small fire pit he had dug and delved in his pocket for some dry lint to try to start the fire. The bracken and twigs they had collected flared into flames, and he placed a pot of water on it to heat.

Jerrol squinted at the fire. "That was quick. I think we'll let you do fire duty all the time. I'll take the first watch, Birlerion, you get the middle watch and Jennery, you take the morning, I can't see us getting any further today." He handed around mugs of chicory tea: not as nice as coffee, but hot and steaming.

It was a cold and miserable afternoon. Jennery began

rubbing his horse down as Birlerion started on his horse. Zin'talia started to complain. *"I'm wet, it's cold. I hate Greenswatch,"* she moaned, swishing her tail. *"It's much warmer in Terolia. Let's go there."*

Jennery eventually soothed her as he began to rub her down. Birlerion unwrapped his bow and dried it off, before rewrapping it and then checking through his quiver.

"Why do you strap it under your saddle? Shouldn't you carry it on your back? Easier to get to?" Jennery asked, watching him.

"In this weather, it's unlikely I'll use it. When I was in Terolia, I used to carry it like this; heat can warp as much as water, and it wasn't so obvious."

"What were you hiding from?"

"Nothing, I was just trying to blend in, not be so noticeable."

Jennery snorted. "Before or after you turned Sentinal?"

Birlerion gave him a brief grin. "Both."

"And how successful were you?"

"Pretty much. Wrapped in scarves it's difficult to tell one from the other."

"True," Jennery murmured as he watched the Sentinal roll himself up in his blankets, trying to get some sleep.

Jerrol peered out into the misting gloom, the soft voices comforting. All was still except for the dripping rain, pattering on soggy leaves and splatting into the sodden moss. The smell of rotting vegetation and collecting water was strong. The chill air found its way into his clothes, making everything damp to the touch and uncomfortable. Even the horses were miserable, with Zin'talia making a point to shudder when she caught his gaze.

He was still amazed by the gentle link that connected them, comforted by its constant presence. The first time he had ever seen a Darian was when he was a child. It was the first time he had ever met his friend, Torsion. His Darian was silver-grey, elegant and very intelligent. She had wrapped every single stable lad around her elegant hoof, the pampered soul that she was. He hoped Zin'talia didn't expect the same cosseting. If so, she was going to be out of luck on this journey.

Jerrol shook Birlerion awake later that evening and rolled himself in Birlerion's warm blanket. He soon dozed off but was roused when he heard Birlerion changing with Jennery in turn. Jennery's low voice carried on the damp air, complaining bitterly about catching a chill in this awful weather and why hadn't they stayed at the inn. Jerrol commiserated. He had a valid point.

Jerrol must have dozed off again because suddenly he was wide awake, Zin'talia screeching a warning in his head. He reached over to grab Birlerion's arm, but he needn't have bothered. Birlerion was awake and moving. There were faint wisps of grey streaking the inky black sky, and the rain had eased to a fine sifting mist. He slid his sword out of its sheath and rose as Birlerion melted into the darkness.

A shadow launched itself at Birlerion, closely followed by a second, crowding Jerrol's arm and pushing him back against the stone outcrop with a breath-stealing thud. Jerrol dropped his sword and slid out his daggers as the bite of cold steel sliced across his ribs.

He struck upwards, hard, connecting with something soft, and parried a second thrust towards his shoulder. He twisted out of the man's embrace and danced back towards the opening, catching a glimpse of Birlerion taking his man down with a flash of his blade; of Jennery, there was no sign.

His opponent dropped into a crouch before sliding forward with a scything motion, trying to take out Jerrol's legs and flipping himself back to his feet in one smooth motion. This was no amateur thug; this was someone who knew his craft.

Jerrol feinted to the left, before twisting into a thrust towards his opponent's chest. The daggers screeched to the hilts as he moved in counterpoint; they leapt apart and circled until his opponent collapsed to the ground as Birlerion slugged him in the head with his sword. Jerrol swayed, clutching his hand to his side as he watched Birlerion sheath his sword before checking the man. Birlerion grimaced, and he knew the man wouldn't be standing up again.

"Jennery?" Jerrol gritted his teeth as he straightened up.

"He's out cold, looks like they took him unawares. He is going to have a major headache on top of his cold." Birlerion tutted unsympathetically.

"Bring him in under the shelter; let's make him comfortable at least," Jerrol said as he turned away to inspect his injury. Not good. A long, jagged slice across his ribs stung, sluggishly bleeding along its length. Not down to the bone, but it would need stitching nonetheless. His jacket had blunted much of the thrust; otherwise, he would be the one lying on the floor and not rising.

Jerrol rummaged in his saddlebag and slapped a cloth against the slice, tying the ends together and tucking his shirt in tightly to hold it in place; they needed to get in the warm and get some light so that they could tend their wounds. He squatted beside Jennery, who was very pale and beginning to groan. Hopefully, it was only a concussion though he was wheezing alarmingly.

"We can't stay here. We need to get Jennery somewhere warm before anyone else finds us."

Birlerion peered out at the misty forest. "I'm surprised anyone found us at all in this."

"You can't say they aren't persistent. We need to get to Greenswatch, it's only a couple of miles further on."

Between them, they managed to get Jennery upright and steered him out to his horse which Birlerion had saddled. "Do you think you can stay on if I help you up?" Jerrol asked, gripping his friend's arm to keep him balanced.

"I'll help him," Birlerion interrupted. "You'll make your side worse." He must have seen Jerrol's makeshift first aid. "Wait for me, and I'll help you with your horse."

Jerrol leaned woozily against Zin'talia, who was nickering with concern. He had lost more blood than he had thought and was feeling lightheaded. Maybe he should return to Old Vespers and clear his name; he was beginning to get fed up with being attacked.

He stared out into the dark forest. The wind was starting to rise; his cloak flapped in the strengthening breeze, a precursor to the next deluge. The rustling trees swished ahead of him, and slim saplings swayed as a sudden downpour drummed on the sodden ground and drenched them.

15

GREENSWATCH

The little mackerel-coloured Arifel popped into view in front of Jerrol, scolding him about his location. He hovered, unimpressed with Jerrol being out in the rain when he could be warm and cosy inside. "Believe me," Jerrol muttered, shivering inside his cloak. "I would much prefer to be warm and cosy." The Arifel flitted away from the outcrop before returning to hover in front of Jerrol again, chittering pointedly.

"Hmm, Ari is saying he can take us to shelter, better than a night amongst the rocks," Jerrol called behind him as he watched the little Arifel.

"Huh, you gonna believe that fluff ball?" Jennery wheezed. "He doesn't even know where we are!" The Arifel popped into view in front of Jennery, scolding energetically, flapping his wings in Jennery's face. "Okay, okay, I'm sorry!" Jennery cried, surrendering to the little creature.

The Arifel shook himself over Jennery, squawked and disappeared again. Jennery sighed and shook his head as Birlerion helped lever Jerrol carefully into his saddle. Birlerion paused to look up at Jerrol in concern before mounting his horse; he took Jennery's reins and led him down the track after Jerrol and the Arifel.

About half a mile down the track Jerrol saw a dim light wavering amongst the trees. "Come quickly," a voice called, "there is a barn to your left you can put your horses in. Reese will see to them for you."

As Jerrol approached the structure, a large man opened the barn door, spilling golden light out into the night. "Quick, bring yourselves inside, this is no night to be out," The man's voice reached them through the rain as they approached.

Jerrol slid to the ground, leaning heavily against Zin'talia as he caught his breath against the jarring. He straightened as a wave of energy emanated from her, his bloodied hand convulsing on her mane. She tossed her head in agitation, whinnying softly.

The man took Zin'talia's reins from Jerrol's nerveless hand and led her into a stall. "Don't worry. I'll give her a good rubbing down. She'll be fine," the giant of a man said, his thatch of red hair glinting in the light of the lantern. He towered over Jerrol, even broader across the shoulders than Jennery. He soon had the saddle off and passed the saddle-bags to Birlerion, who turned to help Jennery dismount. "Go on, get yourself in and dried off." He reached for Jennery's horse and led him into another stall. "I'll be in in a moment, let me settle these for you," he repeated, shooing them towards the cottage.

Jerrol and Birlerion exchanged a glance but did as he bid and steered Jennery towards the small cottage to be greeted by the welcoming smell of coffee in the warm moist air. A slender woman with masses of reddish-blonde curls stood ready to welcome them. "Come in, take off your cloaks. Here, dry yourselves off, it's such a terrible night."

"Thank you. You are very kind." Jerrol wiped his face

with the towel she handed him. She turned back from hanging up his cloak to take Jennery's. Her smile lit up her face. "These cloaks protect well, but even the Lady can't stop the rain."

Jennery groaned. "But that means she can't stop the mud either," he said, looking down at his mud-splashed trousers.

"She can do many wondrous things, but you have to put up with the mud." She hung Jennery's cloak up and stopped to pet the Arifel who appeared in front of her. "Yes, well done, you brought them here," she said, running a gentle finger down his chest. Ari preened before swooping to perch on a wooden pole extending out of the wall over the fire-place. He muttered to himself as he began to groom his wet fur.

She froze as she saw Birlerion. "Oh my, an Arifel is one thing but you..." She stared at him; her eyes wide. "You're a Lady's Guard, a Sentinal, aren't you?"

Birlerion grinned, relaxing the strain on his face. "Yes, Guardian."

"Oh my," she said again. She caught sight of Jennery's face, which was congealing as she spoke. "What happened? Ari didn't say you had injuries." She emptied the fruit bowl on the table and steered Jennery to a seat by the fire, placing the bowl in his lap and a blanket around his shoulders. "What about you two?"

"I think the Captain here needs a seamstress," Birlerion said as Jerrol sat at the table. Birlerion helped him ease off his jacket, scowling in concern as Jerrol's blood-soaked shirt was revealed. Jerrol raised a bloody hand to stop an apple rolling off the table as he leaned back in the chair.

The room was homely, dominated by a large brick fire-place with a stack of wood, burning merrily. A basket piled high with logs sat to one side. Two armchairs faced each other from either side of the fire, a small footstool in front of one of them.

Oil lamps sat on a square table in the middle of the room, the wicks turned down and providing a gentle glow. On the floor was a cheerful woven rug in hues of red and blue, brightening up the room. Jerrol quirked a weary eyebrow. "My name is Jerrol; these are my friends Jennery and Birlerion."

"I am Silene; you met my husband Reese out in the barn. Let me look at your side. Birlerion, please sit by the fire, you must be chilled to the bone. The weather has been unseasonably wet," she instructed as she moved towards the kitchen where she put a pan of water on to heat. "Please sit. I'll soon have the Captain here sorted. Then I'll make a hot drink."

She placed a basket on the table and turned the wick of the lamp up high. Moving to Jerrol, she unwrapped his makeshift bandage and pursed her lips. She bathed his side, revealing the ugly gash. "You're lucky it's not deeper," she murmured.

"The Lady protects," was all Jerrol replied as he gritted his teeth against her gentle probing. "You can see the Arifel," Jerrol said, watching Ari on his perch.

"Oh yes, isn't he beautiful? I've read about them but never seen one. They disappeared after the Lady cracked the stone, no one knew where they went, and over time people have forgotten about them."

"And a great many other things as well, I fear."

"True," Silene said, threading a sharp needle. "Fortunately for you," she said with a twinkle in her eye, "not everyone has forgotten. I remember."

Jennery hugged his bowl, listening to the low toned conversation. "You remember?"

"Oh yes, I know all the histories and myths and legends. I teach the young, at least those who will listen, and I am often consulted by Lord Hugh or by councillors across the whole of Vespiri on points of law or land."

Jerrol tensed as Silene began to sew the edges of the wound together; a sheen of sweat covered his face, and he winced as she progressed around his side.

Birlerion watched Silene, and then he pulled off his boots and left them by the front door next to Jennery's, before padding damply over to the fire. His feet left faint footprints on the wooden floor. He perched on the edge of the chair and leaned towards the flames, the warmth relaxing his tense muscles.

Jennery sat in the other chair, groaning and hugging his bowl, not interested in anything but the fire. His big toe poked out of the hole in his muddy socks and his mud-splashed trousers dripped on the floor, creating a small pool that steamed in the warm air. A clock ticked in the silence, the regular sound soothing the tense men.

Silene finished her grisly work and dusted the wound with white powder before wrapping it securely with a bandage. She inspected Jerrol's tattered shirt. "Do you have another?" she asked, wrapping a blanket around his shoulders before checking his eyes. "You'll do," she said as she collected the scraps and the bowl of blood-tinted water and took them out to the kitchen.

She returned with one of her husband's shirts. "Here," she said, removing the blanket and shaking out the shirt. She helped Jerrol ease his arms into the sleeves without further comment. The shirt shimmered into the same collarless linen shirt he had been wearing before, and she grinned in appreciation. "You truly are the Captain."

"So it seems," he agreed. The sound of the bubbling water drew her back into the kitchen.

"Don't worry about the mud," Silene said reassuringly as she re-entered the room with a tray. Birlerion leapt up to take the tray from her and placed it on the table. "Thank you," she said, smiling up at him.

Birlerion smiled back, instinctively. Silene was the type of person that made you feel comfortable straight away. She was assured and calm, and although not what he would have called beautiful, she was striking. Her movements were sure and economical, and she soon had them seated again with a hot mug of coffee.

"You're a Rememberer," Birlerion said.

"A Rememberer?" Jerrol asked, glancing from Silene to Birlerion.

"Yes, a Guardian of the Lady's Lore; her history, her people and her land." Silene gestured at Ari. "Your Arifel popped in earlier with a request for shelter, so we knew to expect you."

"I'm not sure he's mine exactly," Jerrol said. "He appeared yesterday morning, and he goes where he wants."

"Oh, he's yours alright," Silene chuckled. "The Lady's Captain always had an Arifel. They act as messengers and are very intelligent as you can tell; he brought you here." She looked up as the door opened and Reese strode in on a blustery gust of damp air. He ducked through the door; straightening up, he barely missed the beams in the ceiling. He shucked off his boots and coat and turned towards the fire rubbing his hands.

"You lads alright? It's a wild night out there," he said, running his hands through his windswept hair.

"Yes, thank you, sir, it's kind of you to take us in," Birlerion said as he stood and extended his hand.

Reese shook it firmly. "Silene wouldn't hear of leaving you out there, not after that young chap turned up." He grinned, his blue eyes crinkling. "She wanted to speak with him further, I think," he teased his wife. He waved Birlerion back into his seat.

"You," said Silene pointing her finger at Jerrol, "don't move until I tell you. Drink your coffee, it is well sugared, it'll help with the blood loss."

Reese pulled up a chair and sat as Silene handed him a mug of steaming coffee. "Ah," he sighed, gratefully taking a sip. "Blood loss? What happened? I didn't realise anyone was injured."

"We were set upon about half a mile back down the track. Jennery suffered a bad blow, but we were fortunate to fight them off. I'm afraid there are a couple of bodies left out there." Jerrol glanced across at his friend. He didn't look the part, drooping in front of the fire, periodically sneezing.

"How did you know I was the Lady's Captain?" Jerrol asked, turning back to Silene.

"Not only does your appearance shout it to those with eyes to see, the histories tell us that when Lady, Land and Liege are under siege then look out for the Lady's Captain who will lead the charge to reverse the threat and restore that which was sundered back to its former state. There have been multiple signs, and the Arifel confirms it. Birlerion here, well, he seals it. He wouldn't be awake if there weren't a Captain."

"Why does the Arifel confirm it?" Jennery asked, drooping over his bowl.

"Because there has been no magic in this world since the cracking of the stone, but the magic must be leaking back in if the Arifel can appear. When the people desperately need help, when the Liege is struggling to hold his oath, when the Land itself is under threat, then the Lady will step in and appoint a Captain. A Captain who will protect the Land from those who wish to destroy it; who will protect the Guardians from those who do not understand and support the Liege to reassert his power."

"I'm supposed to do all that?" Jerrol gasped, appalled,

watching Birlerion lean back in his chair and rub a hand over his face.

"That and more, but not on your own and not tonight! There are many here to help you. The Guardians will help, we will help you." She indicated Reese and herself.

"Do you know who or what is threatening us?" Birlerion asked, staring at the fire.

Silene shook her head. "That is for the Captain to find out."

"Can you tell me more about the role of this Captain. I mean, are there any instructions captured somewhere?" Jerrol asked, a plaintive note creeping into his voice.

"The Lady will reveal what you need to know when the time is right. She will provide you with the companions you need; you have Birlerion, and Ari here, for example. They are both living myths and quite unexpected. I'm sure Birlerion can tell you more."

"And your white mare," Reese interrupted. "She has got to be a gift of the Lady, you don't come by Darians very often."

Silene looked at Reese. "A Darian?" She was shocked. "In our barn?"

Reese took up the conversation. "A right beauty she is too, and she knows it." He grinned. "The councils are where you should start, lad. They are undermining the Lady, targeting Guardians. You need to discover what their purpose is. Deepwater lost its Lord recently, and the heir will not pick up the mantle. Word is that he turned away from the Lady; the councils' influence, we believe."

"We saw signs of that at the Grove, histories twisted, unexpected advisors, the smithy was set on fire, and we were unable to save the Guardian, Sylvie."

Silene gasped, raising her hands to cover her mouth. "No, not Sylvie, you think it was deliberate?"

"Even more so now. If what you say is true, and we have a coordinated threat from the councils to overcome, then all Guardians are at risk. Yourselves included." Jerrol paused. "How far are we from Greenswatch?"

"Not far, only a couple of miles as the crow flies. Lord Hugh keeps an eye on us. He values our knowledge, we tutor his children, though not so much Simeon of late."

"Maybe you should consider asking Lord Hugh if you could stay at Greenswatch for a while," Jerrol suggested. "You are not safe here."

Reese shook his head. "We can't leave here. We have animals to look after. Anyway, no one will bother us here. We are out of the way and, if necessary, I can protect us."

Silene shifted in her chair. "There are many pointers in the histories. You should visit the records room at Greenswatch; you might find something there. I remember there being a record of all the holdings and their grants of land. It was organised by events rather than dates, events like the great Vesp flood or the storm that felled the King's Oak. It had descriptions of the events and notations about the Guardians and who they were. The best records house is the Scholar House in Old Vespers; your challenge will be the fact that much of it is still uncatalogued. You need a seer who can find the signs; the signs are only visible to seers or the Oath Keeper. Unfortunately, I don't think there have been either for the last three thousand years."

"A Seer? Is that as likely as a Lady's Captain?" Jerrol asked with a wry smile.

"Good point," agreed Silene. "Your odds are looking better, and there's something else about you, I can't see it clearly," she said thoughtfully as she stared at him, "though it does mean that we are approaching a major event."

"A major event?"

"Yes, when such mythical people like yourself begin to

appear, if the Lady can intervene, then you know she is intervening for a good reason. Something or someone is trying to change the course of our history. You'll find mention of them in the archives. Major events occur more often than you think and in the most unlikely of places!"

They were interrupted by Jennery having a sneezing fit by the fire. Silene looked over. "I think we need to get your friend to bed and dose him up with a hot toddy, catch this chill before it gets worse. He's going to have a nasty headache by the looks of him. Ari will keep an eye on him.

"See if you can eat some stew, warm you up, then I think it's best if you rest, and we can talk more later. Sit by the fire, Captain Jerrol. The heat will do you good. Reese, help Jennery to the back room," she instructed as she walked into the kitchen to dish up the stew.

16

CHAPTERHOUSE, OLD VESPERS

Taelia sat outside the Deane's office and twisted her hands in her lap. She didn't remember much from last night, but she did know that Torsion was home safely. That was one of her worries solved. She frowned in concern as she remembered how bitter he had sounded. Maybe his venture had not fared so well. He had been gone for many months.

She rose as she heard the door to the Deane's office open. The Deane's soft voice bid her enter, and she raised her chin and walked forward, her hand questing for the door frame. She stubbed her fingers as she found it and curled them around the wood. She entered the room.

The Deane spoke, her voice guiding her into the room. "Sit, Taelia." Her hand guided her to the chair.

"Thank you, Deane," she said, sitting in the offered chair. She heard the Deane sit and then clasp her hands on her desk.

"Taelia, do you remember what happened last night?"

A fleeting expression of bewilderment flashed across Taelia's face. "Deane?"

"Scholar Torsion found you asleep in the courtyard. He said you were worried about Jerrol."

Taelia stilled. Her expressive face was open and vulnerable.

"Do you remember what woke you?"

"I was frightened; something was wrong."

"Do you know what was wrong?"

"No," Taelia said hesitantly.

"Torsion said you were concerned for Jerrol."

"He was hurt." Taelia gripped her side. "I felt it."

"Do you know where he is?"

Taelia shook her head.

"What made you go to the courtyard?"

"I needed to see the moon."

Liliian refrained from making the obvious statement. "Why the moon?"

"The Lady was watching."

"Watching what? What did you see?"

"I saw the Sentinals, led by their Captain. They wait, they have been waiting a long time."

"What do they wait for, Taelia?"

"For the Captain to awaken them."

Greenswatch

The morning sun crept around the house and blazed through the bedroom window, waking Jerrol. He lay still, basking in the warmth, assessing his body's complaints; his shoulder ached, his ribs were a muted throb; otherwise, he felt fine.

As he ruminated over the earlier discussion, he sensed Zin'talia's contentment, a soft embrace that meant he wasn't alone. Magic, he thought; magic was leaking back into the world.

A result of shredding the Veil? Was it even possible to shred it, and if so, who could do it? He hadn't realised the Veil was a physical thing. A question for Silene—and on that thought he got up and dressed carefully. Leaving his shirt loose and carrying his jacket, he went downstairs.

He found Birlerion sitting at the table, a half-empty bowl of left-over stew before him, impossibly playing with a blue flame, rolling it across his fingers, before lighting the candle and blowing it out again.

"How is that not burning you?"

Birlerion looked up, startled. Flushing, he relit the candle and picked up his spoon. "I thought I'd lost the knack, but it seems to be back," he said.

"You've been letting me struggle all these weeks, and you could have lit our fires for us."

Birlerion grimaced. "I thought it was a lost skill; it didn't work, to begin with." He rubbed his fingers, and the flame appeared again. "It's only since the fire I've been able to do it again, and I did offer."

Jerrol snorted. That wasn't the only thing that had changed; it was as if something had relaxed in the Sentinal, he was certainly more talkative. "Without telling us how you were doing it, could you teach me?"

"I don't know. If you don't naturally have the ability, it's unlikely to manifest now."

"Well, who could do it? Is it a Sentinal thing? How did you learn?"

"Sit down and eat," Silene interrupted them as she came into the room with another plate and a mug of coffee. "Eat and afterwards I'll check your side."

"How's Jennery?" Jerrol asked, glaring at Birlerion as he obediently sat.

"Still asleep. He took quite a crack on the head, he's lucky they didn't just stick a knife in him," Birlerion mused as he pushed his empty plate away.

"I think they were only paid for one death," Jerrol said.

"Possible," conceded Birlerion. "Reese and I went down and moved the bodies. They're in the shed for you to take a look. I must admit I didn't notice anything that would tell us who sent them, though we can guess."

"Yes, it seems Kharel is getting impatient. I suppose the fact he is sending assassins means he's determined to execute me. Though I think I'll have to disappoint him." Jerrol focused on his plate of stew; it was delicious. He relaxed back into his chair and, looking up, caught Silene frowning at him. "Is something the matter?"

"No." Silene's face relaxed. "Not really, but you are a bit of a conundrum, Captain. I can see the Lady's hand, but there is also another. One I cannot see clearly."

"Well, let me know when you find out what it is." Jerrol grimaced. "I think the Lady's influence is enough to manage for now. Last night ..." Or was it this morning? He shook the thought out of his head. "When we last spoke, you said you thought magic was leaking back into the world. How is that possible?"

Silene sat at the table opposite him. "Captain, as you know, the Lady's Veil is what separates the Lady and the Ascendants from this world. It is a barrier that was erected by the power of the Lady and the sundering of the Bloodstone. Legend says that the Ascendants have been trying to find ways to breach the barrier for centuries. On occasion, they find something that can penetrate, and they focus on trying to widen the gap. Their goal is to bring down the Veil and ascend to power here."

"Wait, you mean the Ascendants are still alive? I thought they all died when the stone was destroyed."

Silene smiled at him sadly. "A common belief, but mistaken. The Ascendants certainly exist, but whether you would call it alive in the manner of our people, I'm not sure. The Guardians and the Ascendants were cut from a different cloth to us and had very different powers. Remember the Lady is our deity, worshipped from afar, our only link to the civilisation that existed here all those centuries ago."

"The Ascendants were not so different to us, and nothing like the Lady," Birlerion said, his voice low.

Silene stared at him. "I keep forgetting you know what actually happened. What we know, we pieced together from those early records. You will rewrite history."

"I'll leave that to Serillion. He is the historian."

"And what are you?" Silene asked, suddenly intent.

"Just a Sentinal doing the Lady's bidding," Birlerion replied with a wry twist of his lips.

"Somehow, I doubt that," Silene murmured. She turned to Jerrol. "Captain, I fear you will need to return to the Chapterhouse in Old Vespers and search for that old civilisation. If they found a way to penetrate the Veil, you'll need to find a way to prevent them from returning. The Watch Towers above Velmouth is another important location. The Veil Watchers are underestimated and often forgotten."

"Silene," Jerrol asked, "have you ever heard of a Veil-shredder?"

Silene's eyes dilated as her face drained of all colour; she leapt to her feet and took a step back. "Who mentioned such a thing?"

"Sylvie said she would tell me about them, but she didn't have a chance."

Silene sat at the table with a thump. "We try not to speak about them, the less said, the better."

"What are they?"

"If Sylvie mentioned it, then she must have been

concerned." She looked up. "The Veil can be damaged. Some people have the power to reach out with their minds: those who have trained their skill to such an art that they can reach the Veil. They try to force a breach, to split the weave. The Veil Watchers should be watching for it, though; it's their job to repair it."

"The Veil Watchers can repair the Veil?" Jerrol sat forward, watching Silene.

"They used to. I'm not sure if they are capable anymore," Silene admitted. "They have become forgotten, lost in time. I doubt they are even aware of what is happening around them. They are so old. I doubt they know how anymore."

"Shouldn't we be keeping them alert and watching? To protect us from this very occurrence?" Jerrol's stomach dropped at the thought the current difficulties could be their own fault.

"It's been over three thousand years," Silene said. "People forget, things don't seem so important when the threat is non-existent. The purpose of the Watch Towers has long been forgotten, the people inside a distant memory. Not everything is passed on as the people forget its purpose."

"The Watchers are three thousand years old?" Jerrol slumped back in his chair in shock.

"What's left of them," Silene said.

"They were first instigated when the Lady created the Watches," Birlerion said.

"But how?"

"Much like the Sentinals, I would think. The Lady blessed her guards with her protection," Silene said.

"The Lady said they were stirring, that I need to awaken them," Jerrol said, squeezing his eyes shut as if he could block out the idea. He had to waken Sentinals and the Watchers?

"Then you should wake them," Silene said, watching him open his eyes, which gleamed silver. "Captain," she finished softly.

His eyes widened. "How?"

Silene shrugged. "I am sorry, Captain, I do not know, that is your job." She turned to Birlerion. "Tell me, is it true the Lady Leyandrii and Lady Marguerite lived in the palace in Vespers?"

"Where else would they live?"

"I knew it. What was Marguerite like? There is so little written about her. What happened to her?"

"She was a beautiful young lady. Mischievous and full of life. Very attuned to the Land. She spent much of her time in what is now called Elothia. She supported Leyandrii at the end, did what was needed."

"Is it true she bonded with the Land?"

Birlerion stilled. "What makes you ask that?"

Silene patted his shoulder as if to reassure him. "Don't worry so, I am attuned to the Land as well. And sometimes I think I sense her."

"You would be in no doubt if you met Marguerite," Birlerion said with a small smile. "As I said, she did what was necessary."

Jerrol sat stunned; he didn't know why he felt so shocked, but he did. It was if every myth he had heard had stood to attention and proclaimed they were real. His mind couldn't grasp the enormity of it. And yet, the Lady had told him, not in so many words but if he had listened the message had been there. He rested his head in his hands as Birlerion stood and went to check on Jennery. He straightened as his side twinged.

Silene was beside him immediately. "Let me check that for you," she said, pulling his shirt up. He took off his shirt and let Silene fuss over his wound. "That looks fine, no sign of infection." She dusted it with more powder and tied the bandages back on. "You'll need those stitches out next week. Otherwise, it should all heal itself if you take care."

"Birlerion and I need to go and speak to Lord Hugh. We thought if Jennery was still poorly, we could leave him with you and pick him up later this evening?"

"That is probably best." Silene looked up from her wrapping as Birlerion came back in the room.

"He's not with it, best we leave him here if that's alright with Silene and Reese?"

"Let's go saddle up and see what Lord Hugh has to say to all this." Jerrol stood and slipped on his jacket.

They were riding down the track towards Greenswatch before they spoke. "You should wake the others," Birlerion said. "We need their help."

Jerrol stared at him. "I don't know how I'm supposed to wake them."

"Knock on the door and tell them to come out," Birlerion suggested with a gleam in his eye.

"If only it were that easy."

"I think we need them. If the Ascendants have found a way to shred the Veil, we are at risk."

"They must have help on this side of the Veil," Jerrol said.

"They would have supporters just as the Lady does. The council's new advisors?"

"To name a few, no doubt," agreed Jerrol. "They definitely have influence; persuasiveness doesn't seem to be a problem for them, does it?"

"It never was," Birlerion said as they turned on to a well-kept treelined road leading to Lord Hugh's home. The trees parted to reveal a grey-stoned manor house. A stone archway led to an internal courtyard, which reminded Jerrol of the keep at Stoneford where he had grown up.

Birlerion looked around with interest, though he did not comment. As they approached the stone-slabbed courtyard the relaxed nature of the guards was proof that Lord Hugh had yet to arrive; there was no bustle or confusion in the yard.

Lord Hugh's steward Garrick came to greet them as they dismounted, frowning at their unfamiliar garb. "Captain Haven?" he said uncertainly, recognising Jerrol from previous visits.

"Garrick, it's good to see you again. This is my colleague, Birlerion of the Lady's Guard. We hoped Lord Hugh would have returned from Deepwater by now." Jerrol handed his reins to a young lad who was staring in awe at Zin'talia.

Garrick blinked at Birlerion who was inspecting the courtyard. He shook himself. "We expect Lord Hugh within the day; please join me inside." Garrick led the way through the dark doorway as the lads took the horses around the back.

Jerrol followed, relieved they hadn't heard of his fall from grace. "I was hoping to visit your records room, if that is acceptable? If Lord Hugh hasn't arrived by the time we finished, we'll head out to meet him on the road. I need to travel on to Stoneford anyway."

"Of course, let me show you the way."

They followed Garrick through a stone archway leading inside the mansion; the stone walls were softened by coloured drapes, and the air cooled imperceptibly. In the centre of the entrance foyer was a sweeping staircase leading to the galleries above. Below the stairs, corridors wove behind and under, leading to offices, storerooms and the Greenswatch records room.

Garrick stopped at a wooden door. "The records room. I'm afraid Lord Hugh does not allow food or drink inside, we've had accidents in the past that damaged essential papers. Refreshments will be laid out in the room next door for you. Please do not take them into the records room."

"We understand. We appreciate your hospitality," Jerrol said as he entered the room. He inhaled the familiar odour of musty books and dust that seemed inevitable in all records rooms.

"Silene mentioned a section for historical events?" Jerrol turned around, inspecting the books. Wooden shelves lined the walls, and every shelf was full of books, scrolls and manuscripts. There wasn't a single empty shelf.

Garrick gestured at the shelves. "This whole room records events; it is a personal perspective as to whether it is major or not. I imagine she was referring to the Elemental scroll. It records any change in power, unusual storms or floods, changes in weather patterns or a change of government, a new king, for example."

"Changes in power," Jerrol repeated, hearing an echo of Silene's calm voice. "That would be it, I think."

Garrick turned the dial on the glass lamp to increase the light in the room and ran a hand down the cataloguing system; he found the reference he was looking for and pulled a hefty tome from one of the shelves. "Here you go," he said, heaving it on the table. "Refreshments will be next door," he said as he left the room.

Jerrol sat down and opened the book, and Birlerion drifted closer to look over his shoulder.

The Elemental scroll was, in fact, a book of loose-leaf parchment pages, which had been sewn into the book individually. He skimmed down the rough pages, letting his eyes accustom themselves to the archaic script. He had learnt to speed read at the Chapterhouse in Old Vespers. He thanked his friend Torsion yet again for persevering with an impatient young boy who preferred to be in the training yard than a schoolroom.

The pages referred to floods, the planting of ancient plantations, the felling of specific trees, or the loss of specimens in storms. It marked the line of Descelles from the beginning and then the Lords who ruled the Greenswatch starting with Lord Warren Descelles, the first Lord Warden of Greens, his son Penner inheriting after him and so on, an unbroken line to the current day.

Jerrol paused over an entry celebrating four of their children becoming Sentinals in the year 1122. Versill, Marian, Tagerill and Birler. And their loss in 1124 when the Lady sundered the Bloodstone. To lose four of your children on one day. Jerrol couldn't imagine the pain that the family had gone through. He looked up and met Birlerion's anguished eyes.

"They were so proud of us," Birlerion whispered, the grief evident in his voice. "To lose all of us would have destroyed them; we were such a tight-knit family. Tagerill would have it we were all tied together, woven tightly, that's why they would never let you go. If only they had known where we were, it might have eased their grief."

Jerrol looked back at the pages and away from the pain in his eyes. There were oblique references to Guardians, though not specific names or locations, loremasters, councillors, temple leaders. His eyes caught on the word descendant. Descendant? He focused on the page and re-read it more slowly.

The Ascendants had descendants. There was a record of a descendant visiting the Greenswatch over a thousand year ago; the descendant had been proud of his heritage, had demanded his due. The people of the Lady's land owed him for the tragic loss of his ancestors. He had searched for something, though there was no record of what he had been looking for nor of him finding it. He had left another descendant in his wake. The birth of his child was recorded, though there was no mention of whether the child's father ever returned. The Ascendants had descendants, and the descendants had descendants. He wondered how strong the belief was that they could find a way to bring their ancestors back.

Jerrol leaned back in his chair and stretched his aching shoulders. He had found the thread he needed. Making a note of the name of the child on a scrap of paper, he skimmed through the book, searching for further descendants. He found an unbroken line to the date that the King's census, currently out of his reach, took over two hundred years ago and the records stopped.

Jerrol closed the book and turned down the lamp. He would leave it for Garrick to return to the right place. Leaving the records room, he returned to the foyer by the grand staircase. Birlerion must have gotten bored and found his own entertainment. Jerrol hoped his homecoming wasn't too painful.

The manor house was still calm and quiet. Lord Hugh and his retinue had not yet returned, even though the day had progressed. He had been searching for two or three hours.

There was a clatter of hooves, and a black horse came to a skidding halt. A small boy slid off the mud-splashed horse and clutched the stirrup to hold himself up as his legs trembled with the effort.

Garrick came striding out of another part of the building. "Norris! What are you doing here? Why aren't you with Lord Hugh?"

"Sir, Lord Hugh bade me give you this, hand it to you and no one else, sir." Norris pulled a twisted screw of paper from his jerkin and held it out. "It's taken me all day to get here. He said I wasn't to be seen, by anyone!"

Jerrol wondered what would have made Hugh so ultra-careful and shivered as a sense of foreboding flashed through him. He joined Garrick.

Garrick dismissed Norris and led the way into his office, gesturing for Jerrol to follow. He sat heavily frowning as he read. He sighed and tossed the paper to Jerrol. "The boy didn't take up the mantle; Deepwater has no Guardian. We need to look at our protocols and protect the land. This does not bode well. Deepwater will sicken, and she will affect our borders." Garrick looked sick himself. "This could be the start of the end," he said. "Hugh is concerned that Simeon will not pick up the mantle, either. There is a groundswell of sentiment in support of the councils. The council's word is gaining more weight than the king. The younger generation is more susceptible to new ideas. The protocols are the precautions to defend from the inside, salvage what we can."

"I'm travelling to visit Lord Jason at Stoneford and Councillor Torsion in Velmouth. Do you want me to take any message with me?"

"I'll get the protocols written up immediately. Lord Hugh mentioned that the Lords of East Watch and Marchwood were expected at the confirmation so they will have them. If you could take a copy to Lord Jason for me, and please keep it discreet as in the wrong hands we would be undone, that would be a great help, and much sooner than I could get a rider there."

"We'll cut cross-country and pick up the Deepwater road so I should meet Lord Hugh on the way."

Garrick paused. "I would spare you a troop to take with you to meet Lord Hugh, but Master Simeon took a guard with him, and I can't leave the Watch undefended."

"Birlerion and I will be fine. I'll go get the horses saddled and find him."

"He walked down to the home Sentinal, round the back."

Jerrol grimaced; of course he had. "If I could impose, we left a friend with Silene. Could one of your lads take him a message for me?"

"Use my desk. I need to find a scribe." Garrick left, paper in hand.

In a surprisingly short time, Garrick was handing Jerrol a fair copy of Hugh's orders, which he tucked away in his pocket. Jerrol thought Garrick might have written them out himself. He gave his message to Garrick, advising Jennery to bring all their things and meet them at the keep at Stoneford.

He walked around the mansion in search of Birlerion and found him leaning against the graceful sentinal near the lake.

"It's Versillion." Birlerion's face was haunted. "I wish they had known."

Jerrol placed a hand on the trunk. The bark warmed beneath his palm, and he saw a broad-shouldered, red-headed man, a broadsword across his back. Versillion, the second eldest son of Greens who had become a Sentinal. The image faded.

Jerrol stood back and frowned. "I don't know how to wake him."

Birlerion closed his eyes and embraced the tree. "You told me it was time."

"No, I didn't, you told me."

"Semantics, it's time. Tell him to wake up."

Jerrol scowled at the tree. "It's not that simple," he said as he laid his hand on the tree. The image came back into focus and Jerrol spoke. "Versillion, it's time to wake."

The image flickered and then faded again.

Birlerion pushed himself off the trunk and frowned up at the leaves. "Lazy sod." He squinted at the tree. "Versill, I'll tell Pa you're skiving off again."

There was no response.

Jerrol shrugged. "We'll try again when we come back, we don't have time now. We need to go and meet Lord Hugh."

Birlerion left the sentinal with obvious reluctance and followed Jerrol around the lake and back up to the house.

Their horses were brought round and, running a soft hand down Zin'talia's neck, Jerrol gathered her reins and hauled himself into the saddle. Birlerion gave Versillion's sentinal one last wistful glance and then swung himself up on his horse and followed.

17

DEEPWATER

They were just joining the Deepwater road, intending to turn towards the manor house, when Zin'talia suddenly bounded forward. Jerrol leapt from his saddle as she skidded to halt before a silver-gowned woman standing beside the road. "Taelia! What are you doing here?"

Taelia smiled up at him, cupping his cheek in her hand. "There is no time, you must hurry. The Lord Captain requires your help." She shifted her gaze to the Sentinal. "Ready your bow, Birlerion. He has been betrayed."

Jerrol stared at her, bewildered. "What are you talking about, and how did you get here?" He ran a hand through his hair. "And how do you know Birlerion?"

"It doesn't matter, the Lady bids you hurry." Taelia pushed him away. "Go!"

Birlerion unsheathed his bow at her word, raising his head, listening intently. "Captain, this way." As Birlerion led the way, the racket of clashing swords drew them off the road. They pushed through a screen of scrub and conifers and came to a horrified halt on the edge of an open field.

Jerrol surveyed the carnage before them. Too few men in the colours of Greenswatch fought a defensive line hampered by protecting two positions, split by their attackers and weakened accordingly. Their discipline held the attackers at bay, but the sheer numbers threatened to overwhelm them. Broken bodies lay across the field in a deadly trail of death and destruction, bandits and Greenswatch alike.

Apart from the clash of swords, the fighting was eerily silent, with men focused on their immediate need: to stay alive and protect their lord. Jerrol's eyes narrowed; how could Lord Hugh be so outnumbered?

Birlerion nocked an arrow and moved closer, picking his targets. Men fell in swathes, and Jerrol gaped at him. His aim was lethal and efficient, his face cold and intent.

In no time he ran out of arrows, and he discarded his bow. He charged his horse straight into the melee, and men scattered. He whirled his horse in front of the suddenly howling men and swung his sword.

Jerrol veered around the battle at the cries of surprise and plunged into the second, smaller clump of men, hacking his way through the barrier of ill-kempt ruffians taking down the well-trained soldiers of Greenswatch.

His sword flickered as Zin'talia barged men aside. His unexpected arrival galvanised the soldiers into a new attack, renewed belief strengthening their arms. The line flexed as the sickening sound of a hammer hitting flesh preceded a physical groan of despair from Lord Hugh's men.

Jerrol spun, but he was too late. Lord Hugh was down. The bandit raised his hammer for another blow and the standard-bearer, screaming in grief, rammed the point of his standard into the man's throat and wrenched it back out. A rush of scarlet blood spurted all over the Greenswatch banner.

The bandit twisted in a final continuation of his move as he drove his hammer into the slight young man frozen in horror before him. The young man stumbled back, senseless. As he collapsed onto the churned-up grass, he drove the pole into the soft dirt; the bloodied standard leant at a drunken angle above him.

Jerrol dragged his eyes from the sight and knelt beside Lord Hugh, checking for a pulse; there wasn't one. He scanned the battlefield. Birlerion was grounded. He was swinging something around his head, and in quick succession three men dropped, their eyes staring fixedly up at the sky. A fourth staggered and Jerrol ran him through before he could recover. Spinning, he sliced his sword across the stunned man's stomach, before pausing to survey the scene as the man thudded to the ground.

He spotted the hub of the soldier's defence. A young girl lay sprawled among the bodies. Her auburn curls were a vivid contrast to the green uniforms around her.

Jerrol hurried to her side. It looked like the girl had taken a brutal fall. He squatted beside her, reached out to check her pulse and then cursed, snatching back his hand as the burn zinged through his blood. She was a direct descendant of the Greenswatch. The black and white Arifel, Lin, popped into view and chittered excitedly.

He stared at the girl; she looked very young and vulnerable. Could she be hosting the Guardianship? When her father fell, the Lady's blessing must have gone somewhere. The girl would have been the nearest acceptable vessel, but it was unheard of for a female to take the Watch Guardianship; there would be questions about that later, he was sure.

If she had, then she was in even more danger. Those trying to eradicate the Lady wouldn't hesitate to kill her too. Lin landed on the girl and crooned.

"Hush," he soothed the Arifel. "I know, but let's keep that quiet for now." Lin meeped in agreement.

He whistled and Birlerion looked up from retrieving his arrows, though most were shattered. "We need to go. We don't want to be here when the next wave arrives."

"I don't think these were just bandits, Captain," Birlerion said. "This was too well-planned. To take down the colours of the Greenswatch?" He shook his head. "Looks like one group took off with the carriage, whilst the rest slaughtered the guard." He led the way to a mound of bodies. "I believe this was the Lord Captain of Greenswatch, Lord Hugh; there is a concentration of bodies around him. His guard fought to the last – well, those that stayed," he said, his lips pinched.

"I think that," Jerrol jerked his head at the unconscious girl, "is his daughter. We need to leave before she's next." He knelt and detached the Greenswatch banner from its staff, folding it over and tucking it in his pocket. He stripped a jacket off one of the guards and covered Lord Hugh's face. Thinking about the behaviour of bandits, he pulled the Watch ring off Hugh's finger and stared at it blindly.

Birlerion took it out of his fingers and inspected it. "I remember the day Leyandrii placed that ring on Warren's hand," he said, his face impassive. He gave the ring back and turned away, yanking an arrow out of a body with unnecessary violence. "Captain, we need to leave," he said.

Jerrol dropped the ring into his pocket with the banner. Lin meeped mournfully and climbed down into his pocket, carefully arranging the folds of the material.

Birlerion tensed and then swung around, thrusting the arrow he held into the chest of the man rising behind him. Bright red blood gushed over his hand. The man gasped, and Birlerion grabbed him by the neck. "Who ordered this?"

The man gritted his teeth, and Birlerion twisted the arrow. "I can draw this out or make it quick. Who?"

"Per'itise."

"A Terolian? What is a Terolian doing in Deepwater?"

The man's breath hissed out, and his eyes rolled, and Birlerion wrenched his arrow out in disgust, letting the body fall.

Jerrol cleared his throat. "How did you know he was behind you?"

Birlerion flexed his shoulders. "Just a feeling." He looked down at the bandit. "Now why would a Terolian embroil themselves in Vespirian politics? They are usually quite insular."

"I have no idea. You're quite handy to have around. What was that you were using earlier, a sling?"

Birlerion's grin flashed across his face, easing his grim expression. "Yeah, surprisingly effective."

"So I saw. Was it your weapon of choice before?"

"A precursor to the bow, you use what works." He looked around at the carnage. The sun was low in the sky, dipping behind the tree line; dark shadows stole across the field, concealing the crumpled bodies, and he exhaled. "In theory, so others don't have too."

Jerrol gazed across the field. "We can't save everyone, as much as we'd like to." He glanced at Birlerion. "We need to go and get Taelia, she is supposed to be in the Chapterhouse. We can't leave her here."

"She won't be there. She is following the Lady's bidding."

"How do you know her?"

Birlerion smiled. "I met her at the Grove. She was the one who gave me the message for you."

"Why didn't you say?"

"I didn't know you knew her."

Jerrol huffed in exasperation, and then extended a tendril

of thought to Zin'talia. "Find a horse. I need you to go and fetch Torsion. He has rooms in the hostelry in Stoneford. Meet me at Hannah's house, it's the last cottage on the road to Stoneford Keep. Discreetly! I don't think we want to advertise any of this." With a tired grunt he mounted Zin'-talia and, looping the rein in one hand, he gestured at the girl. "Pass her up."

Birlerion handed Jerrol the unconscious girl, before stomping off to retrieve his bow and find his horse. Jerrol let Zin'talia wend her way through the corpses and into the dense tree line and then set off for the village of Stoneford, hunching his shoulders against the sound of the carrion crows descending to pick over the dead.

Stoneford Watch

Hannah glanced out of the window. The sun had long since set. A fine rain sifted down from the thick grey clouds that rolled in over the horizon, drawing in the night. She ought to close the curtains and bank the fire for the night, she thought, as she watched her cat lifting his head and staring toward the door.

He gave a gentle sneeze and began grooming his tummy, legs contorted in all directions. And then, grooming finished, he stood and arched his back in a stretch, sniffed her water glass and jumped down to the floor with a gentle thud. He sat like a sentinal, tall and proud, tail wrapped neatly around his feet, staring at the door. The dim light from the wood fire flickered over his ginger coat.

Hannah scowled at her fur-covered pinafore as she prepared to stand: white hair everywhere. She sighed. The cat flicked her a glance and then stared back at the door. Visitors then, and at this time of the night, nothing good.

With the curtains still wide open she couldn't exactly pretend not to be in, now could she? She got to her feet, stretching her stiffening back; she wasn't getting any younger. She shuffled out into the kitchen and wrung out a cloth to wipe off some of the hairs.

The faint jingle of a harness and a muffled curse penetrated the kitchen, and she moved to open the door. The cat led the way; he seemed unconcerned, pausing to block her path on the threshold. A slender man struggled with an awkward burden, and as he reached the light, she saw he was carrying—a child?

"Hannah," he called. "I need your help."

"Jerrol?" she gasped. "What are you doing here?"

"Let me in, and I'll explain," he said as he heaved his burden onto the kitchen table and shook out his arms. "The Greenswatch was ambushed on the road by bandits, all slain or abducted. We managed to save her, but she's unconscious. I don't think there are any broken bones, as far as I can tell, but she took a bad fall."

Hannah checked the girl over and tucked a cushion under her head, making her more comfortable. She hurried to put a kettle on to boil and to stack some towels to warm in front of the fire.

"I'll be right back. Just need to move my horse," Jerrol muttered as he strode back out of the kitchen. He led Zin'-talia off to the looming structure slightly darker than the night shadows. The barn was dry and warm. He rubbed her down with an old blanket, though left her saddled. *"I'll try not to be too long. Sorry about the conditions. It'll be better at Stoneford."* He ran a soothing hand down her neck.

She rubbed her head against him. *"Stop apologising. We may need to move fast,"* she replied. He filled the tub with water and left her nibbling on an armful of hay.

Jerrol returned to the kitchen to find that Hannah had removed the girl's outer clothing and had wrapped her in blankets. She was bathing the girl's face with warm water, the cat by her side.

"There's nothing broken, though she does have a nasty lump on her head," Hannah reported, still gently prodding. She gave Jerrol a searching glance. This was the boy she had fostered so many years ago, now a man in his own right, and one she was inordinately proud of. "You do know who this is, don't you?"

Jerrol shrugged. "I'm assuming she is a daughter of the Greenswatch. Which is why I thought it better to bring her here than leave her on the field."

"Not a daughter, *the* daughter. Lady Alyssa, daughter of the Lord Captain himself." Hannah wiped her hands on a towel. "What are you doing with her? What are you even doing here? You're supposed to be up in Vespers with the king."

"I was just passing through, or so I thought. I can't linger." Jerrol clasped her arm. "I'm sorry to drop her on you, but she is in danger. She was travelling with her father and a large party back to Greenswatch, but they were ambushed. She was supposed to be killed with the Lord Captain today. I couldn't leave her there to die as well, yet she can't go home either until we know what is afoot."

Hannah gasped, her face paling in shock. "T-the Lord Captain?"

Jerrol helped her sit in the chair. He squatted down in front of her, his precious face scrunched up in concern. "I'm sorry. I shouldn't have sprung it on you like that, a bit of a shock I know. You need to be careful who you let in. I'm not sure who is involved. I need to speak to Jason." He rubbed his temple. "I'll be back later, and we can figure out what's best to do. It may be that you go to the council and let them deal with it. I'm not sure yet whether she would be safe. I sent a man to bring Torsion here. I could use his insight into what is going on."

"Torsion isn't here. He travelled up to Velmouth, oh, must have been three months ago. He was talking about the Veil Watchers and wanting to go on to the towers. The council encouraged him to go," she said. "He never said when he would be coming back."

Jerrol stifled a curse. "I'm missing everyone. Is Lord Jason still at the keep? I'll try him first, see what he thinks; if not, we'll have to head up to Velmouth. I can't stay. I'll help you bundle her up in front of the fire, warm her up. If she comes around, she may be able to tell you what happened before we came across them." Wrapping his arms around her, he gave her a heartfelt hug.

Hannah sniffed and hugged him back hard. She tugged at his stubborn chin. "A sight for sore eyes, that's what you are."

He gave her a brief smile. "I'll be back soon. I sent a guard called Birlerion off to find Torsion. If he turns up before I'm back, keep him here; otherwise we'll be delayed even further tracking each other down. Jennery may turn up at some point too." With a nod of his head, he was gone, out the kitchen door and ghosting into the darkness.

Hannah gave another sniff. Jennery was involved in this, too? That meant nothing but trouble. Both her foster sons causing havoc; there would be no peace for anyone.

She looked down at her unexpected guest. She was tucked up in her best quilt in front of the fire. The girl was pale, though her lips had more colour in them. Well, it looked like it was going to be a long night. Keeping an eye on her guest, she sat back down in her chair.

It had to be at least two years since she had last seen Jerrol. Being a King's Ranger kept him busy and away from home. She had been so proud. He had worked so hard to be accepted.

She had recognised him straight away, just the sound of his voice was all she needed. He had gained a few inches, though not as many as he'd wanted, and he was far too thin. He felt like a bundle of bones when she hugged him. On that thought, she stood and placed a pan of soup on the hearth. Whoever turned up would be hungry, she was sure.

Her ruminations continued as she worked. Jerrol had always been a live wire as a child, never standing still. He had boundless energy that invariably led him into trouble until the warden had apprenticed him to the keep and fostered him to her. Between them, they had managed to turn out a King's Ranger. One of the elite soldiers in the king's ranks, responsible for his security, occasionally sent on diplomatic or tricky missions, often on their own.

She sighed as she set to restoring the girl's riding clothes. She sponged off the dirt and the spatters of blood. The clothes were ruined, but she still spread them out to dry. The boots would have to wait until tomorrow. She moved them closer to the heat, to dry quicker. The smell of damp leather soon joined the aroma of drying clothes.

They had even received news here in Stoneford that Jerrol had recently been involved in the negotiations with the Birtolian ambassadors. It was said it would strengthen the relationship with the Birtoli empire for years to come. She stared at her cat. "So what is he doing here, apart from finding trouble?" The cat stared back, unconcerned. He began meticulously to clean his whiskers.

18

STONEFORD WATCH

Jerrol rode up the road to the keep, his mind racing. The moon poked through gaps in the clouds, and he relaxed as it intermittently revealed familiar surroundings. He had left the little Arifel perched on the back of a chair crooning over Alyssa. Birlerion could explain her to Hannah if he had to.

He kept to the edges of the road and concentrated on dampening down the glow that emanated off his clothes again. That was something he needed to think about as well. He hadn't paused since the Lady had blessed him with her presence, but although she might be happy, he didn't want to advertise his presence to all and sundry if he could help it. He'd think about it later. He had other problems to solve this night.

Who would want to remove Lord Hugh from the Greenswatch? It was concerning, following Stefan's accident in Deepwater. And, Jerrol mused, it would mean that relatively young and inexperienced keepers held two key Watches. Easy for the council to worm their way in there if they were not careful, and if so, what were they hoping to gain? Speaking of councils, there were a lot of new faces showing up, and that was unusual as well. Councillors tended to be homegrown, not imported from elsewhere. Who was driving these changes?

The keep loomed up ahead. The crenellated walls caught the moonlight and created deep inky shadows. Jerrol steered Zin'talia off the road and down the sidetrack, which he knew from old led to the midden. The keep had been his old stomping ground when he was a kid; he, Jennery and Taelia had grown up here under the auspices of Hannah and a few frustrated masters. He slid off and led Zin'talia into a small copse of willowy trees. Tying her reins loosely, out of reach of her hooves, he asked her to stay hidden as he scouted out the terrain. The guards' voices drifted on the night air. Jason would have their guts if he managed to slip in without them seeing him.

He melted into the shadows and ghosted along the wall to the small wire gate. It secured the water inlet that ran out under the midden and helped keep the kitchen waste moist, rotting and smelly, ready for the growers to repurpose else-where. He undid the wire closure which was rusting badly, slipped into the tunnel and closed the gate behind him. He was glad he was slight of build as he climbed up the pipe, levering himself into the lower storerooms set below the kitchen.

He paused, listening, but heard no movement in the kitchen above. Jason was a night owl; if he were awake, he'd be in his study on the ground floor, hopefully on his own. Jerrol silently crept down the passageway and up the stairs to the kitchen. Once through the kitchen, he kept to the meagre shadows under the main staircase. The torches were bright, set in the walls. He breathed a sigh of relief as he saw the dull yellow glow beneath the sturdy wooden door which led into Jason's study. He listened for a moment before easing the door open, slipping through the gap and closing it behind him.

Straightening up, he grinned into the surprised face of the keep warden, Lord Jason, sitting behind his desk lit by oil lamps, and surrounded by maps and bits of paper.

"Jerrol!" The warden leapt to his feet in surprise. "What in the world ... how did you get in here? Where are my guards?" His face darkened with anger.

Jerrol held up his hands. "I needed to speak with you, and I didn't want to advertise my presence, or at least not straight away. So, um, I evaded your guards, shall we say?"

Jason looked like he was going to have a fit. "You have no need to creep into my home like a thief, and you know it! But if you can, who else can? Times are not what they were, you know. I can't have security breaches like this. We are exposed." His face was flushed even though he was pleased to see Jerrol.

"Exposed? Who would threaten you, Jason? You're a King's Warden, protector of his lands."

Jason grimaced as he came around the desk and engulfed Jerrol in a hug. Jerrol returned the embrace. "Lady's blessings, it's good to see you. I'm sorely in need of a sensible man for a change. Here, sit, sit!" Jason indicated the chair opposite his desk. "We'll discuss how you got into my keep later. But for now, I am glad you are here. We've missed you, lad, must be over two years now since we last saw you."

Jerrol was shocked at how much Jason had aged; deep worry lines creased his face, his hair was thinning and more grey than black, and he wasn't as stocky as he used to be. "So what's happening for you to need me to be sensible? Never was my strong point," he said, trying to keep his concern out of his voice. Jason had no heir. His wife was long dead, and he had never had children. Jerrol had been his surrogate child as Jason had been Jerrol's father figure, both finding something they needed in the other, and on top of that, they couldn't afford another Watch to be leaderless.

Jason rubbed his face and heaved a deep sigh before starting to speak. "I am surrounded by people who want to act first and think later. I don't know who is stirring them up, but I am constantly drawn into situations where we need to root out dissenters. Yet, when you get to the bottom of it, the council is trumping up charges and against people who legitimately refuse to act against their beliefs."

"Do they have real authority for these charges? Is there a mandate from the king to enforce some new legislation?" Jerrol asked. "I heard something similar in Greenswatch. The council is twisting some of the accepted rulings."

Jason looked down at his hands. "I haven't seen anything, so I think it's all noise, but it's getting worse. The councillors are taking it upon themselves to exact punishments. I've intervened where I can, but I don't always hear of it in time. The punishments are not petty. They are causing real hardship which is what they want. They want to ensure no one else steps out of line. The councillors seem to have forgotten their purpose," he finished, his face stern, the new lines accentuated by the flickering lamp.

"Are there any new councillors? Usually, councils are comprised of local people, but in Greenswatch, there is a new person with supporting henchmen who seems to be orchestrating change in the background. They are targeting Guardians. Though I have no real proof."

Jason grew still. "That is not as farfetched as you might think. There aren't any new councillors, but they are targeting those who follow the Lady. Anyone who visits the groves, asks the Father for a blessing, invokes her name. Now you mention it, it's almost exclusive, though they are not all Guardians."

"But everyone invokes the Lady. She watches us all, who does not?"

"You'd be surprised. There is growing support for the Ascendants. Even among some of my men. They like the idea that they can rule themselves." Jason snorted. "As if they would know how. They believe that the Ascendants are the true saviours, and were persecuted – not true of course, but I hear the rumblings. With the rumours of the King's ill health, and this constant rain affecting crops, people are seeking salvation, and whispers are falling on fertile ground."

"Well, I don't have any good news for you. In fact, I have some pretty bad news." He paused and in a neutral voice reported: "I came across a skirmish on my way here. Lord Hugh of the Greenswatch was attacked as he returned home from Deepwater. The attackers were dressed as bandits, but I would say that this was a deliberate attack. It was too well equipped and orchestrated for it to be a random attack." He pulled out the Greenswatch standard and laid it on Jason's desk. "He fell, his whole guard was wiped out."

The blood drained from Jason's face. "W-what?"

Jerrol rose and poured him a glass of wine from the jug on the cabinet by the wall. Jason sat, stunned.

"I discovered them as we were heading here. Hugh sent his runner back to Greenswatch, in advance of his return home. It was for the attention of Garrick, his steward, but Garrick shared it with me. Hugh was instigating stringent security protocols, and he had updated his instructions for sweeping the Watch. He was doubling the number of sweeps, effective immediately. Garrick was implementing the changes as I left to come here. I have his updated protocols so that you could have a copy as well. Makes you wonder what Hugh found in Deepwater." Jerrol placed the parchment on top of the desk. Jason reached for it instinctively, his mind still numbed by the news.

"I was hoping to cross paths with Hugh on the way here, so I swung further east than I normally would have into Deepwater. We managed to spook the last of the bandits off, but we were too late to make any difference. Well, there was one survivor." Jerrol made sure Jason was listening before he continued. "Lord Hugh's daughter was travelling with him, Lady Alyssa. We scraped her off the field before any of them returned."

Jason's head jerked back. "Is she hurt?" he asked, dropping the parchment.

"When she fell from her horse, she was knocked unconscious. I left her at Hannah's house. I wasn't too sure how safe it would be to come blatantly up to your front door and drop her off."

"I think you'd better. Bring her up to the infirmary. Tyrone can protect her from anyone," Jason said with a slow smile, recovering his composure, "and it will be more official. I can send out a unit to recover Lord Hugh and respond to the threat of bandits, and I can give her my protection as well until we find out what happened."

Jerrol stood nodding acceptance. "I was actually coming here to meet Torsion, but I understand he went up to Velmouth?"

"Yes, and he's been gone for too long. I was debating about sending someone up after him; you'll do nicely. He wanted to go and spend time up at the Watch Towers. He must have left here early spring, that's four months now. He hasn't sent any reports, which is unusual for him." Jason followed Jerrol to the door. "You can show me how you got in here," he said, an edge to his voice.

Jerrol laughed. "You're not going to make me go back the way I came in, are you?"

Jason wasn't smiling. "Oh yes," he said. "I think the fewer people who know we had this conversation, the better. Even here."

The night was well advanced by the time Jerrol was ready to return to the keep with Birlerion and Hannah in tow. Fortunately, Birlerion had been sitting in the kitchen, engrossed in a soft-toned discussion with Hannah when he arrived. Hannah was in full motherly mode; she had seen something in the Sentinal that needed cosseting.

As Jerrol watched them, he wondered how he had ever thought Birlerion cold and aloof. He had won Hannah over and looked at home seated at her kitchen table, drinking a bowl of soup.

Birlerion reported that Torsion's rooms were deserted; according to the locals at the inn, he'd been gone for quite a few months and no one knew when he would return, which matched what Jason had said.

As they prepared to leave, Hannah insisted that she accompany them and the Lady Alyssa to the keep. Jerrol didn't waste time arguing.

Jerrol passed the unconscious girl up to Birlerion and then boosted Hannah up on Zin'talia who protested about carrying someone other than Jerrol—just out of habit, he thought.

Leading Zin'talia up the road, her warm breath huffing against his cheek and chasing away the cold morning air, Jerrol turned back to speak to Birlerion when his face suddenly froze. In an instant, he had thrown the reins at Hannah, unsheathed his sword and slapped Zin'talia on the rump. "Get them to the keep quick," he barked. With a sweep of his sword, he was deflecting an arrow heading straight for Birlerion and Alyssa.

Birlerion and Hannah galloped away immediately, Hannah flailing for the reins. Jerrol charged towards the ambushers, closing in to fluster the archers.

Jerrol sized the opposition up, relieved they were not particularly organised. The two men with bows panicked as soon as he charged them, losing their rhythm, their arrows going wildly off target. Jerrol cut them down swiftly and moved on to the men behind them. They were no match for his speed as he parried a wild swing, flicking his dagger at one trying to circle behind him.

A swift glance noted positions and weapons, and he coldly dispatched them as they advanced. He spun inside the uncontrolled strike of one of the last men standing and hit him sharply behind his ear. The man dropped like a stone to the road. Jerrol hoped when Birlerion returned he would ask questions first.

He retrieved his dagger and vaulted into the saddle of one of the sturdier specimens and was in pursuit of the fleeing horse and rider in moments. Jerrol followed, scowling in disgust. The man was not trying to disguise his route or shake any pursuit. He was travelling in a straight line towards Deepwater.

Jerrol nursed the nag over the faint trails and across fields. It was in no condition to chase fugitives; he was surprised it was still moving considering its poor condition. He closed the distance, checking the tracks occasionally, but the trail didn't deviate.

The sun was overhead as Jerrol reached the outskirts of the grounds at Deepwater. He pulled his horse off the road and tied up its reins so it wouldn't get tangled in them. The horse drooped in exhaustion. It didn't even have the energy to graze; it wasn't going to stray far.

He scouted around the perimeter, noting the positions of the guards and their movements which were non-existent. They weren't expecting any trouble and didn't seem to be concerned with the arrival of a lone horseman in a frantic hurry.

Following the tree line, Jerrol slipped through the shadows and down to the first of the three large lakes from which the land took its name. Tall reeds and grasses lined the lake edges and rustled in the gentle breeze. Gaps revealed swims punctuated with lines and nets tied to tall posts jutting out of the water. Small wooden skiffs made of a few planks nailed together nestled along the shoreline, and bundles of rope freshwater shrimp pots provided ample cover for someone used to sneaking around unseen.

The rotting odour of dead fish and lake weed permeated the air, overlaid by occasional gusts of pungent herbal remedies that cleared the nasal system. Jerrol recognised Malhan weed and the scent of Trealt, a very rare essence only found in the Fuertes district of Terolia and often used to subvert the will of another. Why would Deepwater need that illicit drug?

Jerrol stood in the shadows of the building, assessing the climb and the stability of the wooden trellis attached to the wall. Voices caught his attention from a room on the ground floor. He knelt under the window; it had frosted glass panes, but they were held in by nails rather than the more insulating clay-like paste people were now using. He listened to the heated exchange carefully, his eyes quartering the terrain around him.

A high-pitched voice was berating the unfortunate man. "How dare you ride up here in broad daylight. You were given your instructions; you were to wait for us to contact you, you fool. There was to be no contact. No contact and no connection between us."

"But sir, Per'itise and his men are dead. I can't go back to the camp, not unless you give us the money. The lads are all riled up, spitting mad—you never said nothing about a rearguard." It sounded as if the man gulped nervously. "We did what you said. We caught them unawares and slaughtered them! But them guards killed Per'itise. We followed them over towards Stoneford, but we couldn't catch them."

"You mean you were seen on the field? And you came here?" The man was almost spitting in fury.

"You owe us, we did what you said, we killed them all," the man repeated sullenly.

A lighter voice joined the conversation. "Take it off your back, Peverill. The job's done, and most of the clean-up as well by the sounds of it. Save yourself some money and pay him off. He's stinking up my study."

"My lord." Peverill tried to temper his voice and spoke more calmly. "You shouldn't be seen with this man. You are supposed to be travelling to Greenswatch. You know the plan."

"Yes, yes. I'll go shortly. I wanted to see the calibre of man that bested the best of Greenswatch, and handed that gem into our hands."

"Hush, m'lord. We need to be careful. You know what Var'geris said: the less said, the better."

"Well, he said the fewer witnesses, the better, didn't he?" The man Jerrol assumed was the new lord of the holding spoke coldly. "I suppose we can accommodate him" A muffled thump followed his words. "There, no payment necessary. While I'm gone clean that filth off my carpet, and make sure you remove the blood stains or my mother will be in hysterics." The voice faded as the man left the room.

Jerrol moved. He wanted to be away before the lordling got on the road. He needed to be in a prime position to observe this man's response when he reached the carnage his greed had caused.

Jerrol made his return journey safely. The guards were not interested in guarding, which was interesting. Aaron didn't garner respect from his men, or they wouldn't be so shoddy in performing their duties. He collected the horse from the roadside, but it was done in; it was favouring its foreleg. Probably a strain and the lack of care hadn't helped.

Leading it away from Deepwater, he considered the best way to get ahead of Aaron. He could steal a horse and leave this one in payment, though maybe it wasn't quite fair on the recipient and it would leave an unexplained horse in the town.

He was surreptitiously watching a local hostelry when Aaron and his men swept past. They paid no attention to the other travellers on the road, forcing them to move out of their way, leaving chaos and anger in their wake.

This was to Jerrol's benefit as horses reared in panic and shed handlers, running in all directions. Jerrol snared a sleek bay mare, leaving his poor nag milling about in bewilderment, adding to the chaos. He swung himself up and followed in Aaron's wake. He would ask Jason to return it to the hostelry later.

Transport problem solved, Jerrol returned to the conversation he had overheard. Not only planned but funded by another Lord Holder. It was worse than he had thought; there was a coordinated plan to sow dissent and destruction. They were starting small in some areas, but the changes they were causing in other regions was breathtaking: two major holds fallen, Guardians removed. Vespiri would be overrun from within, and the king was not taking any steps to stop it.

But worst of all was the decimation of the Watches: Greenswatch and Deepwater, both without Guardians. The Land would suffer. The people would suffer. Everyone would suffer in the end. How could they be so blind? Once lost the

Guardianships couldn't be replaced as far as he knew. Losing a Guardianship had been unheard of, until now.

He stilled the faint flutter of panic and the vagrant thought that this was beyond him, and resolutely focused on the road. Slowly he overtook the group in front, passing unseen and unnoticed by the arrogant men travelling ahead of him.

19

STONEFORD KEEP

Birlerion swept into the courtyard with Hannah, yelling at the guards to form up and follow him. Hannah tumbled down from Zin'talia shouting for Tyrone, as Lord Jason strode into the middle of the confusion calling for order.

"Bandits on the road. The Captain is holding them off, need your men," Birlerion rattled off as he handed Alyssa down to Tyrone, who appeared beside him. "Hannah can tell you more."

He pulled his reins so sharply his horse almost rear-ended in his attempt to pirouette out of the courtyard. A few sharp orders from Jason and he was followed by the unit on guard, galloping down the road in pursuit of him.

Tyrone didn't hesitate but strode back into his infirmary, trailed by Hannah and thereafter by Jason after he had instructed a hovering lad to take care of Zin'talia, who was pulling towards the road. Off duty, men had already taken up the recently vacated posts.

Hannah explained Alyssa's injuries to Tyrone, which didn't take long at all, and Tyrone, after depositing the girl on a cot in the backroom, shooed her out. "Leave her with me. I'll call you if anything changes."

Jason arrived to hear his words and herded a reluctant Hannah out of the infirmary. "Yes, yes, come with me. We'll wait for them to return in my study, and you can explain what is going on to me," he said soothingly. "She'll be quite safe with Tyrone."

He managed to get Hannah seated in his study and called for tea. He sat beside her and took her hand. "Now, tell me what happened."

The tea arrived as Hannah started to worry about leaving Jerrol on his own to face the bandits.

"Best you be commiserating with those bandits, they had no chance," he said, handing her a welcome cup of tea.

"They were shooting at us," she exclaimed.

"Yes, but none hit you, did they?" Jason soothed. "You know perfectly well your boy is one of the best rangers ever turned out by the academy, and he had the training of the scholars as well: a potent mix. No bandit is ever going to get the better of him."

Hannah sighed, sipping her tea. "He always seems to be where the trouble is happening."

"Probably because he knows how to deal with it." Jason reached out to squeeze her arm in reassurance. "He always finds trouble; even as a child he was always in the midst of it."

"Is it true? Jason," Hannah said, placing her cup on the table, "is Lord Hugh really dead?"

"Jerrol wouldn't lie, you know that. He brought the Greenswatch standard back with him. That's proof enough for me. I sent Bryce over there to assess what happened and to bring the bodies back. He has a good eye. He'll find out. Let's hope Lady Alyssa comes around soon; it would help to know what she saw."

"Why are they taking so long?"

"I imagine they have gone after Jerrol. They would have been back if they were just rounding up your attackers."

"How can you be so calm?" She clasped her hands in her lap.

"Experience," he chuckled, "and you should know better." He pointed his finger at her. "All the escapades you went through with Jerrol, and you're asking me?"

Birlerion leapt off the back of his horse as he reached the bodies in the road. There was no sign of the Captain, but he hadn't necessarily expected him to linger. He knelt by the body of one of the archers; shaking his head, he moved from one body to the next. They hadn't stood a chance. They were unkempt bandits, paid thugs; even their weapons were poorly made. He instructed the men to load the bodies onto the cart and take them back to the keep. Another he sent to lead the horses.

"Sir, we're a horse short," the man said. "There are nine bodies and we've only got eight horses."

"More like we are two horses short," Birlerion corrected. "Captain Haven would have followed if anyone escaped. See if you can find any tracks, at least we'll know which direction they went."

"Sir," one of the soldiers loading the cart called out. "This one is still alive, looks like he was knocked out."

Birlerion strode over. "Good, at least Haven left us a witness. Keep an eye on him; make sure he stays alive. Lord Jason will want to speak to that one."

"Sir, tracks are leading off to the west, towards Deepwater," called the soldier leading the horses. He scowled. "And none of these horses are in good condition. They've been run into the ground."

"What a surprise," Birlerion murmured to himself. He watched the men swing the last body on the cart. He couldn't achieve anything further here. "Return to the keep and inform Lord Jason what we found. Tell him that I've gone to help Captain Haven."

Birlerion followed the tracks westwards easily enough. The ground was still soft from all the rain, and the horses ahead of him had been moving as fast as their poor condition allowed. The tracks headed straight for Deepwater.

Reining his horse in at the top of a bluff, he looked down at the landscape spread before him; this was a rich land, fertile fields edged by mature timber forests. It looked like they were doing some felling on the West Bank; a number of the ancient trees were down, leaving an unsightly gash in the timberline. In the distance, the first of the three large lakes that gave Deepwater its name gleamed on the horizon.

Inhaling a deep breath of fresh air, he considered what to do. The Lady expected him to protect the Captain. Though the Captain didn't make it easy, much like Guerlaire for that matter. He would have followed the bandit and would be nearing Deepwater by now. The Captain would not be amused if he blundered in behind him; best to leave him to it. From what he had heard, the Captain was better at the sneaky stuff.

He'd wait for him at the ambush site. He wanted to take another look at the strike zone, something had been niggling him from earlier, and he wanted to check it out. Turning west, he followed the trail dropping down until it met the big East Road. He grinned as he found the road; his innate sense of direction was working. He would make better time now and could skirt south of the big lakes.

It was approaching midday by the time he reached the ambush site. He paused and inspected the scene. Bryce's men had begun moving the bodies. They had erected an awning to keep the sun off the mass of bodies piled around Lord Hugh. Soldiers stripped to the waist were busy digging a trench, for the bandits no doubt.

Birlerion watched the work progress. This field was not directly on Hugh's path; it couldn't be seen from the road at all. So, how had Lord Hugh been persuaded off the road in the first place? They had only diverted because of Taelia; she had directed them to the battle.

Birlerion looped his horse's reins around the picket line and asked the lad tending the horses to give him some water. He walked up to join the wiry soldier commanding the activities. "Captain." He saluted. "Birlerion, Captain Haven's guard."

Bryce returned the salute. "Bryce, Stoneford. Birlerion, what brings you here?"

"Captain Haven and I were ambushed this morning on the way to the keep. Just wanted to warn you, you might get some company from Deepwater." As he spoke, Jennery entered the field and approached from the north, an appalled expression on his face as he surveyed the carnage. It was a dismal view.

"Deepwater? I was expecting support from Greenswatch. I sent a dispatch. This is a political nightmare. I have no jurisdiction here, I'm on Deepwater land, with the body of the Lord of the Greenswatch." Bryce grimaced as if in pain. "And no explanation as to why I am here."

Jennery dismounted. "You could say you were just passing. There is free travel on the roads," he suggested brightly.

Bryce snorted.

"Or you could say that a survivor staggered into the keep asking for help, which is almost the truth," Birlerion said, glaring at Jennery.

Bryce ran his hands through his brown hair and refocused on the scene in front of him. "The main concentration of the battle was around Lord Hugh; he was the target. There was a secondary focus area over to the east, but I can't see the reason for it at the moment. There are carriage tracks off to the west. I'd say they absconded with the carriage and whoever was in it; he has a daughter, doesn't he? Could have been her. I've sent a squad to track it and report back."

He walked over to a line of bodies. "These are the bandits. They look like common ruffians to me, clothes and weapons are unkempt, looks like they've been living rough for a while. There're at least fifty of them; we may find more. This is a large number of bandits in one place; they don't normally work together. They are more likely to fight amongst themselves than cooperate. This is highly unusual."

"I imagine it was going to be a good payout," Birlerion said, rubbing his fingers together. He hid his hand as heat tingled on his fingertips, and a blue sparkle flickered over his skin. He tensed; were his powers returning?

"It would have to be," Bryce agreed. "The scholar has captured the salient points. He'll start on the portraits shortly."

"How come you have the talents of a scholar-artist to hand? They are usually in the Chapterhouse in Old Vespers, aren't they?" Jennery looked across at the scholar with interest.

"He's in his journeyman year, happened to stop off at the keep, and Lord Jason invited him to stay and sort out the records room for a while." Bryce eased his shoulders. "He's been after a scholar for ages."

"Well," Jennery said, squinting down the field. "It looks

like your day is either about to improve or deteriorate rapidly." He gestured at a file of mounted soldiers approaching.

Bryce glared at Jennery and strode off to meet the
oncoming party. Birlerion followed behind him. The lead
rider was frowning; he didn't hold out much hope of
improvement.

Before Bryce could say a word, the man approaching him
erupted. "What do you think you are doing here? How dare
you touch these men. I am here to sort this out. This is my
land." He stared down his nose at Bryce. "Explain yourself."

Bryce gave a brisk salute. "Captain Bryce, sir, from
Stoneford Keep."

"Stoneford?" the man snapped. "What is a captain from
Stoneford doing in Deepwater?"

"Report of an ambush arrived early this morning, sir. We
were ordered to assist and recover."

"Why didn't they come to me for help? I am the Lord of
Deepwater and Deepwater is nearer," the lordling huffed.

"Couldn't say, m'lord," Bryce replied blandly. Birlerion
stared at the lord, stonefaced, providing subtle support for
Bryce.

"Well, you can stop now. I am here now, and I will assist
Lord Hugh," the lordling said, glaring at Bryce with distaste.
He paused as one of his men approached and spoke quietly
in his ear.

"Ah, yes. Where is the carriage and Lady Alyssa?" Lord
Aaron twisted in his saddle as if the carriage would magically
appear before him.

"The tracks lead off to the west, my lord. I sent a patrol
to scout."

"That was unnecessary, Captain. Make sure you bury
those bodies. I will save Lady Alyssa." Lord Aaron gave him
a sharp nod and led his men away.

"Pompous ass! Such little surprise and so few questions,"

Jennery said as he joined the stiff-backed captain. "Interesting that he knew Lord Hugh was dead without actually asking."

"Yes, he shows a distinct lack of respect for a fellow Lord Holder, and no concern for the safety of his neighbours or his people. Are bandits so common here in Deepwater, I wonder," Bryce bit out as he turned back to the field. "I expect Greenswatch to arrive shortly. We need to get Lord Hugh ready to return home." He pulled the Greenswatch standard out of his pocket and walked over to where Lord Hugh now lay. Bryce reseated the pole by his head and retied the flag to the end. "Private," he called to a young soldier who was resolutely bending over the feet of another body.

The soldier snapped to attention. "Yessir?"

"Here, stand guard. No one touches him till I say so, " Bryce rapped.

"Yes, sir." The private took position behind Lord Hugh's body and the Greenswatch standard, his eyes front and fixed, his face blank and his posture stiff.

Bryce saluted the standard, before turning back to the grisly work his men were performing. "What a waste," he said, his face cold and severe as his gaze swept the field again.

Jerrol waited for Aaron to leave before he sauntered towards them, leading his wind-blown horse. "Well, that is disappointing," he said as he nodded at Bryce and saluted more respectfully to the standard at the head of Lord Hugh's body.

"What is?" Bryce's voice was sharp. He was at the end of his tether and not appreciating Jerrol's levity.

"That the Lord of Deepwater is not prepared to relieve you of this situation. A bit surprising that, wouldn't you say?"

Jennery snorted. "He couldn't wait to follow the skirts. Break a sweat? I don't think he knows how."

"But how much of this do we think he knew in advance? And how do we prove it to Greenswatch? Do we even want to? I am wondering how distraught young Simeon will be at the thought of ascending to his father's powers." Jerrol frowned. "Do we want to create an all-out war between Greenswatch and Deepwater?"

"Don't you think it would be interesting to see Simeon's reaction to the accusation?" Jennery asked.

"Which we can't make without proof," Jerrol said. "I believe hearsay doesn't count."

Birlerion stared at Jerrol. "What have you heard? You went to Deepwater, didn't you? Was that the source of the attack on us? Surely that is proof. It is a direct link to this." Birlerion waved his hand at the carnage around them.

Jerrol grimaced. "Unfortunately, I don't think I am a reliable witness at the moment."

"Depends who we are convincing," Jennery argued.

"Looks like Greenswatch has arrived," Bryce said, as a long column of mounted riders entered the field, the green standard of Greenswatch leading the way. They came to a halt, and the lead riders dismounted. After a brief conversation, Lord Hugh's steward approached alone, and Captain Bryce walked forward to meet him.

Garrick acknowledged Bryce but continued walking towards the Greenswatch standard, and Bryce fell in beside him. Garrick came to a stop beside the body of his lord, his face pale and strained. He saluted the standard and turned to Bryce. "You are relieved," he said, his voice cold and expressionless. Bryce saluted and stepped back. The Greenswatch honour guard approached in step and took up position at the four corners.

The horse-drawn bier at the rear of the column entered the field at Garrick's signal, and they lifted their lord onto the bier, draping his body with Greenswatch colours. The honour guard retook their position at the four corners, standing at full attention.

Garrick stood stiff and silent, watching. Jerrol approached him carefully. "My lord steward," he said. "I am so sorry for your loss, but there are matters to discuss." He gave Lord Hugh's ring to the steward. Garrick stared at the ring as Jerrol continued. "The Lady Alyssa was recovered from the field and is in the infirmary at Stoneford under the care of Healer Tyrone. Captain Bryce sent a troop after the Lady's carriage, and they are yet to return. Lord Aaron and his men followed them. I regret to inform you that he didn't stay long enough to be informed that Lady Alyssa wasn't in the carriage."

A muscle twitched in Garrick's cheek. "Lady Alyssa is unharmed?"

"She was still unconscious when I left. She took a brutal fall. I followed one of the bandits to Deepwater, and although it is purely hearsay and my word against Lord Aaron's, Deepwater knew. I swear they were involved." Jerrol paused, but Garrick remained silent. "I know you need to escort Lord Hugh home, but if it's your desire, I swear I will protect Lady Alyssa until you are available to escort her home."

Jerrol waited as Garrick stared blindly across the field. "I will accept your oath, Captain Haven." His face tightened in anguish. "I appreciate and honour the support of Stoneford Keep and the King's Rangers, even though the new regime may not continue that in the future. I will return to escort Lady Alyssa as soon as I am able. For now, she is safe, and I have the fallen to honour."

Jerrol bowed. "I will await you at Stoneford." Jerrol turned away as a column of flatbed carts arrived to take up the fallen soldiers. Captain Bryce stepped forward, rapping out orders to his men to assist in the horrible job of moving the bodies to the carts in preparation for the journey home.

Jerrol jerked his head at Jennery and Birlerion to draw them away. "We can't help any further here. I need a horse; mine has had it."

"The horses are over here." Birlerion led the way towards the picket line, where Jerrol selected a horse that looked in better shape than his last poor mount, tiredly heaved himself up into the saddle and led the way from the battlefield.

20

STONEFORD KEEP, STONEFORD WATCH

N ight had descended by the time they reached Stoneford and clattered into the keep's courtyard. Lord Jason met them as they dismounted. Stable boys dashed to take the reins and lead the horses away. He noted their strained faces and sent them off to freshen up with instructions to meet him in the hall as soon as they could.

Jerrol gazed longingly at the bed but stripped off his filthy clothes and washed in the warm water waiting for him. His side was twinging a warning as he carefully dressed in the clean clothes, leaving the bandages untouched. He stamped into his still muddy boots as his clothes shimmered into his uniform of Lady's green. He grinned. The Lady was stubborn.

"Jerrol? Are you back then? It would be nice to know you're alright!" Zin'talia's peevish voice intruded on his thoughts, and he veered out towards the stables to reassure her that he was fine. Hugging her silky neck, he breathed in her musky scent, as she did the same, huffing in disapproval. *"That's the last time I let anyone else ride me. I'm supposed to be with you."*

"I didn't mean to leave you," he said as he leaned into her warmth. *"Jason is waiting for me. I'll come back later."* He reluctantly pushed himself away and headed into the hall.

"You'd better." Her voice followed him.

Jason was seated at a table loaded with food for three hungry men. Jerrol was still the first to arrive, even with his detour, and he carefully sat opposite him.

"Are you alright?" Jason watched his stiff movements in concern.

"We got jumped last night — was it last night? I'm losing track! All this strenuous activity today hasn't helped it." Jerrol reached for the bread and cheese. He was suddenly starving. "How is our patient?" he asked around a mouthful of food.

"Tyrone is keeping her quiet. She came around about an hour ago, but he won't let her talk yet. Hannah is sitting with her. She knows about Lord Hugh; she saw him fall after all." He pursed his lips. "Bryce managing alright?"

"Having the time of his life. I think he might have a few words when he returns. He wasn't too happy with the politics of his situation. I think Birlerion can explain more. He was there when Lord Aaron arrived."

Jason winced. "I can imagine. What a mess!"

"What's worse is that our ambushers originated from Deepwater, and I overheard the young lord and his men discussing the ambush. They were in on it. Deliberately attacking a neighbouring Lord Holder while he was still under their hospitality. Not that anyone is going to believe a disgraced ranger against the word of the Lord Holder, but still, the rot goes deep." Jerrol took another bite and chewed slowly as Jennery and Birlerion entered the room and joined them. "Two key holds without a Guardian. Aaron didn't take up the mantle, and the word is Simeon won't either."

Jason's face blanched. "That is not good news; if there is

no Guardian the land will fail. Once the land starts sickening the people will begin to suffer."

"I wonder if that is the intent. If someone wants to overthrow the current ruler, causing civil unrest would do the trick, don't you think? And that someone riding to the rescue while the current ruler is distracted and ill?

"Both Greenswatch and Deepwater had their councils recently infiltrated by new players encouraging them to promote council rule over the king and Lady. Lord Hugh was so concerned at Aaron's confirmation that he agreed to new protocols with the other lords. Garrick was talking about protecting from within. I think we may even have contention within the holds as well."

Jerrol frowned in thought; he shifted awkwardly as a spike of pain flashed through his side. His ribs burned and, to be honest, he hadn't checked under the bandages when possibly he ought to have; maybe he had overdone it. His stomach roiled as he eyed the food on his plate. "Jennery, share what you found at the Grove," he said, as he surreptitiously wiped the sweat from his forehead.

Birlerion peered at him. "Captain? Are you alright? Have you done yourself more harm?"

Jerrol reached under his shirt and came out with a reddened hand, just as Healer Tyrone entered the hall. Tyrone hustled Jerrol out of the room, complaining under his breath about idiot rangers. He marched him to the infirmary, leaving Jennery and Birlerion to explain everything to Jason.

Jerrol was confined to the infirmary. His wound was painfully restitched, and Tyrone warned of infection. With his foster mother, Hannah, frowning over him in concern, Jerrol stopped arguing. He drank the disgusting potions Tyrone was forcing on him and carefully lay down. Closing his eyes, he caught up on some sleep. It made a change to leave the problems to someone else.

The next morning, he was unable to get Tyrone to release him. Lady Alyssa was still asleep in the bed next to him, a screen separating them. He lay in bed, musing over the incidents in the Watches. Events were happening too fast for it not to be coordinated. He was worried about the King; that last audience with him was even more concerning.

For the king to defer to Prince Kharel was unheard of, yet, as soon as Kharel had entered the room and spoken, the king had stopped mid-sentence, even though he had been talking about oaths, the King's Oath. There had been that resounding crack that echoed across the throne room before fading to silence.

He was also annoyed about the prince confiscating his sword. The king himself had presented it to Jerrol on the conclusion of one of his shadier missions out of Terolia that he wasn't supposed to talk about. He had liked that sword. It took time to train a sword to your hand and that one had been coming along nicely.

His thoughts circled back to the Watches. Who would gain the most by killing off Guardians and destabilising the Watches? Why was it so important to remove him from the equation? What had he been doing that had made him a target? He was only one of many rangers the king could call on. It was true the king did have a preference for using him, but that only meant he got the difficult jobs.

In return, Jerrol had set up some pretty strict protocols around the king which he knew had caused issues with both the chancellor and Prince Kharel. Jerrol grinned viciously; they would find them difficult to overcome. Good. Maybe he had been a thorn in their side, and they had decided it was simpler to remove him.

The evening was drawing in when Jerrol caught Tyrone for a last plea. "I've rested long enough. Give me my clothes, Tyrone, and let me out of here." The inactivity was driving Jerrol mad.

"You'll have rested when I say you have." Tyrone wasn't giving in. "Give your body a chance to heal. As soon as you get up, you'll be tearing off somewhere, and doing more damage."

"I'll be careful. I promise."

They were interrupted by Alyssa's pale face peering around the screen. "Captain Haven?" she asked, tugging her blanket more tightly. "I understand I have you to thank for my rescue."

Jerrol stopped mid-complaint and glared at Tyrone before smoothing his face and smiling at Alyssa. "Call me Jerrol, please, and it wasn't just me," he said, waving his hand in the air. "Birlerion helped too."

"I feel terrible that you were hurt saving me. I don't remember much after I fell off Firefly. Do you know if she is alright?" she asked, her face tightening in concern.

"I expect she's fine. I bet she's munching her way through Lord Jason's feed supplies, and anyway, my condition isn't anything to do with you. I picked this up before we came across you. I just overdid it," Jerrol said while Tyrone snorted in disdain and walked away. "Honestly, this..." and he indicated the bandages around his chest, "was nothing to do with you."

Alyssa's eyes filled with tears. "So many people killed to protect me," she whispered as if he hadn't spoken.

"They were there to protect you, that was their job. They died with honour. I swear by the Lady, my injuries were not caused by you. In fact," he said ruefully, "you can confirm it with Silene. Though please not when I am in the same room;

she will be very upset with me seeing as she stitched me up in the first place!"

"Silene? You know Silene?"

"Yes, we stayed with her and her husband, Reese ..." Jerrol fell silent as he counted back: no wonder he was exhausted! "Two nights ago. We were on our way to visit your father when we got caught out in the storm, and they kindly offered us shelter for the night."

"Oh," she said, closing her eyes. "But you were on the field. I'm sure I saw you and your friend amongst all the bodies." She shuddered as her face paled.

"What made Lord Hugh leave the main road, do you know?" Jerrol tried to distract her from her recent horrors. She looked young and vulnerable perched on the chair next to him with her auburn curls shoved behind her ears, and her brown eyes large in her unnaturally pale face. She should be the one lying down, not him.

"I'm not sure; there was a shout from the front of the column and the guards in front charged off. I think everyone else just followed."

Jerrol nodded to himself: straight into the ambush. He shifted, trying to get comfortable. "How are you feeling?"

Alyssa's shoulders drooped. "I just want to sleep all the time, and I keep seeing things."

"What things?" She had taken the Guardianship after all. She probably didn't know.

"You'll laugh."

"I see things all the time, so no, I won't laugh. Let me tell you what I see. You can tell me if you've seen it too." Jerrol gestured at the end of his bed. "I can currently see a small black and brown fluffy creature that looks like a kitten, but has a forked tail and reptilian wings, sitting on the end of my bed staring at me with big green eyes. How about you?"

Alyssa gasped in relief, holding her hands up to her face.

"You can see it too? I thought I was going mad! No one else has mentioned it."

"That's because they can't see him; he is an Arifel. A not so mythical creature of the Lady's. Only the Lady's Guardians can see him unless the Arifel decides he wants to be seen by others, which doesn't happen very often."

"And you can see him," he said, watching her, "because you are currently hosting the Greenswatch Guardianship, which jumped to you when your father died. And I fear it will stay with you, as I am hearing it is unlikely your brother will pick up the mantle and claim the Guardianship, much as Lord Aaron has done."

Alyssa dropped her hands in shock. "What? How do you know?"

"Well, first because you can see Ari." Jerrol coaxed the little creature up the bed and scooped him up, dropping him in Alyssa's hands, where Ari made himself comfortable, crooning gently. Alyssa's lips quirked up in response as she gently stroked his soft fur in amazement. "He has been watching over you while you have been asleep. And secondly, because I felt it when I touched you."

"What do you mean, you felt it?"

Jerrol glanced around the infirmary. It was so quiet that Tyrone's voice filtered in from the corridor. "It's not common knowledge, and I would prefer to keep it that way," Jerrol warned, easing himself up on the pillows, "but I am the Lady's Captain. Apparently, Ari here appeared because she made me her Captain." The Arifel cheeped in agreement.

Alyssa sat stunned. "B-but, there hasn't been a Lady's Captain since the Lady cracked the stone!"

"So I understand, yet here I am."

Alyssa reached out tentatively and touched his arm; the jolt zinged through her, as it did Jerrol. She petted Ari as he stirred in protest, smiling into his fur. She raised shining eyes. "What am I supposed to do?"

"I'm not sure," he admitted, "though I would recommend you keep it to yourself for now. Although some of the other Guardianships follow the female line, I'm not aware of a Watch Guardianship ever being passed outside of the male line before. Silene might be a good source of information. She might know more." He sighed. "I am sorry, Lady Alyssa, but I don't think you should trust Lord Aaron or your brother with this information, nor anyone else to be honest. If at the Hold confirmation your brother accepts the Lady's protection, he'll take up the Guardianship; if not, it will stay with you."

"Call me, Alyssa, please. I will look after it, don't you worry about that. Lady is my witness," she vowed. The Lady's acknowledgement resonated deep in his bones, and in Alyssa's, too, judging by her widening eyes.

"Witnessed," Jerrol said with a wry smile.

The Arifel popped out of sight as Tyrone returned. "You, young lady, back to bed. You've been up long enough." Observing Alyssa's improved colour, he turned a surprisingly approving gaze on Jerrol. "And you don't move until I tell you so, not until tomorrow, hear me?" he said with a firm nod.

Jerrol grimaced at Tyrone, but lay back down, feeling the hum of agreement from Zin'talia in the back of his mind. Two nursemaids were ganging up on him! At least she had gotten over her resentment with him for leaving her behind. He drifted off, comforted by her presence.

Jerrol woke early the next day, and after a somewhat heated but low-voiced discussion to avoid waking up Lady Alyssa, he managed to get his clothes back and got dressed. Tyrone, surprised that he had kept Jerrol confined for so long, had given in gracefully. He listed the things he forbade

Jerrol to do for the next two days, knowing that it was a hopeless cause. Jerrol airily agreed to all and fled the infirmary.

He was crossing the courtyard as a very weary Captain Bryce and his men trailed in, grubby and exhausted. Even his horse was drooping. Jerrol paused by Bryce's horse, holding his bridle. "What are you doing here? Didn't Greenswatch offer their hospitality?"

Bryce looked down at him; the dust and grime coating his face made him look older. "Garrick did, but the young master was not so inclined. He was berating Garrick for not bringing his sister home, and he dispatched us to get her. He would not allow us to stay while his sister was missing."

Jerrol was horrified. These men had been up for over forty-eight hours straight with little relief from the heart-breaking job of clearing a battlefield of friend and foe alike, only then to travel back from Greenswatch on top of that. "Food or bath first?" he asked.

"Bath," Bryce grunted as he dismounted with a heartfelt groan. "Though there are some things that you can't just wash off."

Jerrol glanced around the courtyard; lads had been roused and were leading off the exhausted horses. Bryce ordered his men to bathe and eat. They were off duty until further notice. The men saluted in relief and dispersed before he could change his mind.

"Go on." Jerrol jerked his head towards the officer's barracks and took the reins. "I'll take your horse. I'll meet you in the hall." Bryce untied his saddlebags before slowly turning away, leaving Jerrol to lead his horse to the stables.

Jerrol led the road-begrimed horse through the archway into the inner courtyard and the stable blocks fanning out around it. A small lad popped up beside him. "I'll take him, sir, I'll see to old Sooty," he said with an affectionate rub of the horse's nose. Jerrol relinquished the reins and turned to greet Zin'talia, who was bombarding him with affection. He hugged her. "Enough! Anyone would think I've been gone a year instead of a day!"

He smoothed a hand down her silky neck; she was looking pristine and full of energy. "Hmm, no gallops for me today, maybe tomorrow, hey? One of the lads can take you through your paces, or shall I turn you out to pasture?" She flashed her eyes at him and shook her head. "Okay, why don't you go for a run." He led her down to the training field, where he released her. Leaning against the wooden rails, he watched her gallop away, frisking all the way, her tail flowing behind her.

He smiled in pleasure at her pleasure as she danced her way back up the field and pirouetted before him. "Now you're showing off," he said as he realised they had gathered an audience of lads, young and old, gazing adoringly at her.

Jerrol caught the eye of the stable master as he walked across the yard towards him. "Now she is a real beauty, and she knows it." The stable master's eyes followed Zin'talia as she frisked away like a young colt. "But," he said glaring at the lads, "we have some exhausted horses here who deserve just as much attention if not more, so off with the lot of you," he barked, scattering the lads back to their duties.

21

STONEFORD KEEP. STONEFORD WATCH

J errol turned back towards the hall, leaving Zin'talia to play, her touch a light and carefree but reassuring presence, the stable master walking with him. "There was a bay mare in the picket, she was from the hostelry outside of Deepwater. I borrowed her the other day; my mount had run out of steam, she ought to be returned."

"I wondered where she had come from. We'll take her back," the stable master assured him, veering off as Jerrol headed for the hall.

The dining hall was sparsely populated: a few guards who had finished their shift, and a sprinkling of Bryce's men silently communing with their coffee, their thoughts far away. Jerrol selected a plate of bread and fruit before pouring his coffee and choosing a seat at an unoccupied table.

He sipped his coffee, letting his mind drift as he relaxed. The low voices around him were soothing. He listened absently to the men behind him as he cut his apple into wedges and began to eat them.

"You should've seen him, proud as punch 'e was, rescuing the ladies. Not that he helped turn the carriage, nor offered us any help on the field. No, that lord won't dirty his hands, yer can tell," one of the guards said.

"And after all that, Lady Alyssa weren't there," a deeper voice replied.

"He weren't pleased," the man said, and the other men with him laughed at the obvious understatement.

"What about going over to Ramila? We've got a couple of days, and there's that speaker on tomorrow."

"Var'geris yer mean? I can't be bothered. I'll go another time."

"We're all going. It'll be a laugh, get some of that Terolian wine in yer, do yer good."

"Give me gut rot yer mean. I remember the last time," the man said.

Jerrol slowly turned his head and studied the men. They were all damp-haired from their recent bath, though they looked weary and drained. Suddenly Jerrol remembered where he had heard the name before; Lord Aaron had said it at Deepwater. *Var'geris* was the name Aaron had said. The way this man said the name, it was quite familiar to him.

Jerrol moved his mug and his plate over to the guards' table, smiling at the men as he sat. "I couldn't help overhearing, were all the ladies alright? I'm sure Lady Alyssa will want to know."

"Yeah, scared stiff and travel-weary, but they hadn't been touched. Not for lack of wanting, so we heard, but one of those wenches had a dagger or two and knew how to use 'em, she made them think twice. They were lucky," the guard nodded wisely. "Very lucky."

"You mentioned Var'geris, is that a person?"

One of the men snorted. "Not been to Terolia lately? It's all you hear, Var'geris this, Var'geris that, apparently it is a new religion sweeping through the nomads. They are falling like flies, never thought to see the nomads bowing to anyone.

Not the families, but they are entranced, can't get enough, so we hear. Makes our life easier, been fewer clashes on the border."

"But the smuggling routes seem to have taken a new lease of life," one of his companions said. "We are intercepting more contraband than ever."

"What sort of contraband?" Jerrol asked.

"The usual: liquor, silk, gems, opiates. All the things the King has a levy on, not large consignments, but enough to be noticeable."

"Any idea who is behind it, or where it is supposed to go?"

"No, they are slippery little buggers. Got all sorts of tricks up their sleeves; you never know what they are going to throw at you. I expect they will be calling this Var'geris down on us next. They keep saying he will come down on us from on high! What was it you said it translated as?" He nudged the fellow next to him.

"Rising up, to be ascendant," the man replied.

Jerrol's stomach congealed. He managed to smile his thanks as he rose from the table. He walked towards the doorway as Birlerion appeared. He jerked his head, and Birlerion followed him out.

"Are you supposed to be up?" Birlerion asked, glancing about as if he expected an unhappy healer to descend on them at any moment.

"Oh yes, Tyrone released me. Where's Jennery?"

"Healer Tyrone dosed him up and sent him back to bed. He was sneezing all over the place."

"Best place for him, then. I overheard the guards talking about Terolia; have you ever visited the country?"

"Er, yes, but it will no doubt be different from what I remember."

Jerrol gave him a sympathetic glance. "I think after we've

visited Velmouth, we are going to need to go on a jaunt to Terolia," and he repeated what the guards had said. "It seems to me the source of much of the trouble stems from Terolia."

"That's not much to go on, though that bandit leader had a Terolian name."

"Then go and find out what else you can. Investigating smugglers should be right up your street. We'll be leaving for Velmouth in the morning." Jerrol started to turn away but paused as Jason strode up; he didn't look particularly happy.

"Jerrol, you got a few minutes?"

"Of course." Jerrol was surprised. He followed Jason back to his office.

"Why didn't you tell me?"

"Tell you what?" Jerrol asked, bewildered.

"That Prince Kharel has a price on your head, dead or alive!" snapped Jason, pacing angrily.

Jerrol was taken aback. "Well, we had that trouble a couple of days ago, but to be honest, with everything going on, I'd sort of forgotten. I know the king doesn't support his view, but the king's voice is not being heard so much lately."

"And how do you know the king's opinion if the prince arrested you?"

"Well," Jerrol expelled his breath, "I was talking to the king in the throne room when I was arrested."

"What? Why didn't the king intervene?"

"I don't know."

"What were you talking about?"

"I can't say. Jason, please, it's not for me to say," Jerrol said as Jason frowned at him. "Honestly, I have my orders and if the king sees fit to leave me adrift, who am I to countermand him?"

Jason sat in his chair. "Lad, what have you gotten yourself into?" His face creased in concern.

Jerrol scowled. "More than I bargained for, I'm sure. I am going to head up to Velmouth with Birlerion, search for Torsion. Then I think we might take a trip into Terolia; there are a few rumours I need to investigate."

"Are you sure it's safe? You've not exactly been discreet whilst you've been here. Oh, I've suppressed this for now, but they will hear the news via other routes. I can't keep it quiet for long, and then you'll have all sorts after you. The amount of money being offered is obscene. What did you do?"

"That's the thing, Jason, I didn't do anything! I have no idea why the prince is determined to kill me. All the charges were trumped up. I was no longer on the chancellor's detail. I'm at a loss."

"Well, you'd better figure it out before it's too late. Who are you taking with you to Velmouth? Jennery?"

"No, I think Jennery ought to escort Lady Alyssa back to Greenswatch. Along with Bryce. I'll take Birlerion. Uh, I don't think I said. He is a Sentinal. I woke him in Old Vespers."

Jason stared at him. "He's a what?"

Jerrol rubbed his face. "A Lady's Sentinal, he was in the sentinal tree in Old Vespers. I woke him up, and he stepped out of the tree, much as you see him now. I ought to go and wake yours up."

"Birlerion is a three-thousand-year-old Sentinal?" Jason repeated in disbelief.

Jerrol grinned at his expression. "Yes."

"And how did you wake him up, may I ask?"

"Umm, by accident. The Lady made me her Captain. It seems the Ascendants are back, trying to overthrow the king and the Lady."

"And you think there are men in the sentinal trees here as well?"

"Yes." Jerrol chuckled at the look Jason gave him. "I'm

not mad. Speak with Birlerion; you'll soon believe me. He'll be chasing me to wake your Sentinals shortly, just you watch."

Jason shook his head and changed the subject. "What about Jennery, what's he doing here?"

"I sent him orders to join me, though I think it's time Jennery returned to his unit. We need to get someone on the inside at Old Vespers, and Jennery could be it."

"I can't imagine Jennery being a courtier." A brief smile flickered across Jason's face at the thought. "Are you sure this Birlerion will be enough?"

"Who else do you suggest? He could always pretend he's arrested me and is taking me back for execution by the prince."

"Don't joke about it." Jason was appalled at the thought. "I was going to suggest Bryce, though I suppose he is not the skulking type either."

"Greenswatch is expecting him to return with Lady Alyssa, so I think he's busy. We'll be fine. We'll be with Torsion." Jerrol tried to reassure him.

"Why does that not make me feel any better?" Jason asked almost to himself.

Jerrol clapped him on the shoulder. "I'll tell Jennery his new orders; you'd better tell Bryce."

Jerrol found Jennery in the guesting barracks, nursing his cold. He took his orders as well as Jerrol had expected, but once he had calmed down enough to listen to Jerrol's reasoning, he was soon nodding thoughtfully. "Do you think Simeon will take the Watch that fast?"

Jerrol rubbed his chin as he considered. "I think the ceremony will happen as soon as Alyssa arrives. I highly doubt Simeon will pick up the mantle; it will stay with Alyssa. You need to help protect her. See if you can delay so you can attend.

"As you are returning to Old Vespers to rejoin your company you could suggest that you escort Alyssa, that will get you in at court. I expect her mother will want to call her to her side once she hears about Lord Hugh. I can't imagine she would miss that opportunity."

"What's the story there? I've never met her."

Jerrol sighed. "Not much to tell, typical daughter of a courtier swept up by a lord, not realising that she would have to live so far from court, and in the 'Wilds of the Watches' as well." He rolled his eyes. "She stayed long enough to beget two children before recalling her promises to the princess that she would return to her duties or some such. And she was gone, leaving Hugh with two young children. Be warned though, she may seem shallow, but she is astute and has the ear of Prince Kharel's wife. Be very careful around her."

"Ah," groaned Jennery, "court intrigue, my favourite. I think I would prefer skulking around Velmouth with you instead, send Birlerion to court."

"Can you imagine a Sentinal loose at court? We will do well together. Let's introduce you to Alyssa. At least you are an official escort!"

Alyssa accepted her new personal guard with aplomb, especially once she realised he was in the employ of the Lady as well. She was enthusiastic about keeping him as her escort for as long as possible. As they seemed to hit it off so well, Jerrol left them plotting their journey and went to search for Birlerion. He had a few plans of his own to set in motion.

He had just exited the inner courtyard when he felt the change in the air. He sidestepped, drawing his sword as he spun into motion and deflected the brutal downward sweep of his opponent's sword. The screech of metal echoing through the hallways was deafening; the sheer force of the blow almost overbalanced the man, who had been expecting it to be a killing blow. Jerrol absorbed some of the energy and used the rest to spin back into the body of his opponent and strike low and hard, to be met with a counter thrust as the man recovered and parried.

The sound of clashing swords drew a crowd of watchers as the fighters traversed the inner courtyard, the swords flickering so fast they were just a blur.

Jennery and Alyssa thrust their way through to the front of the crowd. "Can't you help him?" Alyssa grabbed Jennery's arm as Jerrol went on the offensive, his face cold and stern and very focused. Forcing his opponent back, he began the final movement of his counterargument.

Jennery shook his head. "Too late, I'd only throw him off his stride." Jennery watched Jerrol's opponent falter as Jerrol's unexpected response shattered his timing. The rhythm of the fight was deliberately broken. Jerrol spun tightly and thrust his sword through the man's guard. Jerrol followed the body down to the ground, the deadweight dragging him down. After a short pause to gather himself and breathing heavily, he pulled his sword out and stood back up, blinking blearily at his audience.

"Jerrol, are you alright?" Jennery moved forward to block the view, Alyssa close behind him. "And you," he snarled as Birlerion approached, "where were you? You're the one supposed to be protecting him."

Birlerion stiffened, though he answered calmly enough. "The Captain had it in hand, he is quite capable, you know. I didn't intercede for the same reason you didn't."

Jerrol waved his hand, trying to catch his breath and gripping his side. "Give me a minute." Tyrone had been right; he wasn't as recovered as he thought he was.

Jennery knelt to turn the body over as Jason entered the courtyard. Jason soon dispersed the spectators and was assessing the scene as he approached. "Who is it? Do you recognise him?"

"Never seen him before." Jerrol breathed deeply. "Is he one of yours?"

Jason looked closely. "No," he said slowly. He glanced up and barked out an order to one of the guards who had followed him.

In short order, Bryce arrived, somewhat dishevelled as if he had hastily dressed, and Jerrol remembered he had not long returned from Greenswatch. He grimaced in sympathy as Jason explained what had happened and directed his captain to the body. "Anyone you've seen recently?"

Bryce stared at the body intently. "He may be one of the Greenswatch guards, though I'm not positive."

Alyssa frowned. "I don't recognise him, but then, I don't know all the men."

"Why would Greenswatch send someone after me?" Jerrol said. "It doesn't make sense! They couldn't have known I was here. There was no reason to connect me to the recovery of Lord Hugh."

"Maybe someone at Greenswatch saw you with Garrick?" suggested Jennery. "You were in the archives a while, that might have drawn comment."

Jerrol shook his head. "Only Garrick knew who we were, and we kept out of sight. I can't see how anyone there would have known."

"Unless they were on the lookout for you," Alyssa added. "There are conspiracies we never knew existed, who can tell what they already know? First Lord Stefan, now my father; you can't tell me their deaths are not connected."

The men looked at her in surprise. She raised a very valid point. Alyssa gazed back at them in frustration. "This all has to be connected," she said, sweeping her hand around the courtyard. "Who else is trying to find out what is going on in the Watches? No one but you!"

"Let's move this conversation inside," Jason said. "Bryce,

deal with the body and meet us in my office; the rest of you follow me."

Jason sat behind his desk. His face was creased in thought as he tapped a finger on the arm of his chair. Lady Alyssa sat perched on a chair, with Jennery standing beside her. Jerrol was pacing the floor like a caged animal, still on an adrenaline high as he listed the facts they knew. He paused as the door opened and Bryce entered.

"We know that we have two Watches down." He glanced sympathetically at Alyssa, who inclined her head, her face calm. "That guardians are being targeted, councils suborned, temple leaders converted, even the King is failing healthwise. As Lady Alyssa says, this conspiracy has been afoot for some time, so who is coordinating it? Prince Kharel? The chancellor? Some outside influence? There are rumours of a religious upset in Terolia. Torsion went up to the Watch Towers four months ago and hasn't been seen since. There are rumblings in the northeast; it could be a symptom, or it could be the cause we need to check."

Jerrol held up a finger. "One, we need someone at court to keep an eye on the King and feed us up-to-date information. Two, we need to investigate the rumblings. Three, we need to shore up the watches and begin our defence."

Jason looked at him keenly. "I see your time in the infirmary was well spent," he said as he gestured for Jerrol to continue.

"Seeing as I can't go back to Vespers and I am guessing that is a deliberate act to keep me away from the king, I suggest Jennery goes to court with Lady Alyssa. They have more reason to go than any of us, and I am sure if you drop the right hints, Alyssa, your mother will invite you, and

Simeon will have to agree. He must want to appear to have a tighter alignment with Prince Kharel."

Alyssa tapped her foot gently on the floor. "I'll send a letter to my mother straight away." She glanced up at Jennery, and they shared a fleeting smile.

"Bryce, once you've escorted Lady Alyssa home, you need to detour through the watches to Lords William and Marcus. Check their holdings, agree on the protocols, advise them what has been happening elsewhere and make sure they check out any newcomers to the council. If we can remove them before they can act, we have a chance to weaken their position." Bryce whistled softly, glancing at Jason, who gave him a sharp nod.

"Jason, you need to coordinate with those you trust in the Stoneford council and remove those from power whom you think are the instigators. They can argue the toss once you have them out of position. And this smuggling business..." Jerrol rubbed his nose. "I smelt trealt at Deepwater. If drugs are playing a part in this, we need to cut their supply. Can you try and disrupt the operation permanently?"

Jason chuckled, his eyes bright. "I'm sure we can find a way."

"Birlerion and I will go up to Velmouth; speak to the council, track down Torsion, check out the towers and the borders if possible. Dependent on what we find we'll either head over to Terolia or return here. No matter what, if urgent send a messenger, but within the month, we all need to have reported back to Jason. Then we need to figure out how we win the Watches back!"

Jerrol stopped speaking and looked around the room expectantly. He was greeted by a slightly stunned silence, as they all digested his instructions.

Birlerion spoke up hesitantly. "If there is a deliberate

attempt to keep you from the King, shouldn't you make every effort to reach him?"

"We need proof. Evidence that will prove to the Inquisitors that Kharel and the chancellor are trying to overthrow the king. Otherwise, as soon as I step into the palace, they will execute the warrant and me! They won't have a choice."

"Who else are you taking with you, Jerrol?" Jennery asked. "No offence, Birlerion, but you are only one person."

Jerrol laughed as Birlerion spluttered in protest. "The Lady's guards are not to be underestimated. You'd be surprised how much damage one Sentinal can do. And if there were two, then I would suggest that the Lady meant business."

22

STONEFORD KEEP, STONEFORD WATCH

As Jerrol expected, Birlerion cornered him after the meeting and asked him to awake the Stoneford sentinals. They walked down the winding track to the grove of sentinal trees, Birlerion quietly excited.

The tension flowed out of Jerrol as soon as he entered the grove, the tall sentinals rising above him. He rested a hand on the sentinal's trunk and the leaves above him rustled in welcome. He leaned in to embrace the tree and closed his eyes. He breathed in the invigorating green scent, and as he did so, he became aware of a sense of expectancy.

"Well, wake them up then," Taelia said from behind him. Jerrol spun in shock. "What?"

"They've slept long enough. Birlerion is quite right."

"Tali! What are you doing here?"

Taelia rolled her eyes. "Waiting for you to wake them up."

"I don't know how." Jerrol turned back to the tree.

"Yes, you do. Use the Lady; she's rooted as deep in you as she is Birlerion. She'll help you. She'll always help you, Jerrol, if you ask."

Jerrol laid his palm on the trunk and closed his eyes, reaching for the Lady as the bark warmed under his hand. He opened his eyes and found himself standing opposite a giant of a man; he was well over six foot, black-haired, broad-chested. His high-collared jacket and matching trousers glistened in the silver-green light. He wore a broad sword strapped across his back, the hilt protruding above his head. "Captain, is it time?" The man's silver eyes were bright.

"Time?" Jerrol repeated, hearing the echo of another man asking the same question.

"Time to wake," the man replied with a grin. "We have waited long for this day. We are ready."

Jerrol stared at him; deep down, he knew this man. He knew his name. "Chryllion, yes. I believe it is time."

Chryllion instinctively looked up. "The Veil weakens. You need to seal it soon, or they will breach it."

"I'm supposed to repair it?" Jerrol's stomach dropped.

"You are the Captain."

"I wasn't aware I could. It all happened so long ago that we've lost all knowledge in myth and legends."

"How long ago?" The tall Sentinal stilled, waiting.

Jerrol gulped. It didn't get easier with practice. "Umm, the year is 4124."

Chryllion gasped. "It can't be." His voice shook.

"I'm sorry, but it's been three thousand years since the Lady destroyed the Bloodstone."

"Still, the Veil needs patching."

"I don't know how." Jerrol ran his hand through his hair.

Chryllion gave a brittle laugh. "Of course you do."

"Could you go and patch it?" Jerrol asked hopefully, not sure he understood the Sentinal's words.

"If you command me so, but I will be noticed. Saerille would be better; she has a lighter touch."

Jerrol spun as a woman stepped up behind him. She was tall and slender with long brown hair tied back off her face in a knot at her neck. Her silver eyes, uncannily like Chryllion's and, Jerrol suspected, those of all Sentinals, glared at Chryllion before flickering over Jerrol. "What are you volunteering me for? I never volunteer." Her voice was light and teasing, but her eyes drilled into Jerrol's. Her hand rested on the pommel of the sword that hung at her waist.

"We were discussing patching the Veil," Jerrol said.

Immediately she tilted her head. Jerrol followed her gaze, but all he could see was a swirling mist above them. He looked back down and found her watching him. "Could you patch it?"

"It would only be temporary. The Captain would have to go and seal it." A third voice joined the conversation.

"But could you patch it unnoticed?" Jerrol asked.

Her lips twitched. "Is that a wager I hear? What is my reward if I do?"

"If you're lucky you live." The man walking forward had dark red hair and an expressive face. He was grinning at Saerille, his cheeks all dimples and his silver eyes sparkling.

Saerille scowled over her shoulder. "And you can promise that, Tagerillion? I think that is the Captain's promise to speak. Can you offer that? That I get to live?" She turned back to face Jerrol.

Jerrol froze as he watched Tagerillion; no wonder Birlerion had been excited. Birlerion's brother did not look like him at all, though his resemblance to Versillion was uncanny. Jerrol stared at the Sentinals before him, tall and strong and very intense. He swallowed as he considered all three Sentinals. "I think that is not something I would offer you, Saerille." He spoke slowly, catching the tightening around her eyes and the growing frowns on the men's faces.

"It would be something that I offered to all Sentinals; as your Captain, I look to you all, not just one."

"Well said." Tagerillion slapped him on the shoulder, a grin spreading over his face. "Well said!"

Jerrol relaxed. "Someone is waiting to see you."

Tagerillion looked over his shoulder, and his face lit up. "Birler," he gasped, and he rushed past Jerrol.

They shimmered into the grove where Tagerillion was hugging Birlerion.

"Let the lad breathe," Chryllion said, his voice gruff as he watched their reunion.

Tagerillion released his brother, his face wreathed in smiles. "This is my brother Birler, known as Birlerion." His face darkened. "Birlerion, what happened? We couldn't find you."

"It was chaotic, Tage; you couldn't have found anyone." Birlerion rubbed a shaky hand over his face. "The Lady called," he said.

"And she calls again now," Jerrol said gently, watching the young Sentinal struggling to regain his composure. And he was young; having the older Sentinals beside him accentuated his youth, a fact disguised by his usual air of assurance and self-reliance. Jerrol glanced around the grove, but he couldn't see Taelia anywhere.

"She left," Birlerion said. "She said she couldn't stay."

Jerrol grimaced. "I have no idea how she's doing it. She keeps turning up when I least expect it."

"The Lady sees," Birlerion replied with an enigmatic shrug.

"Doesn't matter," Jerrol said as he noticed the Sentinals watching them. Jerrol gave them a summary of the situation in Stoneford. "I know it's a shock, but anything you can tell me about the Ascendants would be a help. It seems they have returned."

"They can't have, the Lady took them with her," Tagerill said immediately.

"She was supposed to have taken you with her, but you're still here, sort of," Jerrol pointed out.

Tagerill grinned; he was irrepressible. "There's no sort of about it, we are here. Who else is around?"

"Only you three and Birlerion. Though I know Versillion still sleeps in Greens," Jerrol admitted, watching them. They seemed to be accepting the situation very easily. He wondered if they understood what it meant.

Tagerillion turned to Birlerion. "You've seen Versillion, is he alright? What about Marianille?"

"Versillion is still asleep, but at least we know where he is. Marianille is still missing; she isn't in Vespers. There are no other Sentinals in Vespers."

"And Serillion?"

"He still sleeps at the Grove in Greens."

Tagerill released his breath. "Well, that is good news, at least."

Chryllion spoke up, his face grave. "How can we help, Captain?"

Jerrol rubbed his face and stared at them, a pulse beating rapidly under his eye. "Saerille, I need you to patch the Veil as best as you can until I can get back up there. Do not be seen and do not get caught."

"Yes, sir," she replied.

"Chryllion, I need you to stay here and reinforce Lord Jason at Stoneford Keep. You will be responsible for maintaining the keep and the grove until Saerille returns. When you return, Saerille, you help Chryllion and Lord Jason as needed."

Saerille grinned as Chryllion nodded assent and adjusted his broad sword.

"What about me?" Tagerillion waited expectantly, a grin on his face.

"You," Jerrol said, relaxing, inordinately comfortable in his company, "will come with Birlerion and me. I need backup, and you are it." He poked Tagerillion in the chest. "I have a price on my head, and I am fed up with assassins trying to collect it! I need to return to the king and report, and you are going to make sure I get there."

Tagerillion immediately stood to attention and struck his chest, serious for the first time since he had appeared. "As you command, Captain." Then he paused. "King?"

"King Benedict of Vespiri," Jerrol said. He took stock of the Sentinals standing before him in their archaic uniforms, tall and mysterious, and if the legends were right, from a different time when gods walked the land. "Umm, I'm not sure how to tell you this, but the Lady is no longer here. She vanished when she sundered the Bloodstone, taking you, or so we thought, and the Ascendants with her."

"That's not possible." Tagerillion took a step back.

"I'm afraid it is. This is the year 4124."

Chryllion spoke up. "You said the Lady took us all with her?"

"That's been the legend for over three thousand years. When the Lady destroyed the Bloodstone all her Sentinals disappeared, and trees like these," he gestured at the graceful sentinals, "appeared overnight across Remargaren."

"You say the Lady is not here and yet you are her Captain," Saerille said.

"Where is Guerlaire?" Chryllion asked suddenly.

Jerrol shrugged. "I am sorry, but I don't know. The Lady said I needed to find the forgotten and I believe that is you. Your names have been lost in centuries of history."

Tagerillion looked at him, his face pale. "Where are the

others? You said there were other trees? How many are there?"

Jerrol considered for a moment. "Maybe ten or twelve in Vespiri."

"Ten!" Tagerillion was aghast.

"How many should there be?" Jerrol wasn't sure he wanted to know.

"There should be over a hundred," Tagerillion said, looking horrified. His face paled even further. "Our families," he whispered, the blood draining from his cheeks as he realised they would be long dead and buried as well. Forgotten much as they had been.

"I am so sorry," Jerrol said, knowing it was not enough.

"It is not your fault." Chryllion's voice was deep and slow. "The Lady has called, we answer."

"But, Chryllion ..." Tagerillion screwed his face up in anguish.

Chryllion gripped his shoulder. "We serve the Lady, to protect her people. She has called. The Captain needs us."

Tagerillion struggled for a moment, and then he bowed his head. "The Lady calls," he said. When he raised his head, there was a sheen of tears in his eyes. "As you command, Captain," he said, an audible tremor in his voice. Birlerion wrapped an arm around his shoulders.

Jerrol took a deep breath, steadying his nerves. "To work then. Let me introduce you to Lord Jason of Stoneford Watch."

"He's a good man, visits often." Chryllion's deep voice was soothing.

"Ah, but he hasn't met you yet." Jerrol couldn't wait to see Jason's face as he led them down the road towards the keep. The Sentinals kept shoving each other as they pointed out new landmarks and changes in the surroundings. Birlerion and Tagerillion continued a low-voiced conversation, Birlerion no doubt explaining all that he knew. Jerrol led the way through the keep to Jason's office. Fortunately, the sentries recognised Jerrol and waved them through.

"It is much changed." Chryllion spoke from behind Jerrol.

"Even inside? I thought this was all still the original building." Jerrol knocked on Jason's door.

"No, I don't recognise any of this," Chryllion said as he ducked his head and followed Jerrol through the door and into the study. Jason was seated behind his desk, talking with Jennery and Alyssa.

"Lord Jason," Jerrol began, startling Jason with his formality until he saw the three people standing behind Jerrol. "May I present Chryllion, Saerille and Tagerillion, lately the Stoneford Sentinals. Saerille, Chryllion and Tagerillion, may I present Lord Jason of Stoneford, Lady Alyssa of Greenswatch and Lieutenant Jennery of the Lady's Guard." Jerrol stood back and observed their faces. He couldn't help smiling broadly at Jason's bemused expression. Jason glanced from the Sentinals to Jerrol.

"You can't just leave that hanging out there," Jason rapped, glaring at Jerrol. "Explain!"

"My Lord Guardian," Chryllion spoke, "it is an honour to meet you finally. My colleagues and I have enjoyed your visits. We look forward to working with you to rid Stoneford of this Ascendant curse."

Jason gasped. "You woke the Sentinals?"

"These are the original Sentinal guards, confined to their sentinal trees until the Captain returned." A smile flitted over Jerrol's face as Jason struggled with his words. Alyssa and Jennery exchanged amused glances.

Jerrol poured some wine. "Here." He handed one to Jason and, offering the Sentinals a glass, he took a gulp himself. "Sit, and we'll explain."

Jason sat and numbly drank his wine.

"Remember when I told you about the fire at the Grove in Greenswatch? And the loss of the Guardian."

"You haven't told me about any fire at the Grove,'"Jason replied.

"I must have done," Jerrol said, trying to remember.

"If you'd stop flitting around the country for five minutes, you might remember to tell me what you've been up to, but ..." Jason spread his hands.

Jerrol launched into a recap of events at the Grove and Deepwater.

Chryllion's low voice interrupted him. "You mean to say we've lost two Watch Guardians? Greenswatch and Deepwater?"

Tagerillion stirred his face pale. "Greens has lost its Guardian?"

"Yes, the Greenswatch Guardianship currently resides in Lady Alyssa, but I fear the other is lost. Both the heirs have strayed from the Lady's path."

"Your name is Tagerillion? Tagerill?" Alyssa said hesitantly, her diminutive form dwarfed by the Sentinals. "Your father was Lord Warren Descelles of Greens, wasn't he?"

"Yes, he was the first lord, appointed when the Lady created the Watches."

Alyssa held out her hand. "Then we are cousins, many times removed, but family all the same."

Tagerillion's face lit up, and he engulfed her in a hug, the thrill of the Guardianship flowing between them.

Saerille spoke over them, concern in her voice. "If what you say is true, I had better leave straight away. I need to see what is possible. It may be, Captain, that you will have repair the Veil after all."

"We'll worry about that when we have to. What do you

need?" Jerrol hoped it wouldn't come to that. He had no idea where to start.

"A horse and a map. I have all else," Saerille said, ready to leave.

Jason gave the orders and glanced at the excited Alyssa and Tagerillion. Tagerillion dragged Birlerion forward, and Jason shook his head before turning back to Jerrol. "What are you talking about? What's this about a Veil? When were you going to tell me about all this?" he said, his voice rising with exasperation.

"I'm sorry, Jason, I thought I had. Anyway, Ari will prove it one way or the other." Jerrol muttered a command, and there was a ripple in the air as the Arifel popped into view.

Chryllion's face lightened. "An Arifel, what a splendid fellow."

"This is Ari. Ari, I'd like to introduce Lord Jason, Guardian of Stoneford, and his Sentinals Chryllion, Saerille and Tagerillion."

Jason launched himself out of his seat. "What?" As Ari joyfully fluttered above their heads, a second Arifel appeared, and Lin chittered as she landed on Birlerion's shoulder. Alyssa reached out to stroke her white chest.

"He can see them. He's a Guardian!" Tagerillion said with a smirk, regaining some of his former bounce as he interrupted his discussion with Alyssa.

Jerrol called the excited Arifel down to him, attempting to calm him down. "This is an Arifel, and only Guardians can see him, so," Jerrol shrugged, "you must be a Guardian. Now if I have it right, Ari and Lin can speak to us, and we can use them to pass messages back and forth?"

"Indeed," Chryllion rumbled, "when they pay attention, they are a very efficient method of communication, but they tend to have short attention spans." He glared critically at Ari, who cheeped happily in response.

"But you can all call them when needed, can't you?"

"Oh yes, they will respond eventually," Birlerion said as he stroked Lin. The Arifel perched on his hand, preening under all the attention, meeping happily in the presence of so many Guardians.

"Birlerion always had more luck than the rest of us, they seem to like him," Tagerill said, watching his brother.

"Right then, Saerille, make sure you report on what you find before you take any action. We do not want the Ascendants to discover you are abroad until we are ready. That is one advantage we can't afford to lose," Jerrol ordered.

Saerille nodded. "Yessir, I understand. I will be careful."

"No heroics, Saerille. In and out unseen, remember?" Chryllion said.

"Yes pops," she said, with a vivid smile at the older Sentinal. She saluted Jerrol and left the room on the heels of a page who had returned to say her horse was ready.

"Jerrol," Jason held his head in his hands, "what do you mean they are my Sentinals?"

"Well, I suppose they're mine, as I am their Captain and they are part of my Guard, but their allegiance lies with Stoneford. They protect Stoneford Watch. You are the Guardian; therefore, they look to you. Chryllion will remain here with you. Once Saerille has patched the Veil, she will return and help you and Chryllion as needed. Tagerillion is going to come with Birlerion and me and see what is going on at the Watch Towers."

"My friends call me Tagerill, Captain. I would be honoured if you would do the same," the red-haired Sentinal said with a grin.

"Shouldn't Tagerill come with me to Greenswatch?" Alyssa suggested doubtfully.

"Nay, my Lady, the Captain needs me," Tagerill said. "I'll return in good time. Greens is no longer mine, and I doubt I would recognise it. It belongs to Penner's descendants. I belong with the Captain."

Jerrol recognised the need to act, to be of use. He silently agreed with Tagerill. Greens would be a bittersweet return. His gaze paused on Birlerion, still cradling the little black and white Arifel. His face was soft as the Arifel rubbed against him.

What was it about him that caught your eye? For someone so reserved, people deferred to him without noticing. He had morphed from a cold-eyed killer to a man with a history, in a few short weeks. A man with strong emotions and an abiding love for the Lady, someone he knew would become a friend, given time. Even Jennery had gotten over his initial suspicions.

When had Birlerion become such a reassuring presence behind his shoulder? He seemed to have adapted so well compared to the newly awoken Sentinals. And yet there was still something elusive about him, something hidden. Jerrol wondered when Birlerion would finally relax enough to trust him.

23

VELMOUTH, STONEFORD WATCH

Jerrol watched Tagerill in concern as the Sentinal slowly crouched lower in his saddle as they travelled. He had tried to answer his questions, but the more places he pointed out, the more confused Tagerill's questions became. He became quieter and more withdrawn as the miles passed.

Once again, Jerrol appreciated how well Birlerion had adapted. He had to admit that he doubted he would have adjusted to his situation so well. Birlerion didn't seem nearly as displaced as Tagerill did, even though he admitted he knew none of the villages Jerrol was naming. The only time he had wobbled was when he had greeted Tagerill, which under the circumstances was only natural.

Ranks of mature trees lined the roads, opening into arable fields that stretched as far as the eye could see before closing in around them again. Roads led off to small villages and hamlets, through dark tunnels of trees that Jerrol named but meant nothing to the Sentinals.

Birlerion twisted his lips. "It's like being a stranger in a foreign land; now and then you recognise something, and you think you know where you are, but you don't really."

"I spent months posted here in Stoneford, yet I don't recognise any of it," Tagerill said.

"You will learn Vespiri again. Underneath it is still the same, it is still home," Jerrol said, trying to reassure them. "I will awaken more Sentinals, and we will find your friends."

"Not all of them," Tagerill replied, his voice low. "My sister was in Vespers with Birlerion. You say that was destroyed and has been rebuilt. Greens has lost her Guardian." He swallowed and continued. "My father was the first Guardian, that was the last time we were all together. Versill, Marian, Birler and I, we were all rangers before we became Sentinals. We all came home and celebrated the creation of the Watch with my parents and my eldest brother Penner."

"Versill is at Greens, and we have each other," Birlerion said, trying to reassure though his expression matched Tagerill's.

"As Alyssa said, you have family at Greens, maybe many times removed but they will still be your family, Tagerill. I think you will find yourself fortunate," Jerrol said.

Tagerill brightened a little. "At least there is still a Greens," he agreed. "And Versill is there. And Serillion."

"We will stop there on the way to Old Vespers after we find Torsion and discover what is going on up here. Tell me about Serillion, is he a friend of yours?" Jerrol asked.

Tagerill finally relaxed as he started to talk about his friend. The miles passed as he and Birlerion reminisced about their days at the academy. Jerrol shook his head at their antics and looked forward to meeting the Sentinal that meant so much to them both.

. . .

Velmouth perched in the foothills of the Stanton Peaks, a curling spine of snow-tipped mountains that curved around the town and split off to the north into Elothia. The air was crisp and clean and so clear that the vibrant blue sky and the surrounding pine trees popped. The resinous scent of pine permeated the air.

The conical roofs of the grey stone Watch Towers peeped above the ranks of deep green pine trees, wreathed in mist. The Watch Towers were at least another day's ride from Velmouth.

Tagerill took a deep breath. "The Watch Towers seem to be untouched, though I do not remember a town here," he said, gazing about him.

"We have grown. Remargaren is more highly populated now, and new towns are springing up everywhere. Keeps the scholars busy updating the maps."

"There are maps of all Remargaren?" Tagerill's voice rose in surprise. "Guerlaire spent much of his time exploring new lands."

"Oh yes, from the icy wastes of Elothia to the Island archipelago of Birtoli."

"Islands?" Tagerillion twisted in his saddle. "Is Birtoli no longer connected to the mainland?" He looked around as if he would be able to see it.

Jerrol grinned. "I'll take you down to the coast at Mortelin, you can see the main islands of Aguinti and Molinti from there."

Tagerill sank back in shock. "Islands?" he muttered to himself.

They approached the outskirts of Velmouth as wooden houses with small picket-fenced gardens lined the road. The town sprawled at the foot of the mountains and tracks led off in all directions, lined with houses. The main road opened into a central square with empty stalls lining the edges. A small temple stood proudly to the north of the square, its white dome gleaming in the bright sunshine. They rode past busy cafes and taverns towards the hostelry and the adjoining inn.

"Birlerion, go and get the rooms. Tagerill and I will see to the horses. Let's get settled. Then we'll split up and search for Torsion."

Birlerion dismounted, tugged his saddlebags off and walked up the steps into the inn. Jerrol and Tagerill continued into the barn next door. The fresh smell of sawdust and straw blended with the aroma of leatherwork and the musty odour of horses. A small, wizened man came out of the tack room as he heard their voices.

The man gave a sharp whistle, and a young lad scampered in to take one of the horses. "Them over there are empty, pay at the inn with your rooms." Jerrol followed the lad as directed and suddenly turned back. "We're hoping to meet a friend here, Scholar Torsion, do you know him?" The man stared at him and then he shook his head before shuffling back into the tack room, uninterested.

"Where do you think Scholar Torsion will be?" Tagerill asked as he led his horse into a stall.

Jerrol considered Tagerill's question as he followed with Zin'talia. "Well, he is a sometime councillor up here, so I suggest we start at the council building. If not we can check at the temple and the local taverns, though he may be up at the Watch Towers. He has always been fascinated by the Watchers. He will be so excited to meet you. Be warned, he will interrogate you until he knows everything you know."

Tagerill gave a small chuckle. "I'm not sure I'll be much help there. The Lady set the Watchers their task. We merely guarded them."

Jerrol unstrapped Zin'talia's saddle and pulled it off. He slung it over the bar and leaned against the railing. "It concerns me how much was lost. Over time the legends evolved in the telling, the messages lost or diluted. When the Lady did whatever she did in the end, the destruction must have been total. She used all the magic left in the world and took the knowledge of it with her." Jerrol watched Tagerill. "We know so little, and nothing about Sentinals."

Tagerill finished unsaddling his horse and turned back to Jerrol. "The Lady created us about two years before she sundered the Bloodstone not that we realised that was going to be her intent. We were scattered across Remaragen, trying to block the Ascendants'plans and protect the people." Tagerill began to brush the worst of the dust off his horse. "The Ascendants grew out of the Administration; they got used to the taste of power. They were not satisfied with ruling on behalf of the Lady, they wanted it for themselves. That was why the Lady created the Watches. She devolved some of that power into the people themselves.

"The land provided for the people, the people worshipped the Lady, the Lady blessed the Guardians, and the Guardians protected all. I suppose it is to be expected that the regions devolved as they have; it would take much to replace the Lady." He grimaced. "The Ascendants were furious, so it doesn't surprise me their descendants are targeting the Watches today, trying to complete what the Ascendants failed to."

"And they genuinely used magic?"

"They liked to think so. The Ascendants became so focused on the belief that they were special, the pure bloodline that was born to rule, that they forgot that the Lady and her family created Remargaren. They had real power.

"The Ascendants discovered some of the latent power of the land and those clever enough harnessed it, through their minds or through other devices they created. But they couldn't control it properly, and they caused more damage than good. We spent all our time fixing the damage."

"So you have power as well?"

Tagerill chuckled. "The Lady has the power, and her sister Marguerite. They work through us. We are her tools. We do her bidding. We exist to protect the Lady and her people."

"These Ascendants have found a way to control people. They are controlling the councils, and they are turning on the Guardians." Jerrol stepped out of the stall, slinging his saddlebag over his shoulder as a young lad arrived with a haynet for Zin'talia. He cooed over the white mare, stroking her flanks. Jerrol grinned at the sight of another convert. "She likes Baliweed, if there is any to be found," he said, handing the lad a coin. The lad darted off.

Jerrol looked at Tagerill. "They are slowly destroying the King's power in the Watches. We need to find who is behind this. It is bigger than a power grab by Prince Kharel and the Chancellor; they are focused on the King and Vespers. This is more insidious, and it's here in the Watches, and the Lady is the target."

"We will find them, Captain. The Lady watches."

"As the line protects," Jerrol replied instinctively. "We'd better get on with it then," he said, leading the way out of the stable.

They found Birlerion stretched out on a bed in their room, dozing. Jerrol dumped his bag next to a bed, and Birlerion opened his eyes. "Come on. There are a few hours of light left, let's check if Torsion is here or if he's up at the towers. Birlerion, you go and check us in at the council office. Tagerill, you visit the temple and the square. I'll check the hostelries. We'll meet at the tavern in the east corner of the square."

They split up and began searching Velmouth.

Jerrol and Tagerill were first back to the tavern. They slid into a shadowy alcove, exchanging notes while they waited for Birlerion. "According to the smith, he came through about a month ago," Jerrol said as he sipped his ale.

"I didn't find any word of him. If he did stop here, he didn't stop long."

Jerrol tapped the table. "But in Stoneford they said he left three or four months ago, so where has he been?"

"Maybe he went straight up to the towers?" Tagerill suggested, watching the door. "Apparently, there is quite a pilgrimage to the towers lately. People travelling up there to be blessed by the Lady, or so the Father said. I'm not sure why the temple isn't good enough; she's more likely to be there than the towers."

Jerrol relaxed against the wall. "Did the Father say why?"

"No, he kinda clammed up when some petitioners came in, but I did overhear him telling them another trip would take place tomorrow and they could book a place on the wagon at the council office. For a fee no doubt," Tagerill said, with disgust. "It sounds like someone is trying to make some money on the side out of innocent people."

"The council?"

"It will be interesting to hear what Birlerion has to say," Tagerill murmured.

"Where is he? I didn't expect him to take this long." Jerrol shifted restlessly. "Maybe we ought to go find him."

Crossing town, they kept to the main streets and soon arrived at the darkened council office. There was no sign of Birlerion.

It was a two-storey building clad in wooden planks, with an outside staircase leading up to a door on the second floor. The front of the building had wooden steps leading up to a verandah which circled the ground floor. The verandah was bare; no furniture or plant pots adorned it like neighbouring buildings. The front door had a sign pinned to it announcing that the office was closed, which explained the darkness downstairs. A solitary light glowed in the upstairs room.

Jerrol carefully circled the building, checking for guards and alternative entrances, but the stairs were the only way up. The drainpipes looked to flimsy even for his paltry weight. He ghosted up the steps to listen at the door. He heard movement within, but no voices. He was debating about entering when the decision was taken out of his hands as the door opened. The tall, dark-haired man jerked back in surprise at the sight of Jerrol with his hand raised to knock on the door.

The man cursed and reached for his sword and Jerrol launched himself at him, giving the man no time to react. Tagerill followed up Jerrol's strike with a clip behind the ear from the haft of his dagger, and the man collapsed in a heap in the floor. Tagerill produced some cord and tied the man up.

"Who is he?" Tagerill patted the man down as Jerrol searched the room.

"A councillor, I assume, though from his reaction I would suggest we'll find he's one of these Ascendants." Jerrol stared at the man's thin face, committing it to memory; although he had never seen him before, his face reminded him of some-one. His left eye was purpling nicely; someone had hit him, and recently.

"Ascendants were nothing like him. They had power, magic, and they weren't afraid to use it."

"They have enough power," Jerrol said as he displayed five letters he found on the desk. "Look, the council is being suborned, the same as we found at the Grove. I bet they control everything in Velmouth. They are undermining the Watches, and no one noticed." He tucked the letters in his jacket.

As he sat at the desk pondering, he noticed a skewed rug which was snagged on a slightly raised floorboard. He crossed the room and knelt, levering the board up with his dagger. He felt around the hole. Encountering the corner of a box, he lifted it out. Inside was a copy of a pamphlet praising the rise of Var'geris and a small black notebook listing names and words. He suddenly wondered what Nikols had done with the one he had found in Old Vespers.

The man on the floor groaned. Jerrol pocketed the pamphlet and notebook, shoved the box back into the hole and replaced the floorboard and rug. He sauntered over to the window to check the road before hitching one hip on the desk. They had been here too long.

"That wasn't a very nice welcome, now was it?" Jerrol asked as he watched the man. "Do you always attack visitors as soon as they arrive? Where is my friend?"

The man stiffened. "You're too late," he spat.

"Oh, why?"

"He is lost. He won't be able to resist."

"Where did they take him?"

"Once Var'geris hears you attacked his disciples, you will suffer his wrath."

"Really? Where is this mighty Var'geris? I keep hearing about him, but there isn't much substance to him. Does he speak for himself?"

"Blasphemy!" The man struggled to release his hands, desperate to grab Jerrol. "Once Terolia is in his hands, Vespiri will be eager to submit to his rule."

"How do you intend to do that?"

"You'll see, we have the Captain now, he'll show us the way in," the man sneered, rolling over and trying to release his bonds, refusing to say more. He stiffened as Tagerill loomed over him.

"I doubt he will. I think you'll find he won't give you

what you want." Jerrol rose, collected the papers and glanced out the window. "I'm disappointed, Councillor Fortes, that you are not prepared to do your duty to your king and Lady. That is the purpose of the council, you know," he said as he crossed the room. "I think that it is time you retired and allowed someone more suitable to fill the role."

The man's eyes widened in fear. "You wouldn't dare," he spluttered.

"Oh, why ever not? You have no such qualms when you send out your men," Jerrol purred into his ear as Tagerill set to work.

24

STONEFORD KEEP, STONEFORD WATCH

Jason stood in the gate, watching the last of Bryce's men ride around the curve in the road and out of sight. He turned back towards the keep with Chryllion at his shoulder. The Sentinal was a constant shadow. Jason strode towards his office deep in thought, ruminating on what to do first. He had called his captains to his office. It was time to read them into his plans. He would miss Bryce; he was his right hand, but it would do the others good to step up.

He looked up, twisting as Chryllion shoved him from behind. He heard a high-pitched twang and Chryllion deflected a bolt which thudded harmlessly into the wall. Jason dived behind the nearest column before his assailant could reload, calling out to his guards. There was the sound of an altercation on the stairs, and he peered around the column, hefting his dagger ready to throw it if he had a line of sight.

He stood astounded as one of his garrison's unit leaders was hustled down the stairs between two of the on-duty guards, his face starting to redden from a well-landed punch.

"Danilesh, what is the meaning of this?" Jason was horrified.

Danilesh glowered at Jason before staring at the floor. A young private came forward with the crossbow. He was shaking his hand out. "M'lord, he was too busy reloading to check who was behind him," the young man said, handing over the crossbow, having just struck a senior officer.

The two guards on either side of Danilesh jerked his arms back painfully, forcing his head up. Jason took the crossbow, thinking fast. "Was he on his own?"

"As far as we could see, he didn't have a spotter," the young man replied.

"Private Mackie, isn't it?"

"Yessir." The young man stood to attention and saluted.

"Escort Mr Danilesh here to the cells and then join me in my office."

"Yessir!" He saluted again and gestured the men to precede him to the cells.

Jason took a deep breath, trying to control his rapidly beating heart. He stared at Chryllion.

"My apologies, my lord, there was no time to warn you."

Jason waved away his apology. "Thank goodness you were here," he said as they walked to his office, where his remaining captains were waiting for him. He threw the crossbow on his desk with a loud clatter. "Bramon, why was Danilesh trying to kill me?" he asked, his voice cold and harsh.

Captain Bramon stepped back at the ferocity in Jason's voice. "W-what?" He gaped at Jason.

"Danilesh, he is in your division, isn't he? Where is he from? Has his behaviour changed recently?"

"Lieutenant Danilesh is from Appletree, on the borders of East Watch. He's a solid officer, clean record, the men like him. I haven't noticed anything different in his behaviour. He is just back from leave. What happened?"

Jason pointed at the crossbow. "He tried to nail me with that. Now, why do you think he would do that?"

"I-I don't know, sir," Bramon stuttered. "There is no reason for him to target you."

"Well, he obviously thought there was, and we need to find out if there are any others like him," Jason snapped. "You need to be on the lookout for any change in behaviour. I need to know we can trust our men. I need to know I can trust you." Jason took a deep breath. "I called you in here today to bring you up to date. This," and he pointed at the crossbow, "makes it more imperative." He was interrupted by a tap at the door.

"Come," he said.

Private Mackie opened the door, saluted and shut the door behind him. "Lieutenant Danilesh is restrained in the East cell block, sir. I left two guards with him. Umm, I took the liberty of requesting two men from Captain Bramon's unit to man the walls, sir."

"Very good," Jason said. "Captain Bramon, *Corporal* Mackie here shows excellent initiative. I suggest you use him wisely."

"Yessir," Bramon replied.

"Right, sit, gentlemen, this is the situation." And Jason, after waiting for them all to settle, gave them a quick summary of recent events. "We can now see that even our garrison is being affected by whatever disease is spreading through the Watches. We are already spread thin, with the border patrols and increased garrison security; adding a campaign against the smuggling routes is going to extend us further. Suggestions, gentlemen?"

"Why don't we bring our plans for the Fourth Division forward? Drop the other divisions down to two units for now, before we can recruit. Now is probably not the time to bring new people in if we cannot be sure of their loyalty," suggested the second unit commander. "We can tighten the rotations, reduce the leave to garrison only. We are under war conditions in effect."

Bramon spoke up. "I suggest we interview every man who is back from leave; with the unit restructure we could say it's for reassignment, which will be true enough. We don't want all our experience in one division. And a rotation may not be a bad thing if we think there are some rotten apples."

"We should use the cadets, sir, add them to the garrison rotation, slot them into the units. It would be good experience." Mackie spoke hesitantly. As Jason nodded encouragingly, his voice firmed up and he continued. "And help bolster the numbers, which might mean we could keep an extra unit or two. There are duties that they could do, which would relieve some of the pressure on the other units, and most of them are gagging to move up, sir."

"Interesting idea. Go and fetch the drillmaster for me." Mackie left the room as Jason continued. "Recommendations for advancement should be on my desk by tomorrow. Bryce should be back before the end of the month; in the interim, his sergeant will act in his stead. Each of you set up the interviews, and by the end of the week, I want your suggestions for the divisions. I also want to create a floater unit under my command." Jason paused as he looked at Bramon. "In this floater unit I want men you absolutely trust, as we also have another task," and he went on to explain the need for investigating the council.

"But isn't that out of our jurisdiction?" Bramon asked. "I mean, that's the King's business, not the army's."

"The safety of the people in the Watches is our business, and these are unusual times. We know something is going on, and it is our responsibility to find out what, and to protect the King and his people against it. Right, you have your orders, get moving. Report back by the end of the week. Any concerns, raise them immediately, don't wait. Bramon, stay, we need to speak with Danilesh." He dismissed the others.

The drillmaster and Corporal Mackie caught up with them as they descended the stone steps to the cell block. The air was dank and still, the gloom alleviated by lanterns hanging at regular intervals along the corridor.

Two guards bracketed the barred door. The first guard saluted Jason before pulling the bolt back and opening the door. "He hasn't said a word, sir," he reported, standing back. Jason stepped forward, with the drillmaster looming behind him. A soft command and Mackie moved in front with a lantern which dispelled the darkness. Danilesh huddled on his cot, lost and bewildered; gone was the angry glowering attacker.

He lurched to his feet and stood to attention as soon as he saw Jason. He was slightly taller than Jason with broad shoulders and a trim figure. As Bramon said, he was a solid officer and completely reliable until now.

Jason stopped in front of him. "Report," he said.

"S-sir? I'm not sure why I am here. What happened?" Danilesh held his head, frowning. "I don't remember getting here, did I hit my head?" He glanced around the cell with unseeing eyes.

Jason observed him. "You tried to shoot me with a crossbow."

"Never," Danilesh responded. "I would never do such a thing. I would never betray my o-o-..." He coughed, trying to get the word out. He tried again. "My o-o... ugh," and he inhaled as he choked on the words. He began to panic as he struggled to breathe; his eyes rolled as he started hyperventilating. Jason rushed to hold him down as he collapsed on the floor.

"Get Tyrone, quick," Jason ordered over his shoulder.

Mackie handed the lantern off to the drillmaster and ran for the infirmary. The drillmaster knelt next to Jason. "What's going on here, Jason?" he asked, staring at Danilesh as the shudders eased and his body relaxed.

"I don't know, let's get him off the floor." Between them, they lifted the unconscious man onto the bed. Jason gave the drillmaster a quick recap of the morning's events. He had just finished when Tyrone appeared in the doorway.

"Tyrone, I'm glad you're here."

Tyrone moved over to the bed. "Mackie here filled me in. Danilesh had no memory of the event at all?"

"That's what he said. And when he was trying to say such an action would be against his oath, he seized right up, couldn't get the word out. It was strange, Tyrone, I've never seen anything like it, it was if his body was preventing him from saying the words. He started to spasm almost immediately."?

Tyrone checked Danilesh's pulse and eyes. "Let's get him back to the infirmary, and I can investigate further. Once he's conscious, I'll let you know, and you can question him again while I'm observing him. I would recommend we keep him under guard for his safety."

Jason stared at the now peaceful Danilesh. "You think he is a risk to himself?"

"Let's take the precaution. I don't like where this is heading." Tyrone called in his helpers, and they lifted Danilesh onto a stretcher before leading the way out of the cell. Jason ordered the guards to accompany him and dismissed Mackie back to his duties. He walked with the drillmaster. "It was suggested this morning that most of your cadets are ready to step up into the units. At least in supporting roles."

"Depends what you have in mind," the drillmaster rumbled. He was a big man with a barrel chest and a deep voice which could be heard across the training field when he wanted it to be.

"There is a disease spreading through the Watches. Unfortunately, we are infected too, though to what extent I don't yet know. I need to know who we can trust. We are stretched thin with all the problems we are facing. I need to defend the garrison, stop the smuggling trade, patrol the borders and clean up the Watches. If I drop the divisions down to two units, we could create a fourth division. You know we've been talking about it, but we haven't had the men. The question is, how ready are your lads? We would be fast-tracking them, but it might do them good, and buck up the other men."

The master nodded slowly. "As long as you don't rely on them in the front line of a pitched battle, I think they will manage fine. I have thirty lads in their final year. It would only be another nine months before we graduated them. I intended day placing them soon."

"Work with my unit commanders on the best placements. They will provide their recommendations by the end of the week. The earlier, the better to be honest," Jason said as he eased his shoulders. He slowly walked back to his office, suddenly drained.

Tyrone called Jason back to the infirmary that evening. He was waiting for Jason in the outer room, his face grave. "I'm not going to tell you what I think happened. You can question him and see where it goes. I'll be watching his reactions, and I'll be ready if necessary."

Ready for what? Jason thought to himself, but he followed Tyrone into the smaller back room.

Danilesh was sitting up in bed. A guard stood in the

corner of the room with a strange expression on his face, a combination of fascination and sympathy.

Jason stood over him, waiting, while Tyrone drew up a chair and sat, making himself comfortable.

"How are you feeling?" Jason asked.

"Much better, sir. I am sorry, I don't remember what happened. Master Tyrone was telling me I collapsed, but I don't remember."

"Don't worry about it. I am sure it'll come back later," Jason reassured him. "How was your leave? You went to visit your parents, didn't you, in Appletree?"

"Yes," Danilesh said, a frown creasing his face. "Yes, I did. My brother was home on leave too. He is in the King's Fourth Cohort over on the borders with Terolia. My mother was ecstatic having us both home. It doesn't happen very often."

"Terolia, eh? Does he like it? What did your brother say about it?"

"Oh, the usual, soldiers always complain, sir." He made a face. "He was eager to go back. He made quite a few friends over there."

"Did he talk about any friends in particular?"

"I don't know. He might have. I can't remember." Danilesh massaged his temple.

"Was Captain Haven mentioned at all?"

Danilesh reacted as if he had been punched in the chest, gasping for breath as his heart rate spiked. Tyrone leaned forward. "It's alright, Dani," he said. "Deep breaths, that's right, you can control it."

Jason waited patiently as Danilesh got his breathing back under control. Tyrone sat back, and Jason continued.

"I was reading an interesting book yesterday. It was explaining the origin of the Guardians." Jason paused as Danilesh lurched out of his bed, hands reaching for him. His sheets tangled his legs, and he fell, the spasms prostrating him, and Tyrone had a draught ready to pour down his throat around the piece of wood he had shoved in his mouth.

Jason watched Danilesh as the tremors smoothed out and left the young man exhausted.

"One last thing, Dani, say the Lady's Oath," Jason said, watching the immediate subdued reaction, the drug taking the edge off the severity, but there all the same.

"Someone has planted a reaction to keywords in his head," Tyrone muttered, standing up as his helpers returned Danilesh to the bed. "A bit clumsily, as it doesn't matter the context, merely the word."

Jason looked down at semi-conscious Danilesh. "And I am assuming he is a knife at my throat?"

"I'm not sure. It depends if the imperative was for one attempt or to continue until he killed you or died himself. Without knowing the keyword, we'll never know."

"Is there any way of reversing it?"

Tyrone shook his head as he gently covered Danilesh with a blanket. "Without the keyword, it is impossible."

"Who would do such a thing?" Jason demanded — and worst of all, how was he supposed to prevent it from happening to others? Lady help us, he thought desperately; they had no protection against such a threat.

Tyrone straightened up. "One thing, though, you have an easy check for all your men. Get them to recite the Lady's Oath every morning. You'll soon know if someone has been affected."

25

WATCH TOWERS, STONEFORD WATCH

Jerrol worried they had delayed too long explaining the situation to the only councillor in Velmouth not in receipt of one of Fortes' letters. Councillor Sellins had not believed them, to begin with, and had been horrified when he did. They left him rounding up his wayward councillors and threatening Fortes with whatever foul punishments he could think up.

They travelled as fast as they could to Tower Hamlets, skirting the lake which took up most of the plateau and climbing up through the trees to the towers. Birlerion had been in their hands all night. Jerrol prayed he was still alive.

"Where do you think Saerille will be?" Jerrol asked as he dismounted and handed the reins to Tagerill. He stared up at the dark stone towers as Tagerill led their horses into a copse of trees out of sight. The grey dawn attempted to peep through the brooding, black clouds. The air was dense and moist with promised rain. Skirting the walls, he searched for a way in as Zin'talia complained about being left outside to get wet. Sometimes a Darian was more trouble than she was worth.

"I would recommend we don't contact her. She will stay hidden. She will come to us when she needs us," Tagerill said as he followed Jerrol. There was no way in and in the end Tagerill boosted Jerrol up on the wall at the rear as the gate was solidly locked.

Jerrol hovered on top of the wall searching the interior. The cobbled courtyard appeared empty. The buildings were in darkness, and he couldn't see any sentries on duty. He climbed down into the yard. From what Jerrol knew the towers were the home of fifteen Veil Watchers, old men now, who stared at the heavens searching for answers to age-old questions.

Scholars used to visit as part of their journeyman year, but as time passed and no answers were shared the reasons for visiting faded, and fewer came. He wondered why Torsion continued to visit. He also wondered if there were any answers which never made it out of the towers.

Jerrol crossed the courtyard and silently eased the gate open enough for Tagerill to slip inside before closing it behind him. They froze beside a parked wagon as two guards exited a tower and crossed the courtyard, oblivious to the two standing in front of the gate. The guards' voices travelled clearly. "Well, he was a bit of fighter. It will take a while before he cracks, but they always do in the end."

"If only he knew the keywords, eh? I'm sure he'd like to switch it off. To be at the mercy of someone else for the rest of your life, euch!" the other guard responded.

Jerrol exhaled as the guards entered the building opposite. "Keywords?" he murmured, fingering the black notebook in his pocket.

Tagerill entered the tower through the open archway. A wooden door made of heavy oak with iron fittings stood open. The deep grey stone walls were thick and smooth. A wide hallway opened before them with a spiral staircase dominating the centre and rising through the tower and curling down into velvety darkness beneath their feet. As they climbed, blind corridors and dead ends spun off at each level. Jerrol caught Tagerill's sleeve and pulled him down a dimly lit corridor. The air was musty and dry.

Lifting a lantern off the wall, Jerrol entered one of the end rooms. He stopped abruptly at the sight of what looked like a corpse. An ancient man dressed in an out-of-date, black velvet suit lay in a reclining chair staring up at the ceiling. His skin was creased and wrinkled like old parchment.

Jerrol felt the man's neck and the soft beat pulsed slowly beneath his fingers, though the man never stirred at his touch. He glanced around the empty room. Thick red curtains covered the windows and blocked out the light. The suffocating darkness was lifted only by the glow from the lantern.

He jumped when a muttering began behind him. Tagerill entered the room and shut the door.

"One hundred twenty-four degrees East, 31 degrees on the meridian. Veil thinning needs a patch... 125 degrees East, 31 degrees on the meridian. Veil thinning needs a patch..." The scratchy voice continued muttering a succession of numbers as Jerrol looked around the room in concern. There was nowhere to hide if anyone came.

"Boy, I know you're there," the voice growled. "Are you taking this down? We need to do a patch, the Veil is thinning."

"Yessir," Jerrol said, his voice echoing in the empty chamber, "only I don't know how to do a patch."

"Yes you do. I can feel your power. Leyandrii sent you, didn't she? Come here where I can see you," the man instructed.

Jerrol walked around in front of the Watcher. He met the man's luminous eyes as he inspected Jerrol. "They get younger every day," he complained to himself. "Don't just stand there. Write down these numbers," he said, indicating a notebook lying on his lap.

Jerrol reached for the pad. "Sir, I'm not supposed to be here. If the people running this place find me, they will harm me."

"Rubbish, you honour the Lady, no one will harm you. Come, you must patch the Veil."

"I'm sorry, sir, I don't how."

"Are you stupid, boy? What is the Lady thinking of?" the Watcher muttered.

"Times have changed, sir, the people here do not revere the Lady. I'm not sure who they do follow, to be honest."

"Really? That can't be true." The man stared at Jerrol, his eyes glowing. Jerrol flinched at the touch of such an ancient mind, though held firm as the man rifled through his recent memories, leaving an impression of distance and time passing. "No one has been collating the coordinates for centuries? For that long? Has it been that long?"

"Um, can you check if your previous coordinates have been repaired? I think they may have been using them to target the collapse, not repair it."

"Where are my acolytes, my students? Have I been asleep for so long?" The man tried to move, but his body had atrophied. "Has it been so long?" His voice faded, and he closed his eyes, falling silent again.

Jerrol hesitated, pad in hand, but it appeared that the man had returned to his former state. He glanced down at the pad, which was half full of notations. He pocketed it, not knowing where else to hide it, and cautiously backed out of the room. He needed to find Birlerion and report back. There was much more going on than they realised.

Jerrol retreated, closely followed by Tagerill, and they descended the stairs, pausing at the foot of the adjacent tower as the sound of chanting drifted on the air. Someone was either up very early or very late.

Jerrol stepped through the doorway and peered up the stairs. He heard a cold voice which sent shivers down his spine. It was edged with spite and hatred and led the chant being repeated over and over:

"Justice, inheritance, for all to see.
   Bound to these words forever be.
   Support my cause,
   Perform my will,
   Blessed be your service to me."

The words dripped like acid into his mind, and Tagerill cursed under his breath. "They are using *Mentiserium*. It is a mind-control technique."

"Never heard of it," Jerrol replied as they climbed the stairs.

"Hold the Lady in your mind, she will protect you," Tagerill said as he paused outside the door.

Jerrol brought the image of the Lady to the forefront of his mind and relaxed as the pressure building in his head lessened; he listened intently as the chant died away.

"There, that wasn't so bad, was it? Now, tell me your name."

"Birler of Greens." Birlerion's voice slurred.

"Where is the Captain?"

"Not here."

"But you know where? Tell me, you can tell me. I won't tell anyone else," the voice persuaded. There was silence.

"Tear the Veil. You know you want to; you need to. Reach for the veil. It's calling you, Birler of Greens."

There was the sound of a fist hitting flesh and Birlerion's groan broke the silence. Tagerill's face went flat.

"This is taking too long. He should have been under by now," a smooth voice interrupted.

"We will continue until we break him; he can't hold out forever. You can't stay here, Var'geris; you don't have the time. Leave him to me. I'll get it out of him."

"He has silver eyes. Only the Lady's Guard has silver eyes," Var'geris said. "There has to be a Captain to wake the guards; either it's him, or he knows where he is. Make sure you find him, Ain'uncer, we must have the Captain."

"Don't worry. I will. Guard him. I'll be back in shortly," Ain'uncer said as the door opened and two tall, dark-haired men left the room.

"A Captain after all these years. It is a sign that our time is nigh. Well, well, a treasure indeed." The man was gloating.

Jerrol and Tagerill shrank back into the darkness. The men strode down the stairs, black robes flaring. They didn't even glance towards the alcove where Jerrol and Tagerill were hiding.

Tagerill waited until the men exited the tower and then barrelled into the room. He took in the two guards beating up his brother, and he struck, fear driving his arm. Jerrol hovered over Birlerion. He lay restrained in one of the reclining chairs, and he stared glassily at the ceiling. His shirt was ripped and spattered with blood, his jacket lost.

"Birlerion." Jerrol gently touched his shoulder. Birlerion groaned and instinctively strained against the leather straps. Jerrol began unbuckling them.

"Birlerion, it's Tage." Tagerill hissed at the sight of his battered face and carefully helped him to sit up, an arm around his shoulders supporting him. Birlerion leaned against him, his body trembling. Jerrol passed a jug of water, and Tagerill trickled it into Birlerion's mouth. Birlerion gagged, and most of it dribbled back out again and down his neck, mixing with his blood.

Birlerion coughed. "They are after the Captain. They want to shred the Veil." His chest wheezed. "We need to leave. They are using *Mentiserium*." He paused to cough again and spat out blood, wincing as his chest grabbed. "They are very good at it."

"Not good enough, fortunately," Tagerill murmured.

"Tagerill, what is *Mentiserium*?" Jerrol asked, gazing at Birlerion in concern. From the amount of blood down his shirt, it looked as if his nose might be broken; both his eyes were blackened and swollen, and his lip split and puffy.

"It's a mind spell. Controls people's actions, forces them to tell the truth. Once enspelled, keywords control their actions. In theory, saying the word wakes them up, then saying it a second time is the reset. It should negate whatever suggestion they planted and allow you to replace it with another. Though that was then; whether it's the same now, who knows," Tagerill replied, his face grave. "The difficulty is being able to tell if a suggestion has been planted."

"How would we know?"

"There are no obvious signs that a person has been enspelled. The only protection is to call on the Lady." Tagerill checked out of the tower. "We need to move. It's starting to get light."

Jerrol froze. "Then how do we know Birlerion isn't enspelled?"

"He's not," Tagerill said. "There's no way."

"But how do you know? You said there was no sign."

"I'm not," Birlerion said, holding his chest. "I hold the Lady close."

Jerrol frowned at him, concerned.

"We need to leave," Tagerill said.

"I'm not sure Birlerion is quite ready to move." Jerrol folded a damp pad and dabbed it against his bloody face.

"I'm fine," Birlerion said, flinching away. He stood with their assistance, swaying unsteadily as he peered at Tagerill through swollen eyes. "What took you so long?"

"We admired the scenery on the way," Tagerill said.

"We should have gone with you. I am sorry, Birlerion." Jerrol gripped his shoulder.

Birlerion shrugged and then winced. "You couldn't have known. Can we leave now?"

"We haven't found Torsion yet. Do you remember if they mentioned him?"

"No idea," Birlerion said, squinting at the slumped bodies of the guards. "What happened to them?"

"Tagerill," Jerrol said with a slight laugh. "Come on, let's get out of here."

Voices rose across the courtyard, loud in the stillness of the early morning. Jerrol drifted down the stone stairs, and Tagerill supported Birlerion as they reached the ground floor.

"We can't leave yet, looks like the guards are changing over." Jerrol peered down the stairs as they spiralled onwards into velvety darkness. "Maybe we should wait down below, just in case they check up here."

The stairs curved down into the dark where the air was a lot thicker, almost claustrophobic. The lower levels were deserted, unused, full of shadows. Tagerill helped Birlerion sit on the stairs. Their voices were low as Tagerill questioned him further.

Jerrol extended his hand in front of him, carefully feeling for the next step with his foot. The air resisted, and then, just as quickly, he was through, and he was drawn further down the stairs. He jumped as a single drop of water plopped on the stone beside him.

Jerrol strained to see in the soft green light the walls were emitting. The steps levelled out, leading into a narrow passage, and a tiny glow drew him on. The walls dripped with green slime coating the surface of the stones. He wrinkled his nose at the smell of rotting vegetation and algae, trying to avoid brushing up against it.

The passage was a lot longer than it looked. The light drew him on. Frowning, he stopped as a flash caught his eye; something glinted in the wall. Jerrol reached out to trace its edges and pulled his hand back with a gasp; it was sharp. His finger bled. He sucked his finger as he worked his dagger out of his belt, and then dug the point around the stone, easing it out of the wall.

The crystal fell into his left hand, and he hissed as it sliced his palm, sucking in his blood. He tried to drop it, but it stuck to his skin. He shook his hand, but it only absorbed the crystal faster. His blood splattered on the wall.

The crystal began to glow in his palm, the silvery glimmer suffused with pink, as the crystal absorbed his blood, and his hand absorbed the crystal. He caught his breath as he clenched his fist; a blushing radiance escaped. He opened his hand, and a silvery light flared, suspended in the air. The crystal had gone. His stomach fluttered as he raised his hand and looked at the walls.

What had he done?

Markings were engraved in the walls which glowed green in the unnatural light. He traced an image of a tree and the moon, the Lady's mark. Whatever had happened was under the Lady's eye, so maybe he hadn't erred after all. He closed his eyes and tried to calm his frantically beating heart.

When Jerrol opened his eyes, he was staring up at a tall tree looming above him. He lay at the foot of the largest sentinal he had ever seen. His vision was full of silver bark and high above was a canopy of deep green leaves, rustling even though there was no breeze. He inhaled the fresh greenness of the tree and levered himself upright.

His hand hurt. As he lifted it, he remembered the crystal. He smoothed his fingers over the fine, silver scar on his palm.

The Lady approached, her face serene. "You can't stay here," she said, resting a hand on the tree. "You must return and find the rest."

"The rest?" Jerrol asked, watching her in awe.

"The rest of the Bloodstone," she said as his vision shimmered, and he found himself lying on the floor of the underground tunnel below the Watch Towers.

Tagerill was bent over him, shaking his shoulder. "Captain? Are you alright? What happened?" His voice was sharp with concern.

"I'm fine, I think," Jerrol said as he sat up. The damp chill seeped through his clothes and, balancing his hand against the wall, he let Tagerill help him rise. His hand stung, and he realised it still bled. He pulled his handkerchief out of his pocket and wrapped it around the wound.

Tagerill watched in amazement as a silvery light flared above Jerrol's bandaged hand.

Jerrol's eyes gleamed a luminous silver in the light. "The Lady's visits always seem double-edged. You never know what to expect," he said with a wry grin as he looked back down the corridor. Whatever had happened was meant to happen. He was supposed to have found the crystal; he knew it. His veins buzzed as the crystal worked its way around his body. It was part of him now. He sheathed his dagger. A fair exchange, he supposed; he provided a host for the crystal and gained the ability to hold a light in his hand. "Where's Birlerion?"

"I left him on the steps." Tagerill hesitated. "Captain? What did the Lady say?"

Jerrol walked back towards the stairs. "We shouldn't leave him alone," was all he said.

For a supposedly clever man, renowned for his intelligence-gathering skills, he was stumbling from one crisis to another blindly following the Lady's trail. He must be doing something right, though he wished he knew what it was. He climbed the curving staircase. They needed to concentrate on getting Birlerion out.

When Tagerill and Jerrol reached the top of the stairs, Birlerion had gone.

26

GREENSWATCH

C aptain Bryce led his party up the road to Greenswatch and heaved a sigh of relief as the trees opened and revealed the grey stone manor house. They had arrived.

Lady Alyssa waited for the stable lad to position the dismount block before taking the hand Captain Bryce offered and dismounting.

A slim, young man, with hair the colour of ripened corn, hurried down the shallow stone steps. "Alyssa, at last!" he said as he hugged her. He set her back, blue eyes scanning her face. "Are you alright? Why didn't they provide you with a carriage? You didn't ride all the way here?" he asked, appalled.

"Because I didn't need a carriage. I rode to Deepwater, and I am more than capable of riding home again." She wasn't going to allow Simeon to start telling her what she could and couldn't do.

"But you are in mourning for Father. You can't be jaunting all over the countryside as if it was just some outing."

"I can assure you that I am well aware of what happened to Father. I wasn't jaunting. I was travelling home as quickly as possible, and a carriage would have delayed us even further. Allow me to introduce Captain Bryce from Stoneford Keep and Lieutenant Jennery from the King's Guards, who escorted me home safely. Also, Hannah of Stoneford, who assisted me on my journey home." Alyssa indicated her companions who were standing behind her.

"Captain Bryce." Simeon stared at the man he had sent off to collect his sister. "Thank you for delivering my sister to us."

Bryce gave him a stiff nod.

"Ah, Garrick." Alyssa greeted the Watch steward as he entered the hall. "Please arrange for Captain Bryce, his men and Lieutenant Jennery to be accommodated. They will be staying to pay their respects to my father before returning to Stoneford. Also, if you would, please prepare a room for Hannah near me."

"Certainly, my lady." Garrick indicated the way to Bryce and Jennery. "Please, if you would follow me. I will ask your maid Millie to escort Miss Hannah to her room."

"Thank you, ma'am, sir," Captain Bryce said. "We appreciate your hospitality."

"Garrick, please make sure you show Captain Bryce and Lieutenant Jennery where to join us for dinner tonight. I look forward to seeing you gentlemen later. Hannah, I must speak to my brother, but I will join you shortly." She turned back to Simeon and tucked her arm through his.

"Tell me what has been happening here. What is the plan? What have you heard about Father?" she asked.

"Those men will be leaving tomorrow, Alyssa. They do not need to stay any longer."

Alyssa stiffened, releasing his arm. "Of course they will stay, Father would expect them to."

"I'm glad you arrived today," Simeon continued as if she hadn't spoken. "The Leaving is planned for tomorrow and my confirmation the following day. Reid is finalising the preparations as we speak. Come, you must be tired, your maid is here and she can assist you to your room."

"I am not tired, Simeon. I want to know exactly what the ceremony for Father will entail. You weren't going to hold the Leaving without me, were you?" she asked, her eyes glinting dangerously. "I expect to see that the full Leaving ceremony is performed by Silene at the Grove."

"Ah, Silene was not available, so the Father will perform the ceremony," Simeon blustered.

Alyssa came to an abrupt halt. "Why is Silene not available? Have you even asked her?"

"Now Alyssa, don't be difficult. I'm sure you're tired; come, let Millie help you to your room."

"Don't you dare, Simeon. You will honour our father appropriately and request that Silene presides, or you will regret it."

"Don't you threaten me." Simeon grabbed her arm and scowled at her. "I am the Lord of Greenswatch, and I will decide what we will do; you will obey my orders. Don't think you can come here and twist me around your little finger as you could Father."

"What happened, Simeon? Why would you not pay our father the respect he is due?" Alyssa refused to cower before her bully of a brother.

"You're just a girl; you wouldn't understand," Simeon sneered. "I have to make my presence felt from the beginning. I am the new Lord of Greenswatch."

"You would receive more respect from the people around you," Alyssa said, wrenching her arm out of Simeon's grip, "if you gave those people a little respect in return. How can people support you if you don't value them? Our people loved Father. If you can't honour the relationship he had with Greenswatch and its people, then you are to blame for the damage you do to yourself. Can you not see? Let Garrick arrange the Leaving. Reid can spend his time on your confirmation."

Simeon wavered. He stiffened as Reid approached. "Apologies for the interruption, Lord Simeon, but I couldn't help overhearing your conversation. I am more than capable of arranging a Leaving and a confirmation. Please do not be concerned."

Alyssa glared at the thin, angular man her brother depended on. He was dwarfed by his black robes, which accentuated his pale face. "This is a private conversation, and your intrusion is unwelcome," she snapped. She couldn't believe the gall of the man.

Simeon glanced between the two. "Thank you, Reid, I am glad to hear everything is in hand. Please escort my sister to her room. I am sure she is tired after her journey."

Alyssa jerked as anger coursed through her, and her lips tightened. "I am quite capable of finding my way. This is my home too, don't forget!" Simeon flinched at the expression on her face. "I do not require an escort," she said as she stalked off.

When her maid Millie arrived, Alyssa was still pacing up and down her room. "Miss Alyssa, what in the Lady's name are you doing? You need to rest before dinner. Here, let me help you out of your habit. A quick wash will get rid of the dirt, and then you can relax."

Alyssa allowed Millie to help her undress and wash, thinking furiously as she obediently lay down on her bed, as if she needed a nap at her age. What was Millie thinking? She listened to her maid moving around the room until she gathered the travel-stained garments and left, shutting the door behind her.

Waiting for a moment, Alyssa listened intently and then got up, rummaging through her wardrobe for a simple gown she could manage on her own. She would send Jennery for Silene. He knew where she lived, and then Silene would be able to talk some sense into Simeon.

Alyssa paused with her hand on the door latch as she heard voices outside in the corridor. She listened carefully, eyes widening as she recognised the voices of Millie and Reid. That man's voice grated on her nerves; there was something she didn't like about him.

Millie was flirting with him. Alyssa couldn't think of a more disgusting person to get close to than him. She shuddered delicately at the thought and listened harder. Was Millie reporting her movements to that creep? They moved away down the corridor, and Alyssa gingerly opened her door and peered out. The way was clear, so she flitted down to the room she thought Garrick would have provided for Hannah, and she tapped lightly on the door.

She slipped into the room as Hannah closed the door behind her. Alyssa clasped Hannah's hands. "Hannah, you have to help me," she whispered.

"Whatever has happened?"

"I need you to ask Lieutenant Jennery to go and fetch Silene. My brother and his nasty henchman are watching me, and Millie as well. I can't believe Millie would betray me like that. Simeon is refusing to give my father the full Leaving ceremony tomorrow. I need Silene to talk some sense into him."

Hannah took a deep breath. "Let me get this right. You want Jennery to bring a lady called Silene here to speak to Lord Simeon? And that Silene must convince Lord Simeon to give Lord Hugh the full Leaving ceremony tomorrow."

"Yes, he must bring her tonight. Tomorrow will be too late!"

"What is the world coming to when a man's child won't provide his father with a proper Leaving ceremony. My, my, child, leave it with me. I'll go now. Jennery will bring her, don't you worry."

"Oh, thank you, thank you. I am sorry to impose, but I don't think I would reach the barracks unseen!"

"Don't worry, child. It's not for you to be visiting a barracks full of men for sure. You go back to your room and get ready for your dinner." Hannah shooed her out and then bustled off towards the barracks.

She found Jennery leaning against the doorframe of a room in the guest barracks. He looked clean and relaxed, dressed only in his linen shirt and trousers. His blond hair was still damp from its recent wash, and he was laughing at something someone in the room had said. Her eyes dwelled fondly on his handsome face. Jennery straightened up in surprise when he saw her, his shirt moulding to his body as he moved. "Hannah, what are you doing here. The barracks are not the place for women!"

Hannah laughed. "I'm too old to worry about that. Anyway, it's better I come than Lady Alyssa."

Jennery tensed. "Lady Alyssa? What happened? Come, sit down. Bryce won't mind sharing his chair," he said as Bryce hastily vacated the only chair in the room. He was similarly smelling of soap and looked much younger and relaxed out of uniform. His shirt sleeves were rolled up to his elbows, and he was freshly shaven.

Hannah smiled her thanks. If only she were younger, she wouldn't mind being held by those strong arms. She dragged her attention away from Bryce's trim body and looked at her son. "Well, from what Lady Alyssa tells me, her brother Simeon is not going to give her father the full Leaving tomorrow. She wants you to go and find some lady called Silene and bring her back here tonight to talk some sense into him."

Bryce whistled softly from his perch on the end of his bed. "That would be a mistake by the lad, that's for sure."

"And that's not all. It sounds like her brother is keeping a watch on Lady Alyssa's movements, him and that henchman of his. I am not sure what they are planning, but it doesn't sound like it will be a benefit to the girl or the Watch," Hannah said. "So, you had better get on your horse and go fetch this Silene now."

Jennery scowled. "You're worse than the Commander! Yes, alright I'm going, I'm going. Bryce, you might have to give my apologies. I doubt I'll be back in time for dinner."

Bryce waved him off. "I'm sure I'll think of something."

Watch Towers, Stoneford Watch

Tagerill cursed under his breath. "What is he thinking, why didn't he wait for us?" he said, peering out of the door.

"Do you think he is enspelled?"

"Not Birlerion, no way. He must have seen something."

Jerrol scanned the courtyard. "You go and restrain the off-duty guard. I'll find a diversion to distract any others." Tagerill didn't argue. Instead, he moved stealthily across the courtyard.

Jerrol skirted the courtyard and entered the square building opposite the tower. The corridors were silent. He hadn't seen any guards, and he wondered where they were; possibly off duty, he supposed. Hopefully, Tagerill would deal with most of them. He crossed the main hall, once catering to hundreds of students, now echoing emptily. This place was a forgotten place, shrouded in history and deliberate misdirection.

He needed to speak to the King. He would instruct

Liliian to reassess the purpose here. To care for the Watchers and find out how they could patch the Veil. How many years had it been unprotected? No wonder the Veil was shredding, and magic was leaking back in. How could they have forgotten the purpose of the towers? A niggling thought surfaced. What did Torsion know that they didn't? And where was he?

Searching the dining hall, Jerrol couldn't find anything flammable except the tables, and they would make too much noise to move. He needed to be careful; he didn't want to put the watchers at risk, but it had to be a big enough distraction to draw everyone, so he and Tagerill could pick them off. Maybe the kitchen would be better. He left the dining hall and peered around the door to the kitchen.

The kitchen was surprisingly empty. He had expected the cook to be firing up the ovens for the morning baking, but only dust motes spiralled in the silence. The room was dominated by a large wooden table in the centre, with an iron rack suspended from the ceiling. Hanging from the rack was a variety of utensils. The ovens lined the far wall, butting up to an open fire with a pot hanging over it in the corner. To the other side was a stack of kindling wood — piled neatly and promisingly inflammatory.

Jerrol skirted the table, moving towards the hearth. The fire was banked, a sullen red glow at its centre. He scooped up a shovelful of glowing coals and deposited them in the middle of the kindling wood. He piled some pieces on the top for good measure and left it smouldering, and then headed for the back exit.

"Well, what do we have here?" the man almost purred. "A rescue attempt, is it? Have you come to save the Lady's Captain? I knew he was the one; he had to be."

"I think you must be mistaken," Jerrol replied as he met the dark eyes of the thin man across the table. His face was narrow with deep creases around his mouth, his eyes black and pitiless. He wore long black robes that made his skin appear even paler than it was. He was remarkably similar in looks and build to the man they had tied up in Velmouth, and to Torsion, come to think of it.

"Oh no, I have you now. Are you a Sentinal? I know all about the Lady's Guard. We have much to talk about."

"I don't think so," disagreed Jerrol, "unless you're going to explain what you are up to here. Who are you, and where is Torsion?"

The man stared at him intently, his eyes pools of shadow. "Ah, you think you can resist. You all do at first, but you'll see the light in the end. My name is Ain'uncer, I am your friend, and you are mine. You want to help me. Look in my eyes, yes, look deep and see what you can see. You think you see, but you don't. Let me show you the way." Ain'uncer's voice dropped into a steady drone, insidiously working its way into his head and subduing thought. The clatter of Jerrol's sword hitting the stone-flagged floor jerked him back to his senses, and he backed away as Ain'uncer picked it up, chanting continuously.

Jerrol looked around him, frantic. He cast about for the nearest weapon as Ain'uncer began to advance on him. Jerrol found himself holding a ladle as he moved towards the far end of the table, shaking his head as if he could shake Ain'uncer's words out of his mind. How had he affected him so fast? It was alarming how easily this man could control people's minds.

He swung the ladle at Ain'uncer, distracting him enough to stop the chanting. His groping hand found a sieve, and he planted it like a mask over Ain'uncer's face, before the startled man realised his chant didn't have the desired effect. Jerrol grabbed a pan, hefting the ladle in his left hand.

Ain'uncer stepped back in surprise. "It's not possible," he

muttered under his breath. Jerrol parried the sword with his ladle while swinging at the man with his pan. Ain'uncer retreated into the dining hall. Jerrol followed; the aroma of wood smoke drifted in the air. His fire was taking hold.

"Guards!" Ain'uncer shouted as he pointed the sword in front of him, trying to keep Jerrol in the kitchen. "Seize him!" he commanded, as guards entered the hall behind him.

Four guards raced across the dining hall, fanning out either side to pen Jerrol in until one of the guards saw the smoke coming out of the kitchen. "Fire," he yelled, rushing towards the kitchen. Jerrol stuck his ladle out and tripped him up, followed by a stunning blow to his head with the pan.

Dropping the pan, Jerrol unsheathed his dagger and threw it across the room at Ain'uncer, before turning back to the advancing guards. He parried the first blow with his ladle, rolled, retrieving the pan, and spun upwards. His momentum turned him back inside the guard's swing, and he hit the guard with the pan. The guard tumbled into the wall, stunned.

Jerking his other dagger out, he circled Ain'uncer, aware of Birlerion staggering into the hall and drawing off two more guards trying to flank him. He attacked, striking hard with his dagger as he deflected the sword with his ladle, twisting the man into the path of the other soldiers. He darted around the tables towards Ain'uncer and gasped as a burning pain in his back brought him up short. A King's Guard lunged at him as he spun. Jerrol managed to deflect the blade away from his ribs.

Jerrol lurched back as the guard advanced, and Birlerion slid his body between them. Birlerion faltered, his breath hissed out, and he launched himself at the guard, forcing him back across the room, blocking the follow-up strike.

Jerrol took a steadying breath, and Ain'uncer roared as Tagerill arrived. Jerrol gripped his ladle just in case. Birlerion staggered back, and Jerrol grabbed him. His shirt was more red than white, and what he could see of his face that wasn't bruised was far too pale. He eased Birlerion to the floor as he sagged in his arms. Birlerion held a sword, and he waved it feebly as Tagerill waded in.

27

GREENSWATCH

J ennery and Silene arrived back at Greenswatch later that evening, not long after the evening meal had finished. Alyssa flew to embrace Silene before Simeon could utter a word of complaint. Alyssa ushered Silene into the room, passing her coat to a hovering manservant.

She threw Jennery a grateful look as she escorted Silene to a chair by the fire. Silene came to an abrupt halt as she caught sight of Reid beside Simeon. Her eyes widened and her lips tightened, but she held her peace and allowed Alyssa to fuss over her.

"My dear Alyssa, Simeon, allow me to offer my heartfelt condolences. Your father was a good man, and he will be greatly missed," Silene began, clasping her hands in her lap.

"Thank you, Silene." Simeon was stiffly formal. "But you didn't need to rush over tonight; you could have waited until the morning." He glared at Jennery. "The lieutenant takes too much upon himself."

"It was fortunate Alyssa sent word, else I would not have

known. I would not want you to think me remiss in paying my respects."

"Oh Silene, it was awful." Alyssa's voice trembled.

"Hush, child," Silene soothed. "Lady be thankful, you are safe." She patted her face sympathetically and hesitated as the zing of a Guardianship sparked at her fingertips. "You must tell me all later," she said, searching Alyssa's eyes.

Reid shifted sharply behind Simeon and muttered a few words before bowing to the room and leaving. Jennery moved from his lean against the door to allow him to go, watching him with suspicion.

"Simeon, child, are you ready for tomorrow?" Silene asked.

"I am not a child, Silene."

"I know," Silene said. "And tomorrow you will be granted the responsibility of the Watch. Your father so hoped you would not have to take that on so soon."

Simeon drew himself up. "It is my inheritance. He tried to keep me from it, but it is mine."

"He never wanted to keep it from you, Simeon. He was so proud of you. But these are troubled times and holding the Watch will be more difficult. He wanted to protect you for as long as he could."

"Rubbish!" Simeon spat. "He had gotten stuck in the old ways; he was trying to keep control. He wouldn't listen."

"Wouldn't listen to whom?" Silene asked. "Your seneschal? Not a follower of the Lady, I believe. Where did you find him?"

"None of your business. Who I choose as my servants is nothing to do with you."

"It used to be." She watched Simeon closely. "When did you leave the path, Simeon? What made you forsake the Lady?"

Alyssa gasped beside her; raising her hands to her face, she turned stricken eyes on her brother.

Simeon raised his chin. "You are but a teacher for children, Silene, and there are no children here. I suggest you leave before you are escorted out and told not to return."

"Simeon, you cannot banish Silene. She is our family," protested Alyssa, standing between them. "You must allow Silene to preside over Father's Leaving. You may no longer follow the Lady, but he did, and you will honour his beliefs." Alyssa stood before Simeon, her eyes flashing, her face determined.

Jennery thought she had never looked so beautiful. He observed Simeon; he was strung tighter than a bowstring and looked as if he would snap at any moment.

Silene rose. "No, child, for now, it is decided. The choice has been made. He is lost, and his guide will not lead him back." Simeon flinched as he met her eyes. "It is never too late to find the right path. If you ask you will never be refused," she promised. "And now it is late, and I need to go home."

Alyssa turned away from Simeon with tears in her eyes. "I will not stay and see you ruin the Watch," she said, controlling her voice with an effort. "Mother requested that Lieutenant Jennery escorts me to her in New Vespers. I will be leaving after your confirmation."

"You will do as I tell you," Simeon began, but Alyssa flung up her hand.

"No," she replied. "I will be travelling with Lieutenant Jennery to New Vespers."

Simeon swallowed. "We will discuss this in private. But for now, I suggest that your lieutenant," he sneered across at Jennery, "escorts Silene back to where he found her and keeps himself out of Greenswatch business if he knows what is good for him."

Jennery offered a cynical bow. "My lord." He bowed more respectfully to Alyssa, smiling into her anguished eyes. He wished he could hug her, but he restrained himself and turned to Silene to offer her an arm.

Silene looked at him with a twinkle in her eye. She turned to Alyssa and gave her a hug. "Come and see me before you leave, there is much to discuss." She added wickedly, "And your lieutenant knows the way."

Alyssa blushed and hugged her back. "What should I do?" She clutched Silene a little desperately.

"Be careful. There is little you can do. Keep your lieutenant near. I have to go. Simeon is watching."

Alyssa watched them leave before turning back to Simeon.

"What did she say to you?" he demanded.

"She was offering the Lady's blessings for Father for tomorrow since you are not going to. What happened, Simeon? Was your life so bad under the Lady's watch?"

Simeon glowered at her. "You know nothing, and you understand less. Stay out of it, Alyssa, and you won't get hurt."

"Too late." She hissed as if struck. "I have been hurt. I was there, Simeon — where were you? They slaughtered him. They slaughtered our father and all his men; an ambush off the East Road. You never asked; was it because you already knew? Don't you care?" she lashed out at him before she turned away in floods of tears.

He stood stony-faced, watching her stumble from the room. He had been warned not to listen to her wiles. He was to ensure she was offered to Aaron. That had been the agreement and it would get her out of his hair. He swallowed uneasily. Things were not as easy to control as he had thought. He would be glad once he was confirmed. No one could argue with him then.

He looked up as Reid slipped back in the room. "It's done," Reid said. "Aaron will be here for your confirmation to take her off your hands, so stay the course, and it will all be yours."

"What about my mother? Won't she be expecting her in Old Vespers?" Simeon paced, unable to keep still.

"She's lying. There's been nothing delivered here for her. It's all a ruse."

Simeon pressed his lips together. "A ruse for what? Why would she lie?"

"It's all about power, Simeon. You know that. You have it, and she doesn't. She's trying to defy you. You must show them who is in charge from the beginning; don't allow anyone to tell you what to do. Tomorrow you must keep her under control."

"How? You saw what she is like. Headstrong."

"Well, let us say she should be subdued tomorrow. After all, she's not going to embarrass you at your father's Leaving, now is she?"

The day of the Leaving dawned clear and still. There was an air of expectancy. Everyone felt it as if something momentous was going to happen. The Leaving was to be performed at the home lake, where a single, tall sentinal stood guard behind the house.

Alyssa stood on the steps watching her father's bier carried by his honour guard down towards the lake. A dark green cloth covered the casket, the single globular Alyssium bloom for which she had been named lying on the top.

The procession moved slowly. The local people, barred from attending the so-called "private" Leaving, threw flowers at the bier as it passed, bowing their heads in respect. Her eyes teared as she silently thanked Garrick for keeping to the traditions.

Her father's casket had been guarded by Garrick and his men ever since he had returned to Greenswatch. Four of his remaining personal guard had stood on honour guard all day and night. Garrick now led the procession with Alyssa and Simeon following.

Simeon was cursing steadily under his breath. "Who gave him permission, Reid arranged a cart for him."

"You will honour the man who was our father." Alyssa gripped his arm like a vice. "You will pay him the respect he is due."

"No, dear sister, you and the rest will pay me the respect I am due, or you will regret it." Simeon's face was cold and unyielding. "You will do as I say; those who don't will pay," he said, staring at Lieutenant Jennery, who was standing stiffly at attention with Captain Bryce and his men as they passed. Alyssa gaped as she saw him. His face was badly bruised, his eye bloodshot and purpling painfully. He stood awkwardly, he was clearly injured, but he stood stiff and silent, saluting the bier as it passed.

"What did you do?" Alyssa asked, her stomach dropping. "Silene? What did you do to Silene?"

Simeon jutted his chin out, a sneer distorting his face. "You will learn, the easy way or the hard way. Silene will not be returning to visit us." He strode on, dragging Alyssa with him, as she stared over her shoulder at Jennery in horror.

The lake spread out before them, serene and calm, reflecting the blue of the sky and the tall sentinal under which they stood. Drooping spears of green water iris curved over and kissed the still water, the bright yellow blooms providing a splash of colour along the margins.

The guards rested the casket on the wooden chute created to support it on its final journey. The Father stood to the side and began intoning a prayer as the household staff gathered around. They were few, most being advised to stay away, though some had ignored the orders and attended anyway. Alyssa saw Millie standing with the housemaster, blotting her eyes. Hannah stood behind her.

Simeon strode forward. "Who built this here? Who defied my orders, Reid? Didn't you instruct them to build on the other side?"

"Yes, my lord, I did indeed instruct them so. When I checked last night that's where it had been built." He turned to the carpenters hovering behind them. "Who told you to move it here?" Reid demanded, retribution in his eyes.

The carpenter shrugged. "Wasn't us, sir, we built it where you told us to. Must have been the Lady. She knows where the Leaving should take place." He stared at Reid, his face expressionless.

Reid spluttered, but as the murmur spread around the waiting congregation, he shook his head at Simeon. "Deal with them later. Let's get this over with."

Simeon nodded at the Father fidgeting nervously by the bier. "Father, the service, please," he said. "Exactly as you were instructed." He glared at the small man.

The Father bobbed his head and began intoning a blessing, glibly reading the words from a sheet of paper in his hands. "We stand here today in the name of all those who have gone before us, and with the blessing of the Council, to say farewell to Lord Hugh of Greenswatch. He was a respected leader of the community who did his duty well..."

"Father, how could you?" Alyssa strode forward and snatched the paper from his hands. She seethed as she glared at the priest cringing before her. "You of all people!"

She cast a look of scorn towards her brother who was staring at her in disbelief. "How dare you defile the final offering. I could understand you paying lip service to your new masters, but this!" She rent the paper in two.

Reid attempted to grab her arm, but she shook him off. "Lady Alyssa, you are overwrought; please, you are not well."

Alyssa picked up a torch and swung it at him, so he had to jump back. "You!" She pointed at the four guards still standing at attention around the bier. "Launch it," she commanded as she dipped the torch into the flame. It caught straight away.

She waved it before her as if to keep people back, but everyone was frozen in place, gaping at her. Jennery moved to stand at the head of the bier, ready to help knock the restraining blocks out of the way.

"At your command, my lady," he said, his bow stiff and shallow.

As he rose, Alyssa saw the livid bruising across his face; she bit her lip and drew her breath. "Now. Now is the time of Leaving." Her voice rang out loud and clear. "We celebrate the life of Hugh of Greenswatch. A life well-lived, honoured, loved. A life offered to the people of this land, in honour of the Lady and in the name of the King, our Liege. A life dedicated to the Watch and all who live within it. A man respected and true.

"We, his people, offer him to you, our Lady, to watch over in perpetuity. To love and honour in our place. Watch him well." Her voice faded away as she bowed her head and then she threw her torch on the now floating bier, followed by a shower of blossoms. The people of the Watch had crept along the shoreline, and now cast flower after flower towards the casket.

Through her tears, she watched the flames creep higher as it floated into the middle of the lake, a trail of flowers in its wake. The bier blazed high, the dry tinder burning fiercely, the flames reaching for the clear blue sky before a blinding flash of white filled the lake and the casket was gone. The lake waters calmed, and a carpet of flowers bobbed in memory of Lord Hugh's passing.

Jennery turned back from watching the bier and reached for Alyssa as she swayed, her face a deathly white. He caught her arm, offering support, but staggered as Simeon spun him around. Alyssa gripped Jennery's arm to steady him in turn.

"Unhand my sister; you will not touch her."

"Simeon." Alyssa turned on her brother. "You will treat our guests with respect. He is a member of the King's Guard, and you touch him at your peril. He is also my guest, and you dishonour Greenswatch and me by your behaviour." Simeon took a step back at her acidic tone. "Lieutenant," she faced Jennery, "I thank you for your concern and your support." She shot an icy glance at her brother. "It is a shame that my family are unable to offer the same. I am sorry to see you are injured. Nothing serious, I hope?" She searched his face, desperately looking for news of Silene.

"It is nothing to concern yourself with, my lady. It will heal, and all are well," Jennery said, giving her a reassuring smile.

Alyssa breathed a sigh of relief. "Thank goodness, I was worried..." She glanced at Simeon and tightened her lips. "I am so sorry."

"It is not your fault," Jennery reassured her again. "Please, my lady. You'd best return to the house. We will await your orders."

Alyssa let go of his arm and straightened up. "Yes, we have to survive another day," she muttered under her breath, and saw by Jennery's sympathetic grimace that he had heard her.

"Ah, Captain Bryce," she called as she caught sight of the wiry captain. "I appreciate your staying to pay your respects to my father. Please walk with me and Lieutenant Jennery. It is time to return to the house. You will stay and take refreshments with us, won't you?"

"Lady Alyssa, I would be honoured." Bryce offered her his arm, and they walked back up the road, adjusting their pace to Jennery's rather stiff gait, through the waiting locals lining the way. Simeon strode on ahead of them, looking neither left nor right, escorting the Father who was scurrying next to him.

The waiting people reached out and touched Alyssa's sleeve as she passed. "Lady's blessing, miss," they said, shyly ducking away before she could respond. She looked around in wonder as the people slowly melted away before her, returning to their homes but wanting to make sure she knew they had been there for her father. Her eyes misted, and she sniffed as she watched them leave.

"Here." Jennery proffered his handkerchief.

"Thank you. You are so kind to me."

"It is not difficult."

"Not for you, but for some, maybe." She tightened her lips. "Tell me what happened? How badly are you hurt, and what about Silene?"

"I am fine, and so is Silene. We were jumped on the road by supposed bandits. They came off worse, I can assure you. Silene and Reese left for Stoneford. It will be safer for them there."

"Thank goodness they are safe. I can't believe Simeon would hurt Silene, but I was wrong, and you are not fine. Captain Bryce, tell me the truth, you can see he is not well. Will he be able to ride tomorrow?"

"He's just a bit sore, my lady, he'll be alright tomorrow. Maybe he should have an early night tonight. The rest will do him good," Bryce suggested as Jennery began to protest.

"Then that is what he will do, won't you?" Alyssa glared at Jennery until he yielded. "Once we are back, it's unlikely we'll have a chance to speak. You can see what Simeon is like, and that man of his follows me everywhere. I am not sure what Simeon has planned for his confirmation, but I doubt either of you will be welcome. We need to ensure we delay your departure long enough today that you have to stay the night, because I intend leaving with you as soon as possible after the confirmation, and I get the feeling he may make that difficult."

"He cannot gainsay the King, nor your mother," Captain Bryce said.

"I don't think he believes she has summoned me," Alyssa said bitterly. "He thinks he can dispose of me as he wishes. He has been very clear about that."

"Well, we'll have to convince him otherwise, won't we?" Jennery said with a smile, trying to ease her concern.

She gave him a tentative smile in return, though her gaze firmed as she watched him. "Captain Bryce and I will find a way. You will go straight to bed. I will send Hannah with a draught to make sure you do go to sleep."

Jennery's protest died under her concerned gaze and Bryce's glare. "Very well," he said, easing his back; it was apparent he was uncomfortable.

Later that afternoon, as he dutifully climbed into bed, Hannah arrived with a sleeping draught and strict instructions for him not to get up until it was time for the confirmation the next day. Her expression grew more determined as she saw the dark bruising across his body. One of Bryce's men was on watch outside his door, and he was to rest.

Hannah arched an eyebrow at him as she presented the sleeping draught. "Lady Alyssa's orders," she said firmly, standing over him as he drank it. He eased himself back on the pillow, trying to stifle a groan.

Hannah tutted and tucked him in. Her fingers gently brushed his hair back from his cheek and hesitated over the heat of the bruising. She sat in the chair and watched him until his breathing smoothed out, and he relaxed into sleep. He still looked strained, a crease between his eyes even in sleep. He was hurting more than he had let on. It was fortunate she had slipped the pain relief into the draught as well. He would no doubt need more of them on the morrow.

Her face softened as she watched him sleep. Jennery and Alyssa, she so hoped they would make a go of it. She had grown fond of Alyssa. She would be perfect for keeping Jennery out of trouble.

28

WATCH TOWERS, STONEFORD WATCH

A in'uncer took a step back from the advancing Sentinal, and swept his black robes around him, disappearing in a swirl of cloth.

Tagerill took a deep breath and turned towards Jerrol. His heart stuttered at the sight of the Captain holding his brother in his arms. They sprawled in a pool of blood on the floor.

His sword clattered to the floor as he knelt beside them, his heart hammering as he searched for a pulse. His frantic check reassured him that Birlerion was still alive. He looked up as Jerrol cursed. "He just waded in, got between the guard and me. He was unarmed. Tagerill, why would he do something so stupid?"

"You are the Captain."

"You don't even know me."

"The Lady chose you, and she instructed Birlerion to protect you. He would do whatever is necessary, as would all of us."

"But not to sacrifice his life for mine. He's already taken a beating for me, and now this."

"If that's what it takes." Tagerill bent over Birlerion, staunching the deep puncture wound in his stomach and a slice down his arm that would not stop bleeding. He needed his sentinal. This was an injury he would not recover from overnight.

Tagerill glowered as he padded and bound the wounds as tightly as he could with the cleaning cloths Jerrol found. His hands shook as he worked; he was reminded of Clary's last attempt to kill his brother.

They had nearly succeeded that time and would have if it hadn't been for Leyandrii. He took a deep breath, tenderly brushing the hair off his brother's bruised face; they would not be losing him this time either. Between them, they carried Birlerion out to the wagon that was pulled up beside the gate.

Birlerion groaned as he regained consciousness. He hissed through his teeth and opened his eyes. "What happened?"

"You got in the way of a sword, you idiot; didn't you learn anything in the sparring ring?" Tagerill growled. He spun, expecting a new threat as the guards who had been off duty pounded on the locked door of their barracks. The pounding reassured him they were still contained.

"You prefer I let him skewer the Captain?"

"It would be better if none of us got skewered," Jerrol said over his shoulder as he hurried to unbar the gate and swing it open. He was unsurprised to see Zin'talia and Tagerill's horse waiting outside. Zin'talia was particularly wild-eyed, and he took precious minutes to reassure her before he pulled her into the traces and harnessed her up.

Tagerill climbed up beside Birlerion and rested his brother's head in his lap, flipping a blanket over him. "Why didn't you wait on the steps for us?"

"I saw Clary," Birlerion replied, his voice low and filled with pain.

"Birlerion, you know that's not possible. You are imagining things."

"I saw him. He was older, a bit thinner, but he had that same arrogant expression."

Tagerill wiped the sweat off Birlerion's face. His skin was clammy: shock setting in. He piled a few more blankets on him and hugged him tightly. He wasn't really surprised Birlerion had acted if he thought he had seen Clary; after all, for him, the attempt on his life wasn't all that long ago. "It couldn't have been Clary, Birlerion. The Lady took all the Ascendants with her," Tagerill said, hugging his brother. Tagerill continued to chastise his brother as Jerrol harnessed the other horse next to Zin'talia and without wasting any time climbed up on the wagon and set off.

It took them two days to reach the keep at Stoneford, Birlerion dozing in Tagerill's or Jerrol's lap as they took turns to drive the wagon, only stopping to rest the horses. Lin appeared, meeping in concern as she crouched on Birlerion's chest. Her green eyes were huge, watching Birlerion's greying face intently.

The wagon clattered into the well-lit courtyard as darkness was falling on the second day. Lin flitted on ahead to rouse the keep, and Tagerill relaxed as the newly familiar walls rose around him. Jerrol jumped down from the wagon as Jason strode into the courtyard, Lin chittering above his head. Jason followed Jerrol around the back of the wagon and began shouting instructions to his guards. "What happened?" he asked, climbing up beside Tagerill.

Tagerill winced. "We met with a slight problem at the towers," he said as Tyrone arrived with a stretcher. He glanced at Chryllion as he hovered beside the wagon. "They are using *Mentiserium*," Tagerill said, his face bleak.

Chryllion's face paled. "I thought that practice was banned."

"Not anymore. They were trying to enspell Birlerion."

Chryllion stared at the semi-conscious Sentinal. "I take it they didn't succeed."

Tagerill grimaced. "No. But we found the Ascendants, and they are searching for the Captain." He turned to Tyrone. "I staunched his wounds as best I could, but he's lost a lot of blood. They need stitching. Once he's stabilised, my sentinal can help with healing him."

Tyrone nodded absently as he transferred Birlerion to the stretcher. He inspected Jerrol. "What about you?"

"I'll be fine, just a few bruises."

Tyrone scowled at him. "I'll be the judge of that; bring him too." His attention returned to Birlerion, and he hustled his helpers inside.

Tagerill jumped down and herded Jerrol before him. "A Velmouth councillor ambushed Birlerion. We tracked him up to the towers where they were trying to enspell him. They enspelled a whole unit of King's Rangers, and they attacked us." Tagerill grimaced at Jason. "I don't think the Captain is taking it too well."

"That would be an understatement," Jason said as he led the Sentinals into the infirmary. "We've had a spate of illnesses, and the number is growing. Men are behaving irrationally, trying to disrupt the keep. I'm glad you're back, even if it is in such dire straits. I wish Bryce would return as well. We are getting short on men we can trust." Jason shook his head. "It's like a plague slowly spreading over the whole garrison."

Tagerill looked around the infirmary with new eyes, as he noticed that all the beds were occupied by sleeping men.

"And these are not all; we've had to conscript one of the barracks as well," Jason continued.

"It's not an illness as such," Tagerill said. "It's a mind spell. The Ascendants are trying to brainwash everyone, remove free will. Most of the Velmouth council is affected. We will need to send some men up to Velmouth to help them remove the spell."

"I've seen a form of this mesmerising before, but not on this scale," Tyrone growled as he came out of the back room, wiping his hands. "You, over here." He pointed at Jerrol who, with a martyred sigh, sat on the bed Tyrone pointed to.

"How is Birlerion?" Jerrol asked.

"That is not the first stomach wound he's suffered. He's close-mouthed about it. Any of you like to explain it to me?"

Tagerill sighed. "Let's just say we had problems in our day, and Birlerion took the brunt of them."

"Mathew is sewing him up; he has a more delicate touch." Tyrone helped Jerrol remove his shirt and checked his side. "You're lucky you haven't ripped it open. It looks like he only caught your shirt. Birlerion must have fouled his blade."

"He and I will be having words about that."

Tyrone grimaced in agreement. "How old is he? He doesn't look old enough to have as many scars as he has."

"He's nineteen, a year younger than me," Tagerill said briefly.

Jerrol was appalled. He had thought he was older.

"The lot of you need to be more careful. I have enough on my hands without you as well." Tyrone glared at Jerrol. "We can't do anything for the others without the keywords."

"Which is why it's fortunate I came across this, isn't it?" Jerrol waved the small notebook in front of the healer.

"And that is?"

"A list of affected people and their keywords. The first

word triggers the behaviour. Repeating it is a reset. It seems to leave them open to a new suggestion."

"Where did you find that?" Jason reached for the book and began flipping through the pages. "Here's Danilesh," he said, his eyes bright as he stopped at a name he recognised.

"Councillor Fortes had it. He has been enspelling people in Velmouth and up at the towers."

"At least we know a way to reverse it now," Jason said with relief. "I'll do a compare to everyone we've sedated, see if they are all in the book. I think you have your hands full with Birlerion for now," he said to Tyrone.

Tyrone tapped Tagerill's arm. "You said your sentinal could help him — how?"

"He can speed up the healing process, as long as Birlerion is stable and the wound sealed. We can transfer him to my sentinal, and he will assist with his recovery. I know the Captain is desperate to get to the King."

Tyrone looked at Jerrol and Jerrol shrugged. "It's worth a shot. He's only going to fret in a bed in here. He may as well sleep in the sentinal if there is a chance we can get him healed quicker." He grimaced. "I need him."

"You must tell me more about your Sentinal's healing powers," Tyrone said as Tagerill followed him into the back room.

Jason turned to Jerrol. "Let's go back to my study. We can compile a list of questions and decide where to start. Maybe Danilesh?"

Tagerill helped carry Birlerion down to his sentinal. He scooped him up in his arms, ignoring Birlerion's protests, and shimmered into his tree. Birlerion relaxed with a sigh as the sentinal spun golden strands around him. The strands pulsed brilliantly as Tagerill watched. *"Do what you can,"* he thought.

The air pulsed around Tagerill, and he sat on the chair that materialised under him. A flush of energy washed through him, and he straightened, easing his shoulders. "Thank you," he murmured as his sentinal checked him over. He sat watching the pulsing strands as his sentinal began to heal the worst of his brother's wounds. His mouth tightened; they had almost lost him. Again.

Jason and Jerrol were in deep discussion, reviewing the best way to remove the spells, when they were interrupted by a page who burst in breathlessly. Before Jason could reprimand him, he was speaking. "My Lord, a man and a woman have arrived from Greenswatch; they claim sanctuary under the name of Lieutenant Jennery."

Jason pinched the bridge of his nose. "Advise them I am coming," he said, rising. When he arrived in the courtyard, a large red-haired man was sheltering a small woman from the threat of the guards.

"Lord Jason," Silene gasped with relief, as Jason entered the courtyard.

Jason strode forward. "I am sorry, but you have the advantage of me?"

"I am Silene, lately the Greenswatch Lore Master. This is my husband, Reese."

"Silene, Reese. What are you doing here?"

"We found the Greenswatch no longer good for our health, and Lieutenant Jennery insisted we leave and come here. Captain Haven was right. Greenswatch is no longer safe for us." Her eyes widened as she saw Chryllion behind his shoulder. "My Lord," she whispered in awe. "I see the Captain is assembling his guards."

"Indeed." He gestured towards Chryllion. "This is Sentinal Chryllion. Please, let us go inside. We can talk more easily in my office. Mackie," he called his aide over, "arrange for some food to be sent to my office, and request that a guesting suite is prepared."

"Yes sir." Mackie saluted and ran off without asking any further questions. Jason closed his eyes, blessing the boy before turning to follow his newest guests.

He paused on the threshold of his office watching Jerrol greet them. "I am sorry. Please, you are welcome. This has been a long day," he said with a wry grin.

"We are sorry to be another burden on you." Silene sat awkwardly in the chair.

Jerrol leaned forward. "Are you alright? Were you injured?"

"I'm fine. I fell off my horse when we were set upon and wrenched my shoulder, is all. It is a little sore after the journey here, and nothing time won't fix," Silene replied.

"But what happened, who attacked you?"

Silene eased back in the chair. "Your Lieutenant Jennery came to get me at the behest of Lady Alyssa. She was concerned her brother wasn't going to perform the Lady's Leaving ceremony for her father. She wanted me to talk some sense into him. I failed miserably. His feet are set on a different path, and he wouldn't listen to reason. Alyssa was furious." She shook her head. "I do hope she is alright. Simeon instructed Lieutenant Jennery to escort me back to where I came from." Silene hissed as she shrugged, forgetting her injury. "We were set upon on the way home. Lieutenant Jennery managed to fight them off. I fear he took some injuries as well, but I damaged my shoulder when I fell off my horse. The Lieutenant managed to get me home, and I must admit I was somewhat overwrought and agreed to allow Reese to bring me here. Now we are here. I am not so sure we should have left Alyssa."

"We have a healer here who can look at your shoulder for you. I am sure he has something that will ease the pain,"

Lord Jason said. "You are both welcome to stay as long as you need to." He was interrupted by a light tap, followed by a young woman carrying a tray. "Ah, Mary, please, on the desk will be fine." The maid dipped her knees, and after staring around the room, her eyes wide, she left, closing the door softly behind her.

"Please, help yourself," Jason said, leaning back in his seat and cupping his mug.

"Thank you for your care. We appreciate it," Silene said, staring at Chryllion. She inspected his unusual uniform and the silver eyes that seemed to glow and then blushed as he smiled at her. "I am sorry. I can't believe I am meeting another Sentinal. It seems unreal."

Chryllion's laugh was a deep rumble. "I feel the same way, believe me," he said, shifting his sword. "It is strange to be awake and the world so different. Though I suppose not so different after all."

"True, underneath it all, it is all about power. Those without trying to grab more. Usually at the expense of the innocent." She stared at Jerrol. "You are attracting a lot of trouble, Captain, very quickly."

Jerrol grimaced. "I know."

"Guerlaire was the same. Leyandrii was always saying he should take better care," Chryllion said.

Silene's eyes widened at the casual mention of such legendary people. "You knew the Lady Leyandrii as well?"

"Oh yes, she was such a young lass to have such a heavy burden." His lips quirked. "I guess she wasn't as young as she looked. Marguerite appeared even younger."

"Marguerite? The Guardian of the Land? You knew her too?" Silene looked as if she might faint.

"Yes, she was a little tyke, always vanishing, had the palace in uproar half the time, 'til Taurillion calmed her down." He paused, wrinkling his brow. "I wonder where he is now — where they all are. The Captain says there are only twelve Sentinals in Vespiri. There should be far more than that."

"There are a few in Terolia, but not many," Silene said with an air of caution.

"We will find them," Chryllion said, Silene thought more in hope than in real belief.

29

STONEFORD KEEP

T he next morning Birlerion awoke early. His stomach fluttered uncomfortably; something was wrong, but he couldn't remember what. A comforting hum filled his head, and he knew where he was. He opened his eyes and squinted at the glowing strands surrounding him. A fleeting touch and the glow began to dim; the strands were fading as he watched.

Bemused, he sat up on a wooden cot which extended out of the curving wall. A soft silvery glow lit the room, revealing smooth silver bark for walls. Above him, a swirling mist took the place of a ceiling.

Memory came flooding back. He had seen Clary; he was positive he had. Tall and venomous, black hair tied back off his face. The same supercilious expression, which had changed to horror when he saw Birlerion. What had he been doing at the towers? And why was he afraid of him? Not his typical behaviour.

Tagerill appeared before him, relaxing as he saw Birlerion sitting up. "Thank goodness! How do you feel?"

Birlerion's brow creased. He was still tired. A lassitude

dragged at his body, but his stomach no longer burned, nor did his arm. "Much better, I think," he said, running a hand over his healed skin, the new scar a thin pink line parallel to the other one. "Where are we?"

"My sentinal, he healed you. We are back in Stoneford."

Birlerion stiffened. He had taken the blade for the Captain; he had to learn to stop doing that. Leyandrii would no doubt tell him off. "How is the Captain?"

"Upset at you for risking your life, but otherwise he's fine."

Birlerion rubbed a trembling hand over his face. "How long have I been here?"

"Just a day, the healer stitched your wounds. My sentinal helped you along. I expect you will still feel a little tired; the body needs time and sleep to heal. Time I thought we didn't have. The Captain wants to get back on the road, but he won't leave without you," Tagerill said, watching Birlerion swing his legs over the side of the cot. He handed him a shirt that he pulled out of thin air. "Birlerion, you took a foolish risk. Why did you leave the stairs? If you had stayed there, none of this would have happened."

"I told you I saw Clary."

"You couldn't have."

Birlerion peered at him, his silver eyes still red-rimmed and bloodshot, though significantly less swollen. "He ran away."

"That doesn't make him Clary."

Birlerion grinned. "He looked horrified when he saw me."

"I imagine most people would be, the state you were in. Not a pretty sight."

Birlerion chuckled softly and let Tagerill help him stand. Tagerill watched in concern as he swayed, trying to tuck his shirt in. "The Captain is waiting for you up at the keep. Also,

Loremaster Silene and her husband, Reese, arrived yesterday, claiming sanctuary."

Birlerion turned and almost fell. He felt so weak. He took
a steadying breath as his brother held him up. He hadn't felt
this weak since — he shied away from the memory. Since the
last time.

"Maybe you should stay here a little longer?"

"No, I'll be fine. I just need a minute to adjust." Birlerion
ran an unsteady hand through his hair. "And something to
eat," he said as his stomach growled.

Tagerill escorted him back to the keep, his hand hovering
behind him, but Birlerion seemed to regain his strength as he
walked. By the time he reached the keep, he looked as if he
had just awoken from a deep sleep instead of a near-fatal
injury.

Jason and Jerrol were seated in Jason's study, deep in
conversation when the Sentinals arrived. Once Birlerion was
safely seated, Tagerill went off to get him some food. Jerrol
inspected him. He was still pale. "Are you sure you should be
up yet? Tyrone will have a seizure if he sees you. He was
saying you would be bedridden for at least a week."

"I'm fine. Tagerill's sentinal healed the worst. I can't
remember when I last ate; I'll feel even better after I've eaten.
"

Jason leaned back in his chair. "We were just discussing
this *Mentiserium*. Chryllion and Tyrone worked up a list to try
and remove the compulsions. Jerrol was just explaining it
to me"

"At least you Sentinals have some idea of what it is and
how to use the keywords," Jerrol said.

"Yes, the Ascendants were good at it back then, as well,"
Birlerion said, twisting his lips.

Jason continued. "We've been checking the men each
morning by getting them to swear the Lady's Oath. That's

how we could tell who's been affected, but we're down to the bare minimum. I drew all the patrols in to guard the garrison."

"I think they plan to cause civil unrest. Incapacitating you and the Watches prevents you from intervening, means the King can't protect his people."

"The Ascendants intend putting their people in power. That is the bigger game," Jason said. "Just as you said. Corporal Danilesh tried to put a bolt through me. That's why we clamped down so fast; we had to know who we could trust."

"*Mentiserium* is rife through the Watches, Velmouth and the towers. Where councils have new advisors, you can be sure they will be affected. We need to get word to Bryce and Jennery, warn them to be careful."

"Tagerill was saying you wanted to get on the road. I imagine that will be you carrying that word?" Jason asked.

Jerrol nodded, concern clear on his face. "I fear the king is in graver danger than we first thought. I can't delay, not with everything that is happening in the Watches. You should be able to get Stoneford back on its feet, even clear Velmouth. Councillor Sellins was unaffected; he holds the Lady close. Work with him to remove the spell.

"At least we can foil their plans here and in Old Vespers. I have the list for Old Vespers and the court up here," he tapped his temple, "once we get the King back on his throne." He shifted in his chair, easing the aches. "The Watch Towers are out of our control for now. The King will have to address that, maybe send you some more men to help. We can't risk the Watchers, they are more important than we realised, and the Ascendants control them." He paused as Tagerill entered with a plate of food, followed by a maid with a tray of mugs.

Jerrol reached for a mug of coffee, relaxing as he took his

first sip. His face tightened as he watched Birlerion struggle to eat a pastry.

"Until we clear this *Mentiserium*," Jason said, "the garrison is at half strength. We've not been able to shut down the smugglers as we planned. If we can get these men back on duty, we can address that."

"Trealt removes free will. It is certainly part of the puzzle. If you could shut down that supply, it would help," Birlerion said, looking up from his coffee. Jerrol saw he had given up on the pastry. He met Birlerion's eyes and recognised the deep weariness behind the façade of the speedy recovery he was trying to convey. He needed to get Birlerion back to his sentinal even if Birlerion was going to pretend otherwise.

"How virulent this mind spell is at court, I dread to think. Hopefully, they haven't got that far yet. Though the more I think about it, it would explain much. I don't know how they got to the king. I'll find out more when I see him." He placed his empty mug on the desk. "Jason, I am sorry to leave you with all this, but I need to get on the road. Silene can fill you in on the Guardians and their responsibilities."

"Thanks, I think. Just you be careful on the road; make sure you look after him." Jason glared at the Sentinals.

"With my life," Tagerill promised solemnly. Birlerion just twisted his lips.

30

GREENSWATCH

The day of Simeon's confirmation as Lord of the Watch dawned grey and miserable. The rains sifted down as Reid ordered the servants about, setting up awnings and sheltered pathways to shield the guests from the inclement weather. He scowled up at the sky. It was supposed to be summer.

Lord Aaron and his entourage arrived mid-morning, causing a welcome distraction from the tension brewing between Simeon and Alyssa. Alyssa stood at the bottom of the steps waiting to welcome Lady Olivia as she dismounted from the carriage, which pulled up behind the men. Shaking out her skirts, Lady Olivia turned to greet Alyssa, her face drawn and pale. Alyssa exclaimed over her as she drew her in. "Lady Olivia, you look half frozen; please let me escort you to your room."

Aaron gave her a keen stare. "Lady Alyssa, exquisite as always," he said with a gleam in his eye.

Alyssa kept a smile on her face. "Why, thank you, Lord Aaron. It is a pleasure to see you. I'll return after I show your lady mother to her room." She led Olivia away, trailed by her maids.

Alyssa's maid, Millie, hovered in the corridor and Alyssa was quick to put her to work. "Millie, please escort Lady Olivia's maids to their rooms. Let them decant their things and direct them back to the Pink Room, where they may attend Lady Olivia."

"Yes, m'ady," Millie said as she bobbed a curtsey. "This way, please." She led the way down the corridor to the back stairs.

Alyssa led Lady Olivia to the room and closed the door behind them.

Lady Olivia removed her cloak and gloves. "What a relief to be away from their mindless chatter," she said as she sat in the pink upholstered chair with a small sigh. The chair seemed too big for her. "My dear, it is so nice to see you again, but I am so sorry it is under such circumstances. You have my heartfelt condolences. Your father was a good man; I will miss him."

"Thank you, Lady Olivia. Please, call me Alyssa. Apologies for cutting you short but I need to speak to you before the maids return." She knelt by the side of the chair and looked up into Olivia's careworn face.

"My dear, whatever is it?"

Alyssa took a deep breath. "You of all people know how the Guardianship of the Watches work." She paused as Olivia stilled. "You must know that Aaron didn't take up the Guardianship. His vows never mentioned the Lady; he ignored her completely. I don't know where it went, or who now holds it, if anyone. I believe that Simeon won't pick his up, either. That Seneschal of his is controlling him. He is following a different path, and he set my maid, my own maid," she clenched her fists, "to spy on me."

"Hush, child." Lady Olivia touched her shoulder. "I

understand, but I don't know what I can do. Councillor Peverill restricts me; he commands my every move. Aaron intends to force me to Join with him."

"Simeon is going to try and Join me to your son. In other circumstances, I expect it would have been the right decision, but I can't, not now."

"I still don't understand how I can help."

Alyssa bit her lip. "After Simeon's confirmation, I am going to visit my mother at court. Captain Bryce promised to escort me, but I need you to support me. I am going to say that I wish to speak to my mother before I'll Join. I'll promise to Join with Aaron when I return and not before. You could use it to delay joining with Peverill as well, say you want a double joining." Alyssa's shoulders drooped.

"They won't listen to me," Olivia said, knowing it for truth.

"You could make them listen if you wanted to. I am sure Lord Stefan would have wanted you to protect the Guardianship. If we don't, no one else will. The king has to come and stop all this, this chaos," Alyssa finished, waving her hands in the air. "The maids will return soon. My room is three doors to the right. Lady Olivia, please think about it. I won't let Greenswatch go down without a fight!" Alyssa stood, adjusting her dress.

"I would have been proud to have you as a daughter." Olivia held out her hand as she stood. "And I know Stefan would have too."

"I would have loved it too," Alyssa said, blinking back tears as she took Olivia's hands and kissed her cheek. They both felt the zing that passed between them, and they stared at each other wide-eyed before they smiled in recognition and hugged each other fiercely.

"Call me Olivia," Olivia whispered as they stepped back. "We'll see what we can do." She straightened her shoulders as renewed vigour coursed through her veins. Alyssa was right, Stefan would have wanted her to protect the Guardianship with her very last breath.

Alyssa walked down the stairs slowly. As she reached the bottom, she heard the rumble of voices in the long drawing room, so she turned towards the door. She raised her chin as she pushed the door open and entered. Lord Aaron and Councillor Peverill were seated in a huddle with Simeon, deep in conversation. Aaron noticed her first. He stood and gave a shallow bow. "Lady Alyssa."

"Lord Aaron, Simeon, Councillor Peverill," Alyssa acknowledged them. "Simeon, shouldn't you be getting ready?" she asked. "You're not dressed yet."

Simeon's lip curled. "Women and their fripperies. I am ready. Once Lady Olivia arrives, we will proceed to the pavilion."

"Pavilion? Are we not going to the lake?" Alyssa asked, dread in her heart.

"Reid has it all arranged. We do not need to travel down there. Ah, Lady Olivia, a timely arrival, and Captain Bryce. I wasn't aware that you were still here, haven't you a home to go to?" Simeon glared at Bryce.

"Lady Olivia required an escort. I was happy to oblige," Bryce replied, ignoring Simeon's blatant hint.

Alyssa grinned in appreciation. "You are welcome, Captain Bryce. If it hadn't been for you and Lieutenant Jennery, I wouldn't be here today. Where is Lieutenant Jennery?"

Bryce escorted Lady Olivia to the nearest chair and turned back to Alyssa. "He went to check the horses and ensure everyone is ready to leave on your command."

"Leave?" Simeon stiffened. "I've already told you, Alyssa, that you are not going anywhere. Though the captain and his men are free to go anytime."

"Oh?" Alyssa's eyes glinted a challenge. "And I have already told you that I am going to court to stay with mother. Captain Bryce and Lieutenant Jennery are escorting me."

"Absolutely not," Simeon declared.

"I think you are presumptuous, Lord Simeon. You forget that you are not your sister's guardian, your mother is. Lady Alyssa wants to be with her mother after all that she has been through. It's enough to give any woman the vapours," Lady Olivia said firmly.

"Mother," Aaron spoke over her, "this is none of your business."

Lady Olivia gave him a withering glare. "It is certainly none of yours." She turned back to Simeon as Aaron gaped at her.

"Perhaps I should escort Lady Olivia outside, maybe some fresh air while you continue the discussion in private," Peverill interjected, standing up.

"That is not necessary, councillor. Please sit," Alyssa waved her hand, forcing the councillor to sit back down. He threw a look of desperation at Simeon. "I am not going to be bullied in private. If Simeon has something to say he will say it now."

They were interrupted as Reid entered the room, closely followed by Jennery. "My lords, ladies, and gentleman, we are ready to begin the confirmation." He was blithely unaware of the tension in the room.

Simeon exhaled. "Very well. Alyssa, we will continue this discussion after, privately." He led the way out of the room.

Lady Olivia accepted Captain Bryce's arm before Peverill could cross the room, and they followed Simeon. A slight smile hovered over her mouth. Alyssa allowed Aaron to escort her. His arm was rigid under her fingers and cords in his neck stood out prominently as they left the room. A shocked Councillor Peverill and Jennery followed on behind.

The pavilion was full of seated dignitaries; councillors from the Grove, Lord William from Marchwood and Lord Marcus from East Watch were also present, seated together with their wives and talking intently. Garrick stood at the back amongst the household staff, a heavy frown on his face. Reid ceremoniously led Simeon to the front of the stage and faced the audience.

"Quiet, please," he called out. "We are about to begin the service for the confirmation of Lord Simeon of Greenswatch." He bowed to Simeon before stepping away.

Alyssa scowled as a tall dark-haired man joined Simeon. She turned around to the man seated behind her. "Councillor, who is that?"

"Councillor Meritas, he brings great momentum to our council." He smiled benevolently before he sat back.

Alyssa watched in confusion, numbly listening to the travesty of a service. Her eyes filled with tears as Simeon vowed to keep the rule of the council and swore fealty of Greenswatch not to the king and Lady, but to the council. She bit her lip and clenched her fists, concentrating on keeping her seat; she wanted to launch herself at Simeon and shake some sense into him. How had it come to such a pass? How could Greenswatch be brought to its knees so effortlessly?

"So be it, in the name of the council," Meritas finally proclaimed. "I give you Lord Simeon of Greenswatch. The council looks forward to a strong and prosperous union."

Alyssa stood, unable to keep her seat any longer and confronted her brother. "Congratulations, Lord Simeon, Councillor Meritas." She held herself rigidly; if she relaxed, she wouldn't be able to control her growing despair. Her jaw ached with the effort. "But haven't you forgotten something?" she bit out.

Simeon stiffened. "Not now, Alyssa."

"If not now, then when?" Her voice cut through the silence. She turned to the room, her face pale and stern. "Isn't there something missing? Was the Lady's blessing for Greenswatch invoked and accepted? If so, I fear I missed it in all the councillor's smooth words."

Lord William rose from his seat. "Lady Alyssa is correct. I was surprised at the lack myself, and at this location." He glanced up at the canvas awnings. "I fear that your Watch is exposed, Lord Simeon, and that puts the rest of us at risk in turn."

Simeon drew himself up, his cheeks flushed as he addressed the Marchwood lord. "I think that Lady Alyssa is overwrought with recent events, and certainly behind the times—as it seems is Lord William. The council's voice is ascendant here in Greenswatch." He drew in a slow breath. "Councillor Meritas will be pleased to explain it to you."

"Oh, that will not be necessary. I understand completely," Lord William said before retaking his seat, nodding at Lady Alyssa.

Councillor Meritas stood forward, frowning at the lord. "Ladies and gentlemen, please." He waved towards the exit. "Lord Simeon invites you to accept the hospitality of Greenswatch, and to join him in celebration of his confirmation."

A murmur rose as the audience slowly filed out. Jennery fell in beside Lord William. "Lord William, Lady Imelda," he said. "You risk much, my lord; best keep your men close. Remember what happened to Lord Hugh."

"Lady protect us in these trying times," Lord William intoned, placing his hand over his heart. "As the Lady wishes so it will be, but leaving that child to face those usurpers on her own—I just couldn't do it." William inspected Jennery. "What unit are you? I don't recognise the uniform."

"Lieutenant Jennery of the King's Guard, seconded for

the duration to Captain Haven of the Lady's Guard, sir," Jennery said. "I am escorting Lady Alyssa to Old Vespers later today with Captain Bryce of Stoneford. Maybe we should travel together, at least until we reach the East Road," he suggested as Garrick approached them.

"Liaise with Roberts, he's the captain of my guards." He indicated a bluff man standing behind them.

"I'll leave you in the safe hands of Garrick here," Jennery said as he and Roberts sized each other up as they entered the grand hall. The musicians were playing a lively dance.

"Your lord just painted a huge target on his back," Jennery murmured to Roberts as Lord William, Lady Imelda and Garrick traversed the hall, garnering much attention. Lady Imelda patted her husband's arm and moved off to join Lady Olivia seated at a table by the wall. Captain Bryce stood behind her.

Roberts looked resigned. "Nothing new there, he was a great friend of Lord Hugh. He's been itching to say something ever since the news reached us. And then not to be invited to the Leaving." Roberts spread his hands. "It was bound to happen. I brought an extra unit with us to make sure we make it home; they are camped north of the Grove."

"Good. Unfortunately, you may need them." Jennery scanned the room. Neither Alyssa nor Simeon were present, and nor was that smarmy councillor that Alyssa had taken such exception to. "Excuse me a moment." Jennery skirted the dance floor.

"Bryce, did you see where Lady Alyssa went?" he asked as he reached Lady Olivia's table. Olivia looked up in concern.

Bryce tilted his head towards the far exit. "She went through there with Lord Simeon."

Jennery observed Simeon's seneschal stop someone

leaving and turn them back into the hall. He caught Roberts' attention and signalled. Roberts drifted to the other end.

Lord William approached, his blue eyes alert. "What is the matter?"

Jennery grimaced. "I'm not sure, but the doors are all guarded, and no one is being allowed to leave."

Lord William pinched his lips as he inspected the room. "Nothing for it then, eh Garrick? Must be time to dance with the ladies." He offered a hand to Lady Olivia.

Garrick grinned in response. "Lady Imelda, it would be my pleasure."

31

GREENSWATCH

Alyssa paced the drawing room like a caged animal, trying to calm her anger. Simeon was insufferable. If he thought he could keep her locked up, he would be mistaken. And that new councillor of his, well!

The lock clicked, and Simeon entered the room followed by the councillor, Meritas. He was a dark shadow behind Simeon's shoulder with glittering black eyes that drew her attention. She tried to ignore him.

Alyssa gripped her hands together, ready to pounce on her brother. "Where have you been? How dare you lock me in?"

"You bring it upon yourself by this unbecoming behaviour. Our guests do not want to see you so distraught. Before you make yourself ill, Councillor Meritas wishes to speak to you. He will help you overcome your unnecessary distress. I recommend you listen. It would be easier for you in the end. Now sit." Simeon pointed to the chair.

"No, I will not sit, and I will not listen to either of you. You will let me out."

"All in good time," the smooth voice of Meritas interrupted. "Please, I mean you no harm. Sit, and we can begin. My lord, why don't you return to your guests; you will be missed. Keep them there. I will be along shortly," he instructed.

Simeon inclined his head and left the room.

"What have you done to my brother?" Alyssa asked as she moved behind a chair, her fingers curling like claws around the rigid back, determined not to look at him.

"Nothing that will harm. Just helped him find the true path, as will you. Look at me, Alyssa. Such a pretty name. Look at me and listen, listen to my voice; it will help you relax and free you of these anxieties." His voice droned, a continuous stream as he circled the room, closing in on her.

Alyssa shook the intrusive buzz out of her head and moved away from him. She chanted the Lady's Oath under her breath, concentrating on the words. Dear Lady, she beseeched, help me. She moved in counterpoint to the man who was slowly backing her into the corner. She knew what he was doing, but she couldn't see a way out, the chair between them her final barrier.

"That's right. Listen to my voice, you know you want to, my voice is the door to all you need," Meritas crooned as he moved forward. His eyes glinted as he cornered her. Lunging, he brushed the chair out of her hands as if it was matchwood and pinned her against the wall. He lifted her chin. "Stare into my eyes, and sink deep, deeper, you are feeling relaxed, and at ease."

Alyssa struggled against his relentless grip. "You are relaxing, as you sink deeper and deeper." He muffled her mouth as she attempted to bite him. "You are tired. It is time to sleep, Alyssa, time to close your eyes and sleep." Her struggles lessened as she stared up into his severe face.

"Is that how you always get your women?" A sharp voice

broke the spell. "It doesn't seem very honourable to me. Does it you, Tagerillion?" Jerrol raised his brow at the tall Sentinal standing beside him.

"No, he must be taught those manners that he seems to have mislaid." Tagerill stared at the man. "Most unseemly behaviour."

Before Meritas could react, Tagerill crossed the room and slammed him against the wall, forcing him to release Alyssa, who gasped as she slid out of his grasp.

Jerrol was by her side in an instant, helping her to a nearby settee. "Lady Alyssa, are you alright?"

Alyssa sniffed and rubbed her face. "He was trying to make me go to sleep. His voice," she shuddered, "it was creepy. I was struggling to ignore it. Captain Jerrol, Tagerill, you arrived just in time!"

"Who is he?"

The man struggled against the grip that pinned him against the wall, his feet dangling as Tagerill whispered in his ear. The man's face blanched.

"He is the new councillor, Meritas. Apparently, head councillor, as he performed the confirmation ceremony, if you can call it that. I've never seen him before, but the rest are in thrall. He has done something to Simeon, I am sure of it."

Jerrol helped Alyssa rise. "I need to have a quick chat with him. Do you think you can return to the hall and pretend to be in thrall too? Just agree with Simeon or Aaron, appear docile? I'll be along shortly."

Alyssa leaned on his arm. "Thank you for saving me, and thank you for saving Greenswatch, Captain." She kissed his cheek. They both felt the Lady's thrill as they touched. "I will help in any way I can."

"Well, we haven't saved it yet. But Lady willing we will.

Don't be alarmed when you pass the guards who appear to be sleeping on duty. We will help them later."

Alyssa chuckled with delight, a little colour returning to her cheeks. Tagerill winked at her impishly, making her smile broaden.

Jerrol escorted Alyssa to the door, opening it quietly to check the corridor. "All clear." He opened the door wider. Alyssa slipped through the door and lifted her chin, assuming a vapid expression on her face. Casting a saucy glance at Jerrol, which made him grin in appreciation, she skipped down the corridor. Shaking her head in disbelief, she passed the slumped body of one of her brother's guards.

The strains of a waltz grew louder as she approached the doors of the grand hall. She smiled at Birlerion, who stood guard outside the door. He grinned back at her and opened the door, allowing her to slip in and shutting it behind her.

Jennery and Bryce were skirting the dance floor, looking alert. She cast them a vapid look before approaching her brother. "Simeon," she said. "It's ages since we last danced. May I have the honour of this dance with our newest lord?"

"A pleasure, my dear." He took her in his arms. "So, did you enjoy your chat with Meritas?" he asked, watching her closely.

"Such a nice man, so soothing." Alyssa gazed at him, emptying her head of all thought.

"Good, I'm glad. He will be good for the Watch, I believe."

"I'm sure," Alyssa replied dreamily as they circled the ballroom.

"And here is Lord Aaron, I believe about to cut in." He surrendered Alyssa into the arms of the Deepwater lord.

Jennery watched Alyssa spinning around the dance floor. She didn't look right. He caught her eye, and she distinctly winked at him before her face resumed its vacant expression. What was going on?

He drifted towards the door and met Simeon barring his way. "Please, Lieutenant. You wanted to join the celebration, stay. Lady Cynthia needs a partner," and Simeon smoothly diverted him away from the door.

As Jennery guided the young lady through the steps, he suggested delicately that she dance with Lord Aaron, a venture she was happy to agree to. He gradually manoeuvred them closer to Alyssa and Aaron. "'Change." He offered Cynthia to Aaron, and Aaron had no option but to relinquish Alyssa.

"Smoothly done," Alyssa said with a small smile.

"Has something happened?" Jennery asked with concern, spinning Alyssa away from Aaron.

"Oh yes," she sighed into his chest. "Captain Jerrol is here with Tagerill and Birlerion. They have put all the guards to sleep. I left them having a chat with Meritas." She beamed up into his face.

Jennery blinked. "Ah, I see, I think."

Her laugh was rich and warm and just for him. "Whatever Simeon is planning, he is about to be thwarted. You dance well, Lieutenant. I think you should dance with me again later."

He tightened his embrace and drew her closer. "It would be my pleasure," he said as he buried his nose in her hair, breathed in the scent and shivered.

Alyssa tilted her head back so she could see his face. "Are you alright, Lieutenant?"

Jennery smiled into her eyes. "Oh yes," he purred as she laughed with delight.

The music came to an end, and the couples paused on the dance floor, looking expectantly towards the musicians.

Jennery drifted closer to Bryce, standing near the outer wall. "Jerrol is here," he murmured as they passed.

"Lady preserve us," Bryce muttered with a grin.

"Lords, ladies and gentlemen," Simeon began. "It is with pleasure that I welcome you to Greenswatch and the new age. An age of prosperity, union and growth. Today we will share our vision, and you will understand why you will join us. You will leave this room enlightened and as eager to spread the word as we are. I'd like to introduce you to Councillor Meritas, who will lead the way. Brother Meritas, everyone," and Simeon gestured to the large double doors, which opened right on cue. Only it wasn't Meritas standing on the threshold.

Simeon clenched his jaw as a slight young man entered. "What is the meaning of this? Who are you?"

"I regret to inform you, Lord Simeon, that, ah, Councillor Meritas declined your invitation to enspell all your guests." Jerrol's voice carried in the silence.

"Reid, call the guards," Simeon said.

"I'm afraid if you mean the guards who were preventing your guests from leaving, they are delinquent on duty. They all seem to have taken a nap," Jerrol said not very apologetically. "You'll have to talk to them about their sense of duty when they wake up. Ah, Captain Bryce." Jerrol caught Bryce's eye. "I suborned your men to take their place. I do hope that is acceptable."

Bryce changed a bark of laughter into a cough. "Captain Haven, thank you for the advisory. I will speak to them in due course."

Jennery stifled a snort as Bryce shook his head. You could always rely on Jerrol to do the unexpected. He grinned as Jerrol's gaze landed on him, knowing his spectacular bruising would catch his eye.

"Lieutenant Jennery." Jerrol's eyes widened, and then he

moved on to Alyssa with a smile. "Lady Alyssa, I think we may want to adjourn to a smaller room and allow your guests to continue to enjoy the hospitality or leave if they so choose."

"Just a moment." Simeon ran a finger around his collar. "Who do you think you are, ordering everyone about? This is my Watch."

Jerrol swung towards Simeon. Whatever Simeon saw in Jerrol's face made him take a step back. "Lord Simeon, I believe we need to talk privately."

"I am not going anywhere with you," Simeon blustered. "Reid, Aaron, where are your guards?"

Lord William stepped forward. "Sir, I am not sure what you saved us all from, but I am sure it wasn't going to be pleasant. But I am afraid I don't recognise your unit either."

"He is the Captain," a voice spoke from behind Jerrol, "and you would do well to listen to him." Tagerill stood foursquare in the door, an imposing figure dressed in the same archaic uniform Jerrol wore.

Lord William's eyes widened as he looked from the tall man with silver eyes standing in the doorway next to Jerrol. Jerrol gave a slight bow. "Indeed, I am Captain Jerrol Haven, Lady's Guard."

"You're that King's Ranger. Prince Kharel has a warrant out on you for treason." Councillor Peverill said as he peered around Aaron.

"I believe that is a different Captain Haven," Jerrol said with aplomb, his silver eyes flashing.

Lord William chuckled. "I am sure it is. Marcus," he called the other Lord Holder over. "We will attend this meeting with Lord Simeon and Lord Aaron."

Aaron spoke up at that point. "I am not staying to listen to any of this nonsense. I will be leaving immediately." Councillor Peverill muttered in his ear, and he extended a peremptory hand to his mother. "Mother, come."

Lady Olivia approached Jerrol. "I think I will stay and hear what the Captain has to say," she turned to her son, "as should you."

Aaron scowled. "You will attend me now. We are leaving."

"I think not. The Captain here will escort me home, won't you?" She held her hand out to Jerrol. He took it instinctively, stilling as the Lady's power passed between them.

"It would be my honour, my lady." He gave her a brief smile. Lady Olivia nodded with satisfaction and moved to stand beside Captain Bryce, outstaring her son.

Aaron retreated with Peverill. "You will allow me to leave," he commanded.

"Of course," Jerrol said, and Tagerill stepped aside. Aaron hesitated at the sight of a second, intimidating Sentinal in the corridor, but strode on regardless. Peverill scurried behind him.

Jerrol raised his voice. "Ladies and gents, I apologise for the disruption. Please enjoy the festivities. You are free to leave whenever you choose." He turned to Simeon and Reid. "Gents," he indicated the door, "after you. I believe we are using the drawing room." He waited for Lord William and Lord Marcus to precede him before turning to Garrick. "Garrick, could you hold the fort here? I'll explain everything before I leave," he promised. "Your men are not hurt; we'll release them from the spell, as soon as we have recovered Lord Simeon. Captain Bryce's men moved your men to the barracks, so your guests won't be alarmed."

Garrick gripped his arm. "Thank you, Captain," he said as he turned back to face what were now his guests. Jerrol fell in with Jennery and Bryce as they walked down the corridor.

"Well," Jennery breathed, "you do like to make an entrance, don't you?"

Jerrol grinned. "It was the best way to get everyone's attention."

"You managed that," Bryce agreed. "I'll speak to my sergeant, and I'll be in."

32

GREENSWATCH

J errol paused to speak to Tagerill before entering the room, slipping the notebook Tagerill handed him into his jacket pocket.

He stopped on the threshold as seven pairs of eyes swivelled to him. He took a deep breath and entered the room. "Please sit. 'Black Door,'" he said smoothly, watching Simeon slump in his chair.

"What did you do?" Alyssa leapt up in concern.

Jerrol walked forward. "Maybe Reid would like to explain? No? 'Blue Stone.'" He waited as Reid collapsed to the floor.

"What you are seeing is the result of the mind spell that the Ascendants are casting all over Vespiri, removing free will and planting suggestions that support their requirements. In this case, the neutralisation of Greenswatch."

Alyssa gasped, and Lady Olivia sat back in shock as she realised the ramifications.

"You mean Aaron is affected in the same way?" Lady Olivia turned haunted eyes on Jerrol. "Why did you let him leave?"

"I don't know his keywords. I couldn't release him as I hope we can Simeon here. But let's hear from Simeon what he has been persuaded to do, though I expect his speech earlier pretty much summed it up. Please let me ask the questions. I don't want to confuse him with multiple instructions."

He walked around in front of Simeon. "Lord Simeon, tell me what Councillor Meritas instructed you to do."

Simeon sat up and opened his eyes. "I believe in the right of the Ascendants' claim to power. I will support their every edict and defer to Brother Mer'iteras or Seneschal Reid for all decisions within Greenswatch. I am to ensure that Greenswatch is held ready for the Ascendants, prepare for the arrival of our new leader and take every opportunity to disavow the Lady." Simeon stopped speaking and stared straight ahead, unblinking.

Jerrol glanced around the room at the stunned faces. "Who is your new leader?"

"He will be revealed when the Ascendants' rule is confirmed."

"What of the people in your Watch?"

"They will support the council and the Ascendants."

"Who are the Ascendants?" Jerrol asked.

Simeon looked at him in confusion.

"What are their names?" Jerrol clarified.

"I've only met Mer'iteras and Var'geris. But many others are waiting to be called."

"What happened to King Benedict?"

"Prince Kharel took him to New Vespers and he will accede the throne on his father's death."

Jerrol's voice deepened. "How does Kharel intend to kill the King?"

"I don't know. But his death will be the signal for the councils to rise."

"Lord Simeon, what happened to Lord Hugh, your father?"

"Lord Hugh was killed on the battlefield. I am his rightful heir. I am confirmed as Lord of Greenswatch."

"What are your intentions towards Lady Alyssa, your sister?"

"Alyssa is to be Aaron's prize for taking Deepwater," Simeon intoned as Olivia gasped.

"Well?" Jerrol faced his dumbstruck audience. "Is that enough?"

Lord William shook his head in disbelief. "More than enough. Is that what they intended for us today?"

"Yes, or a variation to enthral you. I expect they planned to instruct you individually once they had control."

"Lady's blessings," Lord Marcus breathed. "It would be unbelievable if I hadn't seen it myself. What happens next?"

"I'll release Simeon. Jennery, Bryce, be ready. He will convulse, hold him still until it passes. He won't remember anything of the period he has been under their spell, so be warned. This isn't pretty, but I haven't found a way to avoid it. He is unlikely to realise Lord Hugh is dead, or that he had his confirmation today."

Alyssa held her hands to her face in horror as she watched Jerrol release Simeon. Her brother convulsed off his chair, but Jennery and Bryce caught him and held him down until he stilled.

After a moment, Simeon groaned. "My head, what did I drink last night?" Jennery helped him sit up. Simeon saw Alyssa staring at him. "Alyssa? What's going on?" He looked around the room and paled as he saw the other lords. "Lord William? Lord Marcus? What are you doing here? Where's Father?" he asked, bewildered.

Jerrol spoke into the sudden silence. "Lord Simeon, I think you should rest for a moment. Bryce, help him to the settee. You've had a bit of a turn. You'll be alright in a moment, and we'll explain. Jennery, is there any water in those jugs?"

Jennery checked the jugs. "It's all wine. I'll request some." He went to open the door and bumped into Tagerill who was blocking the entrance. "Tagerill, we need some drinking water, could you get some for us?"

Tagerill raised his hand and a young page came running. "We need some water, young sir," he requested of the young boy, who bobbed his head in awe and scurried away, returning with a jug.

Jennery grinned at the boy and took the jug. He poured a glass for Simeon and waited as he gulped it down. Simeon held the glass out for more before he sat back, resting his head and closing his eyes. Alyssa sat next to him and reached for his hand. "Simeon?"

Simeon opened his eyes and rolled his head towards her. "What happened?"

Alyssa looked at Jerrol helplessly, tears springing into her eyes.

Jerrol stepped forward. "I am sorry to inform you, Lord Simeon, that you befell an Ascendant plot to take over Greenswatch." Jerrol's face tightened. "There is no easy way to tell you this, but they killed your father, Lord Hugh, intending to place you as their puppet in his place. Today was your confirmation as Lord of Greenswatch."

"What?" Simeon looked frantically around the faces in front of him. "But that can't be true. Lord William?"

"I am sorry, son," William said, "but it's true. We attended your confirmation today, that's why we are all here. We just saw the spell removed."

"I would never betray the Watch or my father," Simeon protested.

"Not deliberately, no." William raised his hands. "But there is much we don't understand going on. The Ascendants are powerful, and they have magics we have never seen before. Son, it wasn't your fault. What befell you almost befell us today."

"And Aaron is still affected. How do we help my son?" Olivia clasped her hands together.

"Aaron?" Simeon peered at Lady Olivia. "What happened to Lord Stefan?"

Lady Olivia paled. "He was killed in a hunting accident; shot by his men," she said bitterly.

Simeon swallowed as he understood what she wasn't saying. "And our men? Where's Garrick?"

"Garrick is representing you in the ballroom where all your guests may still be celebrating your confirmation," Jerrol replied with a grim smile.

Simeon blanched even further. "Lady's blessings," he murmured, rubbing his eyes. "Do I have to face them all today? What did I say?"

Alyssa hugged him. "I am so glad you are back," she said, her relief evident.

"Let's deal with Reid first," Jerrol suggested, turning to the man who was still slumped on the floor.

"Who is he, and what's wrong with him?" Simeon leant his arms on his knees as he peered down at Reid.

"He is in the same state you were. And as to who he was, he was your Seneschal. As to who he is, let's find out, shall we? Reid," Jerrol said clearly. "Tell me your true name and your purpose here."

Reid opened his eyes and sat up. "My name is Kor'aderil. I am to prepare the way for the Ascendants' glory. Greenswatch will be cleansed ready to welcome the new leader. I will do what must be done to provide the brothers with the platform they need to overthrow Vespiri and bring it under the thrall of the Ascendants."

Jerrol ignored the gasps of horror behind him. "And who is Meritas? What is his purpose?"

"Meritas?" Kor'aderil frowned, momentarily confused. 'Ah, you mean Mer'iteras?"

"Mer"iteras," Jerrol confirmed.

Kor'aderil's smile didn't reach his eyes. "Mer'iteras is the foremost expert in *Mentiserium*. He is spreading the word and helping the people to find the truth. He will wipe the Lady's name from the world."

"*Mentiserium*? How did they discover that?" Jerrol stared at the man.

"Var'geris found it. He discovered he could control the minds of others. It is a skill very few possess or can learn. Only the Ascendants' direct descendants have the power. And the beauty is that the people don't even know they are affected, so no one can tell," Kor'aderil boasted.

"Who are the direct descendants?" Jerrol probed.

Kor'aderil's eyes flickered around him. "I am not supposed to know, but Mer'iteras has a brother called For'teres, and there is another who's never named."

"For'teres, I've met," Jerrol grunted, regretting he had allowed him to escape. "Are you a descendant?"

"Me?" Kor'aderil gave a sharp laugh. "No, I'm not a descendant. I'm not of the bloodline, but they welcomed me into the brotherhood all the same."

"Who were you before you entered the brotherhood?" Jerrol asked, fascinated.

"I came from Terolia, a son of the Kiker, not deemed important to be anyone. But they will see. I will show them all!"

"Where are your marks? You display no family allegiance."

"I am a brother. I am no longer a Kikerian. I do not need

family allegiance. The Ascendants removed the marks for me."

"Are you sure you joined the brotherhood of your own free will?"

Kor'aderil hesitated. "Of course I did."

"Where did you join, was it in Terolia?"

"Yes, I had escaped from the Kiker conclave while we were encamped outside Il Queron. I found the true path in Mistra when I heard Var'geris speak. A true descendant."

Jerrol looked around the room. "Anything else I should ask before I release him?"

"What will happen to him when you release him?" Simeon asked.

Jerrol grimaced. "I'm not sure, but I think he will revert to the Kikerian he is supposed to be. I think this whole brother thing is imposed on him, much like they imposed on you. How he will take that is anyone's guess. It sounds like he has been under this spell for many years."

"He must have been, to reach a position of authority and to be trusted to manage Simeon," Jennery agreed, preparing to restrain the man.

Simeon winced at the reminder.

Jerrol turned back and commanded Kor'aderil to forget all imperatives and never to be susceptible to *Mentiserium* again. Jennery and Bryce leapt to hold him down as he convulsed. His eyes rolled back in his head, and he collapsed to the floor, unconscious.

Jerrol sighed, observing the man. "I imagine the removal hurt a lot more for him because it was ingrained for so long. I suggest you take him to the infirmary and keep a guard on him. I don't know how he will react when he wakes up."

Bryce grabbed the man's shoulders, Jennery his feet, and between them, they carried the unconscious man out of the room.

Jerrol rubbed his face; his mad dash across the country-side with Tagerill and Birlerion was catching up with him. He wondered how Birlerion felt. He gave Simeon a fleeting smile. "I recommend you advise Garrick of all this. He is your closest ally, and he will need to understand how to remove the spell from all your men." He handed Simeon the notebook. "There is a list of names and keywords in there. As long as you remove all previous imperatives and block the effect of this *Mentiserium*, the words should be useless."

"Thank you, I will deal with this immediately." Simeon took the notebook eagerly. "Captain Haven, I can't thank you enough for your help. Where Greenswatch would be if you hadn't intervened, I dread to think. That the Ascendants have such power is frightening. Where is the king's defence?"

"I think you are looking at him, and I need to go and brief the king next. That was where I was going before I detoured here. I need to inform the king about what is going on. We will need his help to release Deepwater and the towers, and to protect the other Watches."

"If there is anything you need, anything we can do for you," Simeon gripped his arm, "please, don't hesitate to ask." He turned to his sister. "Alyssa, we need to speak before I go and address our guests. If you would excuse us for a moment." Simeon bowed to Lords William and Marcus and Lady Olivia. "Please, rejoin our guests and enjoy the hospitality. We will be in to address everyone in the grand hall in a moment."

33

GREENSWATCH

The soft green cushions on the window seat coaxed Jerrol to lean back and close his eyes: just for a few minutes, he thought. The emotions buffeting him in the room had taken their toll as he had tried to find his way. They all believed he had the answers, but answers were woefully sparse. The strain of meeting everyone's expectations was wearing him down. He dozed in the warm afternoon sunshine that was weakly penetrating the clouds until Tagerill's voice woke him.

"Captain."

Jerrol reluctantly opened his eyes. "I am sorry to disturb you, Captain." Tagerill apologised, acknowledging the exhaustion on his face. Jerrol waved the apology away. "Saerille sent a report. She patched the Veil, but it won't hold. She needs to stay and keep repatching until you can go up and seal it."

"I don't understand, why can only I seal it?" Jerrol asked with a slight frown. Surely if the Sentinals could patch, they could seal?

"The power to seal is the same as the power to shred; as

you can heal, so you can injure. That power must be controlled. Therefore only the Captain may truly heal. Otherwise, the risk to the Veil is too great."

Jerrol paused. "I don't know how to seal it," he admitted.

"You will when you need to."

"I hope so. So be it; advise Saerille to hold station. Can you call Ari?"

"I'll see to it," Tagerill promised. He blushed and shifted awkwardly. "Birlerion told me the Greenswatch Sentinal is Versillion. If you wake him, Birlerion could rest better in Versillion's tree."

Jerrol cursed under his breath as he rose. "How could I have forgotten? I tried to wake him before, only I didn't know how. Where is Birlerion?"

"I managed to persuade him to rest upstairs. I'll go and wake him and meet you at Versillion's tree."

Jerrol hurried out of the manor house, thankful no further catastrophe had befallen the Watch whilst he had slept.

Skirting the lake that was rippling in the light breeze, he approached the tall sentinal. He rested his hand on the smooth trunk, thought of the Lady and reached. The image of the broad-shouldered Sentinal came into focus, and Versillion stepped forward. He was taller and broader even than Tagerill, but the family likeness was clear. Tousled red hair framed a firm face, silver eyes bright.

"Versillion, it's time to wake. Greens needs you."

"Captain, I have been waiting."

"I know, I'm sorry. But it's time now, and I need you." He stepped back and Versillion shimmered out of the tree. Tagerill rushed up from behind him and engulfed the startled man in a hug.

"Tage? What's the matter?" Versillion looked around

him, frowning at the unfamiliar view, but his expression eased as he saw Birlerion. He hugged his brother back.

Tagerill shook in his arms, incapable of speech, and Versillion looked across at Jerrol. "Captain, what happened?"

Jerrol grimaced and ran a hand through his hair; what could he say? "You've been asleep for three thousand years. The Lady brought down a Veil which banished all magic, to defeat the Ascendants. But that meant she and Guerlaire left along with the Ascendants. Her guards, she encased in a protective sentinal tree." He gestured at the tree. "I awoke Birlerion in Old Vespers about two months ago, Tagerill a few days ago and now you."

Versillion blinked and tightened his grip on Tagerill; he reached an arm towards Birlerion, and Birlerion stepped into his embrace. "Three thousand years?" he repeated, hugging his brothers.

"I'm afraid so. The Lady needs our help, and there is a renewed threat against Vespiri. Guardians are being targeted, killed. Administrators influenced against their better judgement."

"Birler?" Versillion whispered.

Birlerion raised his head, wiping his tears away. "Sorry."

"Hush, nothing to be sorry for, you've had no one. I at least have you."

"It's all so different," Birlerion whispered.

Versillion gave a sour laugh. "It's been three thousand years. The house will have been rebuilt many times; of course it's different. But it's still Greens, and it's the land, not the house, that makes it Greens."

"It's called Greenswatch now," Birlerion said.

"Greenswatch," Versillion repeated. He gave Birlerion a little shake. "It's still home. Our home."

Birlerion gave him a strained smile. "It has a lake," he said, indicating the water behind them.

Versillion spoke more sharply. "It's our home, Birlerion, don't you dare say otherwise. We are still your family. Don't upset Greens."

Birlerion stilled and then sighed. "I know." He looked up, concern in his eyes. "Marianille is not in Vespers. I don't know where she is."

"We'll find her," Versillion promised as he hugged him.

The three brothers stared at each other and then laughed, and Jerrol looked away at the intensity of their reunion. "I'll leave you to get reacquainted. A couple of hours, Tagerill, I'll meet you back up at the house." He left them shimmering back into the tree.

Jerrol's stomach growled, and he went to find some food. Following his nose, he managed to reach the kitchen before anyone found him and sweet-talked the cook into dishing up a bowl of stew and letting him sit at the kitchen table to eat it. Jerrol and the cook were discussing the intricacies of bread puddings when Jennery tracked him down.

"Jerrol, I been searching all over for you; you're not trying to get an advance on dessert, are you?" He glanced around the kitchen. "What have you done with your Sentinals?"

"They're around somewhere. How is Simeon doing?"

"He's not a bad lad, and now he's got rid of that chip on his shoulder, he'll be fine. He had the guts to address his guests and promised to rearrange the confirmation where they would welcome the Lady to Greenswatch and celebrate his father's life."

"Good. What about everyone else?"

"Garrick has removed the spell from some of his men, and they are recovering in their barracks. Captain Bryce and Captain Robert's men secure the perimeter. Lieutenant Jennery, Lady Alyssa and the gentlemen are all in the Picture

Room, which is off the ballroom. I believe most of the guests have now departed."

"Good, I think our work here is done." Jerrol massaged his temples, trying to rub the ache away. "Let's finish it off and get back on the road."

Jerrol and Jennery were about to enter the Picture Room as Tagerill and his brother Versillion approached. Jennery stopped at the sight of the two Sentinals, clearly related and talking intently. Tagerill was waving his hands about as he shared some tale or other, while his brother just shook his head in disbelief. They broke off and saluted as they reached Jerrol.

"Captain," Tagerill burbled, his joy at finding his brother overflowing, "we await your command. What do you need of us?"

Jerrol returned the salute. "Let's introduce Versillion to his Lord Guardian. And then we need to return to Old Vespers."

"I explained what happened here. Versillion is ready."

"Indeed, Captain, it would be my honour to stand by Lord Simeon."

"Good," Jerrol said with relief, "let's get on with it." Following Jennery, they entered the drawing room.

Alyssa stood and crossed the room. "Captain Haven, thank you for returning my brother to me."

Jerrol bowed over her hands. "I'm glad I could help; we were fortunate."

"Indeed, we were." She moved to stand beside Jennery, her hand unconsciously reaching for his arm.

Jerrol watched them, a brief smile flitting across his face before he turned to Simeon. "Lord Simeon, I have someone to introduce to you." He gestured for Versillion to step forward. "Sentinal Versillion is here to help protect Greenswatch as he has done for the last three thousand years or so," he announced into the stunned silence as Simeon's jaw dropped and everyone stared at the tall man with the dark red hair.

"My Lord Simeon." Versillion bowed, his voice low and sincere. "It is my honour to serve the Guardian and the Watch."

"W-what?" Simeon stammered.

"Versillion, Tagerill and Birlerion lived here in Greens when the Watch was first created. They are your family and Versillion will stay here and help you hold the Watch. He will protect you and the Lady Alyssa until you can hold the confirmation and invoke the Lady's protection. You don't need to fear the Ascendants taking hold again, Versillion will prevent that," Jerrol said.

"S-sentinal Versillion, it is a very great pleasure to meet you." Simeon stared at the Sentinal in awe.

Alyssa approached Versillion. "Welcome home," she said as she took his hands. His silver eyes widened as the Lady's thrill passed between them. "Guardian," he said with a low bow.

"Haven," Lord William said as he rose to his feet, "how is this possible?"

Jerrol grinned sympathetically. "I did tell you I was the Captain of the Guard; what I omitted to say was that my Guards are the Lady's Sentinals."

Lord William stared at him hopefully. "Can you wake mine up? There is a Sentinal standing guard over Marchwood. And Marcus has two. I think we need all the help we can get."

"I have to report back to the King first. I suggest that when you return home, you engage with the Sentinals, explain the situation. They are stirring and will hear you. I will return once I have seen the King. Lady Olivia, I would recommend you stay with Lady Alyssa for now until I can speak to the King. Once I know the King is secure, I will come and escort you to court, and we can request his help for your son."

Alyssa spoke up immediately. "Olivia, you must stay with us until we can return you home."

Olivia smiled her thanks. "Do you think waking the Deepwater Sentinal would help Aaron? I hate to think of him under their control and so helpless. The damage they could do to the Watch if we don't stop them could be irreversible."

Deep down, Jerrol agreed, but he had delayed too long already. The urgency to return to the King was building. "I need to go to Vespers first, then we will plan our next steps. Bryce, if you could accompany Hannah back to Stoneford and report, so Jason knows what is going on. Hopefully, Chryllion has routed out all those that were affected by now."

"Chryllion is awake?" Versillion was delighted.

"And Saerille," Tagerill replied with a grin.

"Yes, and Simeon, I am sure you will need to check out the councillors at the Grove. Versillion will help. Their names may even be listed in the book. I am sure they have been affected," Jerrol said.

"Once Garrick has finished with his men, we will move on to the council. We will keep Mer'iteras confined here until you send the King's word," Simeon agreed.

"Be very careful who guards him. You heard what Kor'aderil said. Mer'iteras is the expert; his voice is all he needs," Jerrol warned.

"We'll be careful," Simeon promised. "You'll come back for the confirmation, though, won't you? And you, Lieutenant Jennery?"

"Can't promise anything, but we'll try. We have to return

for Lady Olivia so that may well work out quite well," Jerrol said. "Send word when you have the date set."

"I'll send Ari." Alyssa interrupted the soft conversation she was having with Jennery to look over at Jerrol.

Jerrol noted their quick tete-a-tete though he refrained from comment. "Right, Birlerion is out front, it's time we left."

Zin'talia was complaining at being roused by the Sentinal. *"He doesn't like me,"* she grumbled. *"Why doesn't he like me?"*

"He does likes you, don't be silly," he soothed. *"Be nice."*

Versillion spoke. "By your leave, Captain, I will assist my brother. It may be some time before we see each other again."

Jerrol waved assent and turned to Bryce. "Warn Jason to patrol the Stanton passes. They must be coming over from Terolia. It sounds like that is where the trouble is brewing."

Bryce shook his hand. "I will, and you be careful in Vespers. In both of them," he said, his face grave. He took his leave of the ladies and left the room to find Hannah.

Pausing at the top of the stone steps, Jerrol surveyed the men and horses waiting for them. If he hadn't seen it for himself, he would never have believed the Sentinals had awoken, yet here they were, tall and mysterious. The material of their unusual uniforms shimmered in the evening sunlight. He swallowed the lump in his throat. Greens should be celebrating the return of three of its sons. That such a momentous occasion had passed almost unnoticed was not right. The three men stood close together, their bond visible, and he thought that maybe Greens was celebrating: busy tying her knots, as Birlerion would have it.

Three Sentinals from Greenswatch and there were more down at the Grove. He ought to wake them. Simeon was staring at him with awe. He supposed he looked as strange as his Sentinals with his silver eyes. His only comfort was the fact Taelia wouldn't notice any difference. He admitted to himself he missed her, and Zin'talia snorted and shook her head.

"Jerrol, I can't thank you enough for all your help. I hope you can return for my confirmation. We'd be pleased to see you."

"Do my best," Jerrol said as he mounted Zin'talia and, casting a glance around his companions, he led the way down the road.

34

OLD VESPERS

I t took all night to reach Old Vespers, and that was only after Jerrol insisted they detour via the Grove to wake up the Sentinals. He slid off Zin'talia as they approached the trees guarding the Lady's temple and stood in the centre by the stone table, where he simply said, "The Captain has returned and requires your presence."

Jennery still couldn't quite believe that five tall, silver-eyed men stepped forward out of a swirling mist and crashed their fists against their chests. "As the Captain commands," they responded in unison.

Jennery eyed the three men riding behind him a little suspiciously. Jerrol left the Sentinal called Parsillion to guard the Grove and sent Frenerion to join Versillion at Greenswatch. The three accompanying them seemed worryingly like Tagerill, a little too enthusiastic for Jennery's taste. They all wore the same archaic uniforms as the ones he and Jerrol wore. Each had one of those brutal broadswords across their backs, and they all greeted Tagerill and Birlerion like long-lost brothers. They continued an intense low-toned discussion with the blond-haired Serillion as they rode.

Jennery frowned at the three of them. Birlerion had become more withdrawn and silent as more Sentinals were awoken. What did he fear? The exuberant Tagerill naturally drew the attention, but it seemed as if Birlerion took a step back and watched from the shadows, eyes alert.

Darllion appeared to be the eldest. His grey hair denoted his seniority. Fonorion was black-haired, lean and predominantly silent, a little older than Serillion and Tagerill, who were of an age and knew each other well.

They were all shocked that it had been three thousand years since they last breathed the air of Vespiri. Even worse was the news that the Lady was no longer present and that Remargaren was a very different place to what they remembered. Yet they accepted Jerrol's authority without a single complaint.

Jennery shifted his gaze to Jerrol; he was different too, as if the awakening of the Sentinals was changing him. He seemed more — of what Jennery wasn't sure, but he had a presence about him that he didn't have before, and his eyes flashed silver like those of the Sentinals. Jennery was struggling with the fact that he took it for granted that he could just walk up to a tree, conjure a man out of it and then command him to follow him.

Passing under the golden stone arch of the East gate, Jerrol called a halt on the outskirts of Old Vespers by the temple gardens. The sky was streaked in red and gold as the sun rose and the tower bell in the Chapterhouse called the scholars to break their fast. Tying Zin'talia to the fence, he led the way into the gardens. Soft green foliage edged the paths, sheltering them from view.

He had been aware of Jennery's scrutiny for the last few miles. He didn't know what Jennery was searching for or expected. There were few answers to his questions, so he focused on how to get four distinctive guards through Old Vespers without making a commotion or setting off the garrison.

"Right, we need to get a lay of the land," Jerrol said once the Sentinals had gathered around him.

"A lay of the land?" Darllion asked.

"Yes, I've been gone for nearly two months. We need to discover what's happened to the King, and what the chancellor and the prince have been up to. Jennery, do you think you could see if Nikols is still there? See what you can find out?"

"What are you going to do?" Jennery kept his voice low as his eyes flicked around the quiet gardens. Birlerion drifted off and shimmered into his sentinal tree, and the tree trembled. The pointed green leaves rustled above them.

"Speak to Liliian, see what she can tell us. I think we need to disguise our companions here. The scholars seem the best option to me. Unless you have any better ideas?" Jerrol waited expectantly, but as they shook their heads, he continued. "That is, if Liliian is here. Tagerill, you come with me, the rest of you wait here with the horses. The scholars are peaceful historians who support the Lady. We don't want to scare them; they are not soldiers. Whatever happens, if an alarm goes up, protect those in silver robes; do not hurt them. Understood?" Jerrol looked around the group of tall men surrounding him.

They all nodded. "As you command, Captain." Darllion appeared to be their spokesperson. "Though this Chapterhouse does not look like the Lady's Chapterhouse; the buildings were much taller, and there is no palace. I cannot sense the Sentinals – were they lost?"

Tagerill stiffened. Serillion lifted his head as if searching and Darllion gripped Tagerill's shoulder in sympathy. "I regret, but Marianille is not here."

"I didn't realise this was the Chapterhouse of Vespers, but she would have been up at the palace, not here. Where is the Lady's Palace?" Tagerill surveyed the town before him. "The Lady's Palace is gone, and the Captain's bridge is missing. This can't be Vespers."

"We couldn't protect the buildings and the people," Birlerion said from behind them.

Serillion moved as if he was about to speak, but he held his tongue as Jerrol spoke. "There has only ever been one Sentinal in Old Vespers," he gestured at Birlerion, "and never a bridge. The Chapterhouse before you is the only Chapterhouse of the Lady's Order of Remargaren in Vespiri. Legend has it that the old city was engulfed by a huge landslide at the end of the Ascendants' rebellion when the stone was sundered. The scholars are still excavating the archives below the Chapterhouse." He looked at Birlerion. "The temple and your Sentinal were only discovered in the last hundred years or so."

Birlerion's eyes widened, but he remained silent.

"Remargaren," breathed Tagerill. "The Lady still watches."

"She never stopped," Jerrol said. "I will signal if it is safe and you can bring the horses in; otherwise, you wait here. Understood?"

"We will await your signal or your return. If the alarm goes up, we will come to your rescue. We will not harm any of the Lady's scholars," Darllion repeated.

Jerrol closed his eyes. He sincerely hoped he would not set off any alarm. He couldn't imagine what havoc his Sentinals would cause coming to his rescue.

Jennery grinned at the Sentinals. "You gonna rush to my rescue if the garrison gets upset?"

Darllion smirked, a glint in his eye. "As the Captain orders, it would be our honour. Are we allowed to harm the soldiers?" he asked, straight-faced.

Jerrol glared at Jennery. "Don't encourage them," he said. "They are the King's soldiers. They are just misguided. The King would be unhappy if we disabled his garrison. We need to cause as little disturbance as possible. You can cause havoc at New Vespers. The Prince will have his men on duty; you can deal with them as you see fit. I'll need a diversion to get to the King anyway."

Serillion, a quietly enthusiastic young man whom Jerrol hoped would not turn out to be another Tagerill, returned from a self-imposed sortie around the Chapterhouse, his face alight with anticipation. "Guards on the main gate, none at the back. If there is a patrol, it must be inside," he reported.

"Very well, the back it is; somehow I doubt we would pass inspection."

The Sentinals grinned viciously in anticipation. "We will bide until your return. Walk silent, my Captain," Darllion said before glaring at the other Sentinals. Serillion pulled Birlerion to one side and began talking fast. Jerrol wondered what they were discussing.

Jerrol and Tagerill slipped around to the back of the Chapterhouse. As Serillion had reported, there were no guards in sight. Tagerill paused at the double gates; he gave them a tentative push, but they were barred from the inside. "How about I give you a boost, and you open the gate for me?"

Glancing up at the stone walls, Jerrol estimated the distance was a good fifteen feet above him. He searched Tagerill's face. He was serious.

Tagerill continued. "There are no signs of patrols on the walls, very sloppy," he finished in a disappointed tone.

Jerrol put his foot in Tagerill's linked hands and was

shortly landing on top of the wall. Tagerill peered up at him as he searched the courtyard, before spotting the stone pegs drilled into the walls an equal distance apart. A simple stairway leading down. He climbed down and unbarred the gate, opening it enough to allow Tagerill to slide in unnoticed.

35

CHAPTERHOUSE, OLD VESPERS

J errol headed across the courtyard towards the cloisters and then under the arch which led into a walled garden. A small fountain tinkled to itself in the quiet evening: a gentle counterpoint to the soft cooing of doves roosting in the eaves of the buildings rising either side of the gardens. A peaceful oasis bathed in the evening sun.

"The Deane's office is in the north tower. We need to go this way." He led Tagerill down the passageway behind the golden stone columns which lined the garden, pausing in the shadows as scholars crossed before them, intent on the scrolls in their hands and oblivious to their surroundings.

Jerrol's lips twitched as he heard Tagerill tsking behind him. They reached Liliian's tower and her gatekeeper, seated at his desk at the base of the stone stairs, having traversed the length of the Chapterhouse unnoticed.

The scholar-secretary lurched to his feet in surprise as Jerrol hovered in his doorway. "Captain Haven, what are you doing here? How did you get past our guard dogs?"

Jerrol grinned. "They are not attentive, and they are only

posted at your front gates. So they are not very serious about it, whatever they said to you."

"Attentive enough to keep us contained." The man curled his fists.

"We only saw two, are there any inside?" Jerrol asked.

"There is supposed to be a roving patrol inside and out, but they only check once a day, fortunately. But they won't let any of us leave unless it's at the chancellor's behest."

"Is Liliian here?"

"Yes, she's in her office. Let me warn her you're here. Can you give me a moment?"

Jerrol waved Tagerill into the small antechamber. The looming Sentinal filled the space, and the secretary peered up at him as he skirted the tall guard, before hurrying up the stairs. He returned immediately, gesturing for Jerrol to go up.

Jerrol mounted the stairs, closely followed by Tagerill. Scholar Deane Liliian was on her feet behind her desk when Jerrol entered, her eyes widening as she saw the tall man behind him.

"Jerrol! Thank goodness, where have you been?" Liliian exclaimed before he had a chance to close the door.

"Travelling the watches, avoiding assassins, you know, the usual," he replied with a flash of a smile.

"Don't joke. The situation is dire. The prince controls the king, and the chancellor controls everything else. We are under house arrest here."

"How is the king?"

Liliian scowled. "Not so good, the last I saw, and that was over three weeks ago. Prince Kharel moved him up to the palace at New Vespers. He was confused. I can understand why Prince Kharel is starting the proceedings to take over as Regent. The king deteriorated visibly in the few weeks he was here."

"Has the King's Justice been invoked yet?"

"Not yet, but with the chancellor pushing him, it won't be long. The chancellor is all cosied up with the Elothians, some special relationship he brokered. There is a state dinner in their honour next week in New Vespers. Not that I'm invited. I think he intends to invoke the process then."

Jerrol's eyebrows rose. "Elothians, huh? This new relationship is not that new, I think."

Tagerill loomed behind him. "Who is this chancellor that seeks to overthrow the Lady's champion?" His silver eyes glinted dangerously.

Liliian stared at the tall man standing by Jerrol's shoulder. He wore the same unfamiliar uniform Jerrol was wearing, casting him in a mysterious light. "And who is your tall friend?" She narrowed her eyes.

"My apologies." Jerrol gestured at Tagerill. "This, my dear Deane, is Sentinal Tagerillion of Greens. Tagerillion, Scholar Deane Liliian of Remargaren," he said with a gleam in his eye and paused, waiting.

Liliian made a gurgling noise as she watched the tall Sentinal bow in turn and murmur, "My lady."

"A Sentinal? You managed to wake them?" she asked, awe tingeing her voice.

"Indeed, my lady, it is an honour to serve the Captain."

Liliian's eyes narrowed. "You are the Lady's Captain?"

Jerrol grinned. "Afraid so. Vespiri may have disowned me, but the Lady staked her claim instead while we were saving the Watches." His eyes gleamed silver like his companion's.

Liliian closed her eyes in despair. "Sit," she commanded. "I expect to hear the long story at your earliest convenience, but the short story will do for now." She sat down behind her desk and leaned back in her chair as if exhausted. She had forgotten how exasperating Jerrol could be.

Jerrol sat, waving Tagerill to the other chair. He paused,

collecting his thoughts; so much had happened. "Short story, the Ascendants are trying to destroy the Veil and weaken the Lady's protections by killing off the Guardians. I have been travelling the Watches to discover the cause and reverse the damage they have been doing.

"I believe they have spread from Terolia, casting dangerous mind spells that have influenced the behaviour of everyone they manage to taint. Including the councils. We happened to be in the Grove when they attacked the local Guardian. The Guardianship temporarily sat with me until the rightful heir could accept it. That was when the Lady made me her Captain." His face tightened as he continued. "The Guardians of Greenswatch and Deepwater have fallen; both heirs failed to pick up the mantle, though thankfully Greenswatch has been retrieved."

Liliian raised her hands to her mouth in horror.

He leaned forward, his eyes darkening. "We came across Lord Hugh, ambushed just south of Deepwater returning home after the confirmation of Lord Aaron. We were unable to save him, though we did rescue his daughter, Lady Alyssa. We travelled to the Watch Towers where we found the source of the mind spell and discovered how to reverse it, before coming here where I intend to save the king." He waited for Liliian to comment.

She stared at him. "And that is the short story? I hate to think what you left out."

"Well, I suppose the Sentinals, but I can't explain them now," he said with a resigned shrug.

Liliian placed her hands carefully on her desk and inspected him, noting the new lines around his eyes, the shadow on his chin and his gaunt frame. "Well, Captain Haven, what do you need from me? I assume you are off to save the king next?"

"Straight to the heart of the matter; that's what I love about you, Liliian. Where is the chancellor now?"

"Living it up at the palace, I expect; he has gained a taste for the life he desires. We call him the Pretender." She gave him a sharp smile.

"Pretender?" Tagerill asked.

"He thinks he is the new regent with the king indisposed and Prince Kharel at New Vespers."

"And what does the court think of that?" Jerrol asked.

"If they know what's good for them, they'll toe the line and pay homage to the new force in town."

"And Nikols?"

"Reluctantly biding his time, I think. He has no authority with the king's voice silenced. The chancellor controls the Justice, so be careful. There is still a warrant out for you," she said, her face tight with concern. "There are those who would still collect the bounty."

"They could try," Jerrol said confidently as he stood. "They've failed so far, and now my guards are awakening I think they'll find it even more difficult."

"Guards?" Liliian asked, staring at Tagerill. "Just how many guards do you have?"

"How many Sentinals are there?" Jerrol replied with a grin.

"Jerrol!" Liliian exclaimed in exasperation. "What exactly is going on?"

Jerrol took pity on her and explained. "Well, we are under attack from within and without. The Lady needs our help. The Sentinals are awakening to support her cause. I need to see the king, reinstate his control. Then we can focus on securing all the Watches and deal with the Ascendants."

"How can I help?" Liliian watched Jerrol as he paced. He had changed much since she had last seen him: thinner, yes, but it was more than just appearance. His manner was more authoritative, more decisive. He had a purpose, and he was driven by it.

"I have five Sentinals with me. I had intended disguising them as scholars to get them through Old Vespers, but I think we'll dispense with that idea and just retake the city. The king will want to come home anyway."

Liliian gaped at him. His supreme confidence was astounding. Jerrol grinned at her, his silver eyes lighting up boyishly and reminding her more of the old Jerrol she knew. "I'm not mad," he reassured her as his grin widened. "I sent Jennery up to contact Nikols. If what you say is true, I am the excuse Nikols has been waiting for. He'll take action to depose the chancellor and reinstate the king."

Liliian smiled in appreciation. "Oh, to arrest the chancellor for treason, what irony!"

Tagerill spoke up. "My Captain, we ought to send a message to the others. We have been here too long. I fear their enthusiasm may overrule their caution."

"The Sentinals are a little excited to be back in Vespers," Jerrol explained to Liliian.

A shout at the bottom of the stairs preceded the clatter of feet as someone stumbled up in a hurry. Taelia burst into Liliian's office, a look of horror on her face. "Jerrol?"

Jerrol grabbed her flailing hands and brought them up to his chest. "Taelia! What's happened?"

"The chancellor's men are coming. He knows you're here; he's coming for you. You have to leave," she said, an edge of hysteria in her voice.

Jerrol looked at Tagerill. "Go get the others, bring the horses inside; there is more chance of defending from within."

Tagerill left.

"No," Taelia moaned, "he mustn't find you here. He bought Kirshan assassins, and they accepted payment."

Jerrol stilled.

Liliian's face paled, reflecting the horror he felt. She reluctantly put her fear into words. "They won't stop until they've killed you, not if payment has been accepted." Liliian swallowed. "They don't care who gets in the way. They destroy towns because of their single-minded purpose. You need to leave. They will destroy everyone and everything here to get to you."

"The only way to stop them is your death. What should we do?" Taelia gazed at him in concern.

"Hush." He hugged her close. "Let me think." He inhaled deeply as he gently rocked her in his arms.

"It's not only my death that will halt them, but also the death of the person who paid them," he murmured into her hair. "The question is, is it the chancellor or the prince?"

Taelia heaved a shuddering breath. "I don't feel the prince in this," she said, a little breathlessly; then she hesitated. "I'm not sure it's the chancellor either, though he is aware."

"Well," Jerrol said, his eyes flashing. "I think I ought to have a little chat with our chancellor. I'm sure he's missed me." His voice had an edge to it as he contemplated their meeting.

Taelia shivered. "I can't see him," she said, gripping Jerrol's arms.

"Don't worry." Jerrol kissed the top of her head. "We'll find him. We'll try and lead them up to the palace. Give Isseran a dose of his own medicine," he said, his face brightening at the thought.

At that moment Liliian's secretary burst into the room, followed closely by Scholar Torsion. "Deane, soldiers are approaching, lots of them," he gasped, eyes wide in panic. "What should we do?"

"Nothing," Jerrol said without hesitation. "Stay within.

They are not here for you." He stared at Torsion, trying to see if he looked any different. He had tied his black hair in a queue, drawn off his narrow face, and his black eyes darted around the room; Jerrol had the impression he was searching for someone. "Torsion, thank goodness." He released Taelia to grip his friend's shoulder. "I'm so glad to see you."

Torsion hugged him in return, his severe expression relaxing. "Jerrol, where have you been? We've been so worried. The rumours flying around about you are beyond belief."

Jerrol grimaced. "Never believe all that you hear. How long have you been here?"

"He returned about two weeks ago," Liliian said, watching Jerrol in concern.

Jerrol scowled at the thin scholar. "I've been trying to find you. I tracked you up to the Watch Towers."

Torsion raised his eyebrows. "I can assure I've been here. You do not need to chase me anywhere," he said, his voice bored, though his dark eyes burned at the sight of Taelia in Jerrol's arms.

"He's been here all along. I can vouch for him. Go, do what you must. We'll distract them here for as long as we can," Lillian said.

"Don't take any unnecessary risks; there is no point losing a life over this," Jerrol cautioned.

"What, like you aren't? What do you take us for? Go." Liliian shooed him out of her office. Jerrol hugged Taelia and released her before leading the way back to the ground floor. There was a commotion outside the gates, and as he crossed the grand hall and out into the courtyard, Tagerill appeared, dragging an unconscious sentry through the gate, the remaining Sentinals fanning out behind him.

"Change of plan," Jerrol said. "We need to go to the

palace. It seems the chancellor set some Kirshan assassins on me. We can't stay here."

Torsion followed him. He grabbed his arm, staring at the tall Sentinals in concern. "Jerrol, who are these people? How do you know you can trust them?"

"The Lady claims them, that's why. I'll introduce them later; I haven't time now, you are going to love it."

Torsion hung onto his arm. "Jerrol, it's not safe, wait for the King's Guards. You need support. You can't do this on your own."

"I'm not on my own."

"Violence is not the way. People will get hurt." Torsion scowled at the enormous swords carried by the Sentinals.

Birlerion stepped forward, giving Torsion a close inspection, his face intent. "Captain," he began, and Jerrol cut him off.

"Not now." Jerrol hesitated as he stared at Torsion. "People have already been hurt, this can't be allowed to continue. The king is at risk; we have to help him."

"You think you are some big hero, always racing to the rescue. You are only making it worse." Torsion glared at Birlerion and Birlerion glared back.

Jerrol stared at him, wondering if Torsion had been affected when he was at the Watch Towers. "How am I making it worse? You know it's my job to protect the king and protect him I will."

Darllion broke through the tension. "Captain, Birlerion here doesn't miss. And a Kirshan assassin is good sport, don't you think?" he asked with an evil grin.

Birlerion's face was intent. "It would be my pleasure, Captain," he said, holding Torsion's eyes.

Jerrol looked at them incredulously. "Sport?" Darllion and Birlerion exchanged grins. Each to their own, he supposed, but Kirshan assassins should not be disregarded lightly. If the Sentinals were familiar with them from three thousand years ago, maybe they hadn't been so formidable back then. "You'll be able to pick them out?"

"Piece of cake," Birlerion replied. "They'll be so focused on you they won't see me."

Jerrol choked a little on that, but he let it ride. He trusted the Sentinals implicitly. "Very well. I'm going to lead them away from the Chapterhouse and up to the palace. Darllion, bring the horses in and bar the gate behind us. Protect these people. Birlerion, do what you need to."

"Captain, another force approaches from the west," Serillion's low voice interrupted him from above.

Torsion looked up at the blond-haired Sentinal on the wall in dismay. They were everywhere.

"Could you tell their colours?" Jerrol reached for Zin'-talia's reins, ignoring her mumbled complaints of being left with strangers, even if they were the Lady's.

"The standard is the crown and crossed swords, sir."

Jerrol breathed a sigh of relief. "Is Lieutenant Jennery with them?"

"Can't see him, sir."

"Wait before you engage; hopefully, they are our rein-forcements, and they will turn on the chancellor's men. If not, retreat and meet us at the palace at sunup. Understood? Do not engage if both forces unite."

"Understood, Captain," Darllion said, crisply saluting and turning away to deploy his meagre troops.

"Tagerill, Birlerion, with me." Jerrol swung himself up into the saddle. He gave Torsion a strained smile. "I said I wasn't on my own," he said, and he rode Zin'talia out of the back gates and swung behind the Chapterhouse.

36

OLD VESPERS

Jerrol took the back streets and approached the deserted warehouses that had sprung up under the chancellor's tenure. He glanced at them as he passed; what could he be storing so far inland? Something to check out later.

They kept moving, through the city streets and on past the stone buildings of the King's Justice and up the switchback towards the outskirts of the palace gardens. Dark clouds accumulated on the horizon blotting out the sun: a storm in the offing.

Birlerion muttered a quick farewell as he faded into the gloom.

Tagerill and Jerrol didn't slow; they continued up to the high walls which protected a gently shelving garden, which graduated towards the palace in terraces. Torches lit the paths at each junction that led up to the palace building.

There was a low whistle from above them, and Birlerion's hands flickered. Tagerill translated. "Four coming our way from the east, two patrolling the side gardens."

"Good, watch out for additional patrols; let's get over this wall and deal," Jerrol said as he balanced on Zin'talia's back before levering himself up and over the wall.

The soft thud of his landing was covered by a low thrum and a heavy thump. "One down," Tagerill whispered as he skirted the flower beds and led the way up the slope.

Jerrol heard another thrum and saw a man falter before sliding down off the wall to land in a heap. A black shape launched out of the shadows at Jerrol, and Tagerill blocked the brutal overhead swing with his broadsword, which he had unsheathed in moments.

Jerrol flicked one of his daggers at an approaching guard. The guard dropped as Jerrol spun back towards another oncoming shadow as more of the chancellor's men came charging around the side of the palace. Behind him he heard Tagerill engaging with the chancellor's patrol, having dispatched his opponent, the clash of swords loud in the half-light.

The assassin circled Jerrol as the air vibrated with the passage of arrows overhead, dropping guards around them. Jerrol raised his sword and advanced, forcing the assassin to engage. He drove him back across the flower beds towards Birlerion's arrows and paused, satisfied, as the man gurgled as an arrow protruded out of his neck. He signalled his thanks and turned to help Tagerill, the torches flickering as guards passed before them.

The palace guards faltered and fell back as a unit of King's Rangers entered the gardens. They hesitated, glancing warily at each other before laying their swords on the ground and holding their hands in the air. Tagerill cocked at eyebrow at Jerrol. "They give up too easily. Where's the sport in that?"

"Be thankful. We don't want to kill more men than we have to. Once these men were loyal to the king."

"Then they should be executed for treason," he said, scowling at them in disgust. The guards cowered before him.

Jennery came skidding to a halt beside them. "Why didn't you wait for us?" he puffed as he waved the rangers on around him to deal with the surrendering palace guards.

"Tagerill was having too much fun," Jerrol said as Birlerion strolled up to join them, busy slotting his retrieved arrows back into his quiver. "Nice shot," Jerrol complimented him. Birlerion grinned. "But seriously, Kirshans." Jerrol turned back to Jennery. "We had to lead them away from the Chapterhouse."

Jennery paled. "How many?"

"Well, Birlerion here dispatched four of them, but there could be more. Let's go and speak to the chancellor and find out." He led the way around the side of the palace to the elegant glass doors standing open to the terrace.

"Do you think he is still here?" Jennery asked, following him. "I expect he is long gone. He's the type to save his neck and worry about the rest later," he commented, gazing around him, his opinion of the chancellor clear.

"Best to check though. I need to speak to him," Jerrol said as he contemplated the mess. They had entered through the glass doors into a long antechamber; chairs were in disarray, papers scattered across the floor. He peered into what used to be the king's study: a small carpeted room which faced the formal gardens. He found a similar trail of destruction. "The king is not going to be happy," he murmured to himself as he returned to the ballroom.

"How did you convince Nikols to agree to all this." Jerrol indicated the King's Rangers setting up patrols around the grounds.

"I told him you were arresting the chancellor on charges of treason, usurping the powers of the king, and consorting with enemies of the crown. He leapt at it. I think he was just waiting for the right opportunity, especially when I told him you were on the way to save the king." Jennery paused and looked around. "Shouldn't you be off saving the king? We've got this," he said with a grin.

"I was hoping to have a chat with the chancellor," Jerrol said as a captain of the rangers entered the ballroom.

"Haven," he called across the room. "He's not here."

Jerrol raised his hand in acknowledgement and the man left. "Well, I guess we'll head up to New Vespers." He scowled, thinking fast. "See if you can keep any more assassins off our tail. And don't form up to storm the new palace until I give the signal. I need to make sure we've secured the king first."

Jennery gripped his arm. "I'll wait for Nikols to come up before we follow. Take your Sentinals; they are waiting by the front gate for you. This is a good day's work, go finish it."

"Very well, see you later," Jerrol said. At his signal, the two Sentinals fell in behind him, and they made their way to the front entrance, where he collected the rest.

Darllion grinned as he saw Jerrol. "Captain, the scholars are safe. The Chapterhouse is secure. Lieutenant Jennery brought the King's Rangers, and they quelled those soldiers soon enough. They seemed quite eager to surrender," he said with a frown.

"Doesn't surprise me." Jerrol mounted Zin'talia again. "The chancellor does not seem to have instilled much in the way of loyalty." He grunted as he shifted more comfortably into the saddle, flexing his shoulders to ease the aches. "Right, next the king," he said as he led them down the road to New Vespers.

The brooding storm was approaching fast as they crested the last rise which hid the city of New Vespers. The wind began to strengthen, whipping the trees into a frenzy of rustling leaves. The air was heavy with expectation, and the evening light had a yellow cast, bathing everything in a peculiar shadow. The city seemed to float on top of the regimented streets, which led to the gleaming palace.

Jerrol pulled Zin'talia to a halt and turned to the Sentinals, mere shadows behind him. "These guards will be more difficult to overcome. They will be loyal to Prince Kharel, and the prince suffers no fools. They will be nothing like what you saw at the palace. I don't think the palace guards had their heart in defending the chancellor. They were reluctantly following orders."

"I think a bit of sneaking is in order," Tagerill suggested. "But getting close enough unseen to sneak is going to be the challenge," he finished thoughtfully, observing the open approach. The road was a light ribbon wending its way up the hill lined by flat grass verges. There were few trees to provide cover.

Serillion dismounted and stared at the palace. "How close can we get before they see us?"

"It depends on how fast that storm gets here. If we go straight up the road now, they'll see us as soon as we go around the first bend, assuming the guards are alert. There is an alternative." Jerrol paused, assessing the Sentinals. "We send two of you up to the front door as a diversion, and the rest of us go in the back door."

"Objective?" Darllion asked.

"First, secure the king; that's my job. Reinstate his control of the palace and impound the prince and his supporters; that's where you come in."

"What about the waystone?" Serillion suggested, slowly rotating.

"Waystone?" Jerrol watched him scan the horizon.

"Why don't we enter through the waystone? You could

create one up at the new palace. I suggest up by where that tall tower is situated." Serillion pointed at the tower towards the north of the palace.

Jerrol stared at him. "What is a waystone?"

Serillion gaped back at him. "You don't use waystones anymore? Why, waystones enable us to travel from one place to another almost instantly. Saves a lot of time. There's one in each Watch. The Landgard was the Captain's Bridge; it connected the Chapterhouse with the Lady's Palace. Guerlaire built it as he did the Chapterhouse, and all the archives below." Serillion grimaced. "He was always adding new rooms; he never had enough space."

"The Landgard doesn't exist today except for the marker. It is just a landmark. The reason for it was lost with so much else. I've never heard of a waystone. I'm afraid we would have to excavate it; it is lost as is the Lady's Palace," Jerrol said carefully. "We don't have time to find it."

"The landscape is much changed," Serillion agreed. "But you would find it. You're the Captain after all."

Jerrol made a mental note to interrogate the Sentinals when he had a chance. So much history! The scholars were going to be in their element. "The waystone will be useful once we've found it. When we've finished here, you can show me where it is. But for now, we need to circle that hill and come in from the east down the river valley. Nothing lives up there except sheep and more sheep. The guards tend to pay little attention to the east perimeter. I've slipped in that way before now."

The Sentinals looked at him with interest and Jerrol waved a hand. "We'll swap stories over an ale another time."

Tagerill's eyes brightened, and he shared a grin with Serillion and Birlerion. "Deal," he said with a firm nod.

Jerrol cast about for a stick and then knelt in the dirt. He opened his left hand; the silver glow dispersed the gloom and lit his face, casting his features into shadow. The Sentinals murmured in surprise and gathered round as he began scratching a rough map in the soil. Ari popped into view and meeped as he hovered over him. Ari chittered more sternly and Birlerion opened his hand for the little Arifel to perch on. He wrapped his scaly tail around Birlerion's wrist and leaned forward watching with interest.

"This is the main entrance," Jerrol said, pointing at a gap in the south wall. "It leads into a central courtyard, barracks and stables which are in the west wing. There are three levels, and the king's chambers are at the top of the south tower. The prince's rooms are in the north tower.

"We need to distract the guards long enough for me to reach the south tower and find the king. Then protect him until the rangers arrive, and preferably capture the prince alive on the grounds of treason."

"How many men does he have?" Darllion asked.

"At least two units, about fifty."

"If we can secure as many of the guards as we can in the barracks, we can even the odds," Birlerion suggested.

"Darllion, you take Fonorion with you and see if you can befuddle the guards for us. You need to be inside the palace gates to be most effective, no quarter given. Give us two hours to go around the back, then start up the road. It will take you an hour to ride up the switchback. It is further than it looks." He squinted at the sky. "The storm should be here by then; even if there is a lookout to the east they will suffer the brunt of the bad weather."

Jerrol was surprised when Fonorion spoke. He was the quietest of all the Sentinals and hardly ever said anything, preferring to let the others talk. "Serillion would be best to go with Darllion. He can sweet-talk Guerlaire into parting with his money, even if Guerlaire knows better," he said, his voice low and measured.

Darllion chuckled. "I concur, Captain. Fonorion is right. Serillion is our best befuddler."

"Alright, Serillion, you are on gate duty with Darllion. Fonorion, you're with me, Tagerill and Birlerion. We come in the back door and surprise the rest. Anything else? Questions?"

The Sentinals looked at each other. "See you on the inside!" Tagerill said with a broad grin as they split up.

The remaining Sentinals followed Jerrol down the track and circled behind the hill, approaching the palace from the rear. They left their horses sheltered in a small copse of trees, before working their way up the steep valley, following the little stream that burbled its way merrily through the deep grass.

The storm overtook the last of the daylight. The roiling black clouds made the air heavy and the darkness oppressive. A flash of lightning lit up the fields, followed by a deep rumble that echoed around the hills. Blinded by the rain and the unexpected flash, they stumbled over tufts of grass and hidden dips.

Tagerill cursed under his breath. "In this light, they wouldn't have seen anything," he grumbled.

"Not worth the risk." Jerrol gripped his cloak tighter as the rising wind whipped the rain, driving it against the palace walls.

"If you've entered this way previously, Captain, why didn't you warn the king?" Birlerion asked as they struggled through the tall grass. They reached the base of the palace walls and crouched in a ditch, surrounded by uninterested sheep snuggled against the wall for protection.

"He rarely comes here." Jerrol said as he wiped his face. "And when he does, he stays in the south tower, which is more secure. And anyway, I know about it, so we are always prepared."

Tagerill and Fonorion hunkered down next to them, hair plastered against their heads as the rain suddenly got heavier. A louder rumble of thunder growled across the sky. "The best way in, Captain?" Tagerill peered through the gloom at the high stone walls.

"There is a storm drain at the base of that tower. It's going to be a bit tight, but you should fit."

"We can't get any wetter," Tagerill complained.

Birlerion started chuckling. "You can go in the middle, Tage. That way, one of us can pull you, and the other can push."

Tagerill grunted. "If I get stuck no one else will get through. You puny fellows had better go first."

"Be careful who you call puny, you may need us later! Or we could just leave you there." Fonorion slicked his hair back, which made him look a lot younger.

Jerrol watched them. Their enthusiasm made him feel old, yet they were all about the same age. "Come on, let's get out of this rain." Jerrol climbed out of the ditch and ran towards the tower, keeping low to the ground, and the Sentinals followed. Jerrol used his dagger to lever the grille away and led the way into the circular drain. The roughly hewn walls gave them enough purchase for their feet as they climbed up.

Although the drain was not wide, Tagerill managed to squeeze his broad shoulders through, following Birlerion and Jerrol who nimbly climbed ahead of him, Fonorion bringing up the rear. The reek of damp stone and the sharp tang of water filled the air as a constant stream of rainwater ran down the walls, draining off the battlements.

Birlerion helped pull Tagerill out the other end as Jerrol scouted the outer corridor. He came back grinning. "Serillion and Darllion are above us. It sounds like they made it into the inner courtyard."

They shed their cloaks, and the worst of the rain, as Jerrol led the way through the deserted corridors and up to ground level. A trail of wet boot prints marked their passage, though there didn't seem to be anyone on the lower levels to notice them. The sound of Serillion's commanding voice berating the palace guards greeted them as they crept through the lower corridors and reached the courtyard undetected.

Tagerillion chuckled under his breath, and he exchanged glances with a grinning Birlerion, who was unsheathing his bow. "Oh, that brings back memories."

Fonorion followed Jerrol as they left for the south tower. Birlerion scanned the courtyard for his best vantage point before disappearing into the shadows.

"Keep them contained; if they escape the barracks it'll make more work for the rest of us," Tagerill called after him.

The thrum of arrows and the surprised faces of the guards as men began dropping around them had Tagerill laughing as he strode into the courtyard, swinging his sword indiscriminately around him.

The horrific sound of the remaining Sentinals drawing their broadswords compounded the effect. Birlerion was sure Tagerill's laughter didn't help as the Sentinals methodically took the palace guard apart. Birlerion skewered any man that poked his face out of the barracks, and then Serillion wedged the door shut.

37

NEW VESPERS

J errol led the way to the king's apartments in the south wing, flitting down dimly lit corridors which were surprisingly guard-free. The prince must set great store in his defences, Jerrol thought to himself, his face grim. He arrived at the decorative doors of the king's apartments, still without seeing any guards. Had they all left their posts? He would not have left the king unguarded.

Fonorion hissed a warning, and they flattened against the wall as a guard stomped towards them. He stopped in surprise as Fonorion detached himself from the wall and pointed his sword at his throat. "Do you want to die?" His voice was a deep growl.

The guard raised his hands immediately. Jerrol watched him with suspicion before leaving Fonorion to deal with him. Gently, he eased the carved door open; his fingers traced the shape of the moon carved in the wood. Fonorion reappeared like a ghost behind him and he wondered what Fonorion had done with the guard, but he pushed the thought aside as he entered the room.

The plush red carpet absorbed all sound as they crept

forward. The room was unexpectedly ornate and richly furnished. Thick curtains draped the windows, softening the harsh stone interior; shadowed obstacles became upholstered chairs. Hairbrushes and mirrors gleamed on the table. Jerrol gripped his sword; he didn't remember the king's apartments being so opulent.

The king preferred a more austere environment. His wife passed many years ago, and there was no longer that feminine touch to soften his edges. Jerrol eased the connecting door open and peeked into the chamber. A huge bed dominated the room, the posters swathed in yet more material. He peered around the curtains and opened his left hand; in the silvery light he saw two sleeping forms in the bed. Definitely not the king.

He recognised the dark-haired man and bit back a curse, clenched his fist and began to ease back out of the room. The man jerked and rolled out of bed, rising with his sword in his hand. "Guards," he yelled, awakening his wife who started shrieking as she saw two armed men in her bedroom.

Jerrol winced at her piercing shriek, as did the Crown Prince who growled at her to shut up, but she ignored him, grabbing the sheets around her. She continued to shriek and wail.

"Haven, I should have known you couldn't stay away," he said, squinting at Jerrol.

"Where is the king?" Jerrol gave ground as the prince advanced. Fonorion glanced out the door at the sound of pounding feet and, after a glance at Jerrol, turned to meet the new threat.

Crown Prince Kharel snorted. "He's no use to you anymore. His time is over."

"Do you really think the Ascendants are going to allow you to rule? Was it worth it? To throw away a sure bet for the chance to take the throne early?"

"Of course it was. You don't know what it's like to wait when you know you could do a better job."

"But the Ascendants want everything for themselves. What makes you think they need you?" Jerrol circled the prince.

"They couldn't get to my father without me, not even Isseran could get past you," the prince snarled, lunging at Jerrol.

Jerrol parried his thrust easily. "And once the king is out of the way, what next? I heard Isseran wanted to play regent."

Kharel swore and struck wildly. Jerrol flicked his sword up and twisted, disarming the prince. The prince cowered away from him as he approached and Jerrol flinched as Princess Selvia jumped on him from the bed. She screeched as she pummelled him, trying to gouge his eyes out. He stumbled back, tumbling to the floor under her unexpected weight. The prince dashed for the door, leaving his wife struggling with Jerrol.

"Guards," he screamed, rushing out the door into the corridor. He stopped and slowly backed up with his hands held high, Fonorion's sword at his throat. "You'll regret this, I am the Crown Prince of Vespiri," he began, his voice belligerent.

Fonorion twisted his sword, and the prince shut up. "Kneel," he said, flicking a glance at Jerrol still struggling on the floor with the princess. The prince took one look at Fonorion's face and knelt. "Arms behind your back." Fonorion circled him. He grabbed the prince's wrists and, dropping his sword, tied him up with a thin cord he unravelled from his waist. He tied the prince's hands to his feet just for thoroughness and stood watching Jerrol.

"Having fun?" he asked as he hauled the princess off him.

Jerrol scowled, rubbing his sore face. He had long scratches down his cheek, slowly oozing blood. "Who would have known the princess has more oomph than her husband," Jerrol said in disgust. Fonorion tied her hands to the bedpost. She let her breath go as Fonorion glared her into silence. The threat of gagging was enough to make her obey.

They left the chamber. After a swift, low-voiced conversation, Fonorion reluctantly agreed to guard the prince and he tied the doors shut while Jerrol hurried back towards the north tower where he knew the prince originally had his rooms. A brilliant flash lit the corridors, and Jerrol peered over the bannister into the empty courtyard. A loud crash of thunder vibrated through the palace and grumbled off into the distance.

At the sound of voices, he stilled, blending into the shadows of the long gallery which led to the north tower. Servants' voices? The voices faded as they moved away from him. He padded down corridors and up stairs, working his way through the warren of passages and rooms, relentless in his search.

He surprised a guard at the base of the north tower and struck immediately, crowding the man against the wall. The man sidestepped and whipped around. His wrist flicked, and Jerrol grunted as pain bloomed in his thigh. He staggered, and the man pressed his advantage, forcing him back down the corridor. An arrow buzzed past Jerrol's ear and struck the guard in the throat, and the guard faltered; his sword slipped from his fingers as he collapsed to the ground, gurgling.

Birlerion appeared beside him. His face was grave as he saw the dagger protruding high on Jerrol's left thigh. Glancing around, he eased Jerrol against the wall; bracing him, he pulled the blade out, staunching the wound with a folded piece of cloth he tugged out of his pocket. Jerrol trembled with the effort of remaining standing, waves of hot burning pain flashed through him.

"You should not be alone, Captain," Birlerion murmured, pressing down hard against the wound.

"We need to find the king." Jerrol closed his eyes against the deep ache in his leg and the concern in Birlerion's eyes.

"We will," Birlerion said, undoing his belt and cinching it tightly around the wound. "Ready?" He helped Jerrol stand, keeping a bracing arm around his back.

"The king must be in the north tower, in Kharel's old rooms on the third floor."

Birlerion supported him down the corridor. Peering up the stairwell, he wrapped Jerrol's arm around his shoulder and with one arm around his waist he began climbing, tightening his grip as Jerrol stumbled and in the end carrying him up the last few flights.

He propped Jerrol against the wall and checked the corridor. "Can you stand?" he asked, and then he let go of him and disappeared down the hallway. Jerrol heard a clash of swords and the Sentinal was back, wrapping his arm around Jerrol's waist. "The tower is down the end; it's clear now." He assisted Jerrol down the passageway. They were halfway down when a door opened, and Chancellor Isseran peered out.

He froze in shock at the sight of two armed men, and then he slammed his door shut as Jerrol raised a wavering sword.

Jerrol lurched for the door. Forcing it open, he fell into the room. Birlerion stepped over him and reached for Isseran as he spun his cloak around him. The cloth whipped out of Birlerion's hand as he disappeared, leaving the Sentinal hissing in pain.

Jerrol grimaced as he heaved himself to his knees. "We'll deal with him after; the king is more important."

Birlerion helped him up and dragged him down the corridor.

"Where did he go?" Jerrol asked.

"Not far. We need to get to the king before he does. It seems these Ascendants have discovered more of their ancestors' skills." Birlerion stopped speaking as he heard a knock at a door around the corner, followed by the door opening and closing, and the soft snick of a lock turning. Checking the corridor, he assisted Jerrol into the room to the left of the chamber and dropped him in a chair. Searching the room, he returned with a thicker towel and a thin scarf. He undid his belt and pressed the thick pad against Jerrol's leg and tied it in place. Jerrol groaned, stuffing his hand in his mouth, his face pale.

Birlerion knelt beside him. "I don't know your king; you make sure it's him, and I'll defend the door."

With Birlerion's assistance, Jerrol leant his ear against the wood panel and listened. He didn't recognise either of the voices. They were quite clear as they made no effort to lower them.

"He's getting more difficult every day, how much longer we got to keep this up?" a voice was whining.

"Stop moaning, your job is easy; he sleeps most of the night," replied a colder voice.

"You sure you're giving him the right dosage? All he does is spout nonsense," the whiny man continued.

"It's what they said to give him; the next batch will be arriving next week. We're almost out, and you know we don't have enough to increase the dosage." The man broke off with a gasp.

"Prepare the king. I need to move him." Isseran's harsh voice interrupted them.

Jerrol jerked the door open, and Birlerion followed, crowding the men in the antechamber. "Stop him," Jerrol shouted, pointing at the squat man backing away, swirling his cloak around him. Birlerion launched himself across the room; he slammed Isseran against the door, and it burst open beneath their weight. They tumbled through the door, a mass of arms and legs. Birlerion hung on to the chancellor and hissed as Isseran's fist caught his face.

The air shimmered, and Isseran lurched across the room towards the king, his black cloak swirling around him. "Curse you, Haven, you never learn, do you?" His bony fingers curled like claws around the king's arm. A knife flashed in his other hand.

"Learn what?"

"That your presence is not required. Benedict's reign is over. Long live the Ascendants." Isseran swung towards the king, and Birlerion flung out his arm, pointing at the Ascendant.

"No," he shouted, and Isseran flinched back. Birlerion stared at his hand, bemused as a faint blue light flickered out.

Jerrol scrambled over the king and launched himself at Isseran, who stumbled back under his weight, releasing his hold on the king. They grappled, rolling around on the floor. Jerrol gritted his teeth and hung on, both hands gripped around Isseran's wrist until Birlerion hauled Isseran off him. Birlerion slugged the chancellor, and he folded to the floor.

"Are you alright, Captain?" Birlerion crouched beside him. Helping him sit up, he tightened the binding around his leg. Jerrol groaned, sweat beading his brow. "Hold this a moment." Birlerion placed Jerrol's hand over the pad and checked the room.

Birlerion threw a withering glance at the cowering servants retreating out the door, tied Isseran's arms behind him and after a quick search covered his head with a pillowcase.

"What are you doing?"

"If he can't see he can't disappear," Birlerion said as he tied the material in place.

Tagerill loomed in the doorway, his silver eyes gleaming in the dull light. The servants dangled in each hand like game hung out to rest. Jerrol's eyes narrowed as Birlerion helped him stand. "What have you given the king?" he demanded, flipping Isseran's knife in his hand.

"N-nothing," the man gasped, his eyes bulging with fear.

Birlerion loomed behind Jerrol's shoulder, and the man gulped. Jerrol glanced at his Sentinal's face and shivered; he started speaking fast. "Your life means nothing to me. Prince Kharel chose the wrong side, and so have you. I can kill you quickly or slowly, your choice." He waved his hand at Birlerion, who took a step forward.

"J-just trealt. The prince wanted the king to tell him the Mysteries."

"The Mysteries?"

"The king's secrets. His connection with the Lady and the Land, he wanted the truth. Prince Kharel wanted to know what it was so that they could use it."

"And did he tell you?" Birlerion pounced and twisted his fist into the man's chest. Tagerill raised the man higher.

The man swallowed, his face pale. "D-don't kill me, please. I'm just a messenger."

"You're more than that, I think." Birlerion tightened his grip. "Did he tell you?" he repeated, making his words a threat.

The man shuddered in his grip. "No, no, he speaks nothing but nonsense."

Birlerion eased his grip as feet pounded up the stairs. The man stirred, thinking he was about to be saved, but he blanched as another tall silver-eyed man appeared instead.

"All secure," Serillion reported, his eyes widening at the scene before him.

Tagerill grimaced. "We'll lock them up until the king is ready to speak to them," he said, thrusting them out of the room and out of his brother's reach. "Serillion, guard the corridor. I'll come back for that one."

Tagerill dragged the terrified men away.

Jerrol turned back to the king. There was a strong aroma of incense hanging heavy in the air, but it wasn't strong enough to cover the lately familiar scent of trealt. Jerrol cast a quick look around the room. A large bed dominated it. Apart from the bed, there was a table against the wall supporting what looked like a whole apothecary kit. Stacked underneath the table: a bedpan, water jug and bowl.

Reaching up, he turned down the flame of the incense and let some much-needed air in as he eased open the casement. A gust of rain-drenched air blew in and, taking a deep breath, he turned his attention to the king.

As Jerrol limped to the side of the bed, the mackerel-striped Arifel popped into the room. Chittering softly at Jerrol, he flew towards the bed, perched on the frame and observed the king.

King Benedict was a big man, big in body and big in character. A man of high intelligence and a cutting wit which kept his court alert. All were absent here. This man was grey and shrunken, ravaged by drugs and enforced illness. Jerrol was appalled at how much the king had been affected. How had he managed to become so isolated, so vulnerable?

Jerrol knew he was partly to blame. He had allowed Prince Kharel and Nikols to bundle him out of the king's sphere, leaving the king exposed and unprotected, as had most of his other supporters. No more, Jerrol swore to himself; he would find a way to reverse this or die trying.

The sound of clashing swords from the hallway made Jerrol stiffen. Birlerion left to help Serillion. The king's glazed eyes were open and watching him. Ari chittered, and the king's gaze moved to the end of his bed, a frown creasing his forehead.

"Sire." Jerrol took a deep breath, and stepped over Isseran's body; he hovered over the king. The king convulsed as he saw the figure hanging over him. "Sire, it's alright," Jerrol said, catching his hand and looking the king firmly in the eyes. "It's Jerrol Haven. Please, sire, I mean you no harm."

"Jer, Jer, Jer," the king stuttered, his voice thick.

"That's right," soothed Jerrol, "it's me, your King's Ranger, Jerrol."

"Jer," the king repeated more clearly.

"Yes, sire. They've been giving you trealt, sire. It's what makes you feel so ill. The only remedy I know of that is to hand is alcohol. It counteracts some symptoms, distracts the brain, but only for a short time, and it will make you violently ill after." Jerrol spoke slowly and clearly, watching the king's face.

"D-dink," the king said.

Jerrol looked up as Birlerion hovered in the doorway. "Bring a glass of brandy in for me, would you?"

Birlerion returned, sloshing the brandy into the glass. He passed it to Jerrol, who was sitting hunched over on the bed. The king observed the tall Sentinal with a slight frown on his face.

Birlerion propped the king up with pillows, mouth pinching at how frail the man felt. He took the heavy crystal glass from Jerrol and wrapped the King's fingers around it. He helped guide the shaking hand to his mouth. "The palace is secure. Serillion guards the corridor, Fonorion guards the Prince, there were no other Ascendants apart from Isseran," Birlerion reported, his voice soft.

"Surprising but good news," Jerrol replied, watching the king. He glanced at the Sentinal. "What was Isseran afraid of?"

"His own shadow, by the looks of it."

"You went to do something, and it distracted him long enough for me to reach him."

Birlerion sighed and twisted his wrist. "There is no magic in Remargaren anymore; it didn't work."

"The Ascendants have magic. Ari is magic."

"They must have more crystals. It enhances their skill. Magic is leaking in through the rift in the Veil, enough to awaken but not enough to use. You need to seal it, Captain."

"What will happen to you if we seal the Veil again?"

"What the Lady wills," Birlerion said, his eyes bright.

The king managed to swallow a few more mouthfuls before leaning back against his pillows, exhausted. Jerrol took the glass and rested it in his lap, patiently waiting. The king opened his mouth and Jerrol gave him the rest of the brandy as the king watched him intently.

"Tick tock," Benedict muttered.

"It should work quite fast, but we don't have much time." He took a deep breath. "Sire, the situation is not good." The king snorted gently in reply.

"I know, but your Kingdom is being attacked from all angles. Prince Kharel is in league with others, the chancellor for sure, but there seems to be some outside influence coming out of Terolia. They are targeting the Guardians. They may even have instigated it, instead of exposing it for what it is, and they are using it to drive dissension and fear." King Benedict gripped his hand.

Jerrol continued with his report. "We've lost many Guardians, Lord Hugh and Lord Stefan among them. Their sons have not picked up the mantle; the lands lack their Guardians."

"Tall and Proudies?" the king's voice rasped.

Jerrol grinned at Birlerion. "The Sentinals are awakening. A few are here with me today; this is Birlerion." He waved his right hand at Birlerion and paused as the king stared wide-eyed at the Sentinal.

"Your Majesty." Birlerion ducked his head.

"The Watches are cutting the timber. Isseran was hoarding the wood. Something to do with the Elothians," Jerrol continued. "We discovered there is a group called the Ascendants, and they are using a mind spell called *Mentiserium* to control your people."

"By the water, no-eyes washes her hands of knowledge, pick it up," the king said cryptically.

"You mean the scholars and Taelia especially? They know about the Ascendants?"

The king struggled to push his words out. He crossed his eyes in frustration, which would have been amusing on another day in another life. "T-the ball and chain hold the beginning," he managed.

Sweat trickled down Jerrol's back, and his leg trembled with a deep ache that drained his energy, but he concentrated on the king. "There is so much knowledge, history that we have lost. I'll start with the Sentinals and Liliian. She is going to be ecstatic when she realises she has living history in her hand. Prince Kharel discharged me, sire. Accused me of treason and placed a bounty on my head. I'm not supposed to step foot in the city."

The king glared at Jerrol, paused as he gathered some semblance of clarity and spoke clearly and concisely:

"Do your Duty, Never Falter, Never Fail,
  Lady, Land and Liege obey.
  All are one, entwined ascending,
  Keeper's Oath never ending."

Jerrol froze, eyes widening; this was what the king had tried to say that day he was arrested in the throne room. He had reached the third sentence when Prince Kharel had interrupted them. "S-sire?" The words resonated through his body; he knew these words, he knew the oath, but it had never been invoked. Those were the words carved in the wall above the throne in Old Vespers.

"Never Ending," King Benedict said firmly.

"Lady, Land and Liege obey," Jerrol repeated. "Keeper's Oath never ending." He spread his hand across his heart and bent his head before his king. He felt the Oath acknowledge his response and lock into place with a resounding clang in the vaults of the Land that made the ground tremble. The Lady's response was more visceral, rooted deep within; her presence branched out inside him, entwining them as one. Her greenish hue flared up as a jolt of energy shot through him, and he took a deep breath as he straightened, his eyes luminous in the dim light. The Arifel chittered excitedly as he fluttered around him.

Birlerion watched him in concern. He had thought the Captain was going to pass out, he was so pale, but now he could see both Leyandrii's and Marguerite's touch. The Captain was bound thrice, and there would be no escape. He gave a wry smile. The Lady was possessive; she wouldn't be releasing him any time soon.

The king swallowed reflexively and swallowed again as the blood drained from his face, leaving him a sickly grey; a sheen of sweat glistened on his skin. "Ah." Jerrol stood and grabbed the bowl.

He placed the bowl in front of the king, just as the king heaved and was violently sick. Birlerion handed Jerrol a towel, and Jerrol gently wiped his face. Birlerion offered more brandy, but the king shook his head. "Tick tock. "Another spasm shuddered through him, and he vomited into the bowl again.

Birlerion left to check the corridor.

Jerrol was loath to leave the king in such poor straits, but he had his orders and knew better than to disobey them. He could set some people on the right track though, spoke a few more wheels, remind them they hadn't managed to get rid of him. He smiled ferociously in anticipation.

When Birlerion returned to the room, the king had flopped back against his pillows and was watching the Arifel. "Lost thoughts, travel far, late for supper," the king said, eyes wide with wonder.

The Arifel walked up the bed and squatted on his chest. "Meep," he said, staring solemnly into the king's eyes.

"Chase dreams, fall over, break the glass," the king replied.

The Arifel spread out his wings and chittered sternly.

The king's face brightened. "Paper trails, ears open, yes sir!" He glared at Jerrol. "Already late, be gone!"

Ari rose into the air as the king turned back to heave into his bowl. When the king raised his head again, the room was empty.

38

OLD VESPERS

W hen Commander Nikols and the King's Rangers arrived, the palace was in the king's control. The king's staff had been reinstated, and the king, albeit a little queasily to begin with, gripped his kingdom with an iron fist and began sorting out the mess.

Per the king's orders, Jerrol kept out of sight, constrained to the infirmary to begin with, and then working with the Sentinals and scholars while he waited for the king to relocate to Old Vespers. He worked deep in the Chapterhouse archives, surreptitiously searching for mention of the Oath Keeper and the responsibilities of the Guardians of the Land.

He was soothed by the presence of Scholar Taelia, as she organised the protocols for the search. The Sentinals deferred to her instinctively, and she seemed to have an understanding with Birlerion already. They discussed a variety of topics, often debating quite aggressively.

Her demands kept them hard at work, her insights garnering their respect much faster than Jerrol expected. He relaxed into their old routine of banter and teasing without noticing. The Sentinals watched their interactions with more knowing eyes.

Jerrol made sure no one outside of the scholars knew where he was, and those who did assumed he was another scholar hidden amongst the influx of new faces. The Sentinals, especially Serillion and Tagerill, explored the Chapterhouse in horror. Serillion had reached the point where he was openly wringing his hands, appalled at all the lost knowledge. Tagerill tended to sit up in the bell tower and mourn the loss of the Vespers he knew and loved. Birlerion, when not arguing with Taelia, was usually a shadow behind his shoulder. A reassuring presence, and one he was getting used to.

Torsion followed the Sentinals around, trying to squeeze every piece of information out of them, awed by the living history before him. Birlerion watched him with suspicion, warning the other Sentinals to be careful what they told him. Tagerill and Serillion listened to Birlerion's doubts and shrugged them off; just because Torsion reminded him of an ancient foe didn't make him one, and besides the Captain trusted him. The Sentinals were more interested in learning about the new Vespiri and asked Torsion as many questions in return.

It was some weeks later when Jerrol sighed with frustration; they were getting nowhere. There was nothing noteworthy in the archives. He wondered what was buried beneath their feet and wished the scholars would hurry up. He found their rigid procedures stifling. He needed action.

Seated in the Chapterhouse library, he was idly flipping through an early book on the Lady's administration when Torsion found him. "Here you are, I've been searching everywhere for you."

"Why?" Jerrol asked, raising an eyebrow.

"That Sentinal of yours, Birlerion. He is being difficult. He won't answer any of my questions, yet he was the one here in Vespers. He knew the Lady and Guerlaire."

"They all knew the Lady and Guerlaire."

"I know, but every time I ask about something, the others say, speak to Birlerion, he'll know more. This Birlerion was closer than the others, from what I can make out; he was special."

"In what way?"

"He travelled widely, on behalf of the Lady, yet he is so young — what did she see in him? And at the end, she kept him near her, and sent the others out into the Watches. Why?"

"I suppose she must have trusted him."

"But why him? And not Guerlaire? He could tell us, but he won't. He won't talk to me about anything. I think he's hiding something."

Jerrol laughed. "I'm sure he is. How would you feel being awoken three thousand years in your future? You wouldn't want to share everything about yourself, now would you? Just think what they've lost—would you want to talk about it?"

"I'm telling you, Jerrol; you need to be careful. He is hiding something, and until we know what it is, he is a threat."

"Rubbish, he is a Lady's guard, a Sentinal. He is here to do her bidding, and so far that is what he has done. Just because he won't talk to you doesn't mean I can't trust him."

"He let Isseran escape. Doesn't that make you suspicious?"

"No, he didn't. The King's Guards let him escape. They didn't follow his instructions. I was there when he told them to keep his eyes covered."

Torsion snorted. "We've known each other for years,

Jerrol. I've looked out for you since you were a kid. I only want what is best for you. You are family. You followed my advice then; you should heed it now. Take care, Jerrol, there is much about these Sentinals you don't know."

"And over time we will learn more. Don't rush them, Torsion. We have to earn their trust as much as they earn ours. Give them time to adjust. They report to me. They will obey my orders; for now, that is enough."

"I hope so, Jerrol, for your sake. Speak to Birlerion. We need to know what he knows. Don't leave it too long, or we may all regret it."

Jerrol watched his friend stride out of the library: dark, tall and slim, his robes billowing around him. He frowned as he remembered the Lady's words: *There is one I cannot see, the deceiver, watch for him, my Captain.* No, it couldn't be Birlerion, he had taken a sword for him. Birlerion wouldn't have tried to save him if he were a traitor, would he? He had protected Jerrol ever since he stepped out of his tree. Jerrol trusted him with his life. He trusted all his Sentinals.

He shivered. They would need them if they were going to save Remargaren from this Ascendant threat. First, he needed to understand what being the Lady's Captain meant, then find out how to seal the Veil, and after that he needed to discover who the Ascendants were and how to stop them.

He heaved a deep sigh as he stared across the room. He rubbed his temples, trying to relieve his growing headache. Maybe Torsion was right; he ought to find out more about the Sentinals. He would speak to Birlerion first.

Somehow, he knew his problems were only just beginning. The Ascendants had inveigled their way into the Watches unseen, and they had nearly succeeded in overthrowing the king. He was sure they wouldn't stop there. Whatever it was they were planning, the Lady expected him to stop them. He clenched his left fist; he had two more crystals to find. Standing, he glanced around. He had better get on with it, then.

The End

Did you enjoy Sentinals Awaken? Then please leave a review. Reviews help authors raise awareness of their books and drive visibility to other readers.

Amazon direct review links:

UK: Amazon.co.uk/review/create-review? &asin=B08JQJZKKC

USA: Amazon.com/review/create-review?&asin= B08JQJZKKC

CANADA: Amazon.ca/review/create-review?&asin= B08JQQJZKKC

ACKNOWLEDGMENTS

If it wasn't for my mother, Margaret, instilling in me a love of books, I would never be writing these words today. I wish I had started writing earlier so I could have shared this moment with her because I know she would have loved my characters and the world they inhabit.

I am thankful for my darling daughter, Jennifer, who encouraged me to take the step and self-publish, and go social, and build a website, and take to twitter.

A big thank you goes to my beta readers, Mike Wall and my number one fan, Michael Strick, for reading my early versions and providing detailed and thoughtful feedback, and even putting down *Game of Thrones* to read *Sentinals Awaken*. I appreciate the time and effort you took to read and think about what I had written, and the suggestions on how I could improve it.

To my very dear friend Kaye Adams, who patiently listened to me go on and on about characters, names, plot, and the vagaries of the English language when our crafting evening turned into a writer's discussion group. Thank you for being my sound- ing board and for your constant support and encouragement.

Jeff Brown designed my beautiful cover, (https://www.jeffbrowngraphics.com) and Tom from FictiveDesigns (https:// www.fictive-designs.com/maps) drew the exquisite map of Vespiri.

I hope you enjoy reading *Sentinals Awaken* as much as I

enjoyed writing it, and I look forward to continuing the adventure with you in my second novel, *Sentinals Rising*, which is now available.

LETTER FROM THE AUTHOR

It's funny how all the major events in my life happen at the same time. I graduated from university, got married and started a new job all in the same month. My daughter was born just after we moved into a new house. It seems I need a perfect storm of events to take the next the step.

When my mother passed away four years ago, and my daughter headed off to university, I suddenly had an empty house and time on my hands, and I finally sat down and wrote. The ideas came tumbling out, and there was my first book.

My love of books came from my mum, Margaret. She was voracious, consuming a wide range of books of varied genres. She would sit and knit, watch the telly and read a book, all at the same time. As a child, I inherited the bookworm, though I never picked up the knack of knitting! I devoured Enid Blyton, Elinor Brent Dyer's Chalet School books and moved onto Mary Stewart and Alistair McLean and then we found Anne McCaffrey and then David Eddings, to name a few.

Sentinals Awaken is the first novel in what I originally intended being a trilogy, and although the first three novels fit together, there are another four books with the same characters and world, so I hope you enjoyed the first in the series and stay for the journey. You can follow my progress and find out more about the next book, **Sentinals Rising**, at www. helengarraway.com.

If you would like to stay up to date with news and book availability then please sign up to my mailing list on the above website for a periodic newsletter. I promise I won't bombard you. I prefer to be writing!

If you have a moment please do leave a review and tell other fantasy readers why you enjoyed the book. Reviews are so important to independent authors to drive visibility and to help me to continue publishing. Thank you so much!

Thank you for your support.
    Helen Garraway
    October 2020

Other Books in the series
    One: Sentinals Awaken
    Two: Sentinals Rising
    Three: Sentinals Justice
    Four: Sentinals Across Time
    Five: Sentinals Banished
    Six: Sentinals Destiny

TWO
THE SENTINAL SERIES

SENTINALS
RISING

HELEN GARRAWAY

Printed in Great Britain
by Amazon

36371938R00218